MOST WANTED

MOST WANTED

Mark McHugh

iUniverse, Inc.
New York Bloomington

MOST WANTED

iUniverse books may be ordered through booksellers or by contacting:

iUniverse
1663 Liberty Drive
Bloomington, IN 47403
www.iuniverse.com
1-800-Authors (1-800-288-4677)

ISBN: 978-0-595-43140-3 (pbk)
ISBN: 978-1-4401-2750-2 (cloth)
ISBN: 978-0-595-87485-9 (ebk)

Library of Congress Control Number: 2009924014

Printed in the United States of America

iUniverse rev. date: 4/8/2009

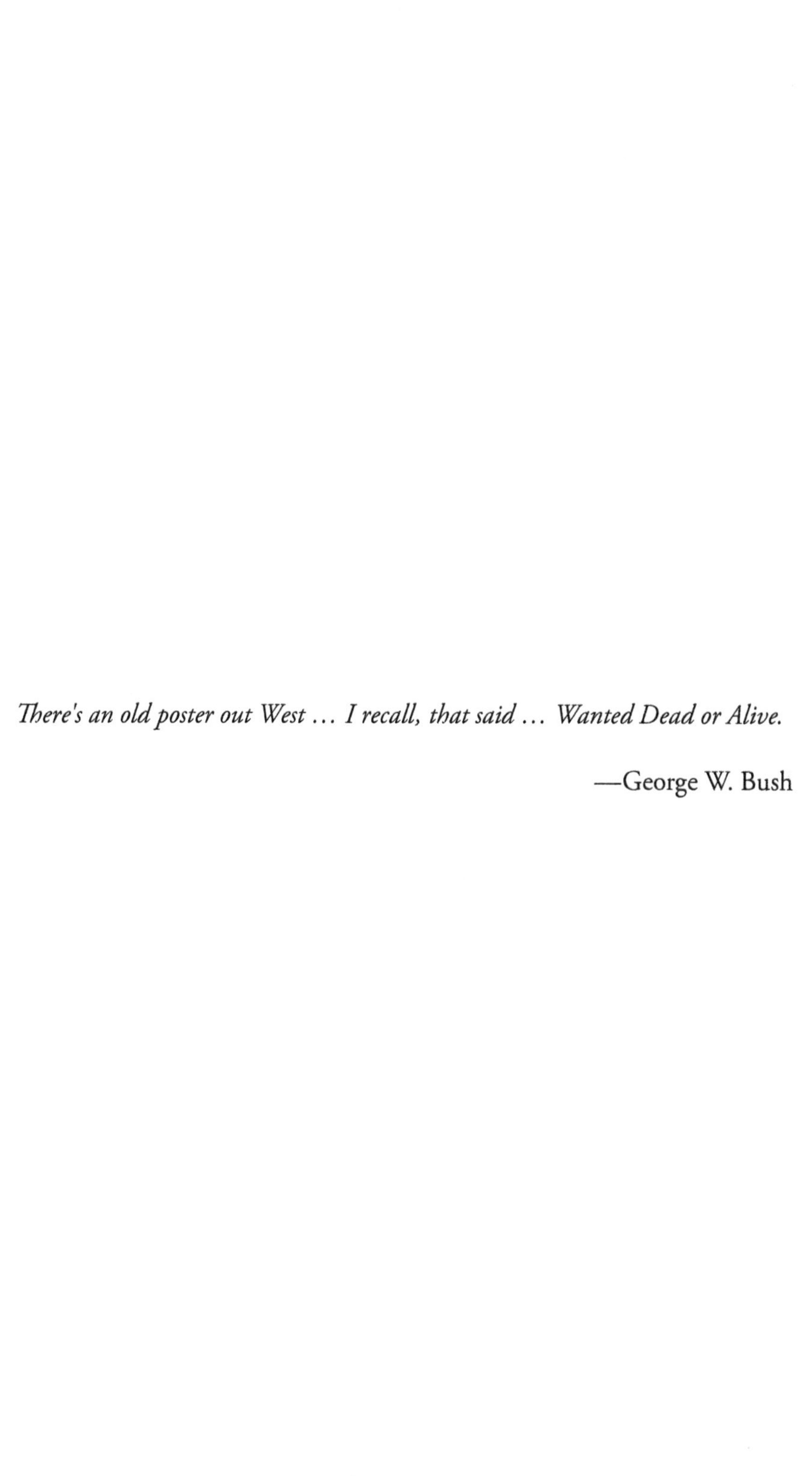

There's an old poster out West … I recall, that said … Wanted Dead or Alive.

—George W. Bush

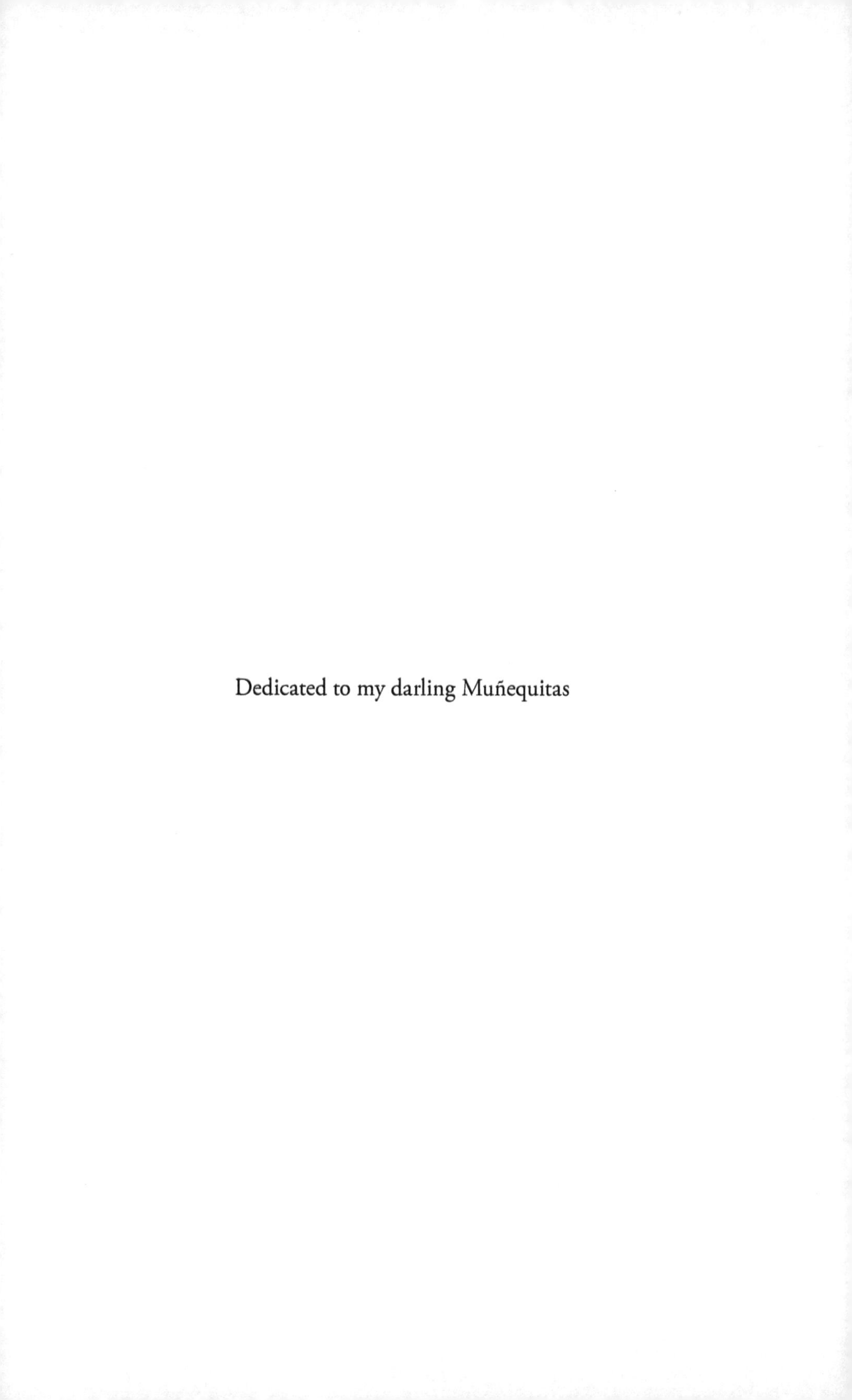

Dedicated to my darling Muñequitas

Preface

I have always been drawn to writing. Put simply, I get great pleasure from the creative process and I was curious to see if I had at least one good book in me. It started as nothing more than a hobby, and for a long time, I was unsure whether I would ever complete the task. I endured healthy skepticism and gentle derision from those who honestly did not believe that I had the makings of an author. Even so, I persevered, and now you can bear witness to the result.

I was keen to entertain by writing in a popular genre. My chief source of inspiration is a generation of action movies and books, which are one of my favorite forms of entertainment. My goal was to produce a well-written modern-day spy thriller, fresh in style and substance. At the same time, I hoped to preserve some of the finer traditions of the great Cold War suspense novels by weaving many unexpected twists and turns into the plot.

The storyline is a flight of my imagination. For authenticity, I leaned heavily on my familiarity with a wide variety of places and cultures from around the globe. My biggest challenge was to make the account both credible and human. As a result, I have tried to avoid stereotypes and endeavored to portray realistic characters in interesting yet true-to-life settings.

I found the time to write during my extensive international business travel. I took advantage of many unproductive hours, which I would have otherwise spent in a sort of suspended animation, either cruising at thirty-five thousand feet or sitting around in hotel rooms on weekends. For this reason, I like to think of this book as a genuine airplane novel—but from a different perspective.

Unsurprisingly, I vastly underestimated the enormity of the undertaking, which absorbed most of my spare time and energy over four years. In the closing stages, as my desire to confound the skeptics and produce a successful novel grew, it became something of an obsession. Now that it is finished, I can honestly say that I derived huge satisfaction from the writing experience and that I am very proud of my accomplishment. I feel I have nothing left to prove, to myself at least.

Like most spy thrillers, the story is based on current world events. A number of true-to-life occurrences, figures, and institutions are referenced to provide context. Nonetheless, the book remains a work of pure fiction; many of the actions ascribed to these persons or organizations are self-evidently make-believe.

Furthermore, while I am convinced that the principal characters have their feet in the real world, they are purely imaginary. To use the well-known cliché, their resemblance to any individuals, living or dead, is purely coincidental.

The backdrop is the international war on terror, which has become such a frightening part of our daily existence. The theme is, as ever, the eternal struggle between good and evil—the good guys versus the bad guys—although distinguishing between them often represents one of life's most important challenges.

This book is intended to be sheer escapism, and it was my hope to avoid being pretentious or excessively demanding to the reader. I trust you will enjoy it, passing time wherever you chose.

Please fasten your seat belts; we are entering a zone of turbulence!

Contents

Chapter 1—
A Decisive Blow

Despite the steady onshore breeze from the Gulf of Oman, the intense heat and accompanying humidity were unrelenting even during the hours of darkness. The air was stifling throughout their departure from the secret military base at Chah-Bahar. On takeoff, Colonel Malek Kalbasi had stayed close by the open tailgate of the chopper, vainly trying to keep cool. He had flown in a helicopter countless times, yet sitting by the open hatch he still could not get over the sensation of weightlessness on takeoff. One second you were hovering just above the ground, and next you were peering out into space.

The regular beat of the whirling rotor blades and the high-pitched whine of the turbines of the Islamic Republic of Iran Air Force *CH-47C Chinook* eliminated the possibility of conversation in the cabin as they carved their way through the night sky. Malek had a headset cupped over one ear, yet he was only half tuned in to the continuous chatter in Farsi on the radio between the pilots and ground control. His mind was racing. He could not shake his nervousness, because their trajectory took them across the Iranian plateau, to within a few kilometers of both the Afghan and Pakistani borders, north of Zahedan. He remained wary of a possible rogue missile from the

Taliban's forces or even the remote possibility of one launched by NATO ground troops.

This was a hazardous mission, and his adrenaline was pumping. He had received his top-secret orders from Mahmoud Ahmadinejad himself. He was in command of an elite squad of eight men from the Quds Force of the Islamic Revolutionary Guards Corps—or IRGC. He sat facing four of his men, who were lined up on jump seats along the opposite side of the fuselage; the other four sat bolt upright along the same side as him. They had all been handpicked for this operation, and Malek could not deny his pride to be leading the best of the best.

The strike force was dressed in battle fatigues with blackened faces. None of them appeared at all concerned about communicating with his comrades. They sat quietly in the helicopter, as they had been trained to do. Their emotions were totally controlled; any personal feelings that they may have had were thoroughly masked behind their grim faces. Each had an accompanying cruel stare that gave him a truly menacing edge.

The men were fully prepared for the operation ahead. Malek had passed the last fourteen hours with them reviewing the mission, starting with their morning briefing. This had given him ample time to go over every detail.

He had begun with a short speech, "Gentlemen, as you have been selected for this operation, you are by definition the finest soldiers in the Revolutionary Guard. The President himself has entrusted each of us to carry out an historic task. However, don't let this go to your head. Over-confidence will make you careless. Keep your focus on the mission and support the other members of the squad at all times."

Malek had a reputation among the men as an outstanding field officer, and for good reason. He commanded the Counter-insurgency Brigade of the Quds Force, and he had previously led several operations such as this—against the Balochi separatist rebels, the Jundallah, or Soldiers of God. His brigade was unusual as the only part of the IRGC that operated exclusively inside Iran. They resembled a conventional Special Forces group and remained under the close operational control of President Ahmadinejad. The rest of the Quds—or Jerusalem Force—was a shadowy organization that carried out subversive operations as a fifth column in most of the conflict zones in the Middle East. By contrast, they were a bunch of ill-disciplined fanatics, only loosely controlled by Supreme Leader Ayatollah Ali Khamenei. They operated with a very broad objective—to spread the Iranian Revolution.

"Men, you're all very familiar with our target—our old enemy, the Jundallah. Recently they have become an increasing threat to us, operating freely in the border regions and strengthening their links with al-Qaeda and the Taliban."

He could see that he had the complete attention of his squad.

"Tonight, we will deliver a decisive blow against the Taliban leadership and the Jundallah from which they will never recover!"

Malek could not forget the notorious incident a couple of months back, when the Jundallah had claimed responsibility for the abduction of a team of IRGC intelligence officers traveling in convoy along the Pakistani border. They had released a videotaped ultimatum to al-Arabiya television, justifying the attack as revenge for alleged Iranian security forces' atrocities against the Balochi people. They had demanded the release of Jundallah members and other Balochi activists detained in state prisons in exchange for the safe release of their hostages.

He was on leave at the time when his comrades were snatched and immediately returned to active duty to see if there was something he could do to help free the captives. His commanding officer—Brigadier General Qassem Suleimani—head of the Quds Force, had insisted that they would not deal with terrorists. At the same time, Iran's intelligence and national security service, the VEVAK, searched in vain for clues to the whereabouts of the prisoners. Malek felt completely powerless, as he sat around the command post for days waiting for news that would allow him to initiate a rescue. He angrily recalled how he had watched the second video statement, three weeks later, showing the execution of his life-long friend, Shehab, among four others.

Because of all this, their mission tonight had a dual purpose for him. He relished the thought of exacting revenge against the Jundallah leadership for the brutal death of his brother officer and close friend. For an instant, Malek felt the hatred well up inside, yet he was only too well aware that he should not let his emotional response cloud his judgment. The Jundallah were secondary; his real target was much too important, praise be to Allah.

Nonetheless, Malek secretly admired how the Jundallah had been playing such a well hidden, but critical role since the Afghan conflict, providing a refuge and protection for key members of Mullah Omar's former regime. Many of the Taliban leaders had been smuggled across the border since late 2001.

Malek considered it a curious paradox. US Intelligence had widely publicized their hypothesis that most of their adversaries in the war on terror had fled after the war to Pakistan and were holed up in the lawless tribal areas along the Afghan-Pakistan border. Some had guessed that Iran was also a hiding place, but no one in western intelligence circles took them too seriously. This was primarily because the Iranian government, as Shia, had been engaged in their own bitter feud against the Sunni Taliban and his international supporters for more than twenty years. Malek recalled, long before the Afghan war, that his masters had frequently warned Washington about the dangers of the Taliban–al-Qaeda axis, all to no avail. More recently, they had cautioned the Americans about the Jundallah. This made it all the more inexplicable for Malek. How could the US pundits so carelessly ignore the role of the Balochi rebels? For unfathomable reasons, the Jundallah were considered inconsequential in the greater scheme of things. In reality, they were the largely responsible for the Taliban leadership surviving intact after the Afghan conflict and Malek knew it.

* * *

The IRIAF Chinook rapidly dropped in altitude to about three hundred feet. Blacked-out and flying close to the deck, they were now making their final approach to the drop zone. It was about five minutes before they landed on an area of flat, rocky terrain. Although he could see from their maps that they were close to the surrounding mountains, it was a cloudy night, and as he peered out of the helicopter's windows, he could barely make out the outline of the valley.

The heavily armed troop disembarked in single file. Malek followed up the rear. They each had a single ear bud inserted and a hands-free microphone to communicate among the squad. There was no idle chatter, according to strict protocol.

They started their silent trek, traversing the edge of the valley for about five kilometers in an effortless trot. After a while, the surface topography became rocky and uneven. Although they were following a goat path along the mountainside, the trail petered out in places, developing into patches of loose scree, where it was easy to lose one's footing. A twisted ankle could easily spell disaster with all the heavy equipment they were carrying. Malek slowed the pace right down until they cleared the most treacherous part of the terrain.

The squad continued to negotiate the rough ground in the darkness. Their objective was an isolated housing compound northeast of Zahedan at Kuleh Sangi, which they were approaching from the east. As they came within half a kilometer, they fanned out and took cover in the rock-strewn landscape. Malek could easily see the compound, which was lit up like a beacon in front of them. Sentries were posted along the wall. The guards would have no hope of seeing them in return, as they peered into the gloom with the light behind them.

Malek counted four men on duty, armed with what he correctly guessed were SMG PK 9 mm sub-machine guns. They are produced in Pakistan based on the famous Heckler & Koch machine gun, which were ideal for close-quarter battle. A firm favorite with the Taliban's personal bodyguard, they are equally the preferred weapons of Malek's own men.

They moved forward silently, closing in on their objective. Sheltering behind the surrounding rock formations, they crawled on their bellies to within one hundred meters of their target. They were now confronted by open ground as far as the wall of the compound. Fortunately, their plan had foreseen this eventuality, and they had carefully arranged a distraction. Two of the group had already worked their way around to side of the compound.

"Now," Malek ordered.

The flash-bangs went off near the front gate three hundred meters away. This gave seven men—led by Malek—precious seconds to sprint across the open terrain and scale the wall at the rear.

"We're in," Malek spoke softly into his microphone.

The next action was for the forward party to eliminate the four lookouts at the front of the compound.

"Done," he heard over the headset, and he grinned.

Accompanied by two of his men, Malek strode in a direct line toward the large building in the center of the compound. With the benefit of surprise, they marched straight through the anteroom, immediately taking out the two heavily armed men posted at the door. Before the sentries had time to react, they each had a small round hole oozing blood from their brow; a second later, they were crumpling to the ground. Once on the ground, they received a second shot to the chest. This was unnecessary, but it was a standard precaution to ensure the kill.

As they entered the dining room, they faced ten or twelve bearded figures—mostly dressed in traditional Arab attire—seated around a T-shaped table. They were clearly startled by the sudden intrusion during their late evening meal. It was impossible not to notice the wizened elderly character at the head of the table, resting almost inertly in a wheelchair with a saline drip attached. With his gnarled features and a pallid grayish complexion, he appeared gravely ill. A male nurse stood nearby. None of the men recognized the old man, except Malek.

In the blink of an eye, the three highly trained Quds assassins swung their weapons to their hips, taking several strides forward in unison and firing in the direction of the assembled group. The result was bloody carnage. They each discharged three thirty-round magazines from their machine pistols. It was all over in less than two minutes. No one was left alive by the vicious onslaught.

Pandemonium ensued in the rest of the compound as the remaining Taliban and Jundallah guards tried unsuccessfully to come to the aid of their stricken leaders. Malek could hear the firefight outside as it intensified. The remaining two sections of his assault force would be well entrenched and could pick off their targets at will. After three or four minutes, there were a couple of explosions, and then silence.

His lieutenant was the first to enter the dining room.

"Sir, we've completed a search for survivors."

"Anything to report?" asked Malek.

"Yes sir, we found fifteen women cowering under a long refectory table in the female quarters."

"I imagine they were waiting for their men to finish before they ate, as is the custom."

"They were all screaming for mercy, sir."

"They must be the wives of the now dead Jundallah or Taliban leaders."

"Without a doubt; most were in Afghani dress of full *purdah*, although I noticed five or six women in more colorful Balochi robes."

"What have you done with them?" asked Malek.

"Well, sir, we took pity on them and just locked them in the room."

'That's okay; they will probably only escape after we're long gone."

"Sir, I have the results of a quick body count too—twenty-five rebels dead, without any casualties among the Quds Force," said the lieutenant.

The rest of his squad began assembling back in the main building.

"You two," Malek ordered, "remove the body from the wheelchair and put it into a body bag. Put the corpse on a stretcher; we'll be taking him with us in the chopper."

There were pools of dark, sticky blood on the floor and bodies strewn all around the table.

"Look for any form of identification," Malek said, motioning toward the remaining corpses.

Both he and his men began to search the bloody torsos for anything that would allow them to confirm the identities of their kill.

"Odd that most of them were armed, but none were fast enough to defend themselves," said the lieutenant.

"They weren't soldiers, just murderous politicians who killed by proxy," Malek replied.

Malek had radioed ahead, and within ten minutes of the firefight, the Chinook landed in the open ground behind the compound in a whirlwind of stones and dust. The pilot feathered the twin rotor blades and lowered the ramp. Led by the two with the stretcher, Malek's men moved in a swift and disciplined manner from their crouched position beside the wall of the compound to board the chopper. Once on board, Malek watched as his men quickly strapped the body bag to the middle of the cabin floor, securing it with a cargo net. They stowed the stretcher and retook their jump seats.

Once they settled in the cabin, Malek spoke to the pilot over his headset.

"Clear for takeoff."

"Roger."

The pilot eased the throttles forward, pulled back on the stick, and the helicopter lifted off into the darkness. The Chinook's flight path was low along the valley, still prone to a chance shot from a handheld surface-to-air missile but well below the radar.

Malek radioed the airbase at Zahedan and relayed a brief, triumphant message to his boss: *The rabbit is in the bag.*

After twenty minutes, they were completely clear of the danger zone and Malek visibly relaxed. The adrenaline had been pumping throughout this remarkable operation, and now that they had achieved all their objectives, without any losses, he was elated. He just sat there beaming for the rest of the flight back.

* * *

As they approached their base, the roof of their underground hangar at Chah-Bahar slid open to give them access. Ironically, the Americans had built this high-tech military base in the Shah's time. A large part of the huge base was underground. MIG-29s, SU-24MKs, F-4s, and F-5s all arrived at the runway by ramp or elevator for takeoff. The Islamic Revolution had been very resourceful in preserving their inheritance and in adding to its operational capability.

As the chopper came to rest in the hangar, Malek commanded his men, "Take the body bag to the high security storage area and wait for me in the debriefing room."

He disappeared into the warren of tunnels below the airbase. Malek was delighted by the success of the operation and continued to wear a broad grin as he strode toward the communications room. His orders were to speak directly to Mahmoud Ahmadinejad—without delay—upon conclusion of the mission. This was his true moment of glory.

He had met Ahmadinejad face to face before, only once, together with a large group of brother officers, shortly after Ahmadinejad's inauguration as president. He remembered being struck by his presence, which seemed to fill the room. He had made such a powerful speech about the importance of Iran becoming strong again, based upon his campaign slogan: *It's doable … we can do it.* Undoubtedly, it was music to the ears of the Revolutionary Guard commanders in attendance.

Arriving at the communications room, Malek was guided into one of the soundproof booths in the corner. Everything had been prepared for his arrival. The technician instructed him to wait two minutes, while he was connected by videocast to Ahmadinejad in his residence in Tehran.

"*Salam! Shoma chetur hastin?*" the president of the Islamic Republic of Iran greeted Malek. "I hear that you have some excellent news for me."

"*Man khoobam, mamnoon*," Malek returned the ritual greeting.

"Congratulations on the success of your historic mission. So, we have finally rid ourselves of this thorn in our side. Send me a copy of your full report once it is ready."

The video screen went dark without Malek having an opportunity to say anything. Curiously, Malek wasn't at all worried by this. He felt proud that he could serve his country in such a momentous manner, even though many would never know about—or even wish to acknowledge—the major role he had played.

Chapter 2— Dawn Breaks

Heyya alas-Salah ... Allah akhbar. The chant from the loudspeaker shattered the early morning calm. The minaret was only sixty meters away from his hotel window. *What an infernal row!* Tom Salter buried his head in the pillow and tried to suffocate the din coming from the malevolent prayer call.

He began to contemplate the hypocrisy of it all. *Millions of Muslims believe in their One God, as do the Catholics in their Virgins and the Jews in the Law of Moses and their Temple. The world continues to commit travesties in the name of their religious convictions. Each faction is continuously trying to impose their version of the "Ultimate Truth" on the remaining population. Each has their own rituals hoping to demonstrate the pious nature of their faith.*

Tom continued to question how Christians, Jews, and Islam could honesty share so many of the same fundamental beliefs yet remain in constant conflict. He acknowledged the many ironies: all three religions are intertwined; the Jew and the Arab are both part of the same Semitic race; Jesus and Moses are prophets in Islam and the Bible corroborates that the Jews and the Arabs are all descended from Abraham. His offspring—Isaac and Ishmael—each became the father of his own nation. Alas, the sibling rivalry continues, with the brothers competing though their bloodlines ever since. The War on Terror—or TWOT in US government parlance—was simply the latest manifestation.

Tom maintained his sense of disbelief. Sometimes the Yanks could make you smile and cringe at the same time, with their foolish acronyms and their penchant for codes understood only by those in the know. It was all comic theatre. Meanwhile, they were now the masters of the universe, the only superpower in the great game. *We all dance to their tune.*

In the good old US heartlands of the Midwest, places like Des Moines, Iowa, and Boise, Idaho, most people couldn't even identify Iraq on a map. Yet today, Americans were being forced out of their shell to police the globe after years of isolationism. It had left them ill equipped to deal with today's ruthless terrorist threat or the harsh consequences, as their young men were being sent home in body bags by the thousands.

Tom's predisposition that all Americans were slightly crazy was based on some of his early experiences in the States about twenty years ago. He was sent over to CIA Headquarters at Langley—near the beginning of his career—to do an important liaison task. Weary after his transatlantic flight from London to Washington, he was just settling into his room in the Hyatt, in nearby Fairfax, Virginia. While he was unpacking, somebody knocked on his door. He thought it was housekeeping.

"Hang on a minute," he shouted, as he scurried to open the door.

To his utter astonishment, there was this sweating middle-aged guy with a paunch and a 44 Magnum in his left hand pointed straight at him. At first, he decided it was some kind of joke, perhaps a try-on by his Agency colleagues, except the slob pushed his way into the room and yelled at him.

"I want your money. Take off your watch and empty out the briefcase—"

"You're wasting your time. I've got nothing of value," said Tom.

"Empty the case now!" the mugger snarled.

"Why don't you just leave and we'll forget all about it, eh?" asked Tom.

"Huh, you must be joking!" he replied. "Now, put your things over there on the bed, where I can see what you're doing."

From his tone of voice and anxious gestures, Tom realized that this lunatic was not pretending. He was obviously a jerk—twitchy as hell and red in the face—not your usual drug addict looking to score. He had the demeanor of an insurance salesman that had fallen on hard times. From his appearance, he wondered if he was suffering from hypertension. It would be just his misfortune if the mugger went into shock, had a heart attack there and then. Somehow, the grieving relatives would sue him. He couldn't believe his luck. *What the hell does this bozo think he is doing? Well, he's picked on the wrong guy.*

Tom was fully trained in unarmed combat and a third *dan* black belt in Shotokan karate; he took all of three seconds to disarm him. Almost instinctively, he grabbed the gun and his left arm and pulled him down to the ground. He kicked his face, putting him out cold with his first blow. He then called 911 from the hotel phone.

About ten minutes later, two cop cars screeched to halt in front of the hotel. Two overweight officers came waddling down the corridor and into his room. He was standing over his assailant with the Magnum loosely pointed at his chest. His aggressor remained out cold. The two cops filled the doorframe as they entered with their guns drawn, mechanically repeating to him, "Drop the weapon, feet wide apart and hands on the wall, now!"

Tom obeyed the command almost subconsciously. Meanwhile, they simultaneously kicked his legs apart, frisked him, handcuffed him, and deftly swung him around almost in one single move. Their bulk was deceptive, as the cops moved swiftly, effortlessly, and precisely after many years of practice on the streets. They began to read him his rights.

"Wait! This guy just tried to mug me," Tom protested.

"Save it for the judge," said the first cop.

The second cop was calling an ambulance for the supposed hapless victim. Meanwhile, Tom, the apparent perpetrator, was dragged off to one of the waiting cars and bundled in the back. Radios were shrieking, sirens were blaring, and the lights were flashing in the background. Nobody was paying attention to Tom, and so further explanation seemed useless for the moment. They set off in the squad car and were soon speeding downtown toward the station. When they arrived, he was thrown brusquely into a holding pen. The sergeant informed him that he would be back in half an hour to take his statement; meanwhile, he could have one phone call.

Two hours later, after the intervention of his contact at Langley—who couldn't hide his smirk on the car ride back—he was in his hotel room. He was desperate to get some rest after his ordeal. Tom wondered if everyone was crazy in this country.

The next evening—just after he got back to his room to change for dinner—there was another knock on his door. Wary after his previous experience, he went to the peephole to check. He was surprised to see his assailant standing with a bottle of whisky and two glasses on the other side of the door. He looked clean and shiny, as if he had just showered and shaved. He was dressed casually yet garishly, in a loud Hawaiian shirt with a gold chain around his neck. He was noticeably calmer and considerably less red faced, but he was still giving off this faintly clammy aura.

"No hard feelings, buddy. Look, no gun this time," he volunteered from behind the door.

Tom opened the door cautiously and let him in.

"I just wanted to let you know I was okay and I'm sorry."

"Huh!" Tom grunted.

"I came round in the ambulance and realized what had happened. Brother, you taught me a lesson!"

He offered Tom a glass. "Scotch?"

"Sure," Tom handed him some ice from the bucket on top of the mini-bar.

"Well, I stake out several hotels in this area," the mugger explained. "I'm always on the lookout for unsuspecting tourists. Europeans are usually the easiest to fleece."

Tom watched him carefully and saw his hand trembling slightly. He looked nervously down at his drink as he spoke.

"I was hanging around in the lobby and I caught your British accent."

Then he looked up at Tom. "I confess I didn't pay too much attention to your physique. The Magnum has always been enough persuasion."

"Hmm," responded Tom.

"With most people it's all over in about three minutes. My average haul is about two thousand bucks."

Tom sneered. "Easy money!"

"People are warned off calling the cops. As a rule, they don't like to get involved with all the hassle."

"I imagine they just file an insurance claim back home."

"In five years of working the area I've never encountered the least resistance. So you came as a complete shock to me."

"Man, you've got balls!" Tom said, after sipping his whisky. "Only in America!"

Despite his misgivings about his American cousins, here he was in Yemen doing their dirty work. In some ways the Brits were America's more worldly allies, with generations of experience administering the unruly tribes of Empire. In the past, they were often chinless wonders thrown into the deep end. Typically, they were sent off to one of Her Majesty's far-flung colonies in their mid-twenties, as district officers or in some form of military capacity. They were forced to adjust rapidly to the local culture. Occasionally, they even started to go native, like T. E. Lawrence.

Even with this heritage, Tom concluded that no natural Brit, European or American for that matter, could ever fully understand Islamic fundamentalism or assimilate completely into Arab culture. It was too remote, too alien, like a westerner trying to blend in and become like the Japanese in Japan. Since the times of the crusades, Christian and Muslim had been competing over the holy places, completely delusional, fighting and dying for their beliefs.

At least the Americans had it half right with their emphasis on upholding human rights. The American Constitution and the Bill of Rights enshrined individual freedoms. Their basic respect for others, and even the way they took up of the cause of freedom in the Arab world was sound in theory—if not in practice. However, they had their orthodoxy and the Christian Right too, whose doctrine was similarly one of religious supremacy. They were conspiracy theorists who thought in terms of the final conflict, who talked of scatological analyses and the anti-Christ, while proclaiming that the return of the Jews to Jerusalem in 1948 signaled that we are in the Last Days.

Sadly, some of these self-righteous convictions about the world's pre-destiny had been absorbed beneath the skin of some of the most powerful individuals on the planet. It had shaped the thinking of America's political leaders, giving them some sort of moral imperative to keep watch over the globe. He speculated they were acting out passages of the Bible, imagining us entering the time of the Tribulation, as prophesied in the Book of Revelations. Meanwhile, Tom figured that if the end of the world was to come, it would truly be—as it says in the Bible—like a thief in the night, when we least expect it. The analyses would be wrong, the timing unforeseen, and the politicians wrong footed.

He knew in that instant that he would never get back to sleep. By now, his head was a seething mass of worn-out, tired political and religious contradictions. He had rolled around in the bed all night, disturbed by the faint, stale body odor that pervaded all the soft furnishings in the room and an uncomfortable stickiness of polyester. There were none of the crisp linen sheets and soft feather pillows of a true luxury hotel.

"Is this the best that Yemen can offer in a 'five-star' hotel!" he scoffed.

It was a sordid and distasteful place. Cynically, he concluded that only European tourists seeking adventure in exotic Arabia—having been duped by their tour companies—or those that were forced to visit on business would stay in this God-forsaken dump.

Yet, then and there, one of those little miracles of nature occurred, as if to contradict his contemptuous view. The ever-present dust in the air combined with the high altitude in Sana'a and imparted a characteristically deep red glow to the dawn. He stuck his head from under the pillow and paused for a moment to marvel at the breath-taking sunrise—or was the altitude just playing tricks with his mind? *Red sky in the morning, shepherd's warning* echoed some recollection from his distant childhood. He wondered what unforeseen consequences this magnificent sunrise would bring.

He tried to focus on the task of the day and the immutable logic that had brought him here to this hostile place. *We have to take the battle to their home territory; we need to strike at the source. The task is clear. Cut off the head of the serpent and its body will writhe in its final death throes.* He was now perfectly placed to do this and poised on the brink of the most important operation of his career, an assignment of historic proportions—Operation Sheikh.

Beyond question, Tom Salter was one of the best-qualified field officers in the Circus—as MI6 was affectionately known in intelligence circles. The name derived from its original home in Oxford Circus and was perpetuated by le Carré's novels. Tom had managed to play the game very, very well to date. He had been in deep cover for years as part of the Middle East Section. His original recruitment was as subtle as the screening was rigorous. Tom was left with a sneaking admiration for the Circus and their modus operandi.

Tom operated under the cover of the Anglo-American Tobacco Company, "vendor of fine tobaccos to the world." As a happy coincidence, most Arabs smoked like chimneys; therefore, his regular presence in this part of the world was easily justified. He pondered that in a curious way, this foul, addictive habit was being used to protect society from worse evils.

All of a sudden, Tom became acutely aware that his mind was wandering erratically; undoubtedly, this was due to his heightened state of anxiety, and he rebuked himself. He had to shake off this nervousness. He had a job to do and he had to stay sharp. His survival depended on it.

He got up and dragged himself into the scruffy shower room. The contrast was dramatic with the Burg al Arab, in Dubai, where he had stayed just last week, with its gold taps and in-room butler. The cheapest room there was about one thousand dollars per night, and it was all outlandishly decorated to Arab taste—Rococo and mock Louis XV. *Chacun à son goût.* Normally, he hated to be so extravagant, but Mohammed—his benefactor—had insisted, without a doubt wanting to impress him. He also knew it was useless to refuse such a courtesy in the Arab world, as it would inevitably backfire.

The shower coughed and spluttered into life, and he recoiled as the water came spurting out as a mixture of brown rust and sand. It was cold! Nevertheless, it was invigorating enough to help him wake up and shake off some of the dark thoughts that had been disturbing his equilibrium since before the spectacular dawn.

Chapter 3—
Before the Storm

Tom had gotten to know Mohammed Saad, the Yemeni minister of commerce, about fifteen years ago as part of his cover in the tobacco business. Mohammed, then a young official in the Government of Unification, was responsible for encouraging inward investment. Tom met him during one of his first deals and spotted his potential immediately. He was brilliant, charming, and intensely ambitious. He was one of a few token southerners brought into the administration after the war, as part of a show of even-handedness. However, from the outset he was treated as an outsider, without real access to the ruling clique. He obviously required help to realize his dreams. At Tom's behest, the Circus had been more than willing to help the aspiring future minister get ahead in government.

Their first project together had been an excellent investment. All had profited from the venture and in particular Mohammed, who had caught the attention of his superiors. At the same time, Tom made sure that Mohammed had become indebted to the Circus in a number of ways all at once. Thus, the hook was set.

Tom recalled how—with a helping hand from the Circus—Mohammed continued to demonstrate considerable flair in wooing foreign investment. Principally this was through Arab investors, World Bank development loans, and Islamic banks. He quickly became the international face of Yemeni business. He developed strong relationships with the Yemeni Diaspora in Saudi, who he persuaded to contribute billions toward the economic development of their native land.

Although his rise was meteoric, it was always self-limiting, since he never was a member of the inner circle who came from the northern tribes. His flamboyant style appeared to generate envy and suspicion. His opponents seemed to tolerate him, but they made it obvious, they didn't like him. Undoubtedly, he had been given the Ministry of Commerce in an attempt to restrain his ambition. It was one of the lesser cabinet posts, unlike Finance, Interior, and Defense. Tom's sources had revealed that the President and Prime Minister rightly wanted him close, exactly where they could keep a good eye on him, but not too close.

Tom had been Mohammed's handler throughout the whole period. However, following the attack on the USS *Cole* in Aden harbor, Uncle Sam had wanted in on the act. The Agency had no significant resource in Yemen and was keen to muscle in on the quality product that the Circus was generating through Mohammed Saad, unimaginatively code-named the Sultan.

Tom remembered saying to the chairman, "I don't want some damn Yank screwing up my textbook operation."

"I am sorry, Tom," replied the chairman, "the director is playing hardball on this one and I'm under pressure from above to cooperate fully with our friends in Langley. You must allow them direct contact with the Sultan."

Mohammed had laughed when Tom told him the news.

"Don't worry, I'll always feed you first."

Mohammed was enjoying this newfound attention from the world's one and only superpower. It was evidently an ego trip for him to go to the Gulf every year and do a clandestine, in-depth reporting to the director of the CIA. The Sultan's slick handling of himself and his formidable connections left a deep impression on his newfound masters, and his product became a major source for Washington policymaking in the Middle East.

Nonetheless, Mohammed was as good as his word. He was very careful not to alienate the Circus and shrewdly kept his finest output exclusively for Tom. Moreover, Mohammed was also very cautious about meeting with the Agency infrequently and then only outside Yemen. In other words, his only day-to-day contact with any covert organization was via Tom.

Mohammed had given Tom instructions before his departure for Dubai to brief the CIA on Operation Sheikh. He'd looked extremely nervous, no doubt because he was betting his whole future on this gambit. His neck was extended further than it had ever been.

"I want you to make sure all aspects of the operation are fully understood by the Agency," Mohammed said.

"We're playing for high stakes," Tom responded.

"You think I don't know it!"

"Don't forget, you've a lot to lose, but also a lot to gain."

"Tom, we've become good friends over the years. I trust you completely. Without you running things, I would never have helped the Circus mount such a delicate operation."

"So, what are you worrying about?"

"I cannot afford any mistakes by people who don't have your level of commitment."

"Weighing the risks, I think you should have bargained for a lot more."

Mohammed grinned back at Tom, but otherwise did not respond. Tom had helped him organize small operations, encouraging armed insurrection in the south. These hit-and-run raids were a way to destabilize the government and undermine Mohammed's political rivals. Now, as *quid pro quo* for his help, Tom was promising him much more—Circus support in a coup attempt.

"Keep your thirst for power well hidden," Tom warned.

"Of course, I'll do just that," he said. "By the way, Tom, is this the first time you'll have met with Kurt Schneider, the new CIA Middle East station chief?"

"Yes, and I'm a little curious."

"I met up with him a couple of months back, on the last of my trips to the Gulf. I confess that I can't trust him without getting to know him first."

"I understand completely—"

"And especially as the Agency has such a critical part of Operation Sheikh."

As Mohammed was a typical Arab, Tom realized his relationships must be built over time, and he had not had a chance to put Kurt's dependability to the test.

"My first impression is that Kurt is too squeaky clean," Mohammed said. "He was sucking up to up the director all the time."

Tom made a face. "How nauseating!" Meanwhile, he was left wondering what to expect.

*　　　*　　　*

Tom had called upon a small and largely anonymous office block in a quiet suburb of Dubai, ostensibly belonging to Terratec Consulting. It was in fact a very thinly veiled cover for the CIA. While it was relatively inconspicuous from the outside, when you gazed around the open plan floor inside and saw only a cross-section of white and African American faces, it was immediately clear that this was no normal regional office of a consulting firm.

"Good morning. How can I help you?" an attractive American receptionist greeted him.

Presenting his Circus ID Tom said, "I'm here to see Kurt Schneider … he's expecting me."

The receptionist made a quick call to verify Tom's details and said, "Please take a seat; somebody will be with you in a minute."

Tom wondered whatever happened to the essentials of tradecraft and blending into your surroundings. He understood that anywhere else in Dubai someone from the Indian subcontinent would have greeted him with some overenthusiastic and archaic courtesy like, "*Welcome, sir! In what manner may I be of assistance? Would you please do me the honor to be seated?*"

"Mr. Salter would you please come with me," said a striking woman, who he assumed was Kurt's assistant.

The name on her badge announced her as Laura. She ushered him in to wait in Kurt's reception area. He didn't know why, but he guessed from her exotic look and her accent that she was probably Puerto Rican—like la Lopez. He had been watching her; her hips swayed gently as she led him down the passageway and he was mulling over her being such an unusual sight so far from her homeland.

"Coffee?" she asked him, breaking his train of thought.

"Oh! Yes please, black, two sugars."

Laura promptly delivered his coffee in a styrene mug, watered down, as was customary back home. Tom realized it was even more subtle evidence that this was part of US government territory. As Tom's eyes wandered around Kurt's reception room, killing time, it was immediately apparent too, that the walls were purposely anonymous. There was no American trophy wall, no picture of the wife and kids; it was completely sanitized. The objective was surely that nothing should provide a clue to the real identity of the occupant or the true function performed here. Of course, it aroused even more suspicion.

Meeting Kurt did not disappoint Tom. He turned out to be a walking cliché—larger than life, the clean-cut all-American. He was clearly the boss, as his office was fully enclosed, away from the open-plan floor.

Tom gave a detailed briefing on Operation Sheikh, but got very little information out of Kurt. True to his profession, in the hour-long interview, Kurt asked a huge number of questions without giving anything away. Tom judged that the meeting was highly unproductive and that Kurt had been rude, but he wasn't going to let his annoyance show. The important requirements that the Americans would provide—satellite cover, drones, and signals intelligence—were established in the first five minutes, and before he left, Tom had codes and co-ordinates delivered on a pen drive, which he carefully slipped into his inside pocket.

Other than that, he underwent an interrogation. They had sat in Kurt's anteroom in two classic wooden chairs. There was a dainty coffee table between them, which Tom thought was going to topple over at any moment. No doubt, it was deliberately to create a sense of unease for any visitor.

"Who are your main operational contacts in Yemen, other than the Sultan?" Kurt asked.

"I'm sorry, Kurt," Tom replied, "but that sort of detail is strictly on a need-to-know basis."

Kurt should have been familiar with the protocol and known better than to try to compromise the mission in this way. Tom suspected that his bosses in Langley were not very trusting and somewhat over-anxious given that the Circus was running the show. He appreciated that they were not used to taking a back seat.

"Who's organizing your logistics?" he persisted.

"My usual crew," replied Tom.

Tom gave little away, deftly talking at tangents all the time, and he could see that Mr. Clean was getting frustrated too. Nevertheless, no more than he deserved. Kurt should have known better than to treat him like a complete rookie.

When Tom had phoned Mohammed after the meeting, the minister had become furious.

"Kurt had clear instructions just to listen and cooperate with providing any necessary backup," said Mohammed.

"Well, he didn't stick to his brief," Tom responded.

"What was he thinking about in the name of Allah? What's he up to? He was not supposed to be asking such questions."

"I'd really like to know what these damn Agency spooks are holding back."

"Me too—"

"I guess we'll find out sooner or later, and I'm damn sure we're not going to like it."

"I hate unpleasant surprises."

"You're not the only one! I also hate the idea that somebody is playing games on such a decisive mission."

"I'll speak to Kurt. Maybe there's a simple mix up."

"Like hell there is!"

*　　*　　*

Despite the fruitless briefing with Kurt, and his seeds of doubt, Tom had relished the opportunity to pass a few days in Dubai before returning to Yemen. It was much more cosmopolitan than the rest of the Gulf. You could still get a glass of beer and there was even pork on the menu in some places.

He headed off downtown past the bustle of the Creek to one of his old haunts, *Trader Rick's*, to see if any of the usual crowd was still around. There was the prospect of sharing a beer and swapping stories of life in the Middle East.

Tom discovered the place half-empty, which was unusual for early on a Thursday evening. Of course, there was the after-office crowd huddled over by the bar, talking shop. Apparently unable to get a release from their daily drug, they had begun to tell each other desperately dull and tedious corporate war-stories. As the alcohol began to seep toward their collective brains, they became louder and louder. Then Tom noticed some of the ad agency mob over in another corner and recognized a few familiar faces. He wandered in that direction.

At that moment, he was struggling to see if Paula was there, with her husband Martin. Now there was one lucky bastard who didn't know when he had it good. *She is one of the most sexy, precious gems of womanhood on the planet and he spends his life screwing around. What a fool!* Tom could hear his own woman shouting abuse at him: "All men are the same—they think with their dicks!" Well, maybe this Neanderthal did, but Tom Salter certainly didn't. After many years of philandering, he had learned the value of a stable relationship. He spun around as he caught Paula's scolding but sensual voice. His heart skipped a beat as he found who he was looking for.

"Wow, you're looking good. Where's that treacherous double-crossing bastard that you call a husband?"

"He's just over there getting the drinks … hey, Martin, another beer for Tom!"

Paula then started to rattle out the latest gossip, "Guess what? We've just bought a stunning villa on the Palm Islands."

Tom immediately thought that Martin and Paula had been suckered like so many footballers' wives into the latest property fad in Dubai. The construction boom was slightly surreal here, and he never ceased in his amazement.

"Prices are skyrocketing right now, just like the buildings, but sooner or later the market will come crashing down," he said.

"Come on now, Tom, you're such a cynic."

"I like to think I'm a realist," he said wagging his finger.

"We paid about a million bucks for seven bedrooms, servants' quarters, and our own private beach with a landing stage. To me that's good value."

His jaw dropped. "To me it's a lot of money!"

"Yes, but you only get a two-bedroom flat for that much in Central London."

"That could be a risky investment too."

"And the builder threw in a Freudian-looking powerboat with 650-horsepower inboard-outboard. It's Martin's latest play thing."

By this time, he was smiling. "Hmm, so it required a hefty bribe as well."

"Tom, why are you so negative! I'm sure we got a good deal. The same villa, next door, is on the market for one point two million."

"You don't have to convince me."

"What on Earth's that curious expression for then?"

"Oh … I'm sorry … I was just thinking how happy I am that I've never been tempted to be part of the latest thing."

"At least come back and see the house; it's on the way to your hotel."

"Okay, I admit I'm intrigued."

"Even better, why don't you come and stay with us?"

"Thanks for the kind invite, maybe next time; although I'll definitely make a quick detour to see the house."

"We'd love you to stay."

"I wish I could, but Mohammed will want to hear all about my night at the Burg, as a way to reinforce his generosity."

"Do you have to?"

"Well, I'm booked into one of the panoramic suites at four thousand dollars a night, which is too good to miss."

Tom saw Paula pout, as if she was pretending to sulk.

"And I want to be on good form tomorrow too, as I've got an invite to go sailing at the Dubai Offshore Sailing Club. I promised myself an early night."

"Oh, all right, but I won't let you off the hook so easily next time."

As they left *Trader Rick's,* he was following behind Martin and Paula's car. While he drove, he began desperately missing Karin, the woman of his dreams and his heart. Karin was hot-blooded, passionate, demanding, insatiable, and jealous. One of those imponderable things in life is why opposites attract. Too much fire in a relationship and you get burned. Too little and you are left out in the cold. All of a sudden, he became keenly aware of his own inadequacies. His inability to express his true feelings was the cause of much of the tension between them.

"Damn!" he said as he hit the steering wheel.

Why? Oh why, had he fallen out with Karin? It was such an ugly fight, as their fights always were. Trying to maintain a long-distance relationship by phone was impossible, and he knew it. He needed to give her time to cool down, but somehow, this time, it was different. Now it was almost two weeks since they had talked. He was devastated, as he had never gone so long without speaking to her.

It was such a stupid quarrel, as she wanted him back home, but because of the mission, he had made some lame excuse.

"Don't lie to me, Tom. You lead a double life. As far as I know you have another woman."

Tom felt powerless to respond, as he did not want her to have even the slightest inkling of what was really going on. Uncharacteristically his smooth talk didn't work either.

"That's just blah, blah, blah!" she said.

"What about your continuing infatuation with that aging Belgian playboy you used to go out with?" he replied. "What's his name, Michel?"

"You're just ridiculously jealous because he isn't a fickle, shallow character like you."

Then she stuck the knife in, "He isn't feeble in bed either."

With his ego bruised, he said, "So what's the real issue here? Let me guess, it's the same old problem—you're bitter and twisted because we can't have kids."

He'd crossed the line and she went silent. They both desperately wanted a child, but she was infertile, by all accounts because she had been raped in her early teens and had a botched abortion. She hung up.

His relentless desire to win the argument had carried him too far, as usual. Tom knew in his heart that he had to stop being so defensive and back down more often. She was hot headed and she knew which buttons to push to get a reaction. What she said really mattered to him, so much so that he found himself forgetting commonsense and starting to trade verbal punches. There were no winners to these rows, just losers. He needed greater sensitivity to understand her insecurity and respond to reassure her rather than escalating things. When would he stop being so emotionally inept and learn how to treat a woman as he should? He cursed his own stupidity.

His only way out was to bury himself in the mission. He had to forget the terrible angst he felt. After all, this was the mission to end all missions. It should be more than enough to keep him distracted. Once it was all over, he would have a lifetime with Karin to make amends.

Chapter 4—Arabia Felix

After Dubai, Tom had spent the past week in Sana'a preparing for the mission. That particular morning, he was on tenterhooks. Tom had an inexplicable sensation that he was being watched as he returned to his hotel room after breakfast. Walking down the corridor, he glanced over his shoulder a couple of times to see if he could make out who was behind him. Seeing no one, he shrugged it off, although he remained alert. He typically lived on nervous energy before any big assignment, much more so on this particular occasion. He needed to calm down, or he was in danger of attracting unwanted attention. He was probably just being overly sensitive anyway.

Regardless of the importance of Operation Sheikh, Yemen was not a safe place to be right now. There were less than two hundred UK citizens in the country. The committee types at the embassy had warned him to leave at the last British businessman's forum, which had been more than three months ago. Most of these pathetic so-called career diplomats and desk jockeys were surely long gone, pruning their apple trees in suburban Surrey, awaiting reassignment by the Foreign Office to a cushy number in a much less hazardous Caribbean backwater.

While walking down the street yesterday he was harassed by some self-proclaimed guardian of Islam—carrying a pole with a picture of Saddam—

yelling anti-Western slogans in Arabic and ringing a bell. He didn't need reminding that he was Infidel. *Huh!* They could keep their cherished land of milk and honey, mythical home of the Queen of Sheba. Yemen was a primitive feudal and intolerant place, still stuck in the Middle Ages. As far as he was concerned, it was a land of poor, ill-educated, and unruly hill tribesmen, whose value system has the Toyota Land Cruiser and the Kalashnikov at the top of their list. Moreover, their superstitious nature and misguided sense of morality was now fuelling their own holy war against the excesses of western civilization.

Then, full of self-doubt for a second, Tom wondered what on Earth he was doing in the middle of it all. Yet, deep down, he had no real reason to feel insecure; he was well trained, passing out top of his year. *Boy, I remember my old man gloating over that. To think it was the only time the old bastard ever displayed an ounce of real emotion at one of my achievements. Nothing, but nothing was ever good enough for him—school, college, my first job—only the best would do, what is more it was always expected.*

Meanwhile, the memory of Tom's walk around the spice souk yesterday came wafting back into his mind; he recalled the bright colors of the spices in the hessian sacks and the lingering aromas. He had wandered into the depths of the old walled city of Sana'a. There were antique rifles on sale, Martini-Henry single shot, pre–Arab Revolt; new coffee pots kicked around in the dust to give them more of an authentic, aged look; and the ambergris, frankincense, and myrrh laid out for the tourists. His imagination was stirred. He pictured this as the land where the biblical kings came from, searching for the newborn Christ. Not much had changed since biblical times.

"Hey, mister! *Sabah al noor ... Ta'faddel.* Come into my shop. Very good prices," a shopkeeper yelled as he passed by.

The pungent smells, with garbage discarded in the middle of the street, goats roaming freely, and the kids romping around, all created a distinctive atmosphere. He noticed one pretty girl about seven or eight years old, running through the bedlam. She was clothed in a charming embroidered green silk dress with bare feet and her hair tied back in pigtails. He witnessed a delightful spark and air of innocence in the little girl. While he observed the youngster out of the corner of his eye, she bounded gleefully down the alley to the right. Other children were close by eating *halwa*—a sweet confection made up of dates, lemon juice, sugar, water, and sometimes oil—a sort of sugary delicate mush. The kids were licking their sticky hands, as flies swarmed around their partially congested eyes.

The women were veiled all in black, waddling in unison down the street. They looked like misplaced penguins far from their natural habitat. When he got closer, Tom could see the henna adornment on their hands—as this is the only bare skin showing—seemingly, they wanted to make it as attractive as possible.

He pondered the enigma of Yemen, or *Arabia Felix,* as it was known in Roman times. Unlike its Middle East neighbors, Yemen still conjured up the illusion of the undiscovered Arabia of not so many years ago, before the oil wealth really came and started to corrupt. It was a time when traditional values and Arab hospitality reigned. The inhabitants of this era seemed to understand their mutual interdependency and thus the importance of demonstrating kindness even to strangers. It was a time, however, that provided only for peoples' basic needs, and most spent their days managing the harsh realities of their existence. They were dealing purely with questions of survival in extreme climatic conditions, with no electricity and few creature comforts. A cruel but simple life had molded a strong Arab identity; but now this was fading into a distant memory. It was being replaced by a consumer society with an insatiable desire for the trappings of modern life.

As Tom sat daydreaming in his room, his reverie was broken by a knock at the door. He was already on edge and since the incident in Washington; he always carefully checked before letting anyone into his hotel room. Through the spy-hole, he recognized one of the members of the Filipino band that had entertained them in the hotel restaurant the previous evening. She was an attractive sight, especially in this austere land. Intriguingly, she was still dressed in the sequined evening dress she wore on stage. She was anxiously clutching her bag. Her hair was disheveled and she seemed very agitated. It looked as if she had been up all night.

Tom asked through the door, "How can I help you?"

"Mohammed sent me," she answered.

Her voice quivered in a way that revealed her nervousness.

"You'll have to do better than that, sweetheart."

"No, please," she began to beg. "I have nowhere else to turn, and if they catch up with me they'll kill me, I know."

Tom decided that the terrified Filipina either was a very good actress or was genuinely in danger, or perhaps both. Against his better judgment, he slid the privacy chain across and unlatched the door. He withdrew his pistol from his shoulder holster and stood back as he opened the door. He motioned to her silently, pointing the muzzle of the weapon toward the table in the corner of the room. Meanwhile, he stuck his head out into to the corridor to ensure there was no one skulking behind her. He swiftly closed and locked the door behind him.

"Okay, what do you want?" Tom demanded, still pointing the gun at her. "Why are you here?"

"My name is Lady. I haven't known Mohammed for long. I was introduced to him after the show a few weeks ago."

Tom got a good look at her ample breasts, as she angled her upper body toward him while she spoke.

"Oscar, our manager, said that he was a very important man and that I was to look after him—treat him special, if you know what I mean."

He looked down at her.

"Mohammed invited me to his home and was very sweet," she said.

Tom sneered. "I'm sure he was!"

"I decided to take a risk and tell him what was happening to me. I was really frightened."

He stared at her.

"And why was that?"

"For several weeks, someone had been leaving evil notes in my locker with nasty threats like, '*Filipina whore, you will receive Islamic justice for your crimes. We will stone you to death. You will never leave Yemen alive.*' I just couldn't believe it!"

Tom raised his eyebrows.

"Oscar told me not to worry. It was just some perverted Yemeni customer who would never really do anything. In any case, he said we were under the protection of the chief of police."

"What did Mohammed have to say?"

"Well, he listened carefully to my story and appeared genuinely concerned. Then he told me that if ever I felt I was in imminent danger, I should knock on your door and you would help me."

Tom frowned, "Nice of him to mention it to me—"

"In the last few days, whenever I left the hotel I've been followed by one or two of those bearded fanatics."

"That's nothing out of the ordinary in Sana'a," observed Tom, who was so far indifferent to her plight.

"Yes, except that last night after the show, I went to change and one of them was waiting backstage. I was scared. You can't imagine how I felt…"

"Please just stick to what happened."

"Well, he put a hood over my head and then handcuffed me. He dragged me to the staff entrance, where two more were waiting."

Tom listened carefully as she described how they had manhandled her into the back of a van and then drove off.

"I had no idea where we were heading; I just sat on the floor trembling. I lost track of time, but guess it was probably a little under an hour before we reached our destination."

Tom was attempting to spot the tell tale signs of a liar as Lady spoke—

hand in front of the mouth, momentary hesitation and dilated pupils—but there were none. Her story did not quite gel for him, and his professional instinct told him to beware. Although she had almost convinced him, he decided that she was not quite the *femme fatale* she was pretending to be. Indeed, he concluded she was a smooth operator and extremely persuasive, but it was all too polished. It was too much of a coincidence that she would turn up at his door, precisely as he was about to embark on such a critical mission. Besides, she appeared to be very nonchalant about his pistol. More to the point, if someone had sent her, whom was she working for and what exactly did she hope to gain coming to his hotel room like this?

Tom was curious to hear the rest of her account. "So what happened next?"

"I think that they were scared to touch me at first, like I was some devil woman. They must have been concerned about preserving their Islamic virtue."

Tom caught a glimpse of her upper thigh as she laughed and crossed her legs.

"Like I was cattle—they prodded me with a stick to get me out of the van, then led me through a series of passageways and locked me in a room."

"Did you have any idea what they were planning to do?"

"By now, I thought they intended to kill me."

"So, how did you escape?"

"Well, my instinct for self-preservation took over. Suddenly, I was no longer scared. I was completely certain that unless I could get away, I'd be dead. I managed to force open a window and fell head first on to the ground outside."

"Ouch, that sounds painful!"

"It was. When I came round, I could make out that I'd been held in a low warehouse. It was in the middle of a large plot, surrounded by a five-meter-high perimeter fence."

"Didn't anyone see or hear you?"

"No, thankfully, I was out of sight and earshot of the main gate. Though I had no idea how I would get past the guards or over the fence."

"So, what did you do?"

Lady leaned her body toward Tom, gazing into his eyes as she gently stroked her hair.

"Well, I headed straight for a small building by the fence line; it was deserted at that time of night. By chance, it turned out to be an office with a door, which exited to the road."

He suppressed his instinct to call her a liar. "How lucky for you!"

"When I found myself in the street, I ran as fast as I could in no particular direction, trying to put as much distance as possible between me and those Islamic freaks!"

"That still doesn't explain how you got back here."

"Well, by chance, I stumbled upon the main road. Almost immediately, one of the front desk staff from the hotel, who was on his way to work, recognized me and bought me back."

"My, my, you were very fortunate. Now, what makes you think that I will help you? How do I know that this isn't some elaborate trap?"

She sat back and her eyes widened. Tom could sense that Lady was expecting a very different reaction from him.

Tom then ordered her at gunpoint, "Stand up and put your hands on your head. Now, turn around and face the wall."

"What!"

He unzipped her cocktail dress from behind and let it fall to the floor. Underneath, she was wearing a seductive set of sheer black lingerie, with a tiny lace thong, stockings, and a garter belt. She was concealing a holster inside her thigh. Tom knew in an instant that his gut feeling about Lady was correct. He reached down carefully and extracted a Glock 33 Pocket Rocket from the holster. Examining the weapon, he could tell she was a no amateur. The gun had been modified, with a trigger job and the machining marks smoothed out.

"A girl has the right to defend herself!" she said.

"Okay, now turn around and keep both your hands on your head," Tom instructed. "Let's start over. This time I want the truth."

Tom took a good look at her and realized how easily he could have been tempted under different circumstances. He wondered how many poor fools had fallen for her fatal charms.

"Mohammed didn't send me," she confessed.

"Who did?"

"I'm from the National Intelligence Coordinating Agency of the Philippines."

"So what are you doing here?"

"Well, I'm working as a contractor to Yemeni Intelligence," she replied. "Several of us were provided as part of an exclusive arrangement to further Philippine interests in the Middle East."

"Go on—"

"Look, if I tell you everything, I'm going to need some help to get out of here; otherwise, they really will come after me."

Tom shrugged. "I suppose so."

"I know you have friends in the right places."

"So, who's your boss?"

"I didn't make that part up—it's Oscar—and even though we're on the same side, he will throw me like a bone to these Yemeni dogs, just to keep them happy."

A convincing tear rolled down her cheek.

"Please help me."

"I cannot promise anything; it all depends if I like what I hear and if indeed I believe that you are telling me the truth this time."

Lady gulped. "I guess I have no option but to trust you."

"Now you're being more realistic."

"Well, I was briefed by the Yemenis to get close to you. They're aware that you work for the Circus and are suspicious about your relationship with Mohammed."

"They must have suspected me for years," Tom remarked.

"Recently they have been monitoring your messages, and although they cannot break the codes, they realize that something important must be going on, because of the volume of signal traffic."

"So, after you got *close to me*, what was supposed to happen?"

"Well, I was due to report back on Wednesday … or as soon as I had something. Then they were intending to bring you in for questioning."

"Sounds plausible, but I'll need some proof that what you are saying is true," he said. "I want the details of your Yemeni contact. I'd also like to know, when, and where they were planning to pick me up. If your information checks out, I'll help you."

Lady quickly scribbled the details down on the hotel notepad and handed it to Tom.

"Get dressed and wait here for me. I'll be back in an hour. Don't leave the room and don't contact anyone."

Tom was taking a bit of a risk leaving her in the room, but he rationalized that it would be a further test for her not to flee. Apparently, a bunch of amateurs had sent her on a futile fishing trip, and she evidently feared the reaction to her failure. Rather than risk their wrath, surely she would prefer to lay low in the hope that Tom would come through for her. He'd find out soon enough.

Tom discretely left the room and drove straight to his office in the business district of Sana'a. When he arrived, he calmly connected the phone to the scrambler and called Mohammed on his private line.

"Hey, Mohammed, it looks like we've got a problem," he said.

"What's up, Tom?"

He told Lady's story and asked Mohammed to check out the details.

"I'll call you in thirty minutes," he replied.

Twenty-nine minutes later, Mohammed was on the phone again. "Tom, it checks out. Although they appear to have nothing yet, this means that my enemies are getting close. We must watch our backs very carefully."

"Khalid is due to pick me up in the morning at the start of the mission."

"Okay, then stay out of sight; spend the day locked in your room with Lady," Mohammed instructed. "I'll arrange an escort for the Filipina and a private plane out to Dubai tonight."

"Perfect!"

"Her minders will come to your room this evening at seven; they will identify themselves with the code words *Private Dancer*."

"Got it," he replied.

Tom packed up his desk, left the building, and was back at the hotel twenty minutes later. As he arrived, Lady was sitting on the end of his bed watching the cable TV. There was some Hollywood blockbuster showing; bullets were flying and there were dead bodies everywhere. The Yemeni version was heavily edited to remove even the most innocuous love scene, yet it thrived on images of gratuitous violence.

"How can you watch that crap?"

She turned toward him and wiggled her dress over her thighs. "Would you like to do something else instead?"

Tom was not tempted in the slightest by her provocative response.

"No, but let's get a few things straight. We've arranged for your safe passage to Dubai this evening; in the meantime, you're to stay here with me—on your best behavior."

"Okay."

"It wouldn't worry me personally if we were to hand you over to the Yemenis."

She swallowed hard, "Oh, I see!"

He gave her a look of contempt. "You know the only reason we're helping you and not turning you over is we want the Yemenis to believe that their little plan has worked."

"Uh huh," she responded.

"I'd say that's a pretty fragile motive for saving your skin, and it wouldn't take much for us to change our minds."

At this, Lady bowed her head meekly and nothing more was said.

Chapter 5—Downhill the Whole Way

Khalid al Querishi had been working for the Circus for three years now; he was young and eager and wanted to be part of the action. He was a Yemeni and an excellent hire; he majored in electronic engineering at MIT and subsequently studied advanced weapons technology on a special graduate program at the Circus training facility near Cambridge, England. His cover was as a salesman responsible for the al-Jahni account. In reality, he was a multi-skilled technician with experience in armaments, radio, satellite—you name it. He had become very excited when he was assigned to Operation Sheikh, which he took as a real vote of confidence by his superiors.

Khalid called for Tom at the hotel in Sana'a before dawn, anticipating the long drive of fourteen or fifteen hours to the al-Jahni fiefdom in Lahij. Tom was already waiting and appeared from the shadows in the car park. Tom climbed into the passenger seat of the specially modified *Range Rover Sport* and threw his kit bag in the back.

"Did you get my message about the Filipina?" asked Tom.

"Yes, I did, and it was kind of worrying," he replied.

"She got off last night without incident. I left my door locked with the 'Do not disturb' sign on the handle and the TV on loud."

"Then I'd guess it will take the hotel staff at least twenty-four hours before they check the room."

"Come on then, let's go."

"Yes, so we are long gone before they notice and besides, the roads are much safer in the morning."

By mid-morning, most Yemenis would have been to the market to buy *quat*. *Quat* was a relatively soft drug, a naturally occurring amphetamine and a stimulant. The ritual involves rolling the masticated foliage into a ball and placing in one cheek, where it is chewed for the day. Driving standards in Yemen were lousy at the best of times, but because of *quat*, they deteriorated noticeably by the afternoon.

Along the route there were constant roadblocks manned by scruffy Yemeni soldiers. At the perimeter of Sana'a, they approached the first such roadblock. Lining-up in front of them were long-distance taxis—antiquated Peugeot 505 station wagons that were crammed with passengers, goats, and bedrolls hanging out of the windows. They were flagged down at the barrier.

"Tom, have you got two hundred *rials*?" he asked.

"Just a moment," Tom replied, fishing in his pocket for the change.

Khalid paid the small bribe and they were waved on without a second glance. This procedure repeated itself on each successive occurrence.

The first part of their drive was boring, along a flat plateau at two thousand meters above sea level. They passed through the occasional village with the characteristic quarried stone houses. Off in the vast expanse ahead of them, they could see some taller rock faces, rising up three hundred meters or more above the flat terrain. As they got closer, some small settlements became visible, hanging in the most precarious places, almost suspended in mid-air. The houses were clinging to the rock face, interconnected by the narrowest cliff paths. Goats, sheep, and some cows could be seen as a group of small dots in the distance clustered along the pathways, being reared, as it were, on the edge of a precipice.

"Khalid, you Yemenis are just like your animals, tenacious bastards!" said Tom.

"Huh!" he grunted, not amused.

They arrived at a small town around ten and he took a detour.

"Hang on a minute. Let me show you what's most important in Yemeni life."

He parked in the central souk, a circular area with battered pick-up trucks spaced around the perimeter. They were all loaded with a fresh consignment of *quat*, tied in bundles and partially covered with cotton rags. It was like a flower market without the blooms. Each customer took away a fresh bunch.

As they walked around he explained, "*Quat* is best chewed the same day it is picked. And, there's a scale of prices, the highest being for the more succulent, newer shoots."

They went shopping, starting with a couple of the smaller trucks and bargaining for the best produce at the best price. Finally, after ten minutes of haggling, they walked away with their bunch.

He laid it on the floor in the back seat, "Let's save this for later."

"Fine by me," replied Tom.

After about eight hours on the road, shortly before Taiz, they turned one corner and arrived at the edge of an escarpment. The panorama was stunningly beautiful. The road twisted downward probably six hundred meters, via a series of hairpin bends. The rocky mountainside was turned green by cultivation on terraces that formed waves and spirals around the edge of the chasm.

"Coffee used to be the staple produce here, but it has been all but replaced by another cash crop," he said. "The parallel economy survives on *quat*."

"A bit like the Colombians with cocaine, then?" asked Tom.

"Yes, one terrace is enough to make someone relatively wealthy."

"That must be very tempting for the farmers."

"See those pillboxes constructed all across the terraces? They contain sentries armed with automatic weapons."

"So, it's tempting for thieves too," observed Tom.

As they rounded the third bend, on their long way down, he swerved abruptly to cut inside a fully laden pick-up truck coming straight at them on the wrong side of the road. They sideswiped the truck, which let out a sort of hollow metallic clunk.

"God damn!" said Tom.

An instant later, they just missed the crash barrier, as he came back the other way. Khalid was struggling to keep control over the vehicle. Tom just closed his eyes. There was either a poorly protected six-hundred-meter drop on one side or a rock face on the other. Thankfully, he missed both and there was no serious damage.

After it all, he just shrugged. "*Inshallah*, all Muslims are fatalistic; they believe it's the will of Allah if their number is up."

"No shit!"

"I'm sure the driver of the pick-up was high as a kite on *quat*, too."

The incident bought home to him that danger could be lurking right around the next corner, literally. Although he was the better driver, it required a lot of concentration to stay alert and he was getting tired after a long stint in the driver's seat. He handed over to Tom at the bottom of the spectacular pass. They progressed steadily for a couple of hours while Tom was at the wheel. Meanwhile, he rested with his eyes half-shut. There was no conversation between them. Both of them appeared to be lost in their own thoughts about the mission.

They finally arrived in Lahij at about 8 PM. It was here in Lahij that they would encounter their guide, who was to escort them on the next stage of their quest.

"All I need to do now is eat and sleep," Tom said. "Remember, tomorrow we are meeting the al-Jahni at nine o'clock."

He looked the other way, as he had other ideas and little interest in sleeping that night. While they were waiting to get past a line of traffic, he leaned out of the window of the vehicle and spoke to a woman in the street *sotto voce.*

"I'm fixed up for the night," he turned and said to Tom.

Tom's jaw dropped.

"Leave me here, take the car, and I'll meet you in the morning."

"What just happened?"

"She's a friend of my sister," he said.

"But, how do you know what she looks like," Tom stammered. "She could be ugly as sin under all those veils?"

"You need to stay on good terms with your sister!" he grinned.

Chapter 6—
Into the Lions' Den

The involvement of the al-Jahni was part of a complex web that Mohammed had weaved for them. Even though Tom had done business with the al-Jahni for nearly fifteen years and they were co-investors in Mohammed's first venture, he still did not trust them. Abdullah al-Jahni, the patriarch and Nabil, his half brother, were both very shrewd businessmen; yet were renowned for being completely ruthless when looking after their own interests. They were close friends of Mohammed Saad and were involved in numerous joint ventures together. Sir Peter Wood—now the Circus chairman—had closed the original cigarette distribution deal with them. Sir Peter was a keen mountaineer and used to go hiking in the hills above Aden with Nabil. This had undeniably created a special relationship, which the al-Jahni was keen to exploit whenever they could. Until now though, there had never been any direct connection to Circus activity—and for very good reasons, Tom felt especially uneasy about changing this arrangement for such a critical mission.

Tom recalled when he had been invited to a dinner at the chairman's home, a fifteenth-century manor house in the beautiful Kent countryside. The manor was nestled in a pastoral setting, on twenty-five acres in the low hills between Tonbridge and Tunbridge Wells.

On arrival, Sir Peter came out to greet him. He shook his hand firmly and gave him a steely gaze. Sir Peter was tall—about six feet—with classic features, a thick head of gray hair, and a sinewy frame. He was dressed casually as befits an English country gentleman and from his relaxed manner and friendly smile, he seemed to relish his role as country squire.

"How about the grand tour?" asked Sir Peter.

"I'd love to," replied Tom.

"We renovated last year with original oak weatherboarding and Kent peg-tile roofing."

"You've done a fantastic job."

As they strolled past the outbuildings, Sir Peter pointed out an early clock tower with weather vane.

"It has a fully restored and functioning movement that chimes on the hour."

"It's magnificent."

Entering the west wing of the manor, Tom had an unrestricted view of the Weald.

"This is very picturesque. It's difficult to believe that all this stunning scenery is less than forty miles from London."

"Look there." Sir Peter pointed at a number of oast houses dotted along the horizon.

Tom peered into the distance, "It's an idyllic scene."

Sir Peter then ushered Tom along the corridor. "Come and see the Great Hall. It's the best bit—with archetypal king-post construction, all made of solid oak."

Tom was suitably impressed. It was resplendent with oak beams. He also observed that Lady Pamela, Sir Peter's wife, had decorated the room classically, tastefully mixing Middle Eastern and English. There was a long dining table with oak divider to the living room, and the oak flooring was covered with antique *kilims*. A variety of weaponry adorned the walls: a diamond studded Omani *kunja*, or ceremonial dagger, with silver and mother of pearl inlay; muzzle loading rifles and a gilded scimitar. Tom speculated that some items were surely gifts, while Lady Pamela must have spent many days scouring the souks of Arabia to unearth the others. He noticed—slightly concealed off to one side—some jaded climbing trophies that appeared to be her one concession to her husband's past.

Sir Peter struck up a conversation with him about his early experiences in Yemen.

"Do you remember Walter Ramsdale?" Sir Peter asked.

"Of course," replied Tom, "he was my first operational supervisor."

"There was something vaguely homosexual about Walter, although he made all pretences of being a red-blooded ladies man."

Tom smirked. "Yes, I recall how he looked on Fridays, when he used to stand around the hotel pool at the Sana'a Hilton in his posing pouch."

"As far as I can remember, he always took very good care of himself and was in excellent shape for a middle-aged man."

"It was embarrassing to watch every weekend though." Tom cringed as he brought to mind the scene at the pool.

"Tell me more," said Sir Peter.

"The first part of his routine wasn't so bad. After a little posing, he used to do a very competent dive, followed by several lengths up and down with an effortless looking crawl."

"Yes?"

"Well, then came the worse bit. After he got out, he would strut around, blatantly leering at the women by the pool, before sitting on a sun-lounger next to one of them and starting on his worn-out chat-up lines."

"Hmm, that must have taken some nerve." Sir Peter stroked his chin.

"Do you know what surprised me most of all?" asked Tom. "How often his corny approach succeeded with lonely airhostesses on stopover."

"The saddest part for me was when Walter was forced to leave the Circus under a cloud," said Sir Peter. "I received a report from the internal audit team, who'd discovered that he had been fiddling his expenses for years."

"I remember the affair very well."

"We found out he'd been charging hotel nights, gifts, and expensive meals to sustain his extra-curricular activities."

"You know, the rumor was that his wife knew exactly what was going on."

"Really, I didn't know."

"I believe she never joined him in the Middle East, as she didn't want to confront the situation."

"I suppose that makes sense."

"She was clearly prepared to turn a blind eye, so long as the checks continued to be deposited in her account every month."

"That must have fuelled Walter's loneliness and insecurity."

There was no malice in their remarks; they both seemed genuinely amused by his antics but saddened by the outcome. It had fallen to Sir Peter to fire him. Sir Peter had been humane about it; he'd protected Walter's pension so his family would not suffer for his misdemeanors. Ironically, this set off a chain of events that created a space for Tom, who was unexpectedly promoted to senior operative for the Arabian Peninsula.

Sir Peter, as he had become entitled after his elevation in the Queen's New

Year's Honours List five years ago, was the sort of Englishman Tom admired, a true gentleman—worldly wise, softly spoken, persuasive, and cogent. His powerful intellect combined with a clear sense of purpose. He perpetually weighed the odds and took calculated risks. He possessed a finely tuned, dry sense of humor, which he used to great effect. Indeed, Tom considered him the arch-proponent of what the Spanish called *humor Ingles*.

Tom listened intently as Sir Peter continued talking about his early years and how he came to join the Circus.

"I graduated with double first at Cambridge in English and PPE but didn't want any particular career, so I set off on a climbing tour, starting in the Atlas Mountains and then Kilimanjaro. I worked my way around the world from Africa to Asia, and ended up in the Himalayas, where I climbed K2."

"I can imagine that was truly the experience of a lifetime!" said Tom.

"But all good things must come to an end. After a year, my uncle intervened. He was deputy governor of the Bank of England at the time."

Tom looked at him wide eyed.

"He insisted that I get a stable career, and he introduced me to a friend in the Foreign Office, who had just the job for me. '*Was I interested in learning Arabic?*' he asked."

"That was intriguing," said Tom.

"Indeed, in those days, the Circus sent two young hopefuls to Lebanon to become Arabists, at a private institute attached to the American University in Beirut."

"What a wonderful opportunity—"

"For sure, Beirut was a melting pot of different nationalities and the most cosmopolitan destination in the Middle East."

"I've heard many tales about the old days."

"They're all true and more. What really sold me was that it was one of the few winter sports centers in the Middle East. I could indulge my passion for skiing during the weekends."

"Fantastic!"

"Yes, it was a great place to live, packed with history, archaeology, and natural beauty."

Tom caught a sparkle in Sir Peter's eyes as he reminisced.

"You were in the cradle of civilization itself."

"It became a personal obsession for me to discover as much as I could about the history and culture of the region. I went on several expeditions to Syria, Iraq, and to Jordan to explore the ancient sites."

Tom smiled, acknowledging Sir Peter's obvious pleasure.

"And the best part was that I was being paid for doing what I really enjoyed. Eighteen months later, after the induction course in Cambridge, much to my surprise, I was picked to take over the Middle East Region."

In the after-dinner conversation, Sir Peter had grilled Tom about his more recent experiences in the Middle East, pumping him for further tales of his exploits and anecdotes about the new players, including the Sultan. Tom could sense his nostalgia for his earlier years with the Circus. Surely, his mind was now filled with the stuff of diplomacy, liaisons with Joint Chiefs of Staff and such. It must have seemed so superficial to Sir Peter—all that politics and mumbo jumbo. Meanwhile, the adventurous spirit appeared to be still there inside, aching to get back into the field. Tom had concluded that he was envious and would love to exchange places.

Indeed, he wondered how Sir Peter would react if he were given the chance to join them on the ground for this particular operation.

* * *

Boiled eggs for breakfast and Tom was ready to face the day, a little worse for wear after a rough night's sleep, but still capable of functioning at near-peak performance. He met Khalid in the lobby and they drove to the al-Jahni compound in the city center. They parked in a cramped parking lot, where they almost dented the car for the second time, as they were jammed into a negligible space. Finally, they managed to squeeze out of the vehicle and walk up a flight of backstairs.

As they knocked on the entrance door, an Egyptian clerk greeted them.

"Please follow me."

He ushered them through a large modern glass atrium into a waiting room.

"Ahmed, will see you soon."

Punctuality is not customary in Yemen, and they were left waiting for nearly two hours. Tom was just starting to get extremely edgy when Ahmed, a junior cousin, appeared as if nothing had happened and invited them into his office.

"Come in and please take a seat," said Ahmed.

They went through the ritual of coffee and polite conversation for fifteen minutes. Then Ahmed turned to business.

"So, you want our help. How will we be compensated?" he asked.

Tom sensed that Ahmed was deliberately creating unnecessary ambiguity around something that had already been agreed upon, and frankly, by this time he was getting tired of the run around. It was classic al-Jahni, and Tom had witnessed the tactic too many times to fall for it.

He snapped, "Look Ahmed, we don't have time for your games. Take us to Nabil, now! Otherwise you'll have to answer to Mohammed Saad."

Ahmed winced.

"He'll pay you in due time—handsomely, I'm sure," said Tom.

Tom's anger appeared to take him off guard. He was not behaving like the usual polite Englishman he was no doubt accustomed to.

They took the elevator to the eighth floor and Nabil saw them immediately. He was the family closer for all key business deals; the most sophisticated of the two brothers and one of the best-educated members of the family firm. He studied Modern History at Cambridge, under a UK government-sponsored program in the early seventies. Used to a more western approach, he skipped the usual formalities. He began by apologizing for Ahmed's behavior, claiming he was acting alone.

Bullshit! Tom knew the whole thing had been staged.

Nabil then lifted the phone and called his secretary, rattling off instructions in Arabic, and within sixty seconds, Hammed materialized in the room. Hammed was a short, wiry Yemeni, with a hooked nose and leathery tanned face; he looked comfortably dressed in traditional garb, *thobe* and *ghutra*.

"I am guide for you," Hammed said. "I take you to the Jebel tomorrow."

"You will need to get some more suitable clothing," said Nabil, "mainly not to be so easily recognized."

"Please follow me," Hammed said to Tom and Khalid. "I find good clothes for you."

Nabil held his hand out to intervene.

"First, I would like to invite you both to lunch."

He led the way to the family dining room.

Lunch was more like a banquet. Abdullah, Ahmed and the rest of the male al-Jahni line were all there waiting for them. Each one performed the small ceremony to wash his hands before the meal, and then Tom and Khalid sat with them on cushions at a low table, set with a fabulous damask tablecloth, crystal glass, and gold cutlery. The drink was *laban*, a smooth, milky yogurt. There were multiple courses of lamb stew, baked chicken, fish and fragrant rice, bowls with all types of salad, more thickened yogurt, honey and pomegranate, and Arabic bread to dip into the food. Astonishingly, Abdullah and Nabil started to serve them before they had even touched their own plates.

Nabil explained, "It's a Yemeni custom that the most senior members of the household should serve honored guests."

"Well, you certainly know how to make an impact!" Tom declared.

The conversation was stilted at first, but after the initial niceties, it became a heated debate about American policy in the Middle East. The al-Jahni family members were foremost businessmen and, by necessity, probably some of the most westernized Yemenis. The family was run just like a business. Each of the new generation was educated in the US in something that would benefit the family: finance, IT, business administration, and engineering. However, despite their US education, apparently their anti-American sentiment ran deep.

"How come US politicians understand so little about our culture," one of the younger al-Jahni protested. "They have a completely myopic view of the region's issues and politics."

"Yes, they blundered into Iraq under false pretences," said another, "and they're now suffering because they didn't think through their exit strategy."

"Will their politicians ever learn to apply the basic lessons they teach us in business school?" added Ahmed.

"Their arrogance and self-righteousness will be their own downfall," railed another.

"They want to impose their cultural norms and religious convictions upon us, because they see us as backward and uncivilized," said the first speaker.

"How can that be?" asked Ahmed. "Their own civilization is barely three hundred years old, whereas ours is nearly three thousand!"

What surprised Tom was their depth of feeling. He couldn't figure out why the al-Jahni was willing to help them, as doing so was clearly supporting the western alliance. This was not about money, as the al-Jahni were fabulously wealthy; it was not about prestige, as hopefully no one would ever find out about their part in the mission; all he could think was that Mohammed was calling in old favors and was therefore concerned that the whole process involved a degree of coercion. This was a bad omen, especially if they were not fully committed to the mission.

It took several hours before the feast was over. Presumably in deference to Tom's sensibilities, there was no subsequent *quat* session to retire to, so the family members just drifted away after the meal, in all probability to chew in private.

Nabil recalled Hammed and he led them off to find their ethnic disguises. Khalid would have no problem blending in, but Tom's height was a difficulty not easily overcome. With the exception of Bin Laden, there were very few Yemenis over six feet and he would stick out like a sore thumb, even in tribal dress. Tom agreed that he would go by mule, as his height was better obscured that way. They were armed with Kalashnikovs, a belt with extra ammo, grenades, and a *jambiya*, or curved dagger, as was befitting a Yemeni tribesman.

It was time to retire and get some important rest before what was undoubtedly going to be a long, decisive day for Tom and Khalid. They arrived at the hotel and went straight to sleep. There was no fun and games tonight for Khalid.

Khalid shook Tom awake at 5 AM and together they dressed silently in their tribal attire. Shouldering their weapons, they left by the rear exit to find Hammed and their mules waiting for them in the car park of the hotel. Hammed had packed some additional ordinance just in case. Yemenis were more confident with extra firepower, and hence Hammed had brought in tow a couple of RPG launchers, a mortar, bombs, and twenty-five kilos of Semtex, plus detonators.

Tom knew that the biggest adventure of their lives was only just beginning.

Chapter 7— The Silvery Moon

Tom and Karin had their own bolt hole, far from the rest of the pack, in the Turneffe Islands just off the coast of Belize. It was a small, exclusive location in a national park, where no further construction could take place. The only industry on the islands, if you could call it that, was the shrimp farm owned by Tom's millionaire friend Rafael, who sold him the land to build. The rest was pure tropical idyll. Their house was nestled away in the dunes in a sweeping bay, with a stunning sandy beach and never another soul in sight, except for the occasional private yacht that anchored there.

The villa was painted with bright tropical colors and had a terracotta roof. It was light, bright, and airy, with hammocks on the veranda that overlook the sunset. Tom had recently spent money on doing it up. Consistent with his obsession for gadgets, he had made it a true digital home. Every function in the house was managed centrally from small computer that fixed the temperature of the water from the thermal panels on the roof, controlled the satellite dish tracking for the TV and broadband connection, and activated the security shutters. It even allowed viewing of the CCTV system right down to the jetty over the Internet from anywhere in the world.

"You can't be too careful," Tom had said to Karin.

To get there you had to own a boat and a degree of determination too, as it was about twenty-five kilometers offshore Belize City. During peak season, they had started a ferry for the tourists to some of the public beaches on the larger islands, but this had not greatly affected their privacy. The only regular means of access was Tom's launch, with a small outboard, normally tied up at the jetty.

The evening was calm. Karin Duval sat out on the veranda swinging gently in the hammock and gazing out at the beautiful seascape. The translucent turquoise water in the bay slowly surrendered to the fiery red sun. It was hot and humid and there was only a very gentle offshore breeze. Time passed slowly as she rocked back and forth. Night fell, and without any lights on in the house, she could see the full moon reflected off the becalmed, dark blue sea, as if in a mirror. She could also hear the waves gently lapping against the jetty, and the surrounding world was totally at peace. It was a soothing sensation, like watching a celestial light show while listening to nature's own mood music.

After about an hour, Karin went into the study to check her e-mail. She was hoping to receive a message from Tom telling her he was all right. She always worried when he was away, and this time she was especially concerned. She had some sort of premonition from the start of this trip that things were going to go wrong. Nonetheless, she kept reassuring herself that Tom was well able to look after himself.

* * *

Her mind wandered back to the night that they had met. She had seen him first through the crowd at a New Year's Eve party in Brussels, hosted by her friend and former classmate Annette, who now worked for NATO.

She had called Karin, "Oh! Please come to my New Year's party. You'll need a break after ten days with your parents."

"I'd love to … can I drag my brother Paul along?"

"There's someone I'd like you to meet too. He's gorgeous—tall, dark, and handsome."

"Oh no, I don't want you to fix me up … you know how I hate blind dates."

She was not at all sure what to expect. Nonetheless, she decided that whatever happened, it would be better than staying at home with her parents and seeing the New Year in quietly *en famille*.

How she had lusted after him from that very first moment. Destiny had somehow drawn them together and she had intuitively known from that first evening it was going to last. They were connected through an irresistible force.

She was immediately fascinated by Tom's looks and the sound of his deep, sexy voice echoing across the room. He was standing chatting to Annette's boyfriend, Pierre, nursing a drink in his hand. It seemed as if Pierre had nudged him and whispered something in his ear. Then he turned to look directly at her. His green eyes pierced her consciousness, and she felt almost naked before him, unsure where to hide.

He had moved purposefully toward where she was standing.

"Hi, my name is Tom. You must be Karin. Annette suggested we should get to know each other."

Her voice wavering a little, she said, "Oh, yes."

"Would you like to dance?"

"Of course, I'd love to."

Fate played its hand: as soon as they set foot on the dance floor, the music changed tempo to a series of laid-back romantic tracks. Karin had stuck to Tom like a limpet for twenty minutes. She was unsubtle at seducing him, brushing her body against his. They barely exchanged a word, yet she could feel that she aroused him. She didn't care, she wanted him like no other man she had met. She knew almost nothing about him, but the mystery was part of the excitement. She sensed she would have plenty of time to discover all his secrets later, to get to know the most trivial things about him. Up till now she went by the packaging, and she liked what she saw—he was tall, handsome and well groomed on the outside—and she felt sure he would turn out to be sensitive and kind on the inside. Her instinct hardly ever betrayed her.

Karin had come home to Belgium from the States for the Christmas holidays to see her aging parents, who lived in Leuven, just outside Brussels. It is part of the national psyche that most Belgians find it a wrench to move ten kilometers away from their birthplace. In that sense, the Duval family was very atypical Belgian, as her father, Paul Senior, was a career diplomat and they had traveled the world in Karin's formative years. They lived in many different places: Washington, Jakarta, Madrid, Budapest, Brasilia, and Kinshasa. What is more, Karin's mother, Irene, was Irish and fifteen years younger than Paul—another oddity, as not many Belgians marry foreigners.

When they sat down to chat, Karin found out that Tom and Pierre were old colleagues, working together on some NATO project. Pierre was a little eccentric, in the nicest sort of way.

"You know, I'm passionate about Porsche 911 Turbos," said Pierre. "I have three of them lined up in the driveway."

"Oh, really?" Karin said. In truth, she was totally disinterested.

"I spend most of my spare time making custom modifications to the engines to try and get more power out."

"I can't imagine why you would want to do that." Karin shook her head in disbelief.

"You know that I engineered my own water-injection system?"

"Pierre, I know nothing about cars. I'm sorry, but you're wasting your time with me," she said, laughing at him.

He turned to Tom, "The engineers in Stuttgart-Zuffenhausen freaked out when I told them. But they checked the limitations of the materials I'd chosen and ran stress calculations for me on modified engine components."

Tom just looked at him and raised one eyebrow.

"The Porsche technicians just love me, as I provide a test bed for some wacky ideas."

"Boys and their toys!" said Karin, beginning to get impatient with the conversation.

"You realize that Pierre is slightly crazy," Tom remarked, "like all those that have a touch of genius."

Karin was conscious that Tom was making excuses for his friend.

"His cars are absurdly fast and powerful. He should be in jail, considering the numbers of times he's been clocked breaking the speed limit," Tom said.

"The Belgian police are inept," Pierre responded. "I have the maximum points on my license."

"You need to be very careful then," said Karin.

"You know, it's impossible to identify the driver from the photograph they send you," explained Pierre. "And so my seventy-five-year-old mother pays the fines. Although she hasn't driven for nearly twenty years, she is close to getting her license revoked too!"

"I'm not sure if that's funny or just pathetic," Karin said.

"Well, I was so shitless the first time I went out for a drive with him, I just shut my eyes and prayed," Tom said. "Going for a ride in one of his 911s is a bit like sitting in a drag racer."

"So what's the big thrill?" asked Karin.

"It's amazing. When Pierre flips the switch you are pinned to the back of the seat, while the car accelerates to two hundred and twenty kilometers per hour in the blink of an eye!"

Karin decided that this was all male bullshit. She really wanted to get Tom out of this juvenile conversation, go somewhere alone together and tease him a little, get him to make her laugh.

Tom must have sensed her disquiet, and he responded quickly.

"It's just a way for him to cope with his male inferiority."

He then turned to Karin and asked her, "Do you want a breath of fresh air? It's getting claustrophobic in here."

"Let's go," she agreed in a flash.

They tumbled down the stairs together and out into the cold night air in the center of Brussels. They were well wrapped in coats, scarves, and gloves. It was eleven thirty and they were getting very close to the New Year. They encountered hundreds of revelers all pushing in the direction of the Grand Place. Tom and Karin were carried with the tide of humanity up the Rue de Bouchers, past the mass of restaurants and cafes. Most were displaying fresh produce outside to entice customers. The aromas were unbelievable. Although Karin tried, she could not physically disengage herself from the moving throng and stop to take a closer look.

Karin tensed a little and grabbed Tom's arm as a firecracker went off in a side street. He pulled her closer and put his arm around her and they continued like this, joined at the hip. It was a cold night, yet they were unconcerned as they gathered warmth from each other and from the seething mass. Everyone was good humored, chattering, laughing and joking in anticipation of the night's main event. The square was packed shoulder to shoulder, and from where they stood on the side street, they could barely see the clock tower.

It was a clear night and the full moon shone down. The beautiful medieval clock chimed midnight with a succession of figurines, each allotted one strike of the bell out of twelve. Karin listened attentively as on the final stroke, the assembled masses let out a loud cheer. People were hugging and kissing everyone in sight, wishing complete strangers a Happy New Year. Meanwhile, the fireworks exploded overhead and the firecrackers draped down the front of the buildings of the Grand Place echoed throughout the medieval square, creating a cacophony so loud that Karin was slightly deafened. Yet she was oblivious, as Tom had taken her in his arms and planted a huge movie-star kiss on her lips. They were lost in each other and in their long, lingering embrace.

She was falling hard for this guy she hardly knew. She felt like a teenager with a schoolgirl crush, and she couldn't believe it. After the kiss, her heart rate took a long time to get back to normal; they just stood there arm-in-arm watching the revelers until the noise subsided in the Grand Place.

Tom then turned to Karin, "Let's go and find somewhere a little quieter, where we can talk."

"I'd love to," she responded.

They retraced their steps as far as the Place de l'Opera and crossed the threshold into the relative quiet of the Café de l'Opera. By chance, they found a cozy and secluded table just beside a roaring log fire. They took off their winter paraphernalia of coats, hats, and scarves and sat pressed together on the sofa. After the cold night air, they basked in the mutual warmth and the heat of the fire. Tom ordered a glass of Belgian beer and Karin an Armagnac and a coffee and they began to talk.

Karin remembered very little of her own conversation, but to this day she can recite almost word for word what Tom had said to her. He was humorous recounting stories of his life in the Middle East, some of his heartfelt ambitions, his rather lonely upbringing at a Scottish public school, and his struggles with his strict disciplinarian father. She found something attractive in his boyish enthusiasm and vulnerability. This charming and handsome Englishman was sweeping her off her feet. They stayed locked in conversation for two or three hours.

In the end, Tom asked her, "Do you want to come back to my hotel room?"

"I'd like nothing better," she replied giving Tom a playful look.

Tom signaled the waiter, "Can you call us a cab?"

"I'm sorry, sir, but at three in the morning on New Year's night there will be at least a one-hour wait."

"Oh well," Tom said, "let's walk."

It must have been about five degrees below freezing outside. She wrapped up well against the impending cold, but after the intense warmth of the café, nothing could have prepared her for the shock as they left their refuge. It was like hitting a brick wall, although it positively re-energized her for the rest of the night. It was about five kilometers to Tom's hotel.

"With a brisk walk it will take us under an hour," Tom said.

All the way, she was anticipating the night of passion that awaited her. She was nervous. She didn't want to give the wrong impression, yet she was more than ready to leap into bed on their first date. She had no misgivings; it just felt right.

When they arrived at the Hyatt, the night porter opened the door for them and gave a knowing smile.

"Happy New Year, Mr. Salter," he said with a tip of his cap.

They hastily crossed the lobby and entered the elevator together. All Karin's thoughts were centered on Tom, paying no attention to the world around her. He pressed the button for the fourteenth floor. They almost fell out of the elevator door and into Tom's suite. As soon as they were inside, they grabbed each other and started to kiss. She led Tom directly into the bedroom, shedding her clothes along the way. They lay on the bed, Tom cupped her breast in his hand, and started to kiss her nipple gently with his tongue, she moaned, almost inaudibly, and tensed. Her hand found him big and hard—a lovely surprise!

She was aching for him, desperate for fulfillment; she wanted him so badly that she grabbed him and placed him between her legs, pushing her pelvis up at him, letting out a sharp cry as he entered her. He was wild and forceful, and they made mad, passionate love. It was amazing, unlike anything she had ever experienced.

"Oh my God!" she screamed in ecstasy, as he finally exploded inside her, after making her come four or five times—she had lost count.

Afterward, they just lay there for almost an hour, their bodies entangled. Karin was in rapture. She became absorbed in Tom's embrace until she finally succumbed to a blissful sleep.

They woke simultaneously at about nine, still locked together. Karin was feeling horny. They kissed softly at first, Tom tenderly running his hands over Karin's naked body caressing her, awakening her senses. She felt his warm, manly presence next to her skin. She pushed him gently onto his back and climbed on top of him and started to rotate her pelvis, slowly at first, feeling him stimulated by her movement. She then began to move more quickly and ardently as she felt his excitement mount. She wanted him so badly, letting out a gasp as he smoothly slid inside her. She felt as if he was going to devour her; the pleasure was so intense, as he began, almost effortlessly, to make love to her again. Their rhythm gathered pace and as she reached climax she let out a scream of delight. They came together in unison, igniting all her senses. Her nerve endings were raw with exhilaration. It was like the poem, *La Mort des Amants,* the Lovers' Death—an out-of-body experience as her soul temporarily left her body. All her energy drained, she collapsed on top of him.

"You selfish bastard!" she cried out.

"What!" he replied.

"Where have you been all my life? From now on, I'm not letting you out of my sight."

They ordered breakfast in bed, room service. Karin called her brother Paul to say that she would not be back until the evening and to make excuses to her parents. She desperately wanted to stay here in bed with Tom, to keep him as her prisoner and have wild abandoned sex all day long. She needed to make sure that this was not going to be a quick New Year's fling and that she would be embedded in his consciousness, so he would never forget her.

Eventually, sometime after breakfast, they decided to get up and brave the cold.

"Let's go for a drive," said Tom. "It is a beautiful day—crisp and clear with lots of sunshine. It's a perfect day to go to the Ardennes."

"Okay."

"I'd love to go to Bouillon to see the Château and enjoy a Belgian lunch. What do you think?"

"You could talk me into anything you want right now."

"All right, maybe we could take a quick look on the way back at the Cistercian monastery at Orval, where they make my favorite beer."

Karin just nodded in agreement, as she was delighted to spend the day with him. He called down to the concierge and arranged a hire car—a BMW Seven Series—to take them in comfort and style along the well-appointed Belgian roads. Karin was thankful that nowhere was far from anywhere in Belgium, as you could drive from one side of the country to the other in a little over two hours. The road system was remarkable. From Brussels, they headed south on the E411 in the direction of Arlon, driving at over one hundred and eighty kilometers per hour. In just over an hour, they reached the Neufchâteau exit. Karin barely noticed their speed as they were cruising along. Only when they came up fast behind another car did she get any sensation of the high velocity at which they were traveling.

As they left the highway, the route narrowed into a picturesque winding and undulating road with forests on both sides and some spectacular views of the River Semois. The town of Bouillon was nestled in a large U-bend in the river with the Château in the middle, commanding views over the surrounding countryside. She was reading the Michelin Guide and explained that Godfry de Bouillon, the leader of the first crusade to Jerusalem in the year 1096, once owned the Château.

They arrived in perfect time for lunch and parked in the hotel car park. The restaurant had an extravagant menu, all based on regional produce. It was a romantic setting, with a magnificent panorama from their dining table across the river valley to the Château. Karin remembered eating very little, yet it was all exquisite food. They started with Kir Royale as an aperitif, with canapés accompanied by foie gras, followed by *vol-au-vent* and a sorbet to clean the pallet. Then, they were served a delicate fish course with a shrimp sauce. The wine Tom chose, a Pouilly Fuissé, blended perfectly with the flavors of the dish. After that, as their main course, they enjoyed a rich *bœuf bourguignon* with a bottle of St Emillion, 1er Grand Cru Classé.

Karin watched while Tom ate ravenously. She sensed that the wine was going to her head and slowed the pace of her drinking. Even so, she was feeling very mellow at the end of the three-hour epic. They finished off with *crepes flambés* doused in Grand Marnier, adding more alcohol in a final flourish. Karin saw that Tom seemed a little unsteady as they left the restaurant, no doubt due to the heady combination of fine food and wine. As Karin had been a bit more cautious in her drinking, she took the car keys from Tom, just in case.

"Let's go for a tour of the Château, to clear our heads," she suggested.

The late afternoon sun was shining bright and low in the sky. It almost blinded her as they wandered down the road.

"This place is amazingly well preserved," Tom said, gesturing toward the

Château. "You can even imagine Godfry preparing to go off to war, never to return."

Karin was reading the guidebook. "It says here that he financed the crusade by selling the Château to the Prince-bishops of Liege, so must have been pretty sure that his destiny laid far away in Jerusalem."

"Fascinating to think that he was the first of many to take arms in the cause of the Holy Places, setting Christian against Muslim," said Tom. "You realize that this was where it all started. He can have had no idea what he was unleashing on the world."

She glanced at him sideways. "I would never have thought of it like that."

They ambled along arm in arm, more like an old married couple than newly encountered lovers would. Having done their quick tour of the Château, they circled back to the car. Karin took the wheel and drove them toward the French border and the Abbey of Orval. However, before long, she noticed that the warmth of the car combined with last night's partying and the epic lunch appeared to weigh so heavily on Tom that he fell fast asleep in the passenger seat. She looked at him out of the corner of her eye and got goose bumps. She felt as if she had known Tom all her life, not less than twenty-four hours. She didn't believe it was possible to fall in love so quickly, but he was definitely *the one* for her. She pressed down on the accelerator, adeptly negotiating the winding road back toward the main highway and Tom's Brussels hotel.

Chapter 8—
A Moving Target

Tom reflected that in similar conditions to Afghanistan, untamed and heavily armed tribesmen had inhabited this mix of rocky and green terraced hills for centuries. He scanned the horizon with his binoculars at the start of their trek.

"No sign of life," he said.

"You're correct to be very wary of Yemeni tribesmen," Khalid declared. "You'll remember back in the sixties when the British army was easily out-maneuvered and forced out of Aden."

"It was hardly a fair fight," Tom responded.

Khalid smiled, "I agree, without proper knowledge of this terrain, they didn't stand a chance."

"Wiry tribesmen used to the landscape and armed with the latest automatic weapons are formidable opponents. They should always command the utmost respect!"

"Without a doubt," Khalid laughed.

"In any case, you Yemenis just love to fight. If you're not fighting the British, you're fighting each other."

Tom raised one eyebrow and looked quizzically at Khalid. "Am I right?"

"Okay … you're right … I admit it. We've always been an unruly bunch."

"You can't deny it." Tom shook his head.

"Well, nowadays, the game has changed completely and the fight is outside Yemen."

"All the same, the armed terrorists roaming these hills are highly dangerous."

"And now they're even more difficult to locate, as they're constantly on the move to avoid detection by American satellites and spy planes."

After Afghanistan was invaded, Yemen was the natural choice to become the principal training ground for al-Qaeda specialists and the hiding place for some of their top echelons in the hills above Aden. Their funding was conveniently supplied by rich Yemeni émigrés with their multi-billion enterprises in neighboring Saudi.

"Here we are at the *Source*, the beating heart of the al-Qaeda organization," Tom said. "I can understand why Bin Laden chose to return here from Pakistan."

"More than that—Bin Laden is the peoples' champion, he has mythical status in this land."

"That must make him even more secure here. And besides, Yemen is endowed with an endless number of hiding places where he can simply disappear."

"What is more, he's extremely well protected by his constant bodyguard—the Aden-Abyan Islamic Army."

Tom's orders for Operation Sheikh were simple: identify Usama Bin Laden's—or UBL's—hideout as quickly as possible; attach the homing device, which would send precise co-ordinates for the target; and then get out. The Sheikh—as his closest followers knew him—would be eliminated. The reward of twenty-five million US dollars would be incidental. History would never discover the assassins' true identities, as Tom and Khalid would melt back immediately into obscurity. The deed would be done by remote control.

"Khalid, we're putting all our faith in your bunker-busting bomb," he said. "Hopefully it'll do the trick."

"Conventional laser-guided bombs cause considerable damage to most targets," responded Khalid, "but UBL's heavily reinforced underground bunker requires something special."

Tom squinted at Khalid.

"The BLU Super Penetrator is the best option we've got. It uses a warhead with a hard target smart fuse, which gives us much greater depth of penetration and precision. It can even be programmed to detonate the bomb at a specified depth."

Tom never ceased to be impressed by Khalid's familiarity with weapons' technology. The bomb was due to be launched by a Harrier jump jet from HMS *Invincible* standing by in Arabian Sea that much he knew. As Tom went over this in his mind, it all seemed too easy. The mechanics of the operation were not complicated. Finding UBL in his bunker would be the main challenge, and that was Hammed's role.

It was remarkable how Public Enemy Number One and the World's Most Wanted Man had evaded capture for so long. Undoubtedly, he was well protected by rich, powerful, and especially wealthy friends. His sponsors could conjure up any imaginable type of armaments, transportation, communications, and, most important, a virtually impenetrable hiding place.

Spy satellites had watched carefully since the National Geospatial-Intelligence Agency—or NGA—observed unusual signs on a construction site about three years back. Close to a small-fortified village in the hills overlooking Lahij, abnormal rock drilling and explosions were noticed. Allegedly, an observatory was being built as a government-funded research project. However, intelligence sources suspected it was a secure bunker.

Regular NGA tracking highlighted that there was suddenly a large amount of concrete being poured, completely disproportionate to the task of building an observatory. Unfortunately, the satellite covering the Southern Arabian Peninsula and the Horn of Africa was only able to gather intelligence for some three hours a day. It was felt that a change in trajectory, regular over-flights by spy plane or a drone, might attract too much attention. Therefore, they had been unable to verify the details of the target completely. It appeared that the wily Yemenis were carrying out the key construction activities out of sight of any prying eyes. A spy plane from Iraq caught a little more detail when it was unexpectedly routed overhead—seventy thousand feet—but there were no dynamic pictures.

Tom was not naive. "We both understand that UBL is highly suspicious and well protected by his fiercely loyal bodyguard."

"And no doubt he's continuously on the move," said Khalid.

"Even if he's in his bunker when we arrive, he will run the instant he gets wind of us," Tom said.

"Right," responded Khalid.

"So," Tom said, "Hammed must somehow deliver the nearly impossible and get us through the outer-ring protecting UBL."

Tom could not understand why Hammed seemed so nonchalant, while refusing to give away any part of his plan. Tom had to trust in Mohammed and the al-Jahni, but he despised not having all the cards in his hands. The al-Jahni usually only played for their own side and no one else's.

Mohammed had insisted, "I've seen to it that the al-Jahni will do their part. Trust me!"

Very skeptical, he had responded, "It's still a big leap of faith for me."

For the time being though, Tom had more immediate concerns. With their mules roped together, they were following a narrow path that wound its way up the side of the Jebel to the north of Lahij. He abhorred riding, especially in such an ambling style. As his mule plodded along the rocky path, he sat square in the saddle and began to feel the sores developing on the inside of his thighs after the first two or three kilometers. He completely lacked finesse on a mount and was unable to get comfortable and successfully synchronize his movements with the mule. In this case, he did not even have to worry about guiding the mule with reins, as he was tied into the caravan. He cursed under his breath, as he persistently shifted about in the crude saddle to reduce the pounding to his private parts.

They had passed some large fields of alfalfa and then some dog-eared corn on their way to the foot of the mountains. The stony fields were poorly tended, as were the farmers' ramshackle dwellings to the left of the path. A Yemeni woman, swathed in black with a terracotta pot balanced on her head, was collecting water from the well. She didn't give them a second glance and scurried off in the direction of her rudimentary home. The path narrowed and steepened sharply, as they began to ascend diagonally across the side of an almost sheer rock face, which rose up about five hundred meters above them. Tom felt very uneasy on the mule, as he peered beyond the edge of the narrow trail at the drop below.

They were all alone on the track and relatively inconspicuous, at least from a distance, as they looked like a typical mule train carrying provisions to one of the villages in the hills. As they moved in and out of the shadows along the path, Tom sensed a noticeable temperature shift. The early morning light spread warmth, as the cool night air was displaced. It cast shadows in the Jebel, and Tom could see the contrasting colors of the limestone and the scrub vegetation. What's more, he could now make out the topography. Later in the day, the sun would bleach out the entire landscape.

They wound in and out of the rock face, and just as Tom thought they were about to reach a dead end, the path opened up again in the opposite direction. They finally emerged at the top of the cliff onto a plateau. Now some five hours out of Lahij, they stopped for a snack. The sun was beating down on them and severely burned any exposed skin in a matter of about an hour. Tom was grateful for his tribal dress, not only as a disguise but also for its practicality. They sat cross-legged on a large round rock overlooking the path and ate in silence, the mules tethered below them. They had brought some Arabic bread stuffed with chicken salad, which satisfied Tom's hunger.

Afterward, he took some long, deep draughts from the water skins. Tom was glad to be off his mule for a few minutes and started to feel much more animated and ready to continue after some sustenance.

Hammed finally broke his silence to point out their route. "Road no good. Al-Qaeda watching."

Tom already realized that not only was the unpaved road to the north some fifty kilometers longer, but they would never have got within twenty kilometers of their objective without being stopped and searched. It would be permanently watched. It was futile to attempt it.

"This way only fifteen kilometers," Hammed indicated in the direction of the observatory.

From the map, he could see that the plateau went on for a further fifteen kilometers, until it reached the rocky outcrop on which the observatory had been constructed.

Hammed pointed to the rear of the observatory. "We must climb."

Carefully examining the contours, Tom saw that they would have to scale a perpendicular rock face rising up nearly one hundred meters. He wondered how he had missed this earlier.

"In night, we climb," he said. "No guards."

Tom immediately understood that al-Qaeda had left the cliff-side undefended.

"Look," said Hammed, as he showed them the rock-climbing gear he had stowed on one of the mules: rope, pitons, karabiners, and climbing shoes.

"It's risky, but I like the element of surprise," said Tom.

After their rest, the mule caravan set off again and wound its way across open terrain for a further five kilometers toward their objective, until they arrived at a small gorge.

"We wait now," said Hammed.

"We're now within striking distance," Khalid observed.

"But, we must take great care as we'll be at our most vulnerable at this point," responded Tom.

"Even so, this seems like an excellent spot to hunker down until nightfall. We'll be well out of sight."

"You're right. We can also leave the mules here, as we'll need to undertake the last leg on foot."

There was a small spring in the gorge and a sparkling clear rock pool. The pool was sheltered from the harsh rays of the sun by a slight overhang. The spring bubbled to the surface from subterranean depths. As Tom looked more deeply, he saw myriad colors that reflected deep into the pool. Here was something magical, as if it were an oasis summoned from an Arabian fantasy.

The first thing Hammed did was to refill their water skins, as fresh water was a scarce commodity in these parts. Tom then stripped off to his shorts and dived into the pool.

He waved them in. "What are you afraid of? Come on in. The water's really refreshing!"

"If it doesn't bother you I'll just watch," replied Khalid.

Khalid and Hammed were more reserved than he was, part of their culture, he guessed. Tom carried on, invigorated by the experience after the arduous journey. He then sat on a rock to dry off and took a quick power nap. Khalid hid in the shade and followed suit. Meanwhile, Hammed tended to the mules.

Tom and Khalid both woke after about an hour and sat discussing their tactics. Khalid had bought some of the NGA images to work with.

Khalid scrutinized the photos. "It's almost impossible to make out the cliff on these images, which is why we must have missed it before."

"I had no idea that it was such a strong feature," said Tom.

"Look, all the gun emplacements are facing forward toward the road, which should have given us a clue." Khalid circled them with a marker.

"You're right." Tom chuckled. "Well, I'll be damned."

"So what's your idea?" asked Khalid.

"Well, Hammed can dig in at the base of the cliff to guard our escape route. He has an arsenal fit for a small army," replied Tom.

"And if the going gets tough he certainly has sufficient firepower to defend himself," Khalid said with a grin.

"If we scale the cliff without being noticed, we can plant the homing device and enough Semtex on a timer to cause confusion and abseil back down to Hammed."

"That makes good sense to me. We should be back here at the gorge in time witness the show."

"Now, what can go wrong?" Tom asked.

They went through the routine contingency planning exercise, exactly as the Circus training professionals had taught them.

"Well, first," said Khalid, "we could be spotted on the approach to the observatory. We'd then be left no option but to scatter and retreat to the best of our ability."

"I think that's unlikely."

"So, second, and equally unlikely in my opinion, if we are spotted on the way up the cliff, we'll have Hammed to cover us."

"Yup—although I guess we'd be exposed when we abseiled back down."

“Finally,” Khalid narrowed his gaze, “I think the biggest risk is if we get caught planting the homing device and the Semtex.”

“You’re right, and then we’ll probably end up in a firefight. But hopefully we can sow enough confusion with a few grenades and get back to our jumping off point.”

“That ought to do the trick, I agree.”

“After all, we’ll have the element of surprise in our favor.”

* * *

They headed off purposefully at dusk, marching in the direction of the observatory, dressed in fatigues with blackened faces—all with the exception of Hammed, of course, who kept his traditional attire. The ropes and climbing gear were in Tom’s backpack; Khalid carried the Semtex, the light arms, and the homing device; and Hammed had one mule loaded with all his armaments. The mule was muzzled to avoid any inadvertent braying. It took a little over ninety minutes at a brisk pace to reach the base of the cliff. It was a cloudy night, so there was no moonlight for them to see, or be seen. Mercifully, Hammed was sure footed and picked his way through the rocky ground with skill. Tom and Khalid just traced his steps.

As they arrived at the cliff, Tom was very edgy. He could hear little noise from the camp above, except the hum from the generator sheds about three hundred meters away and for an instant, he was puzzled by this. They began to cling to the rock face, with Tom setting off as lead climber. Tom was a little shaky, as it was a long time since his youthful rock-climbing instruction in the Cairngorms. He had been highly proficient back then, regularly mastering climbs categorized as severe and very severe. He quickly became lost in concentration and forgot any nervousness and he surprised himself by remembering most of the moves. *Huh … it’s just like riding a bike!*

Until he got to near the top, he had few difficulties with the climb. However, at this point, he had to swing out and then grab on under an overhang. He used a couple of pitons to secure the rope for Khalid, who he could see performing manfully at the rear. He was anxious about attracting unwanted attention as he hammered each of the pitons into the rock face. As an extra precaution, he wrapped them in cloth to deaden the ringing. Fortunately, the generator was creating enough background noise to mask any sound.

Tom swung over the lip with his gun at the ready and emerged behind a handy rock. Unsure of what to anticipate, he could feel his heart pumping fast. He immediately flipped his night vision goggles down to scan the field of view. He couldn't see a soul in sight. Over by the road was the accommodation hut. Its lights were on, but there were no signs of movement.

"I can't see anyone," Tom whispered to Khalid as he joined him. "Something's wrong."

They fanned out on Tom's signal, moving cautiously toward the observatory, crouching behind another set of rocks only ten meters from the door. Tom saw the trip wire just in time, just a meter in front of him.

"Shit, this area is mined!"

He signaled to Khalid to stop right where he was.

Tom was no longer worried about meeting any resistance. *They were expecting us.* The observatory looked abandoned. Whoever had tipped off al-Qaeda didn't really matter now. Tom was certain that the smart bomb would no longer do the trick. UBL was in all probability already on the move, and this required completely different tactics.

"Oh, fuck!"

He exhaled loudly as he slumped down facing back toward the cliff. His brain started to recalculate all the options and associated risks. At that instant Tom noticed something odd about the rock he was hiding behind; it was plastic and hollow, like the type you get in garden centers. Presumably designed to give nothing away from the air, but here on the ground it was poorly camouflaged. He gingerly lifted it and glanced underneath, using his flashlight. It was a ventilation shaft, which he deduced originated in the bunker below. He signaled to Khalid to come over slowly, keeping his eye out for more wires. To his surprise, the shaft appeared to lead straight downward for about twenty meters or more, without any trap. These Yemenis hadn't managed to find a specialized military architect, although they clearly had the money. *What a stroke of luck!*

He got Khalid to hand him the homing device, activated it, and lowered it down the shaft using a cord from his rucksack.

"If there is anyone still left in the bunker, they're about to get the very nasty surprise!" Tom said.

"Yup," responded Khalid.

They threw most of the Semtex with timed detonators up against the building, for good measure. Then, treading very softly, they made their way back to the overhang at the point where they came up. Tom's eyes were straining through his night-vision goggles to see any more trip wires, but there were none. Al-Qaeda must have expected them to get closer to the building before blowing themselves up. They would be watching from the road and waiting for the fireworks. Tom could guarantee that they would get their money's worth later.

Tom and Khalid clipped on to the rope with their karabiners and were down to the base of the cliff in less than a minute. After quickly removing their harnesses, Khalid tried an owl hoot, which had been the pre-arranged signal for Hammed, but he got no reply.

Tom shouted softly. "Hammed?" but there was still no response.

After a five-minute search, he made out the mule and found Hammed, with his throat slit, lying among his arms cache. He never even fired a shot. He looked almost peaceful.

"Sonofabitch!" said Khalid through gritted teeth. "It was a setup—bastards!"

Tom signaled with his hand. "Let's go this way."

Tom led at a fast pace. They circled the outcrop and came around by the generator shed. There was about fifteen minutes before the Harrier strike and the timers on the Semtex would go off. They needed a fast escape route. Tom breathed a sigh of relief when he spied a Toyota pick-up just behind the generator. It was locked, but Khalid was in the vehicle in less than sixty seconds. Tom watched open mouthed as he broke open the plastic cradle surrounding the steering column and hotwired the vehicle in another thirty seconds.

"Goddamn!" Khalid screamed. "It's almost out of fuel."

Tom grabbed a hose from the generator day-tank and siphoned off fuel into the pick-up—another precious five minutes wasted. Just as they were about to get in the truck to take off, they heard the unmistakable chatter of automatic weapons and suddenly bullets started flying all around them. By instinct, Tom and Khalid hit the deck and then systematically scanned the field of view to determine the source of the attack. Using sign language, Tom indicated that crossfire was coming from one of the gun emplacements down the hill to their left and from the observatory behind them. The rapid fire clunked and clanged as it ricocheted off the generator.

"We'll never get past that emplacement," Tom yelled at Khalid.

Before Tom could say anything more, Khalid had rolled away to the left and shouted, "Cover me!"

Tom was nervous and sweating, as he emptied a magazine from his AK-47 in the direction of the emplacement. This made his enemies put their heads down for a few seconds, but he was still vastly outgunned. Their reply was a volley of machinegun fire that ripped through the cladding on the roof of the generator shed. He flipped over on his side to reload and pumped a few extra rounds at the gun emplacement and then at the observatory door. Two minutes later, the gun emplacement went silent, and Tom turned his attention to the observatory. Khalid slipped back out of the shadows into the shed. Tom saw him with a grin on his face, wiping and sheathing his blade.

"Okay, boss, we've got about two minutes and thirty seconds to get the hell out of here!"

They mounted the truck, Khalid driving, Tom aiming his AK-47 at the observatory hanging half out of the pick-up door. They rattled around the corner in a four-wheel skid.

"Man, that was close," Tom shouted, with a mixture of exhilaration and relief.

He pulled himself into the truck, closing the door. "Go! Go! Go!"

His senses were alerted as the Semtex went off first, setting off a number of secondary explosions, likely the booby traps set for them. This would have indisputably sent any remaining members of the camp scurrying for the bunker. They couldn't hear the Harrier until it had completed its bombing run. By then it was too late. The BLU Super Penetrator was flown straight down the ventilator shaft by the homing device. Tom looked back as he heard a hollow rumbling from deep within the earth. He was filled with awe as he witnessed the mass of flame that shot skyward out of the top of the observatory.

"Nobody can have survived that," said Tom.

"Not a chance," replied Khalid.

Tom's contingency plan was to get back to the main road and then head for their vehicle and the communications gear in the hotel car park in Lahij. He decided that given the opportunity, they should still try to go after UBL. They would pursue him until they could call in a new strike, or even get close enough to take a shot themselves. Meanwhile, there was only one way down the hill by road, and he was certain their target was not too far ahead. The fugitives would be on their guard after the show from the observatory he was in no doubt.

"There were many more explosions than they would have anticipated," Tom said.

"For sure, they'll be suspicious," responded Khalid.

"I'm betting that they're not yet thinking about being followed though."

After one hour of driving, Tom could make out the lights of four or five vehicles about five kilometers ahead, traveling in convoy.

"Close enough for now," Tom instructed Khalid.

"Roger," he replied.

They maintained their distance, crossing the main road after another hour. By 3 AM, they were cruising along the main highway toward Lahij. Tom started to wipe the camouflage paint off his face and adjust himself to normality after the night op.

"Well, we can be thankful that we're still in one piece."

"Without a doubt!" responded Khalid.

"On the plus side, we destroyed UBL's hideout and remain within striking distance, although we lost a man in the process."

"You realize that it will be much more difficult now that we're chasing a moving target."

"You're right, but we'll give it our best shot."

* * *

When they finally got to the Range Rover at dawn, Tom could hear the prayer call echoing in the streets. They left the Toyota in the adjacent parking place and climbed into their own vehicle. Tom powered up the transmitter and enabled the infrared link to his handheld computer to send a coded message to Kurt.

From: Slater, Tom—ME/2—xxx Scrambled xxx 09:14 GMT
To: Schneider, Kurt—CS Dubai
Objective compromised; received prior warning of our arrival. Target fled ahead of strike. We are in hot pursuit. Send drone to track convoy leaving Lahij. Will revert with update using standard protocol.
T.
+++

He deliberately kept his message short and avoided voice traffic, as he didn't want to give explanations. If someone in the system was passing information to their target, the least data Tom supplied the better.

Chapter 9— Unholy Dash

They resumed the chase, with Khalid driving and Tom navigating. Tom monitored their progress using the onboard computer system. It had a head-up display that simultaneously projected maps and GPS tracking of their own position, plus the location of the convoy ahead of them. Tom was relaying instructions to Khalid over his headset, much as a rally driver's copilot would do. The convoy traveled resolutely along the road toward the Red Sea port of al Hudaydah. The paved road ended about fifteen kilometers outside Lahij, where a new highway was under construction. Tom observed the swirling dust cloud ahead of them, as they followed five *Land Cruisers* along the graded road.

"Ease back a bit Khalid," instructed Tom, "so we don't kick up too much dirt."

"Okay."

"I'd hate to give away our position."

"I daren't get too close, anyway. If they become trapped they'll surely fight out of their corner like wild animals."

"I bet that al-Zawahiri knows about the attack on the bunker by now."

"I'm certain of it. They'll have established a regular communications link."

"So, al-Qaeda will be monitoring the convoy and guiding their escape."

"Yes, although, you can bet they'll be reluctant to use satellite phone, as they risk giving away their position."

A couple of years back al-Qaeda had lost one of their senior Yemeni commanders and five operatives near Marib. It appeared that once their satellite phone was intercepted, the NSA had quickly identified the voiceprint of Abu Ali al-Harithi and directed a Predator drone to launch a missile attack on his stationary vehicle. Ahmed Hijazi, a US citizen and suspected al-Qaeda member, was killed in the attack. More recently, something similar had happened in Pakistan, when Hamza Rabia, al-Qaeda's Syrian operational commander in the region, was among five people who died in a mysterious explosion in North Waziristan. The official line was that the blast was set off as the victims were making explosives inside an alleged terrorist hideout. In his view, it was clearly cover for a US missile strike in Pakistani territory. He believed it was highly unlikely that such experienced senior operatives would have been making bombs, or that they would have been careless enough to set them off.

As the pursuit progressed, Tom's head was spinning with unanswered questions.

"How much warning do you think al-Qaeda had?"

"At least enough time to prepare a trap," replied Khalid tilting his head sideways.

"So do you think they know our current position?"

"If, as I suspect, they have a mole, then it's a dead certainty."

Tom frowned. "I really don't want UBL to discover we're following him."

He paused for a moment, and then asked, "Why do you think Hammed seemed so sure of himself? He must have known that we were walking into a trap."

"Without a doubt he knew more than he was telling; it was so obviously a setup."

"How can we have been so stupid?" Tom asked, shaking his head.

"We should have read the signs better, I agree. Remember how Yemenis think. Hammed must have been well prepared for the ultimate sacrifice to protect his Sheikh."

"No, on the contrary, I believe that he was a victim and we were all betrayed by the al-Jahni."

"Do you think that Mohammed knows something then?"

"No one can be trusted for now."

Back on paved road again, Khalid accelerated, trying to keep pace. For now, they were maintaining a modest distance of about five kilometers between themselves and their quarry. The winding road began to descend the length of a narrow valley. Alongside them ran a *wadi,* with a never-ending trickle of clear water. Ahead the sunlight filtered through lush palm fronds, as the *wadi* widened into a small oasis on the side of the highway. Tom was amazed how such lush vegetation grew in an otherwise barren setting.

As they arrived at bottom of the ravine, the *wadi* disappeared underground and the terrain opened out into a large, rocky basin, with a crossroads at its mid-point. The road slopped downward for about a kilometer, on a mound of fractured limestone about one hundred meters above the floor of the basin. This made them highly visible to anyone on the valley floor. Scruffy looking Yemeni soldiers with a mounted gun turret guarded the intersection. Khalid drove cautiously toward them. The troops were chewing *quat* and appeared oblivious to most of their surroundings. They just waved them through. At the same time, the convoy was exiting the basin about five kilometers ahead on the western extremity.

"I bet they've seen us," said Tom.

"I agree. They'll log a lone vehicle behind them."

"You'd better go more slowly for a while and attempt to open up a bigger gap."

"Okay."

"I think there's little risk of us losing the convoy."

Tom had a direct link to the drone tracking the convoy. He could follow them easily from twenty or even fifty kilometers back without giving away their position.

"Al-Qaeda will be suspicious, especially if they see the same vehicle twice," Tom remarked.

Tom remained intent on following their quarry, guiding Khalid along the main highway toward the coast. They passed the ancient city of Zabid without entering.

"Did you know," said Khalid, "that this is where the Yemenis discovered algebra?"

"What quirk of fate made this the cradle of modern mathematics?" Tom asked with eyes opened wide.

"Don't be so cynical, Tom."

"Yemen is such an unlikely place to have made such a big step in science."

Khalid puffed up his chest. "Don't mock. Muslim scholars were the most advanced in the world in the centuries following Mohammed."

"Please don't get me wrong. I'm not putting you down. Really, I'm impressed."

"If you knew more of our history you wouldn't act so surprised," said

Khalid. "We helped the spread of Islam throughout North Africa and as far away as India and Indonesia. In exchange, we received and passed on the knowledge and wisdom of the Orient."

"It's all part of the paradox of Yemen for me," he said. "The ruins of the fabled Queen of Sheba's palace at Marib show that you have not always been a nation of ill-educated bandits. So, what happened?"

* * *

Continuing downhill toward the coast, Tom and Khalid were now running along a portion of dirt road that skirted a banana plantation. The convoy stopped to take a break. The drone locked on to them, stationary, about twenty-five kilometers west of Tom and Khalid's position.

"Pull in and wait," Tom said.

"Okay." Khalid nudged their vehicle into the space between some banana trees.

Tom later pulled out his handheld device and logged on to receive messages. He saw that he had thirty-two in his inbox from the last nine hours. First he clicked on the chairman's message and pressed the decode button.

From: Wood, Peter—C—xxx Scrambled xxx 14:02 GMT.
To: Salter, Tom —ME/2
Source of leak traced to al-J. Sultan compromised with authorities. Circus is airlifting him to safety. Full support will be provided for your pursuit. Terratec data streaming from target on alpha frequency. Do not approach subjects. Repeat, under NO circumstances approach subjects. New mission objective is to follow and ascertain next destination; then call it in.
C.
+++

Tom read the message aloud to Khalid.

"Well, the chairman is getting nervous," Tom said. "He must be under a lot of pressure from Langley because the strike didn't go to plan."

"I imagine that the knives are out."

"Sir Peter is not a man to cave in under stress," he responded. "I fully expect to have our backs covered."

"No question."

"Remember, Operation Sheikh is still controlled by the Circus."

"The message is clear though. Even if we get a straight shot at UBL, we shouldn't take it. I confess I don't understand."

Tom shrugged. “Me neither. I’m sure it has something to do with politics.”

There was a message from Kurt’s assistant, Laura, with the satellite images of the observatory, and Tom could see that the whole area was cratered. The main explosion had collapsed the walls of the bunker; the dome and telescope had caved inward, leaving a twisted mass of metal covering the access to the bunker below. Farther out, the terrain looked pock marked. There were smaller blast circles that stretched to the generator shed, which must have been caused by a combination of the mines and the Semtex. He was certain no one could have gotten out alive.

There was a detailed message from Kurt confirming that Abu Musab—al-Qaeda’s security chief—and his henchmen were among the group escorting UBL and that some members of the Yemeni Bin Hassan tribe were acting as guides.

“Isn’t Abu Musab that bloodthirsty sonofabitch who directed some of the executions broadcast on the Web?” asked Tom.

“Yes, that’s the bastard!” replied Khalid.

“If we ever get into a fight at close quarters, you realize that we’ll be in serious danger from these characters.”

Despite their own rigorous training, they were vastly outnumbered by well-armed, coldblooded, and brutal opponents. Tom felt inside his holster for his SIG Pro lightweight semi-automatic, with its polymer frame. It was easily concealed and wasn’t readily identified as a weapon on X-ray screening. Fitted with a laser targeting system, it became a highly accurate weapon, especially in close or medium-range combat. It gave him a curiously comforting sensation, like an old friend who had never let him down when things got rough.

Other maps, codes, and target data were waiting to be downloaded into the on board navigation system. Tom promptly switched to alpha mode and typed the command: Execute. Then they were all set.

Some forty-five minutes later, Tom became aware that the convoy was moving again, still heading in the direction of al Hudaydah.

“It’s an odd direction that the convoy is taking, don’t you think?” Tom asked.

“I’m mystified as to what they’ll do when they get to the Red Sea,” Khalid replied.

“Do you think they’ll take a boat? A high-speed motorized *dhow* could take them across to Eritrea, Djibouti … but it makes little sense.”

“Yes, they must know the French Foreign Legion watch that coastline very carefully.”

“Perhaps they’re just trying to throw us off the scent.”

Khalid shook his head. “No, I don’t think so.”

"Then their objective must be Upper Egypt. There are strong ties there between al-Qaeda and Islamic militants, I believe."

"Yes, Gama'at al-Islamiyya—Egypt's largest terrorist group—are their old allies. They would certainly provide a safe haven for UBL. They signed a fatwa calling for the destruction of the United States, Israel, and all enemies of Islam."

Tom drafted an urgent message to Kurt, sending a copy to the chairman.

From: Slater, Tom—ME/2—xxx Scrambled xxx 15:43 GMT
To: Schneider, Kurt—CS Dubai
cc: Wood, Peter—C
Unsure of target's route beyond al-Hudaydah, if they take a boat they will be difficult to follow. Request you enact urgent counter-measures at port.
T.
+++

He hoped that this would block at least one potential escape route. He wasn't sure how Kurt would do it, but that was not his problem.

Tom's thoughts turned to Karin, and with them came feelings of anguish and longing, flooding across his consciousness like a tidal wave. Normally he tried to stay focused on the job, but somehow the backwash had built up and needed release. He would pay dearly for his careless words. He would make it up to her somehow—the next time he saw her, he would dedicate his being totally to her and express his undying love. He was sure that they would weep a little about the cruelty of fate; then they would laugh about their own stupidity before they made love. He was ever hopeful that their physical bonding would ease the sense of loss and emptiness at not being able to have a child. At least they had each other. He longed to feel her next to him. He wanted desperately to speak to her, but knew he couldn't. Finally, he could stand it no more; breaking completely with protocol, he sent a quick un-coded message to her e-mail.

From: Slater, Tom—ME/2—xxx Un-coded xxx 15:47 GMT
To: Karin Duval—KarinDv2@hotmail.com
I love you and miss you. You cannot believe how sorry I am.
Tom.
+++

The downward incline became steeper as they got closer to the coastline. The convoy was already in al Hudaydah according to their tracking device.

They were working their way toward the port and no doubt the outer quay, where the *dhows* tied up to load provisions for their voyage across the Red Sea. Tom crossed his fingers and prayed that Kurt was on top of the job. They had to be stopped or they would lose their objective.

He need not have worried, as a USS *Los Angeles*–class fast-attack submarine had surfaced about five kilometers offshore, in sight of the mouth of the port. No *dhow* would stand a chance against the superior firepower of the sub. Anyone thinking of running such a blockade would be in for a nasty shock.

"What the hell!" Khalid said, gawping.

"Check, but not yet mate," Tom remarked as he witnessed the arrival of the submarine from afar.

The convoy reacted quickly. They veered immediately north and headed toward the mountain passes of the Asir Mountains and the border with Saudi.

*　　　*　　　*

As Khalid drove through the backstreets of al Hudaydah, he asked jokingly.

"Hey Tom, what would you like to eat? I could eat a horse!"

Khalid swerved toward a mud-walled compound where a few scrawny mules were eating hay. Tom, meanwhile, was getting even hungrier, so Khalid's lame attempt at humor went straight over his head.

"Seriously, how's about some fish?" asked Khalid. "I know a good place."

"Fine by me," replied Tom.

Khalid pulled up in front of a rudimentary and dilapidated but busy looking restaurant, open to the street. The tables were covered with plastic tablecloths. The walls were chipped white tiles, and the floor was bare concrete. At the back, there was a large gas oven and a couple of open freezer cabinets, into which a Yemeni on a bicycle had just emptied a sack of fish. Tom and Khalid approached the freezer cabinet and Khalid selected two small *najil*.

Khalid explained, "These red grouper are quite rare these days. They're the most expensive fish you can buy here. We're in luck!"

"Fantastic!" said Tom.

They sat down at a table facing the square as the waiter swept the scraps from the previous meal off the table and onto the floor with his hand. Tom became conscious that the oven was being operated more like a blast furnace. The cook skewered the fish and placed them inside the oven, which roared as he switched on a heavy-duty fan. About two minutes later, two burnt offerings were extracted from the oven, completely blackened.

"Ooops, there goes the *najil*," said Tom.

"Wait, you'll see," said Khalid smiling.

The waiter brought them the fish wrapped in newspaper and laid it down on the table in front of them. He then bought a bowl of red yogurt sauce.

"It's a spicy dip—try it," Khalid said. "Look, like this…"

Khalid showed him how to scrape the charred skin from the fish and separate the morsels of white meaty flesh from the bone with his right hand, dipping it in the yogurt on the way to his mouth.

"Oh my God!" screamed Tom, "that's delicious. I've never tasted fish so good."

He sat licking his fingers.

"Yes, the extreme heat seals in the entire flavor the fish—isn't it incredible?"

The fish was delicate and succulent. It must have been fresh from the harbor, probably been caught in the last couple of hours.

"After such a satisfying meal, I'm ready for anything," declared Tom.

With a spring in his step, Tom climbed back into the vehicle again. He took the wheel to give Khalid some time to rest and struck out on the north road from al Hudaydah. Meanwhile, Khalid rechecked the tracking device, confirming the route taken by the Land Cruisers.

"Perfect," Khalid said into the microphone, "we have them at about twenty-five kilometers range, heading north at a steady one hundred kilometers per hour."

"No worries!" said Tom.

He laughed aloud with pleasure as he drove along the long, straight road northward. He flipped on the cruise control to keep them at a matching velocity. This was turning into a marathon, as in all likelihood they would have little ahead of them for at least a thousand kilometers, except for the Jebel, the desert, and the occasional Bedouin. Tom prepared himself for the long journey.

"The convoy was pretty assertive in their change of direction," Tom said.

"Yes," replied Khalid. "That means there's immediate feedback from their command system."

"Kurt's little surprise will certainly have unnerved them."

"They'll now be acutely aware they're being tracked."

"I imagine that they'll be worried about some sort of aerial activity."

"In their shoes, I would be wondering why the Great Satan had not made his move."

Almost on cue, the convoy began to spread out along the road, leaving about a kilometer or so between each vehicle.

"Undeniably that's a tactic to minimize the threat of an air strike," Khalid said, as he watched the display.

"I agree," said Tom. "A drone could only go for one of the five vehicles at a time."

"But with only a twenty percent chance of hitting UBL, such an action would then provide an immediate warning for the others."

"Who knows what weapons capability they're carrying. They could probably mount a counterattack."

"I guess they might have handheld anti-aircraft missiles, like Stingers or SAMs."

"The chairman's instruction makes more sense now. There's a better chance of a successful strike when they come together again."

As the sun began to set across the Red Sea and the dusk fell across the surprisingly fertile landscape, they started to climb again toward the flat-topped coastal range. They observed several vehicles that had parked at intervals along the side of the road, with their owners kneeling on their prayer mats, bowing toward Mecca.

* * *

The driving became monotonous as night fell. He could distinguish only a few dark shadowy features of the terrain in the gloom. The moonlight was obscured by cloud. From time to time, they lost trace of one or another of the five vehicles. This was partly because of the cloudy sky and partly due to one of them going behind the shadow of the hills. It wasn't a problem for now, as Tom knew that they all had only one road to follow.

"One of the Land Cruisers disappeared more than twenty minutes ago and has just reappeared in the same position," Khalid said.

"Note the grid reference," replied Tom.

"Surely, they don't expect us to fall for one of the oldest tricks in the book?"

"Take nothing for granted … assume they left someone staking out the position."

Khalid looked at Tom with raised eyebrows.

"And just to be on the safe side, let's get a thermal scan from a heat-registering drone," Tom instructed.

"Okay."

"Call it into Kurt."

"Roger," Khalid reached for his handheld device to send the message.

Tom parked up in a lay-by about five kilometers short of the grid reference. All communicator channels were left open. Kurt came back about thirty minutes later, streaming data. Tom watched in admiration of the technology, as sure enough there appeared on their screen a characteristic heat signature of a human being behind a bluff, on a sharp bend in the road, exactly at the grid reference.

As luck would have it, at that precise moment, a battered old Yemeni pick-up full of sheep passed them, heading along the road. They followed, slipstreaming the pick-up and heading straight for the trap. Fifty meters before the site of the expected ambush, Tom stopped the Range Rover and Khalid slipped out of the passenger door into the night. Ten seconds later, the Yemeni pick-up hit the trip wire and was launched skyward, swathed in a sheet of flame and slammed even more forcefully back down to Earth again as a twisted mass of metal, bloody wool, bone, and flesh.

"Goddamn!" screamed Tom. Simultaneously, he withdrew his weapon from its holster and flipped down his night vision goggles.

Tom saw the al-Qaeda fighter come bounding down the slope to inspect his bloody handiwork.

"Sorry, wrong truck," said Tom, as the terrorist reached for his walkie-talkie and Khalid stepped up behind him to slit his throat. He opened his mouth to scream, but nothing came out. Then he crumpled like a sack of potatoes on the ground.

Tom leapt out of the car and came forward to survey the scene, the awful stench of the carnage—a mix of charred meat, burnt wool, and sheep shit adhering to the inside of his nostrils. Although his stomach heaved in disgust, he remained focused on his task. They quickly body searched the operative but found nothing. Khalid retrieved the walkie-talkie and his weapon. Tom ran back to their vehicle, covering his nose and mouth. He got in quickly and drove swiftly past the fetid, smoldering mass of debris strewn all over the road.

"Wow, I'm glad we don't have to stick around to clean up that mess!"

"Now we know with absolute certainty that they're aware of our presence," Khalid said.

"You're right, we've been smart enough to foil an attack this time, but we'll have to be much more careful in the future," responded Tom. "They'll not make the same mistake twice."

"We've lost a lot of time."

Tom accelerated harder.

"One stroke of luck," he said. "We salvaged the walkie-talkie."

"Yes, that could be a real bonus, so long as the battery lasts and they don't change the frequency."

Khalid left it on *receive* and placed it on top of the dash. Tom could hear a voice clearly in Arabic.

Khalid translated, "Adnan, report status, over … Adnan, come in, Adnan, over … Code 42, out."

"Hmm," said Tom, "looks like they figured out that Adnan's in trouble."

"I guess they'll send a scout from the local al-Qaeda cell to reconnoiter," said Khalid.

"That'll probably take a few hours."

"In the meantime, I'm almost certain that they'll shut down this frequency."

"Prepare a new message for Kurt so that he picks up the weapon and the walkie-talkie."

"Okay."

"Maybe the lab boys can make something more of them."

"Yes, they should be able to eavesdrop across the full bandwidth."

Kurt responded promptly that he would send in a chopper to do the pick-up. They were given a suitable position some fifteen kilometers ahead. Tom stayed with the Range Rover and watched while Khalid buried the items under a pile of rocks some twenty meters to the west of the proposed landing site.

Rejoining the chase, they found themselves lagging even further behind, as the convoy was now some forty kilometers or more ahead. At 2 AM, Khalid took over the wheel. By this time, Tom had narrowed the gap by only three kilometers. He slid into the passenger seat exhausted. He tapped his password into his handheld and saw there were another fourteen messages. He decoded the last two from Kurt: The first thanked them for the items, which they picked up safely, and the second was a rap on the knuckles for sending uncoded messages.

"Shit! What do I care?" Tom said to no one in particular.

Tom disliked Kurt even more for this. He knew it was unprofessional, but he didn't need some jumped-up station chief reading him the riot act from his air-conditioned office in Dubai. Meanwhile, he was putting his ass on the line in the field. In any case, Karin would have been cheered up by his little indiscretion. He was sure that she was lonely, probably angry and upset too. He'd felt powerless to do anything about it without breaking the rules. He was aware that she didn't really understand his priorities, and he had no way to explain. His anger and frustration just made him more resolved to complete the mission, so he could be back by her side.

Meanwhile, Khalid had had an immediate impact on their progress. Tom marveled at his talent as a driver—deftly accelerating through the corners and adjusting his speed and line on the road to optimize their travel over the ground. Judging from his skilful maneuvering, Tom could tell that his companion had years of practice in difficult Yemeni road conditions. His anticipation was excellent. Tom even gave up trying to give him the rally-driver's instructions.

Tom and Khalid changed places again several hours later, at the last gas station on the outskirts of Sa'dah, just before the bottom of the pass. Their tracking device had shown the five vehicles in the convoy stopping in turn to refuel, about forty minutes earlier. Before their nighttime approach of the station, Tom had requested a further infrared heat trace from Kurt. It had shown an attendant asleep by the forecourt and two more in the back in bunks. There was not too much to worry about, Tom decided. To be safe, he instructed Khalid to sweep the pump island for explosives prior to refueling. Meanwhile he held a gun to the attendant's head.

"It's clean," said Khalid.

"Evidently al-Qaeda was in too much of a hurry," responded Tom.

"Or they figured out by now that we're not that easily fooled."

As Khalid drove off, Tom grinned at him. "I don't think any pump attendant has ever shaken so much while filling up," he said.

"Or been quite so surprised," Khalid laughed, "when I thanked him politely in Arabic: *Shokran Ma' salaama*!"

Chapter 10—Paradise Nearly Lost

Karin was a very light sleeper and awoke at the slightest unexpected movement. She was conscious that the sound coming from down by the jetty was not part of the characteristic nighttime calm on her tropical island. She rolled out of bed and went to the computer monitor, pleased that Tom had installed CCTV at the jetty. It gave her a more secure feeling, especially when she had to spend so many nights here alone. Although she was content with her own company and adored the tranquility of their beautiful home, she got nervous when Tom was away. Besides, she was troubled by their stupid argument; she knew that she was testing him but forgot how easily he was provoked.

She thought of the message she had received a few hours ago, which was typical Tom. It was brief and to the point, more like a business e-mail than a love letter. Nonetheless, she at least felt acknowledged and appreciated. She hated the Circus and everything that went with it. The secretive messages, the impromptu meetings, and the trips away for weeks at a time all came with the territory. She sensed that there had never been another mission quite the likes of this one, though. Tom was so on edge before he left; she had tried to understand and be there for him, but no doubt, he had misunderstood her probing.

At that instant, her attention was drawn back to the present and to a light flickering on the monitor—or was it a reflection off the water down by the jetty, she wondered.

Karin looked closer and gasped, "Oh my God! I don't believe it."

She recognized the outline of three or four men in the moonlight. They were dressed all in black wet suits, disembarking from their rubber inflatable and wading cautiously toward the shore by the jetty. They could have only one objective. At once, she remembered all that Tom had said about such eventualities and responded practically on autopilot. She slipped on her jeans and black T-shirt lying on the side of the bed, laced up her *Nike* running shoes, and then immediately grabbed the backpack that was always left prepared in the corner of the room.

Karin was trembling as she left the house via the trap door in the lounge. She was concerned not to make a sound and remembered to cover her tracks. Emerging into the confined space below the house she carefully closed the door behind her. She scrambled out from under the house on all fours and looked back toward the jetty. Now she could make out more clearly four armed men striding toward the front of the house. She prayed that they had not seen her. She ran, stooped low behind the garden wall at the back of the pool, heading for the other side of the island.

At the end of the wall, she turned again and looked through the cover of the fruit trees. Her would-be assailants were preparing to enter the house, firing what looked like smoke grenades and pulling on gas masks. They each went though separate entrances with precision timing. It was obvious that these men were professionals. She first heard the sound of breaking glass, and then watched as they adeptly hurled themselves across the threshold. She realized too late that she had forgotten to activate the security shutters.

"What the hell!" she murmured.

Meanwhile she had scurried behind the trees to the east of the house. She joined the pathway that ran behind the small hill at the center of the island, darting behind the scrub to avoid being seen. Tom had stashed a small dinghy by the shrimp farm that would allow a discreet escape to the neighboring island of San Pedro Caye. In ten minutes, she was at the boat. She heard some shouting from the direction of the house that was barely distinguishable. With some curiosity, she noted that the accents sounded British, as she gently launched the dinghy into the water and started paddling for her life.

Her head was buzzing. *What the hell is this about? Is Tom in some kind of trouble? They looked like a heavy mob, Special Forces or the like. Why are they looking for Tom?*

She first saw the flash against the night sky, immediately followed by a loud, sharp bang as a stun grenade went off. It was a full–blown commando style raid.

"Sweet Mother of God—whatever next!"

She was about four hundred meters away from the shore and started up the small outboard. She was crouched sideways in the dinghy, with one hand controlling the throttle, so she could look back to the island as well as ahead to her destination. She was already one third of the way across the strait. Luckily, the wind was in the right direction, away from the house, so the hum of the outboard was carried away on the breeze.

In about twenty minutes, Karin crossed the small channel and hid the dinghy in the undergrowth at the back of the main beach on San Pedro Caye. She then walked down the well-trodden path to the town and knocked on the door of a small boarding house. She rang the bell. The proprietor, a large, buxom Honduran woman, her old friend and soul mate Esmeralda opened it.

"*Tienes espacio para una más, mi amor*?" she asked as she stepped inside.

Esmeralda, with arms open wide, laughing with delight, hugged her.

"What's the matter? You look pale. It must be serious for you to turn up here at this time of night. I hope you haven't been fighting with that gorgeous man of yours!"

"No, that's not it," she replied.

"Well, come and sit down and tell Esme all about it."

They sat together on the sofa. Karin—only half believing the night's events—started to recount the tale of the men in wet suits to her girlfriend, who was unusually lost for words.

"Oh my God ... *No puede ser*!" she exclaimed. "Tom must be in deep trouble."

"I need a safe place to stay for tonight."

"Of course you can stay here. But I imagine that you'll want to catch the ferry to Belize in the morning."

"Yes, sooner or later I'm sure they'll start to search the neighboring *cayes*."

Karin was suddenly very tired after her ordeal, and telling the story just made her even wearier.

"I desperately need to get some sleep," she said.

"Of course, sweetheart," Esme replied.

Esme showed her to a cozy guest room on the ground floor. The moment her head hit the soft feather pillow, she shut her eyes and was fast asleep.

Karin woke about eight fully refreshed. Esme breezed into the room ten minutes later with breakfast in bed.

"Here's a strong cup of coffee and fresh baked bread, just as you like it."

"You know, for a moment there I forgot last night's events," Karin said.

"I can hardly believe it myself," replied Esme.

The painful memory flooded back. Karin recalled how Tom had spoken to her, in one of his most serious and frightening moments.

"Look, if anyone ever comes to the island searching for me, then as a matter of life or death, you must leave everything and run. Don't worry, I will come and find you. Go to a safe place a long way away, where no one knows you. You must travel alone, be very cautious, and trust no one."

Just then, Karin also remembered the warning signal advising against returning to the island. Tom had told her to activate it, so he would know that she was in trouble. He had given her a strange-looking oblong device, which she pulled out of her backpack. She flipped open the guard and pressed the red button.

Then she sorted through the remaining contents of her bag. There were two identical sets of Dutch passports—the first in the names of M. Jan Peter Schipper and Mw Geraldine Schipper; and the second with M. Erwin Van Hasselt and Mw. Marina Van Hasselt. Both sets had photos of her and Tom. The documents were issued in Den Haag eighteen months ago. There was about one hundred thousand dollars in cash, neatly wrapped in bundles of fifties and hundreds, plus VISA credit cards from ABN in both sets of names. There was also a small notebook with what appeared to be details of numbered Swiss accounts and some other less easily identifiable ciphers and telephone numbers. There was a SIG Pro semi-automatic and five spare clips of ammunition. Finally, there was a tourist map of Recife, Brazil. Karin thought they were an odd selection of items. They must have made sense to Tom, but not to her. She sat there just staring at the contents spread out on the bed for twenty minutes, very unsure of what to do next. *Speak to me, Tom. Where should I go now? How will you find me?*

"Enough," she said aloud. "It looks like I am heading for Recife."

She got Esme to call her travel agency in Belize and book Geraldine Schipper on the evening flight from Honduras to Miami. She skillfully decided on leaving via Honduras as an extra safeguard, in case someone was watching Belize airport.

Early in the morning, Esme drove her down to the dock. Karin slipped on the ferry at the last minute as a foot-passenger. She stayed directly in the corner of the mid-deck cabin during the one and a half hour long crossing. She purposefully avoided eye contact with her fellow passengers and watched the television screen for the whole voyage.

She disembarked in Belize port alongside a Carnival Cruise liner, again choosing to wait until the last minute to slip off the passenger ramp and mingle with the crowd at the terminal. She was sure that no one had seen or recognized her. She wandered past the Swing Bridge heading for the tourist shopping. After buying some clothes and other essential items, she went into the Fort Point Shopping Center and bought from the fashionable boutiques, whose usual clients were from the cruise ships. She was paying in US dollars, which was perfectly normal and would raise no eyebrows.

She hired a taxi to take her to the Honduran capital, making sure the driver knew she was a Dutch tourist going to meet her husband. She wanted to make sure that nobody would be suspicious if someone asked the driver later about a woman traveling alone, meeting her general description.

It took about two hours to get to La Mesa International airport, and she had to wait a further three hours before the Miami flight. She checked in early and dropped off her recently purchased luggage, having carefully had it wrapped with plastic first. She had a camera as a carry-on, as well as her new Louis Vuitton handbag. She wanted to appear every bit the wealthy Dutch tourist. Although she was extremely nervous, the SIG Pro passed through the X-ray without incident, just as Tom had told her it would. Once she had completed the formalities, she went to sit at the coffee bar in the departure lounge, ordered a coffee, and read a women's magazine to pass the time.

* * *

From Miami Airport, she took a shuttle bus and checked into the Hilton for three nights, under her new name, Marina Van Hasselt. She decided to leave enough of a break between her arrival and departure dates to make it harder for anyone trying to trace her movements. The hotel was full of transients connecting between flights or on a short stopover in Miami, and so another person doing just the same aroused no suspicion at all. The next morning early, she went back to the airport on the same bus. She booked two seats in business class at the Varig counter, one for herself and one for her husband, from Miami to São Paulo and then São Paulo to Recife.

Subsequently, she took a cab from the airport to the Dolphin Mall, got her hair cut, and dyed from her natural black to a shade of light brown, paying with cash. She also went to the optometrist and bought herself some disposable colored contact lenses in brown. She was determined not to be recognized by anyone who might have picked up her trail.

She was now all set, but she had a couple of days to kill. She avoided contact with her friends, and she did not log on to her e-mail, as Tom had explained that she could be quickly located that way through her IP address. She desperately wanted to speak to Tom, but she knew it was dangerous and that she could easily give herself and Tom away in the attempt. Therefore, she just prayed that he would get the emergency warning signal and figure out that something was up.

She decided to watch some of the latest movies on pay-per-view, having nothing else to do with her time. She laughed aloud at *Mr. and Mrs. Smith* and the double life of two professional assassins. This cloak-and-dagger stuff was nothing like in the movie; she could vouch for that with heartfelt conviction. There was far less glamour and much more suffering.

Chapter 11—
The Bottom Line

Brad Hartman, the associate deputy director—or ADD, as he was usually referred to in the Agency—had conferenced in at 0800 hours to the Belize British army base for the debriefing. He sat in his office in CIA Headquarters in Langley, Virginia, with an intelligence analyst on his staff. He was appalled as he listened to the account of Captain Paul Ingram, who was introduced as the senior ranking officer of the Special Boat Service and the leader of last night's incursion. Brad was aware that the elite SBS prided themselves on being the finest amphibious force in the world. What he had witnessed suggested otherwise; the whole raid had been a fiasco from start to finish.

Even so, he listened attentively on his conference phone to Ingram's version of events.

"We flew into Belize two nights ago, on a Hercules troop carrier from RAF Brize Norton, for the operation."

Brad was wondering why Brits were always so long-winded. *Why can't he just cut to the chase?*

"According to plan, we disembarked at the jetty at 2200 hours. We proceeded to the villa, positioning ourselves at the four entry points to the house."

Brad turned up the volume on his hands-free speaker and waved toward his staffer to move closer.

"After firing CS gas through the windows, we burst in though each entrance simultaneously."

Brad thought that the use of such force was more appropriate to an anti-terrorist operation than such an easy target—a lone woman in a remote location, probably unarmed.

"The house was empty; although we assessed that the bed had been occupied only a few minutes prior to our arrival, as it was still warm. We searched the house thoroughly in approximately three to four minutes and concluded that our target had fled."

Holding down the mute button, Brad rolled his eyes at his staffer and groaned.

"After searching the remainder of the property, I decided that the small annex by the pool was the only other logical hiding place," said Ingram. "So we entered using a stun grenade. Again, we found nothing."

"Any idea at all where she might have got to at this point, Captain?" asked the British CO.

"No, sir, we just didn't understand. This was supposed to be a routine raid; we wondered how the hell she had disappeared so quickly!"

Why do the simple missions always give the most problems? Brad began tapping his pencil on the desk.

"We then set up a line to scour the terrain … we were convinced that it was impossible for her to hide on such a pocket handkerchief of an island, less than a kilometer long and a maximum of four hundred meters at the widest point."

To Brad, the SBS seemed to be compounding their stupidity. Ingram should have realized that by this time it was almost certainly too late, as Ms. Duval must have had a planned escape route.

"We walked from one side of the island to the other, spaced at about one hundred meters apart," Ingram continued. "We were hoping to put something up, a bit like beating game. It took us twenty-five minutes to comb the island, but still nothing, sir."

"It sounds like you did your best," said the British CO.

"Then, sir, then as you already know, you ordered me to abort the mission and return to base," Ingram concluded.

The next report was from the NGA. In the early hours, Brad had asked them to go back over the satellite imagery to see if they could spot anything, they might have missed the first time. Brad listened intently, desperately wanting some clue as to Ms. Duval's whereabouts.

"On further examination of the satellite photographs," the analyst from the NGA reported, "we caught a fleeting image of the woman leaving the house about four minutes before Captain Ingram arrived with his men. From then on, we found nothing."

"Well she can't have just disappeared off the island by magic!" said Brad into the microphone, unable to restrain himself any longer.

"No sir, but later that night, we made a pass with an infrared sensing drone and confirmed that there was no significant presence on the island."

"How can such an easy target have evaporated into thin air, for Christ's sake?" Brad demanded. "Nobody seems to have a clue where she went or even how she got away!"

"She must have been warned that we were coming," said Ingram.

"Don't give me that bullshit," Brad replied. "It was complete incompetence and I'm holding you fully responsible."

"I don't like your attitude," Ingram's CO interrupted. "The SBS are completely professional. They followed the plan exactly."

"Oh, shut up, you pompous idiot!" replied Brad. "I don't give a damn what you think. I am calling it as I see it—you guys screwed up."

"I'll be discussing this conversation with my superiors," the British CO said.

"I don't care. You can discuss it with who you like," said Brad. "But it seems pointless to me. It won't help us find the woman or change the fact that you let her escape from right under your very noses."

Brad sensed that the whole debriefing was in danger of turning into a major diplomatic incident and that it was better not to prolong the agony. He was fuming as he disconnected from the teleconference.

Turning to his staffer he asked, "How could I have given these incompetent idiots so much control of such a critical operation?"

Brad already knew the answer—according to NATO protocol the UK military retained operational priority in Belize. He would have much preferred to use US Navy SEALs, but he was sure that this would immediately raise a red flag at Circus headquarters at Vauxhall Cross. Brad was taking a considerable risk of the Circus finding out in either case. It was less risky, he had concluded, if he was able to keep things very low key and through normal channels. Moreover, he had created a cover story about apprehending a woman linked to the Colombian cartels. Brad was taking advantage of the fact that Belize was a well-known transshipment point for international drug traffickers and a center for money-laundering activity.

He now had a major problem on his hands to locate the woman. She was obviously on her guard and apparently adept at evading capture. She had made no contact with Tom—he was certain. At his instruction, the NSA had placed a trace on her landline, mobile phone, and Internet and was intercepting all of Tom's traffic from Arabia. In any case, based on her performance so far, he did not expect her to make such a basic mistake as calling or e-mailing Tom.

Maybe she had just gotten lucky. More likely, though, she had been well briefed by Tom. *Where on Earth was she headed?* He knew it could be anywhere, and every hour that passed diminished his chances of finding her. His best option was to apprehend her while she was still in Belize. Once she got on a plane, their task would become exponentially more difficult.

He called the Agency station chief in Belize, Miguel Santana, and instructed him to set up surveillance teams at all the main entry and exit points to Belize City. He also got him to post agents at all the local airports searching for her.

"Who do you think she's likely to contact first?" Brad's staffer addressed him.

Brad had read the background file on her thoroughly.

"If I was a betting man, I'd wager that Ms. Duval will get in touch with one of her close friends or relatives. The most likely are the brother in Baltimore and the girlfriend in Phoenix."

Brad had up to one hundred and fifty agents at his disposal. With about three hundred and fifty of Karin's acquaintances on file, he estimated that it would take about four days to check out all options.

"We've got a lot of bases to cover, so let's get moving," he said. "I want two agents to stake out Paul Duval's home in north Baltimore right away."

"Yes, sir!"

* * *

Brad received a report on a secure channel later that evening from one of the agents who was assigned to the brother.

"When we arrived Duval was out. We entered through the garage door and placed wiretaps on the phone and bugs in the four key rooms. We were in and out in five minutes," the agent said.

"I trust that you left no trace, "Brad asserted.

"No, sir, everything went according to standard procedure," he replied. "Then we sat in the car listening in from about a block away. Duval arrived home at about six thirty."

From the file, Brad had discovered that Paul Duval was an equities analyst at a large brokerage firm and lived alone. Neighbors had described him as bookish and something of a loner. Apparently, seven or eight years ago, he had shared an apartment with Karin Duval, when they were both studying at Colombia. After she had left New York to live with Tom Salter, Paul Duval had relocated to Baltimore. Brad surmised that brother and sister were very close.

The agent concluded his briefing. "We're sure there's been no contact with Ms. Duval, sir."

"Okay, but stick with it for a couple of days more," ordered Brad.

At the same time as Paul Duval's house was being watched, two other CIA agents reached Phoenix and disembarked from their Washington flight. They had instructions to keep Isabel Lack, an announcer on the KPHO TV News, under close observation. This process would be repeated in several parts of the country over the next couple of days, as Brad widened the search.

A few nights later, Brad sat in Operations Room 4A in Langley, unable to sleep, racking his brains over what to do next. By now, his target could be anywhere. He had forgotten the frustration of such grunt work, as it had been a few years since he had taken direct charge of an individual operation. So far, he'd gone up a number of blind alleys, acquiring a sneaking respect for Ms. Duval in the process. She been very careful about not leaving any clues, making no contact with Baltimore or Phoenix, as his instinct had told him she would. The NSA had confirmed that she had not used her mobile phone, e-mail, or credit cards. Brad had now worked through all but ten of her known associates without generating any obvious leads.

The only thing they had to go on was a possible sighting in Belize, near the harbor. Brad knew that the ferry terminal lay along the logical escape route from the islands. A woman fitting Ms. Duval's description had been seen in a nearby shopping center making a number of expensive purchases, which seemed incongruous for someone on the run.

He called Miguel in Belize on his secure line and woke him up.

"She paid with cash for a set of Louis Vuitton luggage," Miguel reported.

"It could have been anyone off the cruise ships," Brad responded.

"We'll check it out in anyway."

There were too many pieces of the puzzle missing. The one or two pieces Brad had appeared not to fit together at all.

"Goddamn!" Brad said. "She must have had some help."

He shook his head.

"Let's try to pick up the trail from the very beginning. Go to San Pedro Caye in the morning to see if you can unearth any clues," he instructed Miguel.

Mid-morning, Brad received a secure signal from Miguel.

From: Santana, Miguel—LA/43 -xxx Scrambled xxx 15:13 GMT

To: Hartman, Brad—ADD
Got a tape of target on Thursday morning ferry—SPC to Belize. Will check out island today and be back to Belize port tonight to see if we can find her trail.
M.
+++

Finally, they had a lead! Brad made up his mind to go public and contacted the local police to increase his search capability. He would get a decent still photo digitally enhanced off Miguel's tape and circulate it to see if they could find anyone else who had seen her. He also decided it was worthwhile to go back to the shopping center to see if they could get a positive ID. In addition, he sent a message to his Honduran team to provide extra backup to Belize. There were going to be no more *SNAFUs* on his watch, as he would personally take charge of the investigation in Belize.

Brad settled back into his seat as the Beechjet took off from Langley Air Force Base. He took a drink of water from the flight attendant after takeoff, but he had no appetite for anything else. His mind was much more at ease now. At least he had something to go on. He pulled the eyeshades down and decided to get some rest, as it would be a long night ahead. Suffering from a lack of sleep, he fell asleep promptly, just as the jet leveled off at cruising altitude on its way south.

He awoke with a start, taken aback by the stewardess, who was gently stroking the hairs on the back of his arm to wake him up.

"We have about thirty minutes to landing. Do you want to freshen up, sir?" she asked.

Despite being taken by surprise, Brad had controlled his reflex to lash out in self-defense. He had hardly noticed her when he had boarded the plane, but now started to re-evaluate. She was a gorgeous, shapely brunette about twenty-two years old. She was too young for him. In his earlier days as a field agent, he would have seen her as a challenge, but now he was getting past chasing any piece of skirt that crossed his path. As the ADD, he had to set a good example.

Brad was divorced, as the Agency had become overly demanding on his family life. His ex had re-married an engineer, who worked for a software company in Seattle and relocated with Brad's two daughters to the West Coast. He could not object, as he was largely to blame for the breakdown of their marriage. In some ways, his family deserved greater stability than he could offer them. It wasn't that he did not love them; there were just too many conflicting pressures. He had some regrets, but overall the divorce was something of a liberating experience for both him and his career. Suddenly he found he was under much less pressure. He no longer had to conform to the norms of family life, while holding down a ridiculously demanding job. Meanwhile, he felt proud to be a patriot, one of the unsung heroes that defended *Life, Liberty and the pursuit of Happiness*. The price had been high in terms of personal sacrifice.

Chapter 12— The Hunters and the Hunted

The pursuit continued, with Tom driving. His senses were heightened by the adrenaline, while the long night without sleep had drained most of his energy. Although his eyes were still wide open, they were throbbing. He continued scanning the darkness for any signs and then returned his focus to the head-up display to check progress.

Khalid offered him some leaves from the bundle of *quat* they had brought in the market. They both began to chew.

"This will give you a boost. It'll keep you more alert," Khalid said.

"You realize we are only postponing the inevitable," replied Tom. "We'll reach crunch point before too long."

"Yes, I know. But we can't afford to lose them."

Tom nodded. "You're right. We've got to keep going somehow."

With the help of the tracking device, Khalid reported that the convoy was heading out across the desert in single file.

"They've made their move well ahead of the border checkpoint."

"I wonder how they'll negotiate the concrete-filled pipe that the Saudis put in a couple of years back to improve border security?" asked Tom.

A half hour later Khalid reported again, "The convoy is coming to a halt."

"They must have run into the pipe," said Tom.

Khalid informed him after a further ten minutes, "I don't know how, but they've penetrated the barrier and are fanning out on the other side."

Soon they too encountered the barricade, in an isolated part of the desert. Tom followed it until he came to a gap.

"Look at that! There's a clean breach in that section of pipe," Tom said.

"I bet the Bin Hassan took an intense delight in doing that," replied Khalid.

Tom carefully negotiated the gap, ever watchful for booby traps.

During this time of year, the bleak, barren wilderness was close to freezing at night. The rugged landscape of the southern part of the Arabian Peninsula had given way to a mix of scrubland and shifting dunes, as they had left behind the mountain passes and were skirting the Empty Quarter. Tom gunned the motor of the four-wheel drive, and it responded with the high octave screeching sound of the supercharger. He continued weaving in and out of the bumpy terrain, trying to maintain maximum forward momentum.

Tom found that the grayness of the desert provided little contrast at night. Off-road driving was hazardous, as it was almost impossible to make out changes in the topography. They experienced several heart-wrenching crunches, as their vehicle lurched in and out of another crater in their path. Occasionally, they found themselves fleetingly airborne, when an unseen mound provided a take off ramp, only to plummet down to Earth with a thump. He felt a jarring sensation each time the rear shock absorbers bottomed out on impact.

In four hours, due to the rough terrain, they had already gone through two of the four spare tires they carried in the back of their Range Rover Sport. Yet this was by far the best vehicle for speed in this wasteland, chiefly as it had a number of modifications, including a specially developed rear anti-sway bar, gas pressure shocks, and a larger front anti-roll bar. This helped absorb the punishment the rocky, uneven landscape was handing out.

"Tracking all five vehicles independently is a much bigger challenge than when they were in a neat line," said Khalid.

"Yes, these desert tracks spread out in all directions," responded Tom.

"It makes exact navigation a nightmare when there's only a small pile of rocks to mark a change in direction."

"I appreciate that. Focus as hard as you can."

Khalid then looked up at the sky. "Now that it's completely overcast, we can't rely on the satellites anymore and the drones are reaching the limit of their range. I guess we can only expect a sporadic signal from the convoy."

The Predators were operating farther and farther away from their base on the USS *Ronald Regan* in the Arabian Sea. They now had only about an hour over the target before returning to refuel. Tom calculated that they needed to keep about four permanently airborne to maintain the surveillance.

"To make things simpler, I suggest we just try to follow one vehicle and ignore all the rest," proposed Tom.

"How's about vehicle codename *Charlie*?" responded Khalid.

"Okay."

"I bet they'll join together again, in any case."

Having made this decision, Tom began to find the task of following the convoy much easier.

"These guys are good," he said. "They're making rapid progress.

"The Bin Hassan tribesmen know these desert routes well," Khalid responded. "They've spent much of their life smuggling contraband back and forth across this no man's land."

"So, now it's their precious human cargo that's profiting."

"Yes, they say that the men of the Bin Hassan tribe are truly the lords of this largely uninhabited borderland. Did you know their idea of some fun is to go for some target practice?" asked Khalid.

"I've heard some stories about them, but not that one."

"Well, according to the legend, once a month, they load up the back of their Land Cruisers with an arsenal of automatic weapons, grenade launchers, and heavy caliber machine guns. They park their vehicles in an orderly line at the edge of a particular desolate tract, near the Saudi border. Then Qasim bin Hassan, the oldest and probably the most treacherous of the Sheikh Ahmed bin Hassan sons, leads them in a little ritual."

"What on earth do they do with all those munitions?" Tom asked open mouthed.

"Well, I'm told all the sheikh's ten sons direct their massive firepower in unison at some old oil drums, which disintegrate in a hail of bullets," Khalid responded.

"I suppose that's one way to get your kicks!"

"Then—so the story goes—once the drums have disappeared, they home in on some stray rocks in the desert and blast them to smithereens too, until they exhaust all their ammo."

"I'd hate to be on the receiving end of that. Let's hope we never have to tangle with them."

Meanwhile, Khalid was observing the movements of the convoy closely, as Tom drove on into the night.

"Where do you think they're they heading?" Tom asked.

"Well, certainly Bin Laden will not to go his family in Jeddah. They hate the sight of each other. He was disowned by them several years ago."

"What about his Saudi followers?"

"He'll be very careful about contacting them, as the al-Qaeda cells are mostly infiltrated by the Saudi secret police."

"I imagine he'll not stay in Saudi territory any longer than he has to then."

"You're right, there's no refuge for him here. The authorities would kill him without a second thought."

"I'm sure it would be speedy and surgical too—if only to avoid any suggestion of a long, drawn-out martyrdom."

"Yes, *sharia* law insists on swift retribution."

Tom smirked, "You can bet your life that they would make no exception in his case."

They began following what appeared to be a well-compacted trail to the northeast. Khalid announced over the headset that Charlie was fifteen kilometers ahead on the track, doing about ninety kilometers per hour.

"The going's getting much easier," said Tom.

"Sure," responded Khalid. "The first section of desert we ploughed through was very bumpy."

"It's simple enough to keep pace now."

As the sun rose over the dunes at the edge of the Empty Quarter, they were swathed in a red glow reflected from the red sky to the red sand.

"Wow! It looks like some sort of a Martian landscape," Tom said.

"The desert is a place of surprising beauty," Khalid responded.

The spectacle lasted for only about two minutes, until the sun began to ascend rapidly, burning off the cloud and leaving a clear sky.

"Good news," said Khalid. "The satellite tracking should now be fully functional again."

"But the bad news is that any drone operating in the area will be easily spotted," Tom responded. "They're now an easy target for Stingers or SAMs. Send an urgent message to Kurt to retire the drones."

"Don't worry; it's already been taken care of. We're now using a geostationary satellite that covers a thousand-kilometer radius from our position."

"Without a cloud in the sky, Charlie has nowhere to hide."

The track they were following was rutted with the regular passage of vehicles. The repeated hammering by their suspension systems had amplified the unevenness of the surface, resulting in a very uncomfortable ride until you learned to negotiate the bumps at a higher than average speed. Tom was doing about one hundred and twenty kilometers per hour, wary of encountering a major rut or pothole in the surface of the track. This could take out an axle, and it would be game over for them.

"We can afford to take it a bit easier," Khalid said.

Tom decided he was right. "Let's take an early morning break so we don't get too close."

"It's a good idea to allow Charlie run ahead a little."

"I agree we must avoid any visual contact."

They stopped in a small valley with a dried-up *wadi*, containing rough stones and acacias for shade. Tom lit the stove and boiled water for coffee. They ate reconstituted egg and beef sausages from a tin; although a little bland, it was their first warm food for about fifteen hours and went down nicely. Before departing, they filled up the vehicle with gas from their jerry cans and checked the oil, coolant, and water levels, as well as the tires. With a penknife, Tom eased out any imbedded sharp stones that could cause a blow out at speed.

They got underway again, this time with Khalid driving. They proceeded alongside a long escarpment to their west, several kilometers long and about one hundred meters high. The dried up *wadi* snaked across the desert floor in front of them, crisscrossing their path from time to time. Tom was surprised to see the first sign of life for several hours—an old Bedouin alongside the track tending his goats.

Farther along Tom could see birds circling in the distance.

"I wonder what the bait is," said Khalid.

As they got closer, Tom pointed. "Look, it's a dead camel."

Khalid held his nose. "What a foul stench!"

By now, Tom could see the hideous looking vultures attacking their putrid meal with enthusiasm, tearing off pieces of flesh in their beaks and claws. Some were struggling and nipping at each other, trying to keep their opening, like pigs at the trough. Others were circling above, hoping to dive down and find their space.

"Wow, what was that!" asked Khalid.

"No idea."

Tom twisted around in his seat as he became suddenly aware of a very large predator with a huge wingspan that swooped down to within no more than three meters above them. It was flying parallel, casting a shadow twice the width of the Range Rover. The vultures all clamored to get away, fleeing the scene as soon as they saw the massive golden eagle. He was preparing to land with talons outstretched. The magnificent bird was exercising his right and his higher order in the food chain. Tom was astonished by, if not a little fearful of, the colossal eagle, which must have stood almost one and a half meters off the ground.

"Damn, that's incredible. I've never seen anything like this in all my years in Arabia!" exclaimed Tom.

"I'll stop so we can watch some more." Khalid drew to a halt a short distance away to observe Mother Nature's spectacle.

It was such an impressive and powerful sight to see how gracefully the eagle landed, ripped off the flesh from the camel, and ate. After he appeared satisfied, he then tore off the final piece from his prize. Presumably, this remained only partly digested in his gullet, while he launched mightily skyward, off to feed his young. Then, like specters at the feast, a couple of minutes after the splendid eagle's departure, the sinister vultures unashamedly reappeared to continue their decaying banquet.

"It's all part of life's design," said Khalid.

"Yes, although vultures are predators too, all my sympathy is with the majestic bird," Tom responded.

*　　　*　　　*

"If we continued on this trajectory we'll skirt Al Khamasin to the east and cross the main Riyadh-Jeddah highway about two hundred and fifty kilometers to the north," Tom said.

"We have just about enough fuel to make it that far," replied Khalid, "but it'll be touch-and-go if we take any other route."

"So we need to know our next refueling stop with a little more certainty. Do you think I should ask Kurt to standby ready for a fuel drop?"

"In my opinion, that's risky, as it requires an incursion into Saudi airspace. It would be very difficult for a chopper to go unnoticed."

"The US airbase in Riyadh only has stealth fighters, so that's not an option either."

Khalid shook his head. "Any unusual activity will certainly alert the Saudis."

"The less they know about our little operation, the better, I agree."

"Yes, if they get involved they will almost certainly send out half their military and we'll miss UBL in the ensuing chaos."

Tom opened his communicator and downloaded the new day's codes. Then he keyed:

From: Slater, Tom —ME/2—xxx Scrambled xxx 11:25 GMT
To: Schneider, Kurt —CS Dubai
Fuel situation could become critical if fail to reach Riyadh-Jeddah Highway.
Prepare for fuel drop and await further instruction.
T.
+++

He read some of the incoming messages aloud, so Khalid could hear.

From: Wolis: Alfred—Forensic. Int. Langley xxx Scrambled xxx 10:50 GMT
To: Slater, Tom —ME/2
Field Lab Dubai reports FN P90 weapon part of a cache sold to Bin Hassan by Zurich arms trader Von Ludorf in Dec 2005. Same consignment also contained FIM-92E Stingers, M72 LAAW antitank weapon, C-4 Explosive, and Heckler and Koch P2000 machine pistols. Must assume convoy armed with all above. Approach with extreme caution.
A.
+++

"Hmm … so tell me something we don't know already," Tom said.

"Yes," responded Khalid, "they're fucking dangerous!"

Tom and Khalid burst out laughing. When they eventually calmed down Tom continued reading.

From: Burns, Jim—Signals. Int. Abu Dhabi xxx Scrambled xxx 10:41 GMT
To: Slater, Tom—ME/2
Shortwave walkie-talkie is low threshold type. Weak signal capture from satellite. Need ground proximity. I am sending new receiver open on all bands to next drop. You should be able to pick up any unfiltered traffic within range.
J.
+++

"Well, that's slightly better news," Khalid observed, "especially if al-Qaeda continue to use the walkie-talkies. They might just give something away."

"Don't get your hopes up. I haven't a clue when we'll actually get the receiver back," replied Tom.

Tom's jaws were aching from endlessly chewing *quat*. He decided to give it a rest. He wound down his window and spat out a disgusting ball of masticated foliage.

"That's better," he said.

"I agree," Khalid replied, following suit. "I hate that endless chewing, but it's much better than caffeine at keeping you awake."

A little while later, they decided to stop again for a thirty-minute break, just under the end of the escarpment. They heated up lamb stew and rice from a tin of GP rations. Tom devoured his meal. *Quat* suppressed the appetite, so having discarded it, he suddenly felt famished. He washed it down with a large bottle of mineral water and ate an apple. He then boiled a couple of mugs of coffee to drink while driving.

On commencing the next leg of their journey, Khalid said, "I'm going to try to get a nap."

"Okay, as there is little chance of me losing the track," Tom replied. "I'll wake you if I need anything."

* * *

Toward late afternoon, they approached what appeared to be an abandoned Turkish fort on a rocky ledge, somewhere in the middle of nowhere. Tom expected that it was one of the Ottoman Empire's southern outposts used to suppress the Bedouin early in the last century. It would have been a lonely and thankless task to be part of the Turkish military, posted to this fort. The garrison would have been isolated, without any communication with the outside world for months on end and in all probability surrounded by hostile tribesmen.

As they got closer, Tom's sixth sense made him uneasy about something and he decided to shake Khalid.

"Wake up, Khalid! Come on, wake up!"

"What's up?"

"Check out that fort. In case there's the slightest chance of another ambush, I want your full attention."

Tom gave the fort wide berth, diverging from the desert track and taking a route about eight hundred meters to the west, under the cover of a small ridge.

"We've no immediate way of checking if anyone is lurking inside the fort. There's no time for another heat signature," Tom said.

"It's a predictable location from which to mount an attack," Khalid noted. "It has a commanding position over the road."

"Better safe than sorry."

Although Tom had anticipated well, he was still surprised when the rocket propelled grenade exploded on a rock just behind them.

"Shit!" he shouted.

"Here we go again," said Khalid.

Tom parked the vehicle well out of range, behind the ridge. Grabbing their weapons, they started to circle around the fort in a pincer movement.

"Khalid, cover me while I work my way around back."

Crawling behind a small ledge to the north, Tom was able to conceal himself from view of the fort. Meanwhile, Khalid drew fire as he darted across the open space between the ridge and a small rocky outcrop. It was the only feature providing adequate cover to the west of the fort. The machine gun chewed up the ground under Khalid's feet as he ran for his life, feinting both left and right. Their opponent was a lousy shot, as he persistently missed his target. Khalid crouched behind the rock less than four hundred meters from the opposing gunner. Tom could see Khalid pinned down and assessed that the RPG launcher was still a major threat to him. For now, Khalid was only able to respond with the occasional burst that kicked up dust from the ramparts, but he failed to halt the onslaught from the machine gun. Tom crawled faster, hoping to reach his objective quicker so he could relieve poor Khalid.

Tom reached the rear wall in less than five minutes and rapidly scaled the parapet. He sprinted along the battlements until he found shelter in a building that ran the length of one side. Out of the corner of a convenient window, he surveyed the scene carefully. He found to his astonishment that there were as many as five attackers undercover of the west wall. They were in total disarray, bunched together quarrelling behind the machine gun. All were dressed in traditional *thobe* and *gutra* with long beards. From their appearance, Tom was sure that these were definitely not al-Qaeda's crack troops; nor for that matter could they be part of the convoy. Based upon their performance, they didn't posses even the slightest experience in armed combat. He guessed that they were a local al-Qaeda cell and speculated that they had been deployed by al-Qaeda command, who probably thought they could catch Tom and Khalid unawares.

Tom swiftly and mechanically screwed the silencer onto his weapon, and using the laser-targeting system on his SIG Pro, he could just make out the red dot on the back of the white tunic of the main gunner, about thirty meters away. He squeezed off five rounds gently, one by one, moving quickly from one target to the next. He heard a gentle thud as each bullet made its mark. His targets slumped over in swift succession. It was an easy kill, all over as quickly as it had begun.

Leaving the cover of the building, he circled around the top of the battlements, carefully scanning from left to right. He reached and searched his victims, who had all died almost instantly. They had no form of identification. He then ran down the steps to the lower level and found their Nissan truck unguarded, parked at the rear of the fort. Based upon a cursory examination it provided no clues either. Climbing over the rubble in the ruins of the fort, he did a quick reconnaissance to make sure there were no other members of the hit squad lurking. Then he encountered Khalid coming through the main gate, slightly out of breath and looking pale.

"Next time you cover me, okay!" he fumed.

"You had nothing to worry about," Tom replied. "All five were amateurs."

"Maybe, but their bullets were trained to kill!"

They wandered back to the Range Rover without exchanging a further word or glance. Tom was not prepared for an argument. They had orders and the mission to complete; hard feelings, regardless of how justified, were not allowed to get in the way. Once back at the vehicle, Khalid reported the whole incident via encoded chat with Kurt.

"Kurt will send in a ground team to mop up," Khalid announced.

Tom was now keenly aware that al-Qaeda had good intelligence along their route. It was remarkable how precisely they were able to pinpoint their position. They must have scouts on the ground. Moreover, they obviously saw them as an important threat, to be eliminated by whatever means possible. Taking it in turns to sleep was now definitely out of the question.

Chapter 13—Night Flight

Karin got to the airport three hours early, in good time to board the overnight flight to São Paulo, leaving at 10 pm. She was casually dressed in jeans and a top, with little makeup and a few selected items of jewelry, including her gold Rolex. She achieved a cool, nonchalant air and a look of understated elegance.

Keeping up the charade, she explained to the check-in staff in Miami that her husband was on a business trip and had been delayed. She was instructed by the airline to cancel his reservation and leave the ticket open for a later date. All this took an incredible amount of time, as she had to hang around lining up at the check-in and then at the ticketing counter and back at the check-in once more. She felt frustrated by the senseless bureaucracy of air travel and the apparent incompetence of the airlines. *They cannot undertake even the simplest task without making a meal of it.*

She was very glad that she had left extra time, as by the time she had completed this trivial task, she had only thirty minutes to get through the TSA inspection in time for boarding. Again, she encountered another long line in front of the X-ray machines. Realizing there must have been two hundred people ahead of her, she heaved a big sigh. Everyone appeared to be in a similar state of mind, irritated and presumably late for his or her flight.

On top of it all, the government employees in the TSA seemed even more disinterested in making things go more quickly than the airline staff.

"What a nightmare!" she said in frustration.

"I couldn't agree more," said a deep male voice behind her that sounded awfully like Tom.

Karin swiveled instinctively to see who had made the comment. A tanned, well-dressed, very handsome man in his mid-thirties confronted her. She eyed him up and down. He had rugged features that were classically good-looking. His linen jacket was casually draped over his left shoulder, and he was sporting a silk Bahaman shirt and some neat suede loafers.

"Oh, I do apologize. I thought for a moment that you were someone I knew."

"Sorry to disappoint you," he replied smiling, "my name is Javier. What's yours?"

She didn't respond.

"Are you on the São Paulo flight?" he asked.

"Yes, as a matter of fact I am," she replied.

"Don't worry. They'll never go without us; it's far too much hassle for them to offload our bags from the aircraft. This happens all the time."

She was feeling uncomfortable. *The last thing on Earth I want is to be picked up by some stranger in Miami airport. I'm sure he thinks I'm available, since I'm not wearing a wedding band.*

Meanwhile, a little voice inside told her that she would look less suspicious if she appeared to be accompanied. She should accept her own good fortune and all that she had to do in return was to stomach his corny chat-up lines.

"My name is Marina," she volunteered at last. "My friends call me Mari."

Javier smiled again, as he followed her through inspection.

"Can I help you with your carry-on bags, Mari?" he offered.

"Thanks."

Javier took her carry-on and they both headed down to gate E12. Karin discovered that Javier was a male model traveling to Brazil for a photo shoot. He was also in business class, and the airlines staff at the gate gave him the empty seat next to her. Karin learned with mixed feelings that Javier was connecting via São Paulo to Recife too, so she would be escorted the whole way.

Once on board and settled into their seats, Karin began chatting with Javier.

"I am looking to buy a property in Olinda and turn it into my holiday home. I love the old colonial style of the city."

"I've been there once; it's very picturesque."

"One of my best girlfriends bought a place there last year. After a short winter break, I was so impressed that I decided to buy my own piece of paradise as soon as I could."

"It's a good time to buy in Northeast Brazil."

"I'm convinced it is going to be the next big thing, a fashionable tourist destination for Europe's in-crowd."

"You might be right."

"You know the worst thing, so far, is the creepy real estate agent that I spoke to over the phone. His answer to anything was—no problem, *senhora*."

Javier grinned in recognition.

"Little did he realize that these are the three most dangerous words in my vocabulary—whenever I hear them, alarm bells ring!"

"I know a good lawyer that can help fix things. He seems to know everyone in Brazil. I'll put you in touch with him if you like?"

"Thanks, I'll try my own luck first."

She realized that she had better not overdo the damsel in distress act, yet somehow she couldn't resist playing Javier. She stopped herself from becoming too superior, as he could be very valuable to her and she knew it. She was definitely less conspicuous with him.

"Why am I doing all the talking?" Karin asked. "Tell me a little about yourself."

"Well, I never knew my father," he said. "I was bought up by my Spanish mother in London. She struggled to make ends meet."

Karin looked at him with rapt attention. "That must have been tough."

"My mother was an incredible woman. She dedicated her life to making sure I never went without. I would in no way have become as successful as I am today without her sacrifice. I owe her everything."

"She has got to be so proud of you."

"Yes, especially since I've been able to reach the pinnacle of my profession."

"So you're a supermodel," she said laughing.

His chest swelled. "I guess you could say that. My looks were the only good thing I inherited from my father's side."

"Do you have a girlfriend?"

"Not at the moment."

"How can that be? You're such an attractive man."

"Well, I find it difficult to have meaningful relationships. The models I usually hang out with are all so superficial."

"Don't tell me, they're just after one thing, and it's not your money!" Karin grinned.

He frowned back at her. "You have to be so careful when women are throwing themselves at you all the time."

He doesn't lack self-confidence—that's for sure! Is there no end to this man's vanity?

Karin then felt a wave of tiredness wash over her, and her eyes began to feel scratchy. As soon as the flight attendant had cleared her tray, she asked Javier to retrieve a blanket for her. She adjusted the seat and the footrest, inserted the earplugs, put on her eyeshades, and lay straight out, expecting to doze off. However, she couldn't get to sleep; she was over-tired and she was afraid, especially for Tom. A light sleeper at the best of times, she was lingering in a sort of half-awake state, her head buzzing, her mind playing tricks on her.

What the hell is going on? What on Earth did Tom think he was doing placing me in such a dangerous situation? What kind of mean bastards are chasing me?

She was unlikely to get answers to any of these questions anytime soon and she was well aware of it. She glanced over at Javier, who was fast asleep. She decided to go for a walk about the cabin to try to ease the tension. She got up, gently stepping over him, and headed for the galley. Taking a glass of water, she then stood in the space by the exit hatch on the 767, looking out the window at the night sky. There was enough moonlight to see the dense cloud formations below and the starry night sky above. She wondered wistfully where Tom was at that very moment. When she saw him, she would give him such a hard time, but only for about five minutes. Then she would melt into his arms.

Oh my God, I love him so much!

Chapter 14—Pilgrimage

As Tom and Khalid were approaching the city of Madinah, Tom read the Circus briefing on his handheld.

The Prophet's Mosque in Madinah is the second most revered place for Muslims around the world. Millions visit the mosque each year, to worship, to visit the prophet's grave, and to see the city that gave birth to Islam. Madinah has a floating population from about one million three hundred thousand, throughout most of the year, which increases by almost one million during the period of Hajj or pilgrimage.

Usama bin Laden graduated from the Islamic University of Madinah, as did fifteen of the Saudis who participated in the 9/11 hijackings. It has long been known as a prime recruiting ground for al Qaeda fighters.

In August 2005 Saleh Al-Oufi, the leader of al-Qaeda in Saudi Arabia, was killed in a shootout with security forces in the neighborhood of Al-Bahar, Madinah.

He scanned the rest of the write up and discovered that paradoxically the family firm—Bin Laden—won the billion-dollar construction contracts for the reconstruction of the two holy mosques in Mecca and Medina in the eighties. He was already aware of the inescapable links between the Bin Laden dynasty and the House of Saud. Although Usama was now the black sheep of the family, he had been very close to many of the wealthy young Saudi princes during his earlier years. In truth he was one of theirs, only his decision to go and fight a foreign war in Afghanistan had changed his ideology and estranged him from the ruling classes.

The Americans and the Saudis had funded the war, part of the dying embers of the Cold War. They sent many young jihadists like Usama to fight, as nothing more than cannon fodder for the Russians. Little did they realize that the repercussions of this policy would be reverberating around the globe two decades later.

"From memory," Khalid said, "there are Saudi National Guard checkpoints at all the main entrances to the city, and they patrol the desert in between."

"The convoy won't risk detention by the National Guard, I'm sure," Tom responded.

The extra security was because Madinah was *haram,* or forbidden territory, to the Infidel, the non-Muslim, who was not allowed within the confines of the holy city. They watched on the tracking device as about thirty kilometers out, their target left the main road yet again.

"The convoy is skirting the city via desert tracks," said Khalid.

"It will take them a long time to go around Madinah that way."

"Sure, it will dramatically increase their time compared us."

"I estimate it will add approximately one hundred and sixty kilometers."

"They'll be lucky to average much more than twenty kilometers per hour over the terrain to the northeast."

"In that case, I reckon they've just bought themselves at least an eight-hour delay."

"Great, that's plenty of time for us to get some rest and still keep pace."

Tom was running on empty and by now suffering from acute sleep deprivation. His predicament was worsened because of their earlier *quat* chewing.

Tom moaned, "Surely they must be feeling the effect of more than forty-eight hours on the run too."

"But remember," responded Khalid, "they have a big advantage over us—there are enough of them to take it in turns driving and sleeping."

"Look at that … I think we just got an even bigger break."

Tom pointed to the tracking device, which showed that the convoy had come to a complete halt near a small village along the route. They appeared to corral the Land Cruisers, again, as if they were going to settle in for the night.

"It's time to get some well-earned rest," said Tom. "If we don't find somewhere to sleep soon, we'll collapse from exhaustion."

"Huh," was the monosyllabic reply from Khalid.

Tom sent a scrambled text message to Laura asking her to see what accommodation she could come up with based on their current position. Laura came straight back with the co-ordinates of the nearest hotel, Le Méridien, located just outside the city limits. She advised them that they were booked in as tourists on a sightseeing trip from Jeddah and allegedly on their way to see the Hejaz railway.

Tom searched his kit bag and pulled out two *iqamas*, Saudi identity cards, which would get them past the Saudi National Guard. They were both supposedly engineering contractors working for an Irish construction firm, Doherty's. Tom completed two company authorization letters, dating and stamping them to look authentic. He wanted no hassles with the Saudi authorities, who were very finicky about travel permits. They also stopped to fix Saudi plates to the vehicle.

Khalid drove down the main highway from the airport toward the luxury hotel. Ahead, Tom could see one of the royal palaces perched on a hill, overlooking the city. It was bathed in a blue-green light. It stood out against the backdrop of the Jebel in an otherwise featureless landscape. Arriving at the checkpoint, they lined up in their vehicle to pass document inspection. Khalid handed over their papers and responded to the National Guard sergeant's questions in English.

"We are heading to Le Méridien," he said.

The sergeant gave him a dirty look.

"Pull over on the right," he ordered, "and open the rear door."

He started to inspect the contents. Tom realized that this was very risky for them, as he could easily stumble across the weapons they were carrying or his equipment for making false IDs. Mercifully, he started with their kit bags, which contained only clothes and personal items. Tom suspected that he was looking for alcohol or something similar to incriminate them. This required some quick thinking.

Tom whispered to Khalid, "Look, our best bet is to challenge his authority."

Tom asked the sergeant, "Do you know who we are? Give me your name and serial number. I'll be sure to mention it to Prince Naif at our next meeting."

After some radio chatter between the sergeant and his superior, Tom and Khalid were let go.

"Phew, that was a close call," said Tom.

"You realize what it was all about?" asked Khalid. "My *iqama* identifies me as Jordanian Christian. These self-righteous, hypocritical bastards hate all non-Muslim Arabs. It offends them to think that any Arab could be part of another religion."

Tom just sighed, relieved that they had outwitted the sergeant.

"We'll need to watch it in the future, especially if we come across another National Guard checkpoint. It's just possible that the sergeant will check out our story," Khalid said.

"I agree. If he finds out that we lied, they might well be on the lookout for us."

* * *

The two Circus agents promptly reached their destination a couple of kilometers on. The manager greeted them at check-in and gave them a quick history of the hotel.

"Welcome to Le Méridien, gentlemen. This was the most expensive hotel in the world when it was built in the oil boom of the eighties. No expense was spared." He gestured, waving his arms around him.

Tom gazed open mouthed at the splendid lobby swathed in Italian marble, inlaid with gold. It had a domed ceiling supported by magnificent columns carved in the shape of date palms and adorned by chandeliers.

"We have more than four hundred rooms, which unfortunately remain largely unoccupied for most of the year. Outside the Hajj season we are host to twenty European specialists, who keep the presses running at the nearby King Fahd Quran Printing Press, and virtually no other guests."

Tom was astonished by this and wondered how they could afford to keep the hotel open.

"Sadly, now there's very little passing trade. We used to get many tourists on their way to see the Hejaz Railway," said the manager. "I admit that you two gentlemen are something of a rarity today. Most westerners have been frightened off by threat of al-Qaeda."

Undeniably, there were fewer western expatriate personnel in Saudi these days. Most large multinational companies had pulled out any *targeted* personnel and recruited only *non-targeted* Muslim staff to work in Saudi. Many of the westerners that remained were on a managed itinerary, flying in and out of the kingdom with a couple of armed bodyguards riding shotgun. Tom imagined it was not much of a life. He had read that a Frenchman was shot dead the previous week, as he went out to buy milk from the corner supermarket in Jeddah. Tom was certain that for most normal people, staying on was just not worth the risk.

In the meantime, Tom and Khalid were escorted to their suites. Tom didn't even pause to undress; he kicked his boots off and fell face down on the bed. He was asleep instantaneously.

* * *

As soon as he awoke, Tom linked up his communicator and checked in with Kurt. No news to report—the al-Qaeda camp was just stirring and would most probably be on the move within the next few minutes. There was no need for them to rush, as they still had several hours before the convoy would be able to circumnavigate the city.

The manager had explained that the hotel had a staff of about two hundred, an unprecedented ratio of about ten per guest. As Tom came down for a late breakfast, he was leapt upon by the maître d' and escorted to his table, where Khalid was already seated. Their order was taken swiftly. Two waiters each suddenly appeared standing at their respective shoulders; absurdly, one would place the food, while the other was there to remove the empty plate. Tom felt slightly sorry for the staff, as they probably had little practice with real guests. The plates were elegantly laid out, as if the chef were entering a culinary contest with each dish.

Khalid beamed, "They must think we are from the bureau that awards the star ratings to hotels."

"How do they justify all this expense?" Tom asked.

"There have got to be government subsidies to keep this place open all year round," replied Khalid.

"You realize that we now have some time on our hands."

"Yes, about five hours, I estimate."

"I thought we'd meet up in my suite in an hour for a tactical review."

"Good idea."

In the meantime, Tom went upstairs and placed a long-distance call to Belize. He needed to speak to Karin. He wouldn't reveal anything about the mission or his whereabouts; he just needed to talk like two lovers about trivial things that were important only to them. His job could be exciting, but at the same time, it was heart-wrenchingly hard on those closest to you. This would be the last mission, he swore to himself. He would retire after this one and they would go into hiding together.

He had it all planned out—the beachfront apartment in Recife, the new identity as a fun-loving Dutch couple from Eindhoven, who had made their money from their own business in the South West of Holland, then retired early to the sun. He had deliberately not used Circus resources to arrange anything to do with his new life and identity. His money, which was deposited in numbered Swiss accounts, would be laundered through the Cayman Islands and made available to him as a pension from the ABN Bank in the Netherlands Antilles. Nobody would be able to follow the paper trail. He was proud of that.

The operator called back after ten minutes to announce that there was no reply from Belize. Curious, Tom thought, as he recalculated the time difference from Madinah to Belize, which was nine hours back. Eleven in the morning was 2 AM the previous morning. Karin would certainly be in the house; perhaps she was sleeping so profoundly that she didn't hear the phone. It was not at all like Karin. Tom requested the operator to keep trying a little longer. After forty-five minutes, he was getting concerned, but he tried to put it out of his head because of the mission. Could she be so upset with him that she had finally done what she had threatened in their worst moments and left? She wasn't emotionally unstable and he knew it. Something must be wrong. He thanked the operator and said he would try again later in the day.

Tom heard a gentle knock on the door.

"It's me," Khalid said.

Tom let him in; they sat a large walnut dining table in the center of the main room.

"This place is unbelievable,' said Tom. "Look at how this room is so lavishly furnished with expensive period furnishings and chintz fabrics."

"I've never seen anything like it, even in Saudi," replied Khalid. "It's amazing."

Tom spread out the map of the region on the table and started to debate the likely route their target would follow.

"I think that the convoy is now heading north toward the Red Sea coast."

"In which case, their final destination must be Egypt, Sudan, Libya, or Algeria."

"I agree, Iraq is too dangerous for them, because of American patrols and they'll be concerned about Jordan and Syria's uncertain allegiances. I'm still betting their destination is Egypt."

Tom sent a message to Kurt to plan the next drop. They would need Egyptian plates, documents, and decals for the Range Rover, not forgetting some heavier artillery. Tom realized if they got into a firefight with the convoy, their light arms would leave them vulnerable, particularly to surface-to-surface missiles.

Tom called down for coffee and dates. They folded away the maps and all other traces of their discussion as the waiter entered and served them with a typical Saudi treat. The coffee was rich, aromatic, and slightly bitter, with an oily texture and yellow color, flavored with cardamom. It was made from the only the husks of the coffee bean, an acquired taste that Tom had learned to appreciate in his years in Arabia. The dates were succulent, with an almond instead of the pith. They demanded that you ate more.

They sat together in silence enjoying a break.

Khalid spoke first. "I just don't understand it, Tom. Why don't we take them out somewhere in the desert, far from anyone? The US military could easily do a satellite-guided airstrike on five targets simultaneously."

"I don't understand it either. I've no idea why we're playing this stupid cat-and-mouse game!"

"I know we aren't risking offending the Saudis."

"For sure, they would be overjoyed if we wiped UBL from the face of the Earth—even if it was on their soil!"

"I agree; it just doesn't stack up."

Tom had been trying to process the same set of contradictions. Khalid's remarks just underlined to him that he was right to be skeptical about the way their mission was evolving.

"Based upon Kurt's little charade when I was in Dubai, I've had an uncomfortable feeling from the outset."

"What the hell's the Agency up to?" asked Khalid.

"I only wish I knew."

As Khalid was leaving, Tom said, "Let's meet up again for lunch and depart sometime late afternoon."

"Okay."

* * *

Tom stayed in his room and asked the operator to place a new call to Belize. He hung on the line this time, but there was still no response. *Why doesn't she pick up?* He was getting seriously worried.

He went to the hotel business center and logged on to the Internet to check out the security system on the island. The CCTV was functioning normally. He could see nobody—there was no movement. He spent five minutes staring at the pictures on the screen, flicking from the jetty to the front, then the rear of the house, and finally the pool. It was dawn and the early morning light reflected back strongly off the windows. Eventually he noticed what looked like a broken pane of glass in the front door. *Very strange.*

He clicked to minimize the window from the security system, pulling up a new window and logging onto a secure site.

"Shit!" he swore under his breath. "*Code Red.*"

Thank God! If Karin has activated the warning signal then she's most probably safe.

He toggled back to the security site and this time zeroed in on the doors and windows. There had been four breaches. It definitely looked like a precision military raid on their beach home. He also spotted some gas canisters lying out on the porch and could tell immediately that this was not the work of amateurs and definitely not the modus operandi of al-Qaeda. Probably US Navy SEALs or Special Boat Service, he surmised. Now he was even more puzzled. *Aren't we all fighting on the side of the good guys?* In any case, al-Qaeda was highly unlikely to know the identity of those following UBL. This smelled like an inside job. He couldn't fathom why somebody on his own side was out to get him.

Tom returned to his room feeling perplexed. He switched on the world radio and tuned to the BBC to listen to the headlines.

> *Usama bin Laden allegedly warned of fresh terrorist attacks in America in an audiotape broadcast by al-Jazeera, and he also announced a surprising truce in Iraq and Afghanistan to assist reconstruction efforts there. If genuine, the tape represents Mr. Bin Laden's first such address for over a year, following a videotaped message broadcast by al-Jazeera shortly before America's 2004 presidential election.*

Tom was astonished by al-Qaeda's apparent ability to issue taped press releases, even as Bin Laden was fleeing for his life. They clearly should never be underestimated. The US response, according to the BBC, was somewhat predictable.

> *The United States will not let up in the war on terror, despite the threats on the tape, said White House press secretary Scott McClellan. We do not negotiate with terrorists. We put them out of business.*

Tom thought it ironic that this was exactly what they were attempting to do at this very moment, apparently without the full support of Uncle Sam.

He sat down with Khalid in the hotel restaurant a little before two. They went through the ridiculous farce again with the two waiters. Lunch was five courses, so there was much more for them to do. The chef had outdone himself nonetheless.

"What a shame that we are not in more convivial surroundings," said Tom, "and there is no fine claret to accompany the food."

"Stop dreaming, Tom," replied Khalid.

Incongruously, they washed it all down with "Saudi Champagne"—a cocktail of apple juice and sparkling water. They sat completely alone in the restaurant. It took one and a half hours to finish the meal. It was all slightly surreal, and by the end of their banquet, Tom was anxious to get back to the mission.

Chapter 15—Hejaz

Tom and Khalid were now in the real Lawrence of Arabia territory, running alongside the Hejaz railway. It was built by the Turks and repeatedly damaged in fighting during the Arab Revolt. It stretched from Damascus to Medina, through the Hejaz region, and it was originally justified to facilitate the Hajj pilgrimage, although the true purpose was undoubtedly to enhance Turkish rule over this far-flung part of their empire.

From the outset, the railway was the target of attacks by local tribes. These were never particularly successful, but neither were the Turks able to control areas more than a kilometer or so either side of the tracks. Following the breakup of the Ottoman Empire after the First World War, the railway never reopened south of the Jordanian-Saudi border.

Tom continued surveying the surrounding landscape as he drove.

"I can just visualize Peter O'Toole and Omar Sharif in *Lawrence of Arabia* and the scene at the well," he said.

"This vast expanse of emptiness has nothing worth fighting for except for water," replied Khalid.

"Yes, I recall in the movie that a life was taken because a member of the wrong tribe was drinking from the well."

Tom was gathering speed along this sector of the journey, as the road north strung out straight ahead of them into the far distance. In the intense rays of the sun, he could see mirages appearing, pools of water on the road, which vanished as they approached. Then, as if by magic, they reappeared further ahead.

He suddenly braked hard.

"Shit! The Saudi authorities have a crazy sense of traffic control," said Tom.

"You can say that again," responded Khalid.

"Look at that," said Tom, "a speed bump in a completely straight section of road!"

Khalid winced. "I bet there are more ahead—don't you dare miss one of those things."

"I know, at the speed we're going it would cripple our suspension."

Tom strained to see the early warning signs, such as lines of rubber imprinted in the asphalt or the sight of a hapless victim who had hit a bump at speed and then abandoned his vehicle at the side of the road.

"You'd better take the wheel for a bit," Tom said after only a couple of hours of driving. "I can't handle this anymore."

The effort of driving in a straight line, struggling to see against the reflections and the sun's glare, was mind bending. Soon after Khalid took over, they joined a new section of highway in the direction of Tabouk, at al Ula, and things became a little easier.

Tom continued monitoring the convoy on the tracking device.

"Okay Khalid, the Land Cruisers are traveling at a steady ninety-five kilometers per hour and are about twenty-five kilometers ahead, in close formation."

"Excellent—it's just where we want them to be."

"They appear to be a bit reckless, though," said Tom. "This configuration leaves them wide open to air attack."

"Maybe they've figured out that the Americans won't strike on Saudi soil," responded Khalid.

"Who knows?"

As dusk approached, Khalid raced to close in on the convoy.

"We can't afford to lose them at night," said Khalid.

"But let's not get too close," responded Tom.

Khalid slowed down as they passed an Ottoman fort and a railway depot, which had the original locomotives standing in their sheds, well preserved by the desert climate.

Tom was wide eyed. "Amazing! They must have been there since before the First World War."

In the red glow of the setting sun, he could just make out a faint outline against the horizon, a line of dust rising from the desert.

"The convoy is off-road again," Tom said.

"They'll be dangerously conspicuous out in the open desert."

"Not so—by my calculation, they're heading for the ruins at Madain Saleh, where there's plenty of cover."

* * *

Madain Saleh was a spectacular archaeological site with immense stone tombs, originally created by the Nabetians—the same people who built the magnificent Petra in Jordan. The Nabetian Empire controlled the spice routes from around 100 B.C. to A.D. 100. Madain Saleh was an important stop for caravans from the incense-producing areas of southern Arabia to Syria, Egypt, Byzantium, and points beyond. The impressive tombs are carved out of the desert mountainsides, well away from any population. The tribes of Thamud were the earliest inhabitants of this region and were mentioned in the Holy Quran. The story is that the Thamuds denied the message of God, as revealed by Prophet Saleh, and killed the sacred she-camel. Thus, the curse of God fell upon them and they were destroyed and buried under the sand. The isolated site has been uninhabited for centuries, except for the nomadic Bedouin.

The disaffected *mujahedeen* that came back from the war in Afghanistan had been the nucleus around the original call to arms for al-Qaeda. These fanatics wanted *jihad* against the West and especially American hypocrisy. After fighting an ugly war against ill-equipped teenage Russian conscripts, they felt betrayed and used. They had done America's dirty work in an ideological struggle with the communists. Even though by this time, the Russians were a spent force and their heart was not in the fight.

Now al-Qaeda had a new and equally well-trained horde of insurgents, similarly disillusioned with the Americans and the House of Saud. Those that had heard the call to go and fight the Americans in Iraq after the second invasion were now combat-hardened veterans of street-to-street fighting from Fallujah, Baghdad, Basra, and Sadr City.

Unbeknown to the Saudi authorities, al-Qaeda had turned the stone tombs of Madain Saleh into a staging post for the mujahedeen on their way to and from the armed struggle in Iraq. Young Saudi volunteers came here to receive some basic training and to be kitted out with automatic weapons before heading further northward by camel or four-wheel drive, crossing the TAP pipeline into Iraq. The returnees were then used to train and organize the replacement force, before going home and becoming part of one of the embryonic terrorist cells in urban Saudi Arabia.

The rocky outcrops and tombs were the ideal place to hide from the prying eyes of the spy satellites and planes. The area was uninhabited and hence received little attention from the Saudi military.

The news of the Sheikh's impending arrival spread like wildfire among the camp, and the mujahedeen were on heightened alert. They posted heavily armed guards all around the rocky outcrop. Their warrior lord would be well protected while he was their guest.

* * *

Tom and Khalid were completely unaware of the size and the nature of the armed force they were rapidly approaching.

Khalid slowed down as they ventured off road. "Look, the convoy is disappearing from the screen."

"They're hiding somewhere along the main ridge. There, look where the tombs are set back into the rock face." Tom pointed to the screen.

"They'll be parked under an overhang—very smart," Khalid replied.

"They'll be safe there for the night."

Tom told Khalid to pull up against a solitary tomb carved out of a monolith of rock in the middle of the desert some five kilometers from the main ridge. Taking a leaf from the convoy's book, they too parked under the overhang, to be less conspicuous.

As darkness settled, Tom suggested, "Let's stay here for a couple of hours and then go and reconnoiter."

"It will be good to get a better idea of what we're up against," Khalid agreed.

"Great! We'll not say anything to Kurt, or anyone else for that matter."

They blackened their faces, pulled on their rucksacks, containing weapons, night-vision, and a communicator, and set out on foot in the direction of the enemy camp. It would take about fifty minutes to cross the desolate tract between them. They avoided wide-open spaces, finding cover behind the small ridges that crisscrossed the terrain. As they approached the camp, they heard many voices. They spread themselves out flat, on top of a convenient rock-shelf, and observed through their binoculars. There was a big contingent of about one hundred and fifty heavily armed men surrounding a large campfire. Tom couldn't believe that such a large group was out in the open.

"My God, they've got balls!" Tom murmured. "Where the hell did they all come from?"

"Sonofabitch!" Khalid whispered.

"I'd never have imagined so many mujahedeen were hiding out here."

"I think I can make out a taller figure the center of the throng. It's probably Bin Laden, but I can't be one hundred percent sure."

"It's far too risky for us to get any closer."

"Yes, they'll definitely have posted sentries."

Five identical Land Cruisers were parked in a line along the bottom the rock face. Tom could just make out a couple of guards keeping watch around the perimeter of the camp. He decided that the taller figure did genuinely appear to be the Sheikh. He seemed to be encouraging his followers, giving them a motivating speech. It was remarkable to witness the apparent devotion and loyalty of his supporters, who responded enthusiastically to every pause in his discourse with ritual shrieks and tongue clicking. The air of excitement was palpable.

"That's definitely Bin Laden," observed Khalid, "nobody else would provoke that reaction."

"I don't give a damn about the chairman's orders. This is it!" Tom responded.

"I agree. Here's our big chance."

"I'm going to call for an air strike."

"We'll deal a death blow to al-Qaeda."

Tom immediately texted a coded message to Kurt with the co-ordinates.

From: Slater, Tom—ME/2—xxx Scrambled xxx 21:25 GMT
To: Schneider, Kurt—CS Dubai
Have visual contact with UBL in open terrain. Surrounded by 150 enemy personnel. Co-ordinates: N 21.54 W 31.76. Can illuminate target.
T.
+++

"A Tomahawk missile from the USS *Los Angeles* will do the trick," Tom said.

"Great! In twenty minutes it'll all be over," responded Khalid.

Within five minutes came the reply from Kurt, copied to the chairman. Tom pressed the decode button.

From: Schneider, Kurt—CS Dubai xxx Scrambled xxx 21:28 GMT
To: Slater, Tom—ME/2
Negative. Do not engage under any circumstances. Repeat—Negative to air strike

K.

++++

Tom showed the message to Khalid. "What the hell is going on?"

"Goddamn!" he replied.

Tom was open-mouthed.

"Why the Yanks would let this opportunity pass by I haven't a clue," said Khalid.

Tom seemed lost in thought for a moment, slowly shaking his head.

"It's possible we're unaware of all the angles. Remember all good field agents have to be able operate with a high degree of ambiguity."

"I know, but—"

"Don't forget the chairman's explicit order."

"Yes, except he told us to call it in," protested Khalid.

"I realize that's exactly what we did," Tom responded. "Frankly, I was not expecting outright rejection."

"I'm really suspicious."

"I just don't bloody believe it either!"

Tom shook his head once more. "Somebody is playing games with us, but who?"

They slowly retreated to their vehicle, without saying a further word. When they arrived back, they saw that the chairman had sent them a new encoded message.

Wood, Peter—C—xxx Scrambled xxx 22:17 GMT.
To: Slater, Tom—ME/2
Keep up the good work. We want UBL alive.
Do not approach subjects. Repeat under NO circumstances approach subjects.
Mission objective is to follow and ascertain destination; then call it in.
C.

+++

"Oh, so that's the game!" Tom said, shrugging his shoulders. "Those arrogant bastards really think we can herd UBL into a trap, so they can take him alive!"

"Well, I think they've missed their big chance."

"Yes, they'll never get another opportunity like the one we've just witnessed tonight."

Khalid sneered. "Huh! I hate being taken for a sucker."

Tom was unable to deal with all the imponderables. He must follow orders by continuing to track the convoy, at least until they were told to withdraw, but his heart was not in it anymore. He had lost his faith in the system. They were no longer part of a historic mission. In his mind, this was now a routine surveillance exercise. Tom didn't buy the chairman's explanation either. He had a hunch that there was much more behind the Yanks' refusal, and it made him nervous.

They set an infrared perimeter alarm system about one hundred meters from the Range Rover, in case one of the mujahedeen strayed from their camp. Thankfully, they managed to get six hours of sleep in their vehicle without being disturbed, although both of them were restless after the night's surprise revelations.

* * *

The sun was starting to climb over the horizon as Tom awoke. Checking the tracking device, he saw al-Qaeda had broken camp and were setting off along the road north from Madain Saleh. He heard gunfire echoing around the rocky terrain, which he assumed was the mujahedeen firing a salvo into the air, a traditional send-off. He was surprised how little concern they apparently showed but imagined that in such a remote location they thought no one would hear their boisterous salute.

Tom started up the Range Rover. He decided to go round the camp and make a wide circle through the desert to avoid detection.

Khalid was monitoring the convoy on the screen.

"Their vehicles continue in tight formation," Khalid said. "I'd say they are probably forty kilometers away now and are making rapid progress toward the coastal range."

"Funny, they still don't seem too worried about an air attack."

"Last night's events appear to validate their assessment. It seems the Americans won't attack, even given a good opportunity."

"Khalid, I don't know about you, but I don't believe in coincidence."

"I don't either. What the hell—it's like they know that no harm will come to them!"

Tom became lost in concentration, pitting his wits against the wilderness. He was sliding the vehicle around corners at high speed. It provided him with a welcome distraction and the antidote that he needed to calm his fears.

"This detour will keep us well away from the mujahedeen," he said as he glanced sideways at Khalid.

Khalid frowned. "But, we must rejoin the road soon, or we'll be left too far behind through the mountain passes ahead."

"We've been almost two hours doing a full-circle around Madain Saleh, I know."

"Yes, I estimate that we are barely twenty kilometers from our starting point."

When Khalid took the wheel, they started to climb toward the spectacular dark rock formations of the Hejaz Mountains.

Tom observed the map. "The other side of the mountain range is the port of Dubah, where you can take a ferry to the Red Sea port of Safaga in Egypt."

"In my opinion it's highly likely that they will try to get the ferry at Dubah."

"UBL definitely won't risk deviating north to Iraq or Jordan; he wouldn't receive a very warm welcome there."

"And obviously going by road through Eilat and Israel is completely out of the question."

"I agree, without a doubt."

"So, you're still betting Egypt is their final destination?" Khalid asked squinting at Tom.

"It must be … I'll send off a message to Kurt," he replied.

"I'm sure you're right, Bin Laden will be at home, among his largest group of followers anywhere in the world."

"Either way, I seriously doubt if he can be cornered alive, especially once he reaches Egyptian territory."

Khalid nodded. "He'll disappear there easily. It'll be almost impossible to find him."

Chapter 16—
Dirty Work

Back in Dubai, Kurt saw the incoming message from Tom but didn't pay any attention. He was in shock. He felt as if someone had just punched him in the balls. He had been racking his brains since last night trying to figure out what was going on. He was truly impressed when Tom and Khalid had managed to get UBL in their sights.

He remembered thinking that they finally had the sonofabitch. They had even illuminated the target. It appeared as if they would destroy the al-Qaeda network in Saudi and a good part of Iraq simultaneously. It couldn't have been more perfect—out in the desert they were all combatants, so there could be no claims of collateral damage.

Curiously out of place in his chosen profession, Kurt was a moral man who did not believe that the ends justify the means. He began reflecting on the frequent allegations about Uncle Sam's cruelty in killing innocent women and children caught in the line of fire in Iraq. Terrorists played by different rules and thought nothing of killing and maiming innocent civilians. It drew more attention to their cause. Despite the injustice of it all, Kurt fully grasped that his enemies would win if they succeeded in bringing him down to the same inhumane level. War was cruel enough when played by the rules, but the descent into anarchy was a slippery slope, and even the best causes could be easily undermined. Repeatedly, the politics of war proved more important than the fight itself.

He was flabbergasted by the speed with which Ops in Langley had countermanded his instruction to the USS *Ronald Regan*. He couldn't imagine what the hell his old buddy Brad was up to. However, that wasn't the end of it. The blow below the belt came about twenty minutes ago, when he had received a Level Four top-priority order. He stood there in the Ops Room at Terratec with a copy of the decoded message crumpled in his hand, staring into space. He had remained frozen in the same position for some time now.

From: Hartman, Brad—ADD +++TOP SECRET+++LEVEL 4; 04:09 GMT
To: Schneider, Kurt—CS Dubai
Engage and destroy target #517478.
B.
+++

Jesus Christ! I can't do this. He stood there just shaking his head. He was sure there was some mistake. The order was asking him to take out Salter and al Querishi. It was gutting. It was as if he had been ordered to kill his own men—and in effect, it was. The Brits would never forgive them. If the Circus ever found out that the Agency was deliberately targeting their agents, the long-standing relationship between the two intelligence communities would be destroyed.

Kurt learned on his first day with the Agency that Level Four meant an order on the direct authority of the Commander-in-Chief, the President of the United States. At first, he thought there must have been some error with the communication or that someone had falsified the message. He checked the cipher and had the comms operator ping to verify the origin of the message. It all stacked up. He had to obey such an order, and he knew it. He decided to stall and send a message to Brad for clarification. There had to be a mix-up; as soon as he was able to shed light on the situation, then he would stand down.

Laura came up to him and whispered, "Are you all right, boss? You look terribly pale all of a sudden."

"Send a response to the Level Four: please reconfirm target designation; message corrupted; Priority Alpha," Kurt barked. He saw Laura cringe and he was aware that he'd sounded unusually terse. He would have to apologize to her later.

For Kurt this was turning into the nightmare mission from hell. Firstly, they had blown Mohammed's cover, and his best source in the Middle East was now inoperative. Next, they had missed the target on the first attempt and set off on a wild goose chase that had him calling in all sorts of favors from the military. He hated to be indebted in that way. Then, when they had the most significant objective of his career firmly in their sights, he had been instructed to let him go. Now, to make matters infinitely worse, he was being ordered to kill two field operatives on his own side. He wondered what else could possibly happen.

Laura handed him the response from Brad.

From: Hartman, Brad—ADD +++TOP SECRET+++LEVEL 4; 07:24 GMT
To: Schneider, Kurt—CS Dubai
Repeat: Engage and destroy Target #517478. No repercussions—must look like enemy kill.
B.
+++

There was no mistake. He would be in serious trouble if he didn't follow through on the order. He needed time to think and plan very carefully. He also knew intuitively that this could not look like a typical battlefield friendly-fire incident. The Brits would surely demand an inquiry and go through the evidence with a fine-tooth comb. Too many questions would be asked. He responded to Brad to buy more time.

From: Schneider, Kurt—CS Dubai +++TOP SECRET+++LEVEL 4; 08:15 GMT
To: Hartman, Brad—ADD
Copy. Will need some time to set up.
K.
+++

In return, he got the following message:

From: Hartman, Brad—ADD +++TOP SECRET+++ LEVEL 4; 08:22 GMT
To: Schneider, Kurt—CS Dubai
You have 72 Hours.
B.
+++

He decided to call an emergency staff meeting of his key lieutenants. He was going to need help to figure this one out. Frankly, he felt it was just too big to keep to himself anyway. Some shared responsibility would go a long way to making him feel better.

* * *

Kurt walked into the briefing room and called the group to order; they were a disciplined crowd and immediately shut up and turned their attention to him. Kurt explained the new mission. They had never had to handle a Level Four out of Dubai, and there were a few sharp intakes of breath around the room, particularly once the nature of the target was made clear.

"Let me understand," said Frank, the ops man and the most experienced in the room. "We've got to engineer a firefight between our boys and al-Qaeda, in which our side loses?"

"Yup, Frank you got the basic idea," replied Kurt.

"Why we don't just get UBL on the radio and tell him what we want him to do!" he said throwing his hands in the air.

"That isn't as stupid as it sounds," said Kurt. "I think the only way we're going to successfully accomplish this mission is by using al-Qaeda so it looks like we had nothing to do with it."

"So, we have to lead them unwittingly into an al Qaeda ambush," said Todd, the mission specialist.

"Poor sons of bitches," Frank said. "What the hell did they do to deserve this?"

Kurt sensed that he was expressing the sentiment of all of them in the room.

"We've gotten the walkie-talkie working now, sir," said Ron, the comms expert.

"Excellent," responded Kurt.

"If you want, I'm sure we can get a message to the convoy."

"How?" asked Kurt.

"All we need is to be within range," replied Ron. "I have no idea how we can convince them to talk with us, though."

"Well done … good thinking," Kurt encouraged him. "We must find some way to give UBL a sign of our good faith."

"Whatever we do, al-Qaeda will still be suspicious," responded Ray, the senior intelligence analyst.

"How about a free passage across the Red Sea … with no interference?" suggested Ibrahim, the liaison officer.

"Yes, I suspect the Saudis will be all over them if they try to board the ferry at Dubah," observed Kurt. "They must be worried about it."

"In my opinion, although counter-intuitive, the only real option for them is Aqaba, but they still have to cross the Jordanian border," responded Ibrahim.

"You mean, we could offer to get them into Jordan," said Kurt.

"Yes, we'd have to cash in some of our chips with King Abdullah."

"Is that a problem?"

"Well, he owes us so much that it shouldn't be."

"I like it ... more good thinking," Kurt said.

"We can spring the trap in the interior of Sinai. It's completely deserted," said Frank.

"Fine, there should be no witnesses," said Kurt.

"I still don't like the idea of targeting our own," said Frank.

"We must follow orders," said Kurt. "I imagine that our two heroes will be found having fought a brave rear guard action, vastly outnumbered and outgunned. Nobody will be the wiser."

"You cold-hearted bastard," murmured Frank.

Kurt assigned each of them to their respective parts of the operational plan and told them all to be back in three hours for an update.

At the beginning of the next session, Frank kicked off.

"Well, gentlemen, we've concluded that the only way we can keep control of this op is to put a man into the al-Qaeda convoy."

There was an immediate buzz around the room and the usual self-restraint was forgotten for a few seconds.

"That's risky," said Kurt. "How do you think we're going to pull that off?"

"What the hell do you have in mind, Frank?" asked Ron.

"You're fucking crazy! Who would be such a fool to accept a suicide mission like that?" said Ray.

Kurt intervened, "Come on, guys, hear him out."

"Well, we figured that the offer of a free passage across Aqaba wouldn't be convincing on its own. We need to plant our own man in the convoy to guide them."

"It'll have to be someone they know, too," continued Todd. "We thought we could use Abdul Rahman al-Falah."

"But they know we turned al-Falah. Won't they welcome the opportunity to slit his throat?" Ibrahim asked.

"We thought the same, but if UBL thinks we have a hostage—who we'll execute if anything happens to al-Falah—then he might be swayed," he replied.

"Who would give us that much leverage?" asked Ibrahim.

"Well it's not just any hostage. We have the Bin Laden's son, Saad, whom we captured from the Iranians," replied Frank.

For the second time that day, there was a sharp intake of breath around the room.

"When did this happen?" asked Ron.

"Sonofabitch, Frank … sounds like we have a real bargaining chip!" said Ray.

"And it looks like we have a plan," said Kurt. "So let's get Abdul Rahman on the first plane to Jordan."

"Yes, sir," said Todd.

"We are go on Operation Moses!" concluded Kurt.

Chapter 17—Carnival

Karin began reminiscing about her early teenage years in Brasilia. Carnival was the most important festival of the year, even more significant than Christmas. Karin loved the atmosphere as the Carnival approached. She could sense the expectancy on the streets; the air of anticipation was almost electric. Few people were truly concerned with their work, and their minds were focused solely on the impending festivities. She was aware of it immediately as they entered the terminal building in Recife. Javier appeared too self-absorbed to notice anything. They stood chatting waiting for their bags.

"Did you know," Karin asked him, "the Carnival lasts for a full month here, the longest anywhere in Brazil?"

Javier's eyes widened, "Oh … no, I didn't!"

"Along with Rio and Salvador, this is one of three most popular carnivals in Brazil."

"I've been to Rio Carnival. We bought tickets to the Sambódromo and watched the parade of samba schools. It's an amazing atmosphere."

"But, don't you think that Rio Carnival has become debauched? Rio's full of sex tourists who flock to see the half-naked women roaming the streets."

"It was a little sordid in parts, I agree."

"Well, you'll be able to compare that with Olinda, which is free and open to everyone. They start with kids' parades during the first week, and it's common to see kids partying alongside their parents and grandparents."

"I suppose Rio attracts the worst kind…"

"Yes, there are too many foreigners, while Olinda is a true celebration, with mostly Brazilians."

"I'm sure looking forward to experiencing the difference."

"It's great fun. The biggest attractions are the Giant Puppets. They have dozens of huge papier-mâché figures, up to four meters high, which parade along the streets. Some are figures of famous people. I understand that Usama Bin Laden and President Lula are the most popular."

"Ha!" Javier laughed.

"I'm told you can even see the real personalities partying side by side with their replicas."

Javier smirked. "Somehow, I doubt if the real Usama would ever be caught dancing alongside his double."

Meanwhile, Karin didn't have any hotel booking and was wondering where she would go.

"By the way, Javier, where are you staying?"

"I'm heading to a hotel in Boa Viagem, the Atlântico. They reserved a suite for me, with two adjoining rooms."

"Javier, please don't get the wrong impression, but can I tag along with you for the time being? All the hotels will be full because of Carnival, and I don't have a reservation. I can pay."

"Mari, it would be my pleasure. You can have the second room, no charge."

"Great, let's grab a taxi!"

They hopped into a cab together for the short ride to the hotel, winding through the backstreets, squashed in with their entire luggage. Thankfully, it took only a few minutes to get to their destination. Karin checked in as Marina Van Hasselt and Javier's *acompanhante.* She was content that they could sleep in separate rooms. She assumed that she would be able to lock her door, just in case Javier got any ideas in the middle of the night. Moreover, if anyone managed to follow them this far, they would certainly be confused by the ambiguous sleeping arrangements. The hotel would be discrete, as these were very normal circumstances for a traveler in Brazil. If they gave out any information on accompanying females, they could easily lose the good reputation of their establishment.

She felt safe with Javier and was sure that Tom's warning about trusting no one was irrelevant in his case. At the same time, she could not rely on

Javier for more than a couple of days. It was critical that she found her own accommodation and independence immediately.

She was shown her bedroom, which was large and well furnished in a sort of modern Brazilian minimalist style. It had a spectacular view of the ocean. Karin immediately threw open the door of the balcony. She could hear the sound of the Atlantic breakers crashing down on the reef below and the gentle hiss as the waves receded. Again, the crash of the next wave sounded rhythmically in her ears, as the ocean played its ancient refrain. There was something reassuring in the natural order of things, as Karin listened to the immense power of the sea being swallowed up by the shoreline.

She wandered back into the lounge.

"I'm exhausted," she said. "A nap should help me recover from last night's lack of sleep."

Meanwhile, as Javier disappeared into his room, he announced, "I'm going to take a shower and change; then I'm meeting with my agent to discuss the shooting schedule."

"Okay, so I'll see you later."

Karin was secretly pleased that he was going out. Back in her bedroom, she stood alone, gazing out at the ocean for a while, feeling its calming effect. Then she gently pulled the sliding doors of the balcony shut. Dressed in just her T-shirt and panties, she collapsed into bed. She was asleep before her head hit the pillow.

When she awoke, it was early evening. Although she was feeling a bit fuzzyheaded, she was certainly more relaxed. Then she turned her thoughts to Tom and again wondered what he was doing at this precise moment. He was surely in danger too. Worse still, she had no idea when he might turn up or how he would find her. For a moment, she felt completely helpless.

She got up and dressed in jeans and a tank top. She could blend in well here—she could even pretend she was a Brazilian, especially with her contact lenses in. She called down to reception, using her excellent but slightly rusty Portuguese, and she was able to determine that there was a computer in the business center. As Javier had not yet returned, she left a note in the room to tell him of her whereabouts and she went to check the Internet for suitable houses in Olinda. She hoped to avoid using a Brazilian real estate agent by searching for houses on the Web. Unfortunately, she discovered that most of the property on the Internet was aimed at and priced for the foreign buyer. She was going to make little progress by this means and decided to spend the next day in Olinda, doing some scouting on foot.

When she got back to the room, Javier had arrived.

"Can you believe it? The photo shoot is a disaster," he said. "My agent is asleep on the job! It's impossible to shoot an entire men's catalogue in three days, with sixty wardrobe changes and five locations. We'll be lucky to finish in a couple of weeks."

Karin let his tantrum wash over her, much as she would with any attention-seeking child.

"The news reports say that more than two million people are anticipated in Recife and Olinda for the Carnival. How on Earth will we manage to get the right sort of shots with all those people around? It is far too unpredictable," he said, seething. "I'm a top international fashion model, and I expect better than this Mickey Mouse production!"

Once he had calmed down a little, she suggested that they go out for dinner to soak up some of the local culture and help forget about his work.

"I know what will make you feel better, Javier—how about some meat?"

"I'm famished. I could eat half a cow!" he replied.

"I think I know just the place!"

Karin instructed the taxi driver, "Take us to the best *churrascaria* in town."

It wasn't far, about twenty blocks. It was a traditional Brazilian *rodizio* grill. They cooked the meat on a spit over an open log fire in the center of the restaurant. The waiters kept bringing more and more delicious cuts until they could eat no more.

As they finished their meal, Javier enthused, "What a great choice of restaurant!"

"Yes, the meat was exquisite, the best I ever tasted," replied Karin.

Javier had mellowed after a couple of *Caiparinha* and a bottle or two of Argentinean Malbec during the meal. He became even more narcissistic when drunk. Yet, Karin knew exactly what she was doing, filling him with booze after a long flight and a stressful day. Javier was going to be out for the count. She was sure he would not bother her that night.

With the help of the driver, Karin somehow managed to pour him into and out of the taxi. At the hotel, she enlisted the doorman to help get him upstairs to the suite.

"Lay him out on the bed on his side, in case he vomits," she instructed.

Karin gave the doorman a big tip and put her finger to her lips to intimate that not a word was to be spoken. He took the fifty *reals* and left beaming.

*   *   *

Karin was awake early in the morning and got ready to leave immediately. She took a parting look at Javier and saw him lying in the same position on the bed, just as they had laid him out last night. He would have an awful hangover when he awoke, so she was happier not to be around to hear his inevitable moaning.

She took a taxi from the hotel and got out close to the post office at the periphery of the Historic City of Olinda. There were some young kids kicking around a football, barefoot, on a makeshift pitch, and Karin stopped to marvel at their effortless skill with the ball. *Futebol* and *Carnaval* were the national obsessions, and both were carried out with the same flamboyant style and dexterity. Karin reflected that their instinctive talent was an amalgamation of hot blooded, passionate, and slightly chaotic elements. She remembered how her mentor, Henrique, had described to her components of Brazilian culture.

> *We are all great actors, children, or both. We love life and live it with great intensity, for today, not worrying about tomorrow. The need for self-expression and emotion are the sources of our creativity. Appearances always have added importance for us. Never try to scratch beneath the surface, or you risk offending. We do not have the cold-blooded detachment of you Northern Europeans; we love to get involved, and when we are drawn in, we can become fired up about even the simplest matter. We fall in love more easily, more deeply, and fall out of love even more swiftly.*

They were caring words to her as a teenager. At the time, she was struggling with the end of her first adolescent relationship with a very handsome young Brazilian boy who had just dumped her. She knew now that it was just puppy love. Yet it brought to mind the hurt and the pain of her teenage years. She began wondering what he looked like now, guessing that he was some fat old beer-swilling slob with six kids and a nagging wife.

She was brought back to the present with a thump, as the ball landed squarely on her left shoulder.

"*Desculpe, senhora,*" said the tallest boy.

Karin smiled to tell him it was okay. Then she swung around and continued on her way, wandering through the picturesque old city. She liked Olinda, with its colonial style, including many beautiful old churches. The streets were full of character, paved with stones of so many different colors laid at different times.

The Carnival had started here before the rest of Brazil. Many people were still pressing through the crowded streets. Music was blaring from the small bars on every street corner. She could see only a few people drinking in the bars though. By mid-morning, most of the serious revelers had gone home to sleep it off. The band in the main plaza was playing popular northeast rhythms. Part of the crowd was dancing and many were singing along with the band. Gyrating at the front of the stage were three women in full regalia, their hips shimmying in a rapid samba movement. *Wow! You have to be genetically programmed to achieve that level of flexibility.*

She could see many kids dressed in their carnival costumes, including the little ones weaving in and out and underneath the adults' feet. There was a fun fair set up in the second plaza, which was full of screaming children either bouncing around full of energy or badgering their parents to pay for them to go on one of the rides. Each piece of machinery had its own musical accompaniment that blended into a cacophony. Karin's eardrums were being assaulted from all sides. She decided to seek some relative peace and quiet and found herself weaving her way through the backstreets away from the din.

Very little business took place during the Carnival, and she was beginning to question her decision to look for a house at this time. She entered into a small bakery in search of refreshment and was served chilled *água de coco* in the coconut shell by a courteous young man who introduced himself as Emerson. She wandered around inside the bakery, simultaneously browsing and sucking the delicious *água de coco* through a straw.

After a few minutes, Emerson politely asked, "Are you looking for something in particular, *senhora*?"

"Well, actually, I'm looking for a villa. Do you know of any for sale?"

His eyes lighted up immediately, "Come with me, please."

He shot off out of the bakery and around the nearest corner. They climbed toward the northern end of the city via the Ladeira da Misericórdia, which she learned from Emerson was the steepest hill in Olinda.

"It's easier to walk up the cobbled street than the steps at the side, so long as you don't have heels. It's less tiring," he said.

"Okay, thanks," replied Karin.

After about five minutes of climbing at a brisk pace, she was barely keeping up with him. Eventually, Karin found herself out of breath and paused for air. When she looked up, she was facing Emerson, beaming before a spacious historic villa with a For Sale sign in front.

"It's owned by a retired doctor," Emerson explained. "Sadly his wife died recently, which is why he's selling."

He introduced Karin.

"I want to move into something smaller," said the doctor. "I don't have any faith in the local real estate agents. I just put up a For Sale sign and relied on word of mouth."

"Well, it appears we have a common view of real estate agents at least," said Karin and smiled.

The doctor first turned and spoke to Emerson. "Thank you, young man."

Then he turned back to Karin, gesturing. "Please take a look around."

The villa was surrounded by a lovely walled garden and even had a swimming pool. Although it needed some redecoration, Karin judged that it was structurally sound. The triple layer of terracotta tiles on the roof was a sign of the wealth and importance of the original occupant in olden times. They had been recently replaced too, and the inside had a fresh coat of paint. It had very attractive views from pool deck toward the ocean, as it was located at almost the highest point in the north of the city. It also had a large veranda, four bedrooms, and a big kitchen with an adjoining maid's room. The lounge had panoramic windows that opened out on to the veranda. For Karin it was perfect, in a discreet and secluded location. She could move in straight away and with a relatively little work, she could turn it into a stunning home.

After her tour, she returned to sit in the lounge.

"Would you like some chamomile tea?" the doctor asked Karin. "I'll get the maid to make some."

"Yes, that would be nice."

"She immediately liked the old man. He seemed a rather sad and fragile figure, but at the same time kindly and gentle.

"I've lived in this house with my wife for nearly thirty-five years and watched our children grow up and leave home."

"It must hold many fond memories for you."

"Yes it does, although there are too many ghosts of the past, which I can't lay to rest until I move."

"I understand perfectly."

"I want the new owner to be someone that will take good care of this house, which has a special place in my heart."

She felt as if she was being interviewed for the position, and knew she had created real empathy with the old man.

Meanwhile, Emerson was effectively acting as her unofficial broker and helping her to negotiate.

"What's your asking price, doctor?" he asked.

"One hundred and twenty thousand *reals*," he replied.

"You'll never get that on the local market," replied Emerson.

"How do you propose to pay?" asked the doctor, looking at Karin.

"I can pay in cash," replied Karin.

"If it's cash, then I'll accept a lower offer."

"I think a price of ninety thousand is reasonable," said Emerson.

After a pause, the doctor responded, "All right, I'll accept."

Karin smiled in acknowledgement and shook the doctor's hand. Frankly, she was almost ashamed that she was getting the property too cheap. The doctor had little idea of property values; she would have paid more than twice that much. Nonetheless, the deal was done.

"I'll get my lawyer to draw up the sale papers," the doctor said. "Would you like to come back tomorrow and we can sign?"

Karin was struck by the straightforwardness of the whole deal and couldn't believe that she was about to buy a house. She thought of Tom and knew that he would agree with her decision.

As they left, she turned to face Emerson. "Here are five hundred *reals*. Thank you for your assistance."

"No, *senhora*, I can't accept. I am happy to help the doctor, who's an old friend of the family."

She grinned broadly. "I like living in Olinda already. I'm delighted with the house too. Emerson, *thank you*."

Karin took a taxi to the financial district in Recife and went straight to the ABN Bank. She opened an account and obtained a private safe deposit box to put in the remainder of the hundred thousand dollars. She then arranged for a transfer from the Swiss account of fifty thousand dollars and made a declaration to the Central Bank that she was using the money to purchase a house. She established that she would need to provide a copy of the sale agreement before the money would be released. She would get this from the doctor's lawyer tomorrow.

She would say nothing to Javier about the villa. She could hang out with him at the hotel for the next couple of days and then disappear from the scene. Now she was ready to enjoy herself a bit—go to the beach, do some shopping, and behave like a real tourist, enjoying the carnival atmosphere.

* * *

When she got back to the hotel Javier was out. She presumed that he was busy with the photo shoot, which suited her just fine. She chuckled to herself, wondering how "Makeup" had coped with the bags under his eyes from the night before. She was surely going to incur his wrath when he got back. Despite his self-centeredness, Karin had developed a soft spot for him. He was a little eccentric, and his antics amused her. Besides, he had behaved like a perfect gentleman and had been a welcome distraction for her in an otherwise tight spot. When he finally returned in the early evening, he was full of enthusiasm.

"There's this fashion director from São Paulo, Augusto, who I'd never met before," he said. "He's brilliant. He's a genius!"

"That's great, Javier."

"The collection is fabulous and the montages for the photo shoot are inspirational! I love this assignment," he said.

All thoughts of last night seemed to have passed him by, and there were no recriminations.

"I'm meeting up with the modeling crowd later. Do you want to join me?" he asked.

"Thank you, but I've got a bit of a headache," Karin put her hand on her brow, feigning she was unwell.

She wanted to remain as inconspicuous as possible and mingling with such an ostentatious circle would undoubtedly make her stand out. It didn't matter. Javier appeared to respect her decision and did not press her. So she got an early night, while he went out to paint the town red.

They must have had a great time, as Javier returned to the hotel at 7 AM, catching Karin on her way out.

"Well, Mari, honey, feeling better?" he asked.

"I feel fantastic!" Karin said. "I'll be back early this evening. Do you fancy another dinner?"

"Oh, I'd love to. I'll put myself to bed now so I'm in better shape for this evening," he said.

She concluded her business with the doctor in the morning and went off to explore the beach. She found a *posada* with a restaurant facing the ocean and ordered regional fish dish for lunch, served with rice and beans. It was beautifully fresh and delicately flavored. She just sat there after her meal and counted her blessings. She knew precisely all that was missing in her life—all she needed now was for her man to come back to her. She could only wait patiently; yet in her solitude, she missed her friend Isabel and their regular chats. She also wondered how her brother Paul would survive without her support. Then, for an instant, her mood changed to one of anger. *What the hell is Tom doing to me! It's not fair!* Even so, her bad temper didn't last long. It was pointless to blame others for her predicament and after a few minutes, she was relaxed again.

As she left the restaurant, she bought a beach towel from one of the street vendors outside the *posada* and strolled on to the beach, looking for some shade. Her plan was to pass the afternoon daydreaming under a palm tree, before returning to have dinner with Javier. The sun was scorching and she could stay out for only twenty minutes at a time before retreating to the shade. She marveled at the tans of the local girls on the beach, with their dental-floss bikinis, uninhibited sexual creatures taking pleasure in displaying their firm, youthful bodies. Karin was in great shape for her age, but she would confess to a small pang of female jealousy as she watched these amazing young women wander past her.

Time was her only enemy here, and she had too much of it. She would have to wait patiently for Tom and not break the silence. It might be several months before he made contact. Be that as it may, she would endure however long the wait. It was her destiny.

Chapter 18—Cuba Libre

Brad made good use of his first few hours in Belize. He first went to the Fort Point Shopping Center, where the shop manager had remembered the woman in the digitally enhanced photo. He confirmed to Brad that she had paid cash for Louis Vuitton luggage and gotten a tax certificate. After a couple of minutes of rummaging around in his files, the manager came up with a name and address from the certificate. It was Mw. Geraldine Schipper, Pacificatielaan 44, Leiden, Netherlands. Brad sent details scrambled from his BlackBerry to Langley, requesting an APB.

Next, he met Miguel off the ferry and they went to the US Embassy Compound. Here he planned to debrief Miguel—who was anxious to talk—but Brad had stopped him until they were in secure facilities.

They sat down in the communications room and Miguel began to tell his story.

"I checked the passenger manifest but found nothing. Then I spent a couple of hours asking around, but nobody recalled seeing her in the vicinity of the ferry."

"So what next?" asked Brad.

"Well, I found the tourist office and inquired about accommodation on the island. I was given a list of about forty small hotels and boarding houses."

"Yes."

"I did some more footwork, hoping that some of the hotel staff would recognize her."

"I hope that was more productive," he said.

"Well it was, but it proved more complicated than I anticipated."

"Why was that?"

"It turned out that Ms. Duval is quite well known in some of the local hotels. She's a frequent client at the better restaurants."

Brad looked at him sideways.

"But … none recalled seeing her in the last week or so."

"Okay, so did you pick up any leads?" Brad was anxious to get to the point.

"Yes, shortly before I had to take the ferry back," he replied.

"And?"

"I called on a small boarding house on the outskirts of town. I showed Ms. Duval's photo to a large buxom woman."

Brad was getting impatient. *This is like pulling teeth.*

"Well I immediately became suspicious that she was hiding something. Her face reddened and she flatly denied seeing her."

Although his fieldwork appeared to be very thorough, his reporting was long winded; Brad was wondering if Miguel would ever get to the point. He tapped his pencil on the desk.

"Once she had disappeared back inside, I asked the neighbor across the street if she recognized the photo."

"Did she?"

"She replied, 'Of course, it's Karin, Esmeralda's her best friend.'"

"Ah, now we're getting somewhere."

"When I asked her who Esmeralda was, she responded, 'You've just been talking to her.' At that point I realized that I had stumbled across Ms. Duval's path for the second time in twenty-four hours."

"Good work! That gives us a good idea of where she spent the night after the raid."

"Yes, sir, I decided it was better to interview Esmeralda later. Besides, I had to get back for our rendezvous."

"Right, you'll need some assistance to do that."

After hearing Miguel's account, Brad took note of Esmeralda's details and sent a message to Langley to run her through the database. Brad wondered how she had not appeared on the list of known associates of Ms. Duval. Even so, it was now immaterial. He decided to wait on the replies from the research team before taking any further steps.

*　　　*　　　*

Brad invited Miguel to dine with him, "Let's go eat. This is your opportunity to impress me with your local knowledge. I imagine the seafood here is wonderful."

"I know just the place; it's down at the water's edge. My old friends, Rosanna and Greg, have the best restaurant and nightclub on the Yucatan peninsula—La Serenita."

As they walked in, a pulsating atmosphere and a band, playing contagious Latin rhythms greeted them. The place was packed. However, Rosanna quickly found a reserved table for Brad and Miguel on the balcony, with a good view of the stage. Brad ordered a couple of margaritas, finally starting to unwind after all the pressure of the last few days.

Brad found himself mesmerized by the singer. She was beautiful and exotic; her hips swayed tantalizingly to the beat. Miguel leaned over and whispered to Brad, "She's Cuban."

The music was also Cuban style. Brad was enjoying it so much he had to remind himself that he disliked Cubans intensely. Growing up as the son of an East Coast patrician, he learned to hate Castro and all his kind from an early age.

The food arrived right on cue. Greg, a master chef according to Miguel, appeared to have excelled. They started with green-lipped mussels with a parmesan topping, followed by a Caribbean delicacy: grouper with coconut and shrimp sauce. It was served on a bed of wild rice with delicately steamed vegetables al dente. Brad concluded the feast with a mix of *dolce de leche*, fresh cream and strawberries. It was all washed down with a bottle of superb Chilean Chardonnay. He was almost in heaven. He had warmed to Miguel, who by now had more than passed his test.

"Hang on … the best is still to come," said Miguel.

It turned out that Miguel had arranged for the singer to come and sit at their table after her set.

"May I present Gloria, the sexiest woman in the world. This is my boss, Brad. He's one of your greatest admirers."

"Did anyone ever tell you that you look just like a young Harrison Ford?" she asked giving him a captivating smile. "He's my favorite Hollywood actor."

She spoke in heavily accented English, which nonetheless was easy to follow. Brad and Gloria immediately became locked together deep in conversation.

After an hour, she gently leaned across, touching his arm and gazing into his eyes said, "I have to go and do my last set. The band is waiting."

Brad's eyes were popping out as Gloria stood up. *Now ain't that an amazing sight!*

"I'll be back," she whispered in Brad's ear as she headed off to join the musicians who had already struck up an intro.

Brad watched her as she gyrated onto the stage. For him, there was no one else in the room. His eyes pursued her relentlessly. She was gorgeous, with a long cocktail dress that looked like it was spray painted to the contours of her body and beautiful, long, flowing hair. He could swear that she was paying him special attention, giving him a private show. She clinched it for Brad by dedicating a song to her favorite actor while she glanced in his direction.

Eventually, Gloria returned from her final set. She sat down and began smooching up to Brad. She clicked her fingers at the waiter.

"Two mojitos," she ordered.

He wondered where Miguel had gone. Turning round, he saw him exit the bar. He now had Gloria all to himself.

About 2 AM the place was still buzzing. They had cleared away the tables at the front to make a bigger dance floor. There were many couples dancing to the Latin rhythms played by the DJ—salsa, meringue and rumba. Brad thought that these styles of dancing were the closest thing to having sex standing up. The movement was so fluid and passionate; it excited him just watching it. The couples were locked together, with their pelvic areas grinding, apparently joined by some invisible bond and moving seamlessly around the space. Gloria lured Brad onto the floor. He was sure he would make a fool of himself, especially when he compared his clumsiness to the skill of those around him. Yet Gloria seemed to be double-jointed at the hips. She guided him around effortlessly in a salsa. She was employing enough energy for the two of them and making his otherwise pathetic attempt appear relatively proficient.

"Wow, Miguel was right," he said, "you're truly sex on legs!"

"Are you trying to seduce me?" she asked.

"You're so gorgeous, you must get propositioned all the time," he replied.

"Not as often as you might imagine—especially by someone who I find so attractive." Gloria winked at him and began to press her body close to his.

He could hardly believe what was happening. She was one of the sexiest women he'd ever encountered. Brad was going crazy. No woman had paid him this much attention for a long while. He had not had a woman in a year, and he desperately wanted her. Although he knew the risks, little harm could come of it in a backwater like Belize he was sure. He had enjoyed a few drinks—so what? He was confident and convinced himself that there was no harm in a one-night stand. He invited Gloria back to his hotel. They went outside arm in arm and climbed into a taxi.

* * *

Gloria was an agent of the Counterintelligence Division of the DGI, or Cuban intelligence. She had been assigned to Miguel the previous year. She soon learned of Miguel's reputation as a man about town; indeed, Señor Miguel always had a table reserved at all the town's best nightspots. Saying that you were Miguel's friend was a pass key to get into all the fashionable places in town. She observed him spending lavishly on female company, and his apartment always had good-looking women coming and going, never for more than a week at a time. He was not very selective. Many of his conquests were simply the neighborhood whores, who had undoubtedly heard of his reputation as a big spender. They rotated in and out so frequently that she even speculated they might pass in the hallway. He would be an easy mark.

Thus, Gloria effortlessly became one of Miguel's live-in lovers for a short while. Unsurprisingly, she found him both careless and naive, as he fell straight into her honey trap. Gloria skillfully acquired some confidential briefings from Langley during this period. Then she blackmailed Miguel, threatening to expose him to his superiors for passing information.

Miguel had looked bewildered when she confronted him, like a frightened deer caught in a car's headlights.

"What on Earth does Cuban intelligence want with me?" he asked.

"Nothing for the time being," Gloria responded.

"I don't understand," he gasped.

"Let's say we'll call in our marker when the time is right."

"I can't believe it! I cannot give you any useful information. Belize is the back of beyond. Nothing significant ever happens here."

"You may be surprised."

She had not mentioned Miguel's indiscretion again for a long time, until yesterday, in fact, when she instructed him to introduce her to Brad.

"All right," he agreed. "I can't see what harm it will do … I'm pretty sure the deputy director can handle himself."

* * *

Gloria was skilled in the art of seduction, and by now, she had Brad completely under her spell. She was sure he suspected nothing as the taxi headed away from the restaurant.

"The Intercontinental," said Brad to the driver.

They started kissing in the back of the taxi and she could tell that Brad was lusting after her. She reminded herself that she could not afford to become complacent, as this was probably the most important mission of her career. Besides, she must assume that if Brad was smart enough to climb to the top in the Agency, he would be quick enough to spot even the slightest mistake on her part.

Holding hands, they walked rapidly down the corridor to Brad's suite. As Brad opened the door, they became clenched in a long, slow embrace, his mouth finding hers. They started undressing slowly, exploring each other's bodies. She feigned surprise when she encountered his gun and holster. Brad just shrugged it off. His mouth felt warm against her skin. Her nipples became round hard and firm as he cupped her breasts and sucked them softly. She moaned and shifted her hand down to remove her panties and then giggled playfully as she removed Brad's trousers. She pushed him on his back on the floor and mounted him. They rolled around for nearly forty minutes. After Brad came, they moved to lie on the bed, arms wrapped around each other. She could see the lights of the city and the port through the balcony window. There was no movement, as if the world had stopped.

One hour later, they made love again, this time as spoons. She gently pressed her buttocks against Brad, who was half-asleep. She sensed that he was getting excited. In his aroused state, she felt him hard against her skin. She gently guided him inside her; she was still wet, stimulated by their earlier lovemaking. They moved slowly and rhythmically together, building up to climax. Afterward, they stayed joined together for many minutes in silence, while she watched the dawn breaking over the city. Once they separated, she continued to gaze at Brad, until she could see he'd fallen into a deep sleep.

Gloria was keenly aware of her own sensuality and that she had a great body. She had taught herself to become detached, so nobody could tell she was faking it while making love. After all, it was her job, and she was damn good at it! She counted Brad as only the latest in a long line of ill-fated men who had become trapped in her web.

Gloria eased herself gently out of bed and went next door, to where they had so readily abandoned their clothing a few hours before. She went straight to what she was looking for—Brad's BlackBerry. Through a hidden camera at the restaurant, Brad had been watched as he had entered his security codes, and she had been passed the details. She punched the numbers and letters into his machine and, thumbing the wheel, quickly scanned his messages. She rapidly discovered that the ADD was here in Belize on a manhunt, searching for a Belgian woman who lived on the cayes.

She must find out why this woman warranted the personal intervention of the deputy director of the CIA. As she continued to read, more clues were revealed. She saw a communication from Langley, confirming that Mw. Geraldine Schipper was an alias and that no such person existed. Her passport had been issued in The Hague about eighteen months earlier—at the same that her spouse, M. Jan Peter Schipper, received his false documentation. It went on to explain the critical fact that the scanned photos of the Schippers were a close match to their targets: Karin Duval and Tom Salter, a British Intelligence officer. Langley had put out a trace on any usage of the two passports.

Next, there was a brief account from Homeland Security in Miami of how Mw. Geraldine Schipper had arrived in Miami on a flight from Honduras five days ago. After that, the trail went cold. She had given her address as the Turnberry Isle Hotel, but unsurprisingly, she was a no-show. There was no departure record from Miami, but almost certainly, the message concluded, she had left using a second identity.

Finally, in a communication just received, there was an obscure reference from Dubai to something called Operation Moses, with the confirmation—*we are go.*

Gloria replaced the device in Brad's pocket, scattering his clothes randomly across the floor where they had lain. She slipped back into the bed and rolled back on top of him, moaning provocatively and gyrating her hips against his so he felt her soft and warm. She was going to make sure that he would be desperate to come back for more.

*   *   *

The Agency and the Circus had been speculating for years about high-level cooperation between terrorist entities. Gloria smiled as she recognized that they had never managed to obtain conclusive proof. She was one of a select few DGI agents who were also part of the Organization for Intelligence Co-operation among Non-Aligned Nations, or OICAN, which existed as a highly secretive coalition. Its members were united in their profound suspicion or even hatred of the United States. Cuba was a founder member, along with Venezuela, Iran, Syria, Libya, Algeria, and North Korea, in addition to terrorist groups such as the IRA, ETA, Hezbollah, Hamas, and al-Qaeda. Only the intelligence chiefs and the top echelons of the non-aligned governments or the terrorist organizations saw the product, and even then, they were never made fully aware of the source.

Once Brad had left, she began encoding a signal that would find its way to such strange bedfellows as Ayman al-Zawahiri and Hugo Chavez, confirming that the Americans appeared to have lost someone very valuable to them. By implication, if their network could get to the missing woman first, undoubtedly they could exercise a significant advantage over their common enemy.

Chapter 19— The Passage into Egypt

Abu Musab was driving, leading the convoy in the first Land Cruiser. He forked off onto a small track at the bottom of the *wadi*, about ten kilometers short of Dubah. He then wound his way for about five kilometers or so from the main road, until he came to a dead end in a sheltered ravine. He gave the order over the walkie-talkies to circle the Land Cruisers.

He intended to wait until just before nightfall before heading for the ferry, aiming to board at the last moment. This would give them the least chance of being spotted. So far, this was the most dangerous part of their journey. He still had to devise a plan to get them past the port authorities and immigration control in Dubah, an enormous challenge.

As he got down from the Land Cruiser, he was surprised by an incoming call on his radio. Whomever it was calling was using the al-Qaeda distress code and was speaking in Arabic.

"Adel … come in, Adel. This is Wudhu…"

The voice repeated.

"Adel … come in, Adel. This is Wudhu…"

Abu Musab was immediately suspicious. He walked over to consult with the Sheikh.

"My Sheikh, we cannot ignore one of our brethren in distress. He's using the correct protocol. But I'm worried this is a trick."

"Find out who it is," said the Sheikh.

He pressed the send button.

"Wudhu, this is Mohammed. Who are you? Please identify and verify emergency…"

"This is Abdul Rahman al-Falah. I must contact the Sheikh urgently. I have information about Saad."

Abu Musa covered the mouthpiece. "Al-Falah! How does that traitor have the guts to call us?"

"Give me a radio," said the Sheikh.

"I can't recommend it, my Sheikh."

Abu Musa had a sinking feeling in the pit of his stomach. He was now even more mistrustful. He was almost certain now that it was a trap. Yet he handed a spare walkie-talkie to the Sheikh and listened in himself.

"Wudhu, this is the Sheikh," UBL said in a slurred voice.

"*Allah akhbar*. May you live to be one hundred, oh Sheikh. May your enemies always flee from your shadow," said Abdul Rahman. "As you know, I'm a prisoner of the Great Satan. They want me to tell you that they have a trade for safe release of Saad."

"We'll not deal. Saad knows that if necessary, his blood will be spilled along with all the innocent blood of our people.

"Why let him die needlessly, oh Sheikh?"

"This is a holy war. He's ready for death and well prepared."

"But they'll help you and he'll be released if you do what they say."

"And what's that?"

"They are offering safe passage through Aqaba and Saad's release. In return you must help destroy the Infidels that are in pursuit of your convoy."

"Why are they offering us this?"

"I don't know their reasons, but I believe the offer is genuine. How else will you get across the gulf to Egypt? What do you have to lose?"

"How do I know that we can trust you?"

"I will join the convoy myself at Aqaba," replied Abdul Rahman. "You'll have me as a hostage and a guide."

"Wait," the Sheikh commanded.

Meanwhile, Abu Musab was wracking his brains. He wondered how they could trust the traitor.

The Sheikh stared at him intently. "Abu Musab, the Americans—with all their satellites and spy planes—must know exactly where we are. They have been following us for several days and have had many opportunities to destroy us."

"You're right, oh Sheikh," replied Abu Musab.

"So tell me why they haven't."

He shrugged. "I don't know."

"Now they're proposing to help us escape."

"It must be a ploy. They'll try to kill us."

"I don't think so, or they would have done it already."

"What are you saying, my Sheikh?"

"Accept…"

Abu Musab grimaced and responded to al-Falah on his own handset, "Okay."

"Await further instructions … out," replied Abdul Rahman.

The Sheikh asked Abu Musab to call the members of the convoy together. He told them that the Infidel was offering them safe passage and a traitor was coming among them.

"It's the will of Allah," the Sheikh said.

* * *

Tom was initially puzzled when he saw their quarry had stopped, but he took full advantage of the situation to close the gap between them.

"Let's continue along the highway as far as Dubah," said Tom. "We'll overshoot them, but we'll get to the ferry first."

"Good plan," replied Khalid.

"We can easily observe the convoy's movements and stay out of sight in the port."

The Range Rover passed the National Guard checkpoint without incident. Tom and Khalid used their false papers from Doherty's. Evidently, encountering a Jordanian Christian was a more normal occurrence for the National Guard in this region. Then they found their way to the ferry terminal and bought a ticket for the night crossing.

They were tucking into their food at a Lebanese restaurant down by the quay when a message came in that the convoy was on the move again. Returning to their vehicle, they saw the trajectory the convoy had taken.

"But, they're heading for Jordan!" Tom said.

He contacted Kurt immediately via his communicator. Kurt didn't seem to be put out by this news. He instructed them to continue to follow at a safe distance.

* * *

In the early hours of the following morning, the convoy arrived in Aqaba. Their passage through the border was smooth, as the traitor had told them it would be. They immediately converged on the port area. They had received instructions to go directly to the office of the ferry company, where Abdul Rahman would meet them.

They then took the *fast boat,* which reached Nuweiba on the other side of the gulf in about one hour. They were in time for the first crossing of the day. Much to Abu Musab's relief, the five Land Cruisers spent only about fifteen minutes lining up in the port before being loaded up the access ramp.

They arrived on the other side of the gulf in the port of Nuweiba just before nine. The scene was one of total chaos, with teeming crowds swarming around the disembarkation area just as the vehicles and foot passengers came ashore. There were street sellers with snacks and cigarettes yelling at the passers-by. Porters tried to grab any piece of luggage they could regardless of whether the owner had requested help. There was a group of vendors carrying merchandise on their heads, including chicken in cages. However, supply seemed to outstrip demand, as only a few lucky individuals appeared to be doing any business. Relatives greeted the new arrivals, hugging, kissing, and crying out with joy. Others were searching, calling out the names of their loved ones. Abu Musab found it impossible to understand how the passing vehicles did not injure more people, or how someone was not trampled underfoot.

Abu Musab, Abdul Rahman, and the Sheikh had stayed put for the whole passage in one of the Land Cruisers, so as not to be recognized. As soon as their vehicle disembarked, a boy had pushed a copy of the daily newspaper through a crack in the window. He jumped on the running board with one hand hanging on to the wing mirror and the other hand held out for payment. The front-page headlines reported the previous night's ferry disaster with serious loss of life. The Sheikh's eyes widened and then he paled. Abu Musab paid the boy and continued to read the details.

> *The* Al-Salaam 98, *the overnight ferry from Dubah to Safaga, sank last night in the Gulf of Aqaba. It was carrying 1310 passengers, 104 crewmembers, 22 cars, and 16 trucks. It left the port at 7:30 pm. Shortly afterward, there was a fire on the car deck. While the crew tried to fight the fire, a small explosion occurred, as the flames engulfed one of the gas tanks. More and more seawater was pumped into the bilges, as they unsuccessfully tried to fight the fire. This added to the normal ballast. The ship started to list to starboard. After the captain called to abandon ship, he went down to see if he could help fight the fire. He was unable to assist, and the ship turned turtle and sank at 9:42 pm, disappearing from the radar screens without ever sending a mayday message. There were insufficient lifeboats, and only about 300 survivors were brought*

ashore. They are still finding victims in the water. It is the worst maritime tragedy in Egyptian history.

Abu Musab's stomach tightened as the news began to sink in. He saw that nobody at the immigration post was checking passports, as all were intent on watching the TV coverage or huddled in groups. He overheard arguing about who was responsible. He could sense the anger in the air. He also heard part of a broadcast announcing that President Mubarak was flying to Safaga in an attempt to calm the situation and comfort survivors.

"It was undoubtedly a trap," said Abu Musab. "I'm sure it was intended for us and not the poor innocents on the ferry."

"*Inshallah*, it is the will of Allah," the Sheikh said. "He sent the traitor among us to save us from this disaster."

"Allah is indeed merciful. We could so easily have been victims of this tragedy," replied Abu Musab.

"Oh, Sheikh, "said Abdul-Rahman. "This must be the work of the two British agents that have been following you since the attack at the observatory."

"Why would they do such a thing? And how can it be, if they were following us?" asked the Sheikh.

"They had sufficient time in Dubah to set such a trap," replied Abdul Rahman. "These American lackeys must be destroyed for this act of barbarism."

"Yes, they must pay!" replied Abu Musab clenching his fists.

"Let me show you how," responded Abdul Rahman. "But first we must put enough space between us and them to lay an ambush."

Abdul Rahman had re-established a degree of credibility through this incident. Abu Musab listened carefully as Abdul Rahman outlined his plan.

* * *

Tom and Khalid arrived at the border post, some fifty kilometers from Aqaba, and began lining up at the Saudi checkpoint. Tom had been tracking the convoy's progress on the screen. He had decided to aim for the late-morning passage so they would not confront al-Qaeda on the same ferry. For non-Saudi citizens, security was even tighter leaving Saudi than entering. All foreigners had exit visas from their employers to say that they were allowed to travel, as a means to control itinerant workers. He had quickly falsified the relevant documents using his kit. He explained to the Saudi border police that they were driving their car back to the UK at the end of their work assignment. This was common practice for many expats, so they aroused no suspicion.

"How the hell did UBL get through the Saudi border guards?" Khalid asked scratching his head.

"I can only think that they have Saudi documents," Tom replied.

"Even more baffling, the Royal Jordanian Police let them pass border control and then let them on to the boat without further interference."

"I guess they were paid off somehow." Tom gave a quick shrug.

"Or perhaps it was just too big a problem for the Jordanians to handle."

"So you believe they were happy to let the Egyptian's take care of things rather than get involved?"

"Perhaps..."

An hour or so later, they arrived in Aqaba. Tom again read the Circus briefing.

Jordan, Israel, Saudi Arabia, and Egypt all border the Gulf of Aqaba. Taba in Egypt, Eilat in Israel, and Aqaba in Jordan are beach and diving resorts, close together at the head of the gulf. There is a very active al-Qaeda cell in the region, and there has been a lot of recent action. In August 2005, al-Qaeda claimed responsibility for an early-morning rocket attack that nearly struck a US Navy ship docked in the port. It caused damage to nearby facilities and hit adjacent Eilat. There were two previous al-Qaeda attacks in October 2004. Twenty-six people were killed in an attack on the Taba Hilton, and two people were killed in an attack on the Egyptian port of Nuweiba, some sixty kilometers south of Taba. The neighboring Egyptian coastal resorts have also suffered damaging attacks from Islamic militants, with Sharm el Sheikh hit in 2005 and Dahab in early 2006. This has had a serious impact on the Egyptian tourist industry in the Sinai.

They checked into the Renaissance Hotel and went to get a shower and change before eating some late breakfast.

"Nice to feel human again," Khalid said.

"Hmm … me too, but I'm very uneasy here in Aqaba," replied Tom.

"It's not only you. It's this place. Look around; everybody's nervous."

"You know, I feel like I'm being watched the whole damn time," Tom frowned.

"Perhaps it is all the photos of King Hussein and his son, King Abdullah, looking down from the walls!" suggested Khalid.

"No, I'm not imagining things," said Tom, silently nodding toward the reception. "Just look at those sleazy-looking characters in the lobby area with shiny suits and dark glasses. They're secret policemen, or I'll be damned!"

The two were lingering around a little too unnaturally, appearing to spy on the guests as they were checking in.

"Then what about the two swarthy-looking Saudis over in the corner," Tom said.

"Yes, they've been glancing in our direction ever since we began breakfast," Khalid responded.

Tom was glad when they paid for their meal and left.

After checking out of the hotel, Tom put a call in to Kurt, who confirmed that their next drop was due at St. Catherine's Monastery, at the foot of Mount Sinai. They would receive some heavier weapons in case of an engagement with the convoy. Tom was happy, as they would certainly feel less exposed with some extra firepower.

They got to the port in Aqaba in time for the 11:30 AM ferry. Tom was in better spirits now that the chase had resumed. He still had his suspicions about American reluctance to engage and was worried that they were being kept in the dark on a critical part of the mission. However, he reasoned, they had UBL in their sights, so it was not over yet.

The passage to Egypt was smooth, the water calm and clear. The sun was bright and there was not a cloud in the sky. As they set sail, Tom looked back at the almost deserted beach resort and the seafront hotels. Few international tourists were brave enough to come to Aqaba for their vacation these days; al-Qaeda had made sure of that.

While they were boarding up the ramp, Tom had observed that there were a few nervous Egyptians protesting on the dock, apparently unwilling to board the ferry. They were grouped together, talking in Arabic about something. He wondered what it was. Later, while Tom and Khalid were walking around the deck, Tom grabbed an English newspaper from an empty seat. He immediately read about the ferry tragedy that had taken place on the very boat they had been planning to board the previous evening.

"Oh, my God!" shouted Tom waving him over. "Khalid, have you seen this?"

"I don't believe it." Khalid looked aghast.

"Me neither; it's too much of a coincidence. UBL should have been on that ferry—and us too!"

"Who the hell could have done this?"

"Do you think it was the Saudis? Could they have found out something?"

"No way … if they realized UBL had escaped, they would have stopped him at the border."

"What about Kurt … could he have more agents in the field?" Tom raised an eyebrow. "It wouldn't be the first time the Agency had a shadow operation in place for the same objective in case the first mission failed."

"Well, it's impossible that he doesn't know about this," said Khalid, "so why hasn't he informed us of the tragedy?"

"I agree it's very suspicious."

At that moment, Tom noticed out of the corner of his eye, the two Saudis that had been watching them at breakfast. They were leaning over the ship's rail. They seemed to be observing them from a distance and looked away immediately he spotted them.

He turned to Khalid and whispered, "Don't look now, we're being followed."

However, as he turned back to look again they had disappeared. He wondered, why was he was getting so jumpy. Was he just imagining things? No, he was sure. His professional instinct never failed him.

"They've gone. The two swarthy looking Saudis, I mean," he said to Khalid.

"I'm sure they aren't Saudis. But I haven't a clue who the hell they are," Khalid replied.

A chill ran down Tom's spine. Too many people seemed to know about their mission.

Chapter 20—Glory Days

It was purely sexual with Gloria, but beneath it all, Brad felt his permanent sense of loneliness dissipate for the first time in a long while. She was exotic, passionate, yet in some way different from other chance encounters. He was struck by the thrill he felt for her; how he loved just to watch her move and the animal magnetism she emitted. He adored the way her hair fell delicately across her face while she slept. He couldn't get her out of his mind.

Brad went to the embassy that morning with a spring in his step. He left Gloria sleeping in his hotel room. He could still smell the slight scent of Gloria's perfume and although tired from lack of sleep, he was invigorated by the night of raw passion. He was sitting in the morning briefing with the team, yet his mind kept wandering back to the hotel room and the wonderful feeling of sexual gratification.

Whatever happened, Brad needed a fallback plan if Kurt was unsuccessful in taking out the two British spies. He acknowledged that Tom was very smart, and it was likely he would suspect the double-cross before long. Then Tom would surely do the only thing left open to him—run. At that moment, Brad would need to be able to locate him quickly. He was positive that he would run to the Duval woman. Therefore, logic told him he had to get to her first.

Brad agreed to assign a number of agents to pick up Ms. Duval's trail in Miami. He sent Miguel back to the cayes to talk with Esmeralda. He also instructed Homeland Security to search all records of outgoing passengers from Miami for the last week. Even so, Brad was not hopeful. They had nearly two hundred thousand records for women around Ms. Duval's age, traveling alone. This was a daunting task. Brad was sure that she had switched identities. The photograph and description had been sent to all points. There was little else he could do now but wait to see if she would be caught in their net.

* * *

Brad spent two days in Belize completely distracted by Gloria. Meanwhile, the US intelligence and law enforcement machinery continued their exhaustive search for Ms. Duval. However, at the end of forty-eight hours, Brad had no new leads. This was the third morning meeting he had participated in a progress report.

Miguel started with an account of Esmeralda's interrogation.

"I used sodium pentothal to get her to talk."

"A bit old-fashioned but hopefully effective," remarked Kurt.

"Yes, sir—she confirmed that she gave Ms. Duval a bed on the night she escaped."

"Okay."

"She also confessed to booking the flight in the name of Geraldine Schipper, from Honduras to Miami, and to helping Ms. Duval onto the ferry the following morning."

"Anything else?"

"We probed for nearly an hour. I'm pretty sure that she knows nothing more."

"Thanks, more good work," said Brad. "Although we've learned nothing new, it at least confirms what we already suspected."

"Homeland Security has also drawn a blank on lone female passengers matching her description departing from Miami," the intelligence analyst said.

"Nothing on the husband, Jan Peter Schipper, I suppose?"

"No, sir, the trail goes cold in Miami."

"Get Langley to widen the search to all regional airports within a five-hundred-mile radius of Miami."

The analyst continued, "Also, according to the NSA, no fresh contacts have been made with her brother, friends, or for that matter any of her acquaintances."

"Damn, she's good! Where the hell is she?" Brad grimaced.

Brad would need to be patient, but he wasn't sure how long he could afford to wait. Eventually Ms. Duval would make an error—they always did—although to date, her ability to evade capture was admirable. At the same time, he could not afford to sit around waiting for this to happen. He needed to focus all his attention on the most important part of the operation.

"There's little more I can do here in Belize," Brad said as he stood up to leave the meeting.

He decided to fly to Dubai to monitor Operation Moses firsthand. He called the aviation team and arranged for the Beechjet to take him the following morning transatlantic, with a refueling stop in Casablanca, and then onward to Dubai. It was a punishing trip, as it would take about sixteen hours flying time and twenty-three hours, including the time difference, before he landed in Dubai.

I need to get going as soon as possible, but not until after I've said my good-byes to someone very special.

He dialed Gloria's number on his BlackBerry.

"*Hola*, sexy," she answered.

"Oh Gloria, I need you so badly, I can't stop thinking about you."

"I really want you too, *mi amor*." Gloria whispered breathlessly. "The thought of making love to you makes me feel so horny, oooooh!"

"So tell me I can see you soon."

"*Mi corazón, te quiero mucho.* I'm sorry, I wish I could, but I can't get away right now, as I'm rehearsing. Meet me again tonight at La Serenita. I have a show this evening."

He was determined to have one last night of passion; he could always sleep on the plane. When he arrived at 8 PM the place was already packed, even more than it was the first night. Rosanna had held a table for Brad next to the stage so that he could get a close-up view of Gloria's performance.

The band started warming up on an instrumental number, and then Gloria burst on in a fanfare of brass. She moved across the stage, gently nudging her hips from side to side in time with the tropical beat. The regulars greeted her with a rapturous applause. Brad was entranced by the sensuality of her movement and sat there open mouthed throughout her first number.

In any other circumstances, Brad would have been embarrassed by his own behavior, salivating over Gloria like some lovesick adolescent. In the Special Forces, they would have jokingly said that he was suffering from *white-out*. This was the term to describe when a solider had not been laid for a long time and his sperm rose to such a high level that it reached his brain, affecting his decision-making. Oddly, Brad did not care.

That evening for him at La Serenita had a surreal quality, passing almost in slow motion. There was only one thing on Brad's mind, Gloria. Just thinking about her made the hairs stand on the back of his neck. He was torn between his excitement at watching her on stage and his desperation for her to finish. He wanted to take her back to his hotel and screw her rigid.

Brad was in a trance as finally they arrived at his suite around two in the morning. They undressed, again spreading their clothes haphazardly throughout the lounge area. They headed straight for the bed. His mind was on fire as Gloria wrapped her body around his and then tenderly rubbed his groin with the inside of her thigh. He felt as if he would explode with the thrill and the pleasure. She pulled him down on top of her, her tongue began searching his mouth. Then she pushed him on his back, cupped her breasts, and offered him a tantalizing nipple. She stroked herself gently, moving his hand to touch her. He felt her warmth and wetness, while her breathing became more and more pronounced. She spread her legs and guided herself on to him from above. He sensed as her body began to quiver. His hands were on her waist as he pumped harder and harder, until finally they came in unison. He felt the endorphins detonate in the nucleus of his brain and then spread out all over his body in a pleasure wave. Tiny impulses touched the outermost recesses of his nervous system. He was completely and utterly alive. This was the best he had ever had.

"Gloria, you are gorgeous, beautiful, amazing, sexy, unbelievable…," he screamed.

"Wow, that was fantastic!" she replied.

Afterward, he fell into a deep peaceful sleep, totally spent.

* * *

Gloria slipped out of bed and returned to the lounge to locate Brad's BlackBerry. Miguel had provided her with today's code already, which she silently thumbed into the machine. She quickly scanned the messages. At first, Gloria concluded that there was little of fresh interest, except it was now clear that they had lost the trail of the Duval woman. Yet in the final message, there was something quite astonishing—a mysterious reference to the Operation Moses she had noted last time. It was instructions from Brad to the field in Dubai on how the ambush of two British agents should be reported back after the kill, to ensure it appeared as if they had been caught by enemy fire.

To Gloria this was a genuine bombshell. Why would western intelligence services be targeting each other? Regardless of the answer, this morsel could definitely be exploited. She again replaced the BlackBerry in Brad's jacket. She would feed this intelligence into OICAN in the morning. Meanwhile, Brad was softly snoring, as she slid back gently between the sheets and again wrapped herself around his naked body.

* * *

Brad was woken by his wristwatch alarm at 5 AM, still elated by the thrill of the night's lovemaking. He gently disengaged himself from Gloria, feeling a pang of anguish. In his heart he knew that they would never be together again like this, entwined in each other's arms. Her passion had broken through his hard outer shell, which normally protected him from all emotional entanglement. Even so, their separation was inevitable, and undeniably for the best.

While she was still sleeping, Brad kissed her softly on the cheek. He recovered his things and made his way downstairs to find the driver waiting to take him to the airport.

Chapter 21— Slings and Arrows

Tom and Khalid arrived at the foot of Mount Sinai, it was packed with modern-day tourist buses. There was a vast car park with a row of dusty souvenir shops alongside, selling everything from religious paraphernalia to cheap replicas of ancient Egyptian artifacts. They parked their vehicle and worked their way through the crowd toward the fortified monastery. It stood on a raised plateau, silently overseeing the commercial traffic below. It was an imposing sight against the backdrop of the mountain. Tom started to imagine the twelve tribes of Judea camped at the base of the mountain, awe struck and afraid in this very spot. Moses, their leader, had departed to climb the mountain and receive the Ten Commandments. St. Catherine's Monastery is the site of the fabled burning bush, and was his first stop on the way up.

Easing their way through the throng of tourists lining up at the entrance, Tom and Khalid bypassed the main gate of the monastery, finding a side door in the east wall. In true cloak and dagger fashion, they pulled the bell chain, and when the viewing hole slid open, Tom repeated the password—premonition—as he had been instructed.

A monk, dressed in his habit with the hood pulled down hard over his head, let them in without a sound. He signaled for them to follow him. He weaved through the shaded passageways of the monastery, until he arrived at a padlocked door. Tom and Khalid looked at each other in disbelief.

"Well this is corny," Khalid said.

"I know, but remember we're just following Kurt's instructions," responded Tom.

The monk fumbled with the key and finally opened the door to reveal some stairs descending into a tunnel. He locked the door behind them. After about one hundred meters, the tunnel opened out into a large chamber. It was a veritable Aladdin's cave of armaments. Khalid carefully picked out an ERYX surface-to-surface missile launcher and two Heckler and Koch machine pistols. The monk found them four missiles, sufficient ammo, and a box of grenades. They placed all the arms on a small trolley, presumably left exactly for this purpose. The monk then led them further into the tunnel, which eventually surfaced in a storeroom at the back of the row of shops.

"I'll get the car," said Khalid.

Tom helped the monk unload the trolley in the loading bay. The monk handed him a sealed envelope, in which he found Egyptian plates for the Range Rover and a pen drive, presumably containing new encryption codes.

"What about the walkie-talkies?" he asked.

The monk gave him a quizzical look but said nothing.

"You know … walkie-talkies," Tom repeated, pretending to talk into an invisible device.

Either this guy is taking his vow of silence seriously or he's completely mute.

"I'll assume Kurt overlooked the radios," he said finally. "I'll ask him in my next message."

Out of view of all the sightseers, the Range Rover backed up to the loading dock. Khalid leapt out of the vehicle and dropped the tailgate to allow Tom and the monk to load the armaments. The vehicle sagged at the back under the extra weight. They dropped the back seat and moved the main load as close as possible to the center of the truck. This improved weight distribution a bit, but it was still down at the back.

"We'll need to be more careful driving at speed," said Khalid, "as the steering will be light."

"It's a small price for us to pay for the added defensive capability."

Tom covered the weapons with a tarpaulin to protect them from prying eyes. Meanwhile, Khalid used an electric screwdriver to remove the Saudi plates and replace them with the Egyptian ones. The whole loading operation was accomplished swiftly and efficiently in about five minutes.

They drove away from the monastery to rejoin the main road in the direction of the Red Sea, passing the small oasis at Wadi Fieran. A kind of moonscape surrounded them, with rock striations jutting upward and outward and boulders strewn in every direction. All the same, Tom spent little time on the spectacular scenery, as he was concentrating on navigating. Their mission was reaching a critical point. They passed a UN listening station perched on an outcrop in the desert. It was bristling with antenna, fortified with a huge fence and surrounded by razor wire. It was a bizarre sight in this otherwise abandoned place, like a remote outpost colonizing the lunar surface.

He was tracking the convoy, heading northeast along the coast road toward Ras Sur.

"The convoy is now a long way ahead of us—about three hundred kilometers, or a little less than three and a half hours driving time by my reckoning," said Tom.

"We need to focus on closing the gap," responded Khalid.

"It's going be difficult to make that much headway."

"You're right, especially on the open road."

"My biggest fear is that as soon as they cross the Suez Canal they'll scatter and we lose them completely."

Unquestionably, Khalid was going as fast as he could with the additional weapons payload. Meanwhile Tom prepared another message for Kurt.

From: Slater, Tom—ME/2—xxx Scrambled xxx 15:05 GMT
To: Schneider, Kurt—CS Dubai
Successful pick-up at drop, but we now have lost too much ground to convoy. Can you execute delaying tactics to hold convoy prior to the Canal?
T.
+++
P.S. Whatever happened to the walkie-talkie?

They eased out on to the coast road, which was straight as far as the eye could see. All along the shoreline, the sand was white and powdery like talcum powder. The waters of the Red Sea were a pale, luminescent turquoise. The sun sank toward the horizon, as dusk was approaching, shining with a direct intensity through Tom's passenger window. Even with sunglasses on, Tom was partially blinded, making out dark spots on his retinas. They circumnavigated what must have been a cement factory and the only bend in the road for kilometers. It was spewing great clouds of dust into the air, turning the evening sky prematurely dark.

"Khalid, we're struggling here, my friend," Tom said looking ahead at the display, as the convoy passed the small town Ras Sur, at the southern end of the Suez Canal. "We're going to need another small miracle from Uncle Sam."

"I hope Kurt comes through this time."

Tom noticed on the tracking device that the convoy had started to disperse. Then, straight away, he lost the feed from the satellite.

"Why does the technology always fail when you need it the most?" Tom asked. "What the hell are we suppose to do now?"

He tried to signal Kurt, but the communication's link was completely down.

"Shit!" murmured Tom.

"Whatever happens, we still need to close the gap with the convoy," said Khalid.

"You'd best keep going at full speed, while we wait for the resumption of the signal."

A couple of hours later, Khalid slowed, as they went through Ras Sur.

"Still can't get a signal?" asked Khalid.

"It's almost like it was switched off deliberately," replied Tom.

They pulled into a brightly lit Mobil gas station to fill up.

Tom was despondent, "We came so close to our objective, but now they've escaped."

"True, they'll be well across the canal by now," said Khalid. "There's little hope of catching up with them."

"Damn those Agency bastards! We should have taken the shot when we had it."

Khalid went to buy a sandwich and some water in the convenience store. He sauntered back to the vehicle and swung himself into the passenger seat.

He grinned. "Your turn to drive, Tom … we can afford to take it easy now."

Tom got into the driver's seat and took off slowly. They were in an unusual landscape of rolling dunes on each side of the road. In the headlights, Tom recognized these as tank fortifications and thought back to the history of the Arab-Israeli War. Oddly, both sides claimed victory. The Egyptians still celebrated their crossing of the canal in the first days of the war as one of the greatest military maneuvers of all time. They used water canon to penetrate the Israeli defenses. Even so, the Israeli counter-attack led by Major General Ariel Sharon was swift and decisive. If the UN-brokered truce between the Americans and the Russians had not been reached so quickly, he could easily have made his objective and entered Cairo.

"Shit!" he yelled.

As Tom came to a bend in the road, he must have hit a patch of oil, as the Range Rover went into a four-wheel skid. He adeptly turned into the skid without losing control of the vehicle. The wheels picked up some sand from the surface of the road, regaining traction. At that instant, he saw a line of tracer fire coming from a position ahead on the right.

"Sonofabitch! *Incoming*," he screamed.

Thinking fast, he drove the Range Rover head first into the ditch on the opposite side of the road, providing cover from the right. As they nosed into the sand, the airbags inflated. He felt dizzy and his head began to throb from the impact. It took them both several seconds to compose themselves and work free from the wreckage. All they had time for was to grab their machine pistols and roll away, before a grenade, flew by them from the left. It hit the vehicle creating a blinding flash.

Taking advantage of the confusion, Tom and Khalid retreated backward, crawling on their bellies along the ditch. About ten meters back from the burning wreck, they took cover behind a small mound. Tom's heart was racing. Just then, a second grenade hit the Range Rover, this time catching the ammunition in the truck. It set off a rapid series of explosions, which generated a massive blast wave, sending shrapnel and debris flying in all directions. Tom felt physically stunned by the force of the detonations and lost his hearing for a moment. He saw that Khalid looked dazed too. Once they had recovered their senses, each let off a salvo in the direction of their attackers and subsequently slumped back down behind the mound. The response came in the form of heavy machinegun fire on both flanks.

It was overcast and the moonlight that shone through the clouds was barely enough to see by. As far as Tom could make out, there were two groups heavily dug in. They were pinned down and outgunned, but at least had one thing in their favor. Even though their cover was sparse, it would be difficult for their opponents to flush them out without advancing on their position.

"Looks like we finally met our match," Tom said. "Keep your ammo and maybe we can inflict some damage at close quarters."

"They'll never take me alive," responded Khalid.

Every thirty seconds or so Tom and Khalid took turns raising their heads to see what was happening. Occasionally this would provoke another burst of machinegun fire. Their opponents must have had night vision trained on their position, giving them a clear advantage. The stalemate lasted no more than five minutes, but to Tom it seemed like an eternity.

Then Tom heard the unmistakable crack of a high-velocity rifle from somewhere behind them. He anticipated that he would be hit, as they were totally exposed from the direction of the shot. To his surprise, he saw one of the machine gunners slump over his gun, and in rapid succession a second shot whistled past, taking out the second gunner.

"What the hell was that?"

"I don't give a fuck what it was! I'm just pleased whoever fired is on our side!" exclaimed Khalid.

All hell broke loose around them: Three men charged at them from the right, guns blazing, and another three charged from the left. Tom and Khalid swiftly rolled around the mound to get better cover, returning fire from their machine pistols. Tom felt a bullet graze his arm. It stung, and there was some bleeding, but he kept his head and his fire concentrated on one incoming group. Meanwhile, Khalid directed his fire at the second force. Both groups were simultaneously caught in the crossfire with incoming rapid-fire from the high-velocity rifle.

Tom hit one of his assailants, who collapsed on his knees before falling face down in the sand. The unknown shooter had literally blown chunks out of the other two. Similarly, Khalid had hit one of the charging terrorists, while their mystery ally had hit a second and the third had turned tail and fled. Their attackers had been annihilated in a firefight that lasted less than a couple of minutes.

Several engines started within a few seconds of each other, and he watched the convoy regroup from behind the berms fleeing north in the direction of the canal crossing.

"There goes UBL," said Khalid. "That's the closest we're ever going to get to him I guess."

"So what now, my friend?" asked Tom.

It was a rhetorical question, as he saw two men bearing down on them, with their rifles on their hips. Their weapons were pointed straight in their direction ready to fire at the first sign of provocation. From their appearance, Tom immediately assumed that they were Israeli. He confirmed this by the accent as soon as the first man spoke.

"Huh! You are too far away from home, my friends, to be attempting such an operation without backup."

"We had no choice," Tom replied.

"In any case, we decided you could use a bit of ground support," said the first Israeli.

He motioned at Tom and Khalid with his rifle to do a quick check of the bodies, but they found no sign of life. The impact of the high-velocity rifle left nothing to chance.

Then he ordered Tom and Khalid, "Right now, take off your shirts and pants!"

They obeyed without hesitation.

"Put your clothes on these two unlucky bastards," he commanded, pointing at the two bodies that were most intact.

"Now drag them here to the mound."

The Israeli placed the high-velocity rifle by one of the bodies and then pulled the pin on a grenade and lodged it between the two, walking away slowly. All that was left of the two bodies was bloody torsos, some fragments of clothing, and no limbs.

"That should be enough to fool the initial investigation."

"Let's hope so," Tom responded.

"Now, you two follow me."

Tom was bewildered by the turn of events and in no mood to question the Israeli's orders. Still dressed in underwear and boots, they marched the five hundred meters to the Israeli's Land Cruiser.

The first Israeli opened the back and threw a pair of khaki pants and a shirt at each of them. "Put these on for the love of God. I can't bear to look at your scrawny bodies any longer. Doesn't the Circus make you work out once in a while?"

Tom and Khalid pulled on the clothing and smiled at the joke, which seemed to dissolve any remaining tension between them. Meanwhile, the second Israeli passed Tom the first-aid kit to dress his arm.

"Thanks, we really owe you a lot," he said.

"Damn right you do," replied the Israeli. "Now climb in and let's get out of here before the clean-up detail arrives."

Tom had a nagging feeling of déjà vu while he watched the Israeli pair. Only when he visualized them in Saudi dress did he suddenly realize where he had seen them before. He recalled them from the hotel in Aqaba and on the ferry; they must have been following them for some time now.

As the second man drove, the first one spoke. "My name is David, and this is Jacob. We are agents of the Israeli army special intelligence division."

"As I guessed, Mossad," said Tom.

David was medium height with an athletic build and a dark, shadowy complexion. Jacob was taller and thinner with wavy light brown hair, hazel eyes, and softer features. Both were unshaven and dressed in army fatigues with desert boots.

"Our mission is to take out Bin Laden, if you two fail."

"How did you know we would be attacked?"

"We got wind of the trap being set by al-Qaeda and decided to get involved."

"And we're glad you did," replied Tom. "We thought we'd had it for a minute there."

"In fact, we've been following you since Dubah."

"Do you know what happened to the ferry?" asked Tom.

David looked at Jacob, who nodded in assent.

"Yes, we scuttled her, trying to destroy the convoy. Before she sailed we cracked open the sea cocks and then planted incendiary devices on the car deck."

"Was such loss of life really necessary?" asked Khalid. "You're no better than the terrorists."

"What on Earth do you expect!" David replied.

"Apart from the fact that you could have easily killed us too, several hundred innocent people died needlessly," Khalid responded.

"You seem to forget that we are dealing with the most dangerous criminals in the world," said David.

"Our objective may be the same, but our methods are definitely different," remarked Tom.

"Our terms of engagement were to eliminate Bin Laden at whatever cost."

"How did you track him down?" asked Tom.

"You helped," replied David. "We fully penetrated the Agency years ago and were receiving regular updates on your progress from a man well placed in Dubai."

"So we did all the hard work for you?" Tom sneered.

"That's right, all we had to do was to maintain a discrete distance," David said. "We decided to intervene only if there was a risk of the convoy escaping."

Jacob then interrupted, "More to the point, you seem to have upset a lot of people."

"What do you mean?" Tom looked at him sideways.

"You didn't know that your own side set you up?"

Tom's jaw dropped, "What!"

"I thought that the Agency and the Circus were extremely tight. I can't imagine why the Yanks would want to double-cross their most important intelligence partners."

Tom groaned. This confirmed his worst suspicions.

"I doubt if you think like us, but our history has taught us to maintain a solid military capability to counterbalance over-dependence on the Americans."

"Are you telling me they somehow stage-managed all this?" asked Tom.

"No, but they are not always trustworthy, especially when the politics get rough in Washington." Jacob replied

David held his hand up, "I'm sorry, but we can't divulge any more. We must protect our sources."

"But, your little ruse with the two terrorist bodies will be discovered sooner or later. Then they will surely come after us to finish the job. Tell us who," said Tom.

"No, I'm sorry. We can't help you anymore," insisted David.

"Whoever they are, we'll be sitting ducks."

"Then take my advice and disappear until this all blows over."

Tom nodded, "Good advice, I'm certain."

"We can take you as far as the outskirts of Cairo," David said, "but after that you're on your own."

"What will you do?"

"We'll complete our mission and kill UBL."

Tom was left with no doubt about the seriousness of his intent, but he wasn't sure how they would continue to tail the convoy.

Tom and Khalid sat in the rear seats of the Land Cruiser. Tom was quietly observing their progress. Driving alongside the canal, it was an amazing sight to see the ships traveling with their main decks almost level with the bank. The multi-colored lights on their superstructures flickered against the backdrop of the desert night. Since you could not see the water, they appeared like weird vessels cruising on top of the sand. They quickly reached the canal crossing and waited five minutes for the bridge to lower. Soon after they crossed the canal, Tom became detached from the everyday activities in the world outside the vehicle. He was in a reflective mood, highly conscious of their narrow escape. While he was relieved to be traveling with friendlies, he was also acutely aware of the danger that now faced them. They had been betrayed by their own side and were out on their own.

David and Jacob appeared to be absorbed in their own thoughts too, no doubt trying to figure out their next moves. There was complete silence in the truck, as they drove on deep into the night along the main Suez–Cairo highway. Eventually, Tom started to doze off, surrendering to his body's pressing need for sleep.

Chapter 22—
Flying Blind

Brad stood in the center of the Terratec Operations Room, like a captain on the bridge, overseeing the action with Kurt, his trusty lieutenant, at his right shoulder. Twelve specialists sat in front of them in two concentric semicircles, each behind his console. They were all facing a big-screen display. They had poor visibility from the satellite due to the cloud cover. Only a shadowy outline was reflected on the screen.

At the start of the action, Brad witnessed the two direct RPG hits on the Range Rover. He saw the flashes and the heat signatures of the blasts from space.

"Damn," exclaimed Brad. "They'll be lucky to get out of that alive!"

Their last message from Abdul Rahman was followed by radio silence. "Moving in to mop up any survivors. Over and out."

Meanwhile, the screen with the satellite broadcast continued to be almost totally masked by cloud. Brad could see the occasional grenade burst, and he could follow the tracer fire, but he was getting very frustrated by the lack of communication and quality imagery from the combat zone.

"This is a complete balls-up," said Brad.

"We're trying our best, sir," responded Kurt.

"Well it's not good enough! I have no clue as to what's really happening on the ground, and most of all, who's winning."

"I appreciate that, sir."

"So *do* something, damn it!"

"Ron, for Christ's sake, I want Abdul Rahman back on the radio. Do whatever it takes," Kurt yelled.

"I'm sorry, boss. I keep trying, but he's just not answering," Ron responded.

Eventually, they could make out through the obscurity that the convoy was moving out.

"The encounter must be over," said Brad.

"Yes sir, and since the convoy has left the scene intact," he responded, "I'm assuming al Qaeda has been victorious."

"Okay Kurt, given that we can't get confirmation from Abdul Rahman on the radio, we'll need a quick field assessment," Brad said.

"Roger, I'll get right on it and get a CIA clean-up team in place," replied Kurt.

"Hang on a minute … we certainly can't afford to wait for an Agency crew to find out what happened."

"Sir, shouldn't we send in the professionals?"

"Unfortunately, that will take several hours that we haven't got. Who's closest to the scene?"

"The USS *Ronald Regan,* sir."

"Get them to send in a chopper with a small reconnaissance squad. Place the duty intelligence officer in command."

"Right away, sir—"

Brad thumped the desk. "We must get in and out before the Egyptians suspect anything."

"I agree. The last thing we need is for them to send in their bungling military to trample all over the site before we get a chance to discover what happened."

* * *

The Apache Attack Helicopter got to the location about thirty minutes later. From about a mile away, the pilot reported spotting the burned out and almost completely unrecognizable wreck of the Range Rover. In Dubai, they were tracking the chopper, as it circled twice and then landed about two hundred yards away on a flat piece of desert.

The murky night sky was beginning to clear. From the live satellite feed,

Brad could just about make out the reconnaissance crew disembarking and starting their search on the ground. The duty officer was a young lieutenant from Navy Intelligence, and he was accompanied by a detachment of four heavily armed Navy SEALs.

Within a couple of minutes, the lieutenant called in, "Sir, we've found two bodies close to a mound about thirty feet from the wreck."

"Can you ID them?" asked Brad.

"It's difficult, sir, as there's not much left of the bodies, but from a preliminary examination of their weapons and clothing I believe they're the two Circus agents."

"Give them a proper burial," Brad pinched the bridge of his nose and closed his eyes for a moment.

When Brad's gaze returned to the screen, the squad was combing the desert to the east.

The lieutenant came back on the radio again. "Sir, we've found a dismembered torso."

"Any ideas who it might be?"

"It looks like one of the terrorists, sir. Whoever it was, he was completely wiped out."

"How's that?"

"Well, it looks like our boys didn't go down without a fight, sir. There are limbs strewn all over the place. We're walking in a wider arc around the Range Rover."

"Anything else to report?" asked Brad.

"Yes, sir, another body of what looks like an al-Qaeda gunner, who was dug in two hundred yards from the road."

"Okay."

"He was decapitated and blown backward. He didn't stand a chance … It's pretty gruesome out here, sir," he said, his voice shaking.

Brad was irritated by the lieutenant's obvious squeamishness, wishing he would keep such comments to himself. At the same time, he was baffled by the apparent decimation of the bodies.

"Do they look like they were they hit by depleted uranium rounds?" Brad asked.

"Sorry, sir … I can't tell you."

Brad guessed he had never been in a combat situation, let alone witnessed the devastating effects of such munitions at firsthand. He remained tuned in as they completely reconnoitered the combat zone. The lieutenant reported finding four more bodies. After forty-five minutes at the scene, Brad ordered him to close out the search.

"Lieutenant, collect all the weapons and load them into the chopper."

"Roger that."

"Then pull together the scattered remains and cover them loosely with sand."

"Okay, sir."

Brad had no idea when they would get a specialized team to the site, and he wanted to preserve the bodies as best he could.

Within ten minutes, the lieutenant came back on the radio again.

"We're returning to base, sir."

"Good, you'd better get out of there. We don't want to risk getting discovered."

Shortly afterward, the pilot reported, "We're taking off in a southerly direction. Guidance system is engaged. The flight plan has us staying at below three hundred feet, to get home under the radar."

* * *

Brad and Kurt were discussing the implications of what all they had just witnessed. They sat in a fully enclosed, soundproofed room adjacent to the Operations Room.

"Okay, Brad, I hope you're happy now that you have your pound of flesh and UBL is free!"

"Well, it looks like mission accomplished from where I'm sitting. Why are you so nervous?"

"I realize it would be wrong to query Level Four orders … but I don't understand why we were protecting UBL. It just doesn't seem right."

"Believe me there are valid reasons—that's all you need to know."

He could tell Kurt was not so easily reassured. Despite the fact that good intelligence officers were taught unquestioning loyalty, in this case Brad knew he was asking a lot from Kurt and his team. He would have to tread carefully.

"It seems Abdul Rahman achieved the objective but has gotten himself killed in the process," said Brad.

"Huh! There will be no tears shed for Abdul Rahman al-Falah on either side."

Brad tugged his ear. "One thing in particular is troubling me. I'm very curious about the high-velocity rifle and the depleted uranium rounds … where do you think they came from?"

"Maybe the Circus agents added a weapon at the monastery without our knowledge."

"In that case, take a close look at the weapon when we can get hold of it."

"Yes, sir."

Brad's gut feeling told him that something was terribly wrong. To calm some of his fears Brad decided he must focus on the next steps. He had to make sure their backs were fully covered.

"I'll do the President's brief," said Brad. "In the meantime, can you start work immediately on a communiqué to the Circus and a press release?"

Although he maintained his façade of complete control, underneath Brad was very worried. The operation was definitely not going the way he'd planned it.

"We'll need to work fast. If we are too slow in confirming what happened, the Circus will smell a rat."

"Yes, this was their operation, after all."

Examining his fingernails Brad said, "On the press release, maybe it should read, *Off-duty British officers killed by active al-Qaeda cell in Sinai.*"

"Sounds good—I'll make it public through our usual Egyptian press agency."

"We'll have to be careful not to upset the Egyptians. They're very sensitive."

"Cairo will certainly want to hush it up. They'll be more worried about their precious tourist industry than two dead foreigners."

Brad signaled Washington confirming the death of the two agents and that UBL had gotten away unscathed. He reported that the convoy had crossed the Suez Canal and it was now believed to be heading south.

He then approved Kurt's signal to the chairman, which was very different in tone and content.

MOST URGENT
From: Schneider, Kurt—CS Dubai xxx Scrambled xxx
To: Wood, Peter—C
Regret to inform that our agents caught in al-Qaeda ambush in the Canal Zone. Both Salter and al Querishi have been killed in ensuing encounter. US Navy is performing cleanup. Operation Sheikh aborted.
K.
+++

Brad hoped that they had done enough to conceal their involvement. It must look like an al-Qaeda operation or their cover would be blown, with disastrous consequences.

Chapter 23— A Friend in Need

KHALID'S SECOND COUSIN, ALI, LIVED in a new suburban housing project just outside Cairo. The Israelis had dropped Tom and Khalid at the front gate. Khalid managed to raise Ali from the security kiosk by telephone.

"Ali, please help us," begged Khalid. "We'll be gone first thing in the morning. No one will ever have to know we were here. Come on, for the love of Allah, we desperately need somewhere to stay. I'll reward you, I promise."

Five minutes later Ali came to pick them up at the gate in his shiny new *Toyota Corolla*.

"By the way, I don't want your money," Ali said.

Tom climbed into the back seat with Khalid.

"Khalid, your cousin must be anally retentive. His car still has the plastic on the seats," he whispered.

"He's always been like that."

"Are you sure he's going to be okay with us?"

"Ali is nervous to have guests of any kind, and worse still you're a complete stranger."

"Well—"

"Give him a little time to get used to the idea. He'll be all right."

Ali put them up in an unfurnished room, with just a couple of mattresses on the floor.

"Ali clearly doesn't want us to get comfortable and stay," Tom said.

"Yes, but he'll take care of us tonight out of a sense duty to the family," responded Khalid.

"Then what?" asked Tom.

"Don't worry. I have something better in mind for tomorrow. Let me call an old friend of mine, Ahmed El Khabir."

Tom shrugged. "I'm totally in your hands."

"Don't worry. Ahmed was one of my best friends from MIT. He set up an electronics business here after he returned from the States."

"Are you certain we can trust him?"

"I can vouch for him. He's totally dependable More importantly, he's unknown by any intelligence agencies. I'm sure he can help us."

Tom listened while Khalid arranged for Ahmed to collect them the following morning. In the meantime, Tom was very grateful to have found a place to rest after their ordeal. Despite the meager accommodation, he slept soundly and woke late, at around nine, when Ali's two young sons wanted to see their Uncle Khalid. Unable to contain their enthusiasm any longer, they burst into the room and jumped all over Khalid and his makeshift bed. The boys tugged his arm and yanked his hair.

"Khalid, can you play with us, please? Oh! Come on … please."

"Enough!" responded Khalid, but to no avail.

He got up and started tickling them, tipping them upside down and whirling them around to shrieks of delight.

"Again, again ... and it's my turn," were the only responses.

Eventually Alyssa, the boys' mother, came in and scolded them, "Let your poor uncle have some peace so he can get up. Come on, out of here."

Tom watched as she opened the door and herded them out ahead of her.

"We'd better be quick," Khalid said, "Ahmed will be arriving at ten."

Tom looked over toward the door. "I agree. We must leave as soon as possible. We can't afford to involve Ali and his family anymore."

* * *

Ahmed picked them up promptly from outside the house. He greeted Khalid with a bear hug. Then he stood back and took a long look at them both in their Israeli army fatigues.

"*La, la, la, la,*" he clicked his tongue, an Arabic cry translating to *No, no, no, no.* "We must get you a change of clothes immediately; otherwise, you'll be arrested as Israeli spies!"

The chauffeur drove them comfortably in Ahmed's Mercedes 500 S Class, with blacked-out windows. He informed them that their destination was Maadi, an upper-class district along the banks of the Nile and it would take them about an hour and a half to get there through the frenzied Cairo traffic.

"I swear that Cairo gets more congested every time I come here," Tom said.

"Hardly surprising," Ahmed replied. "Cairo has a population of almost twenty million, and it's expanding at nearly one million per year."

"I'll never get used to the driving here," said Tom. "It's truly terrifying."

Sure enough, all along the route, numerous cars seemed to aim directly at them, only to swerve at the last minute. Somehow, miraculously, they avoided any impact. There was traffic and honking of horns in all directions.

"Look at that." Tom pointed to a mule pulling a cart along one of the main feeder roads into the city. "It's holding up an entire three-lane highway!"

"In Egypt, the ancient blends with the modern in a very haphazard fashion," Ahmed said.

They passed a magnificent Coptic Cathedral on a hill.

"Now there's a good example," said Ahmed, "fabulous architecture from the twelfth or thirteenth century next to dusty shantytowns constructed in the last twenty years."

The houses looked barely habitable, made from block work that seemed randomly stacked. This reinforced Tom's sense of order transcending into chaos.

"I always thought it an irony how the Egyptians created probably the greatest of the early civilizations," said Tom, "but are struggling to adapt to the complexities of life in the twenty-first century."

"We have a tremendous legacy, but it is true, modern-day Cairo is chaotic," Ahmed smiled.

* * *

Once they reached Maadi, the streets were well laid out and lined with palm trees.

"This is quite different to other parts of the city," Tom said.

"Yes, it's prime residential real estate," responded Ahmed. "You can tell from the number of foreign consulates and embassies here."

Ahmed first took them to his tailor. Tom and Khalid were kitted out with a stylish wardrobe of Egyptian cotton shirts, combined with designer jackets and trousers. They told the tailor to burn the clothes that the Israeli agents had given them. They then went to a shopping mall to buy accessories, loafers, watches, belts, and toiletries. When they finally finished two hours later, they had spent about ten thousand dollars each of Ahmed's money. Ahmed, still smiling, did not appear to be upset at the cost. Afterward, with their new smart-casual look, they could have easily passed for wealthy executives anywhere in the Arab world.

Ahmed's villa was in the Mediterranean style, secluded behind a ten-meter-high perimeter wall. The Mercedes entered though a remotely controlled aluminum gate and swung into a large courtyard at the front of the house. The villa was enormous, with probably fifteen bedrooms, a pool, a tennis court, servants' quarters, and a beautiful terrace that opened out from the main living area.

Tom was impressed and whispered to Khalid, "There must be money in electronics in Cairo!"

"I think I made a wrong career move," replied Khalid.

"*Ahlan wa' sahlan*—please make yourselves at home," said Ahmed. "There's a buffet lunch already laid out for you on the terrace."

"Khalid, you really came up trumps with Ahmed," said Tom.

They sat down to enjoy a sumptuous meal of Lebanese-style cooking, including *tabouleh*, *hummus*, cucumber with *laban*, *kofta*, *falafel*, *kibbe*, garlic chicken, and fried eggplant. They ate with gusto, hardly speaking. When they were done, they were completely stuffed. Tom eased back in his chair, sighing in contentment. Ahmed's servant bought them some Turkish coffee to conclude the feast.

In the meantime, Ahmed disappeared inside, while Tom and Khalid began discussing their predicament.

"What are we going to do next?" asked Khalid.

"I'm convinced that Kurt had a hand in all of this. I think we should confront him," replied Tom.

"Wouldn't it make our revenge even sweeter if we were able to complete our original mission and take out UBL?"

"What are you getting at?" Tom tilted his head sideways.

"Well, it now appears that the Agency is trying to protect him. Besides, we'd be doing the rest of humanity a huge favor in the process."

"Come on, Khalid, maybe we can pick up the UBL's trail later if we're lucky. That's, assuming our two Israeli friends don't get to him first. Although I'm convinced he'll head for Upper Egypt or even Sudan, either way he'll be difficult to locate. In the meantime, I think it'd be more productive to pay a surprise visit to our friend Kurt in Dubai and find out exactly what he's been up to."

"But won't it give the game away?" Khalid raised one eyebrow.

"No, I don't think so. Why?"

"For starters, everyone will immediately know that we weren't killed in the ambush."

"Not if we are careful. I figure that if Kurt has double-crossed us and we can expose him to his superiors, just maybe we'll be able to save our own skins."

"Maybe, or maybe not." Khalid shrugged.

Tom leaned forward looking intently at Khalid. "Otherwise, we'll be on the run for the rest of our lives—unless you can suggest another way to clear our names."

"Okay, Tom—you win. Even though I'm reluctant, let's go to Dubai."

Ahmed arrived and asked, "What on Earth have you two been plotting?"

"Ahmed, we need help. How quickly can you get us passports and tickets to Dubai?" asked Khalid.

"Oh, in about three days I think. Let me take care of it."

"Thanks—I owe you a lot," replied Khalid.

As Ahmed went back inside the house again, Tom turned to Khalid and said, "We must get going as soon as we can."

"I agree, the longer it takes us to get to Dubai and back, the more difficult it'll be to get another shot at UBL," responded Khalid.

"On the other hand we don't have much option. We should take the opportunity to rest and recuperate a little."

"True, we've been on the road for nearly a week; we've been shot at several times and had a couple of very narrow escapes. My nerves are raw."

"Mine too…"

"Plus we'll need to sort out the logistics: transportation, weapons, and communications."

Tom nodded slowly.

"In Dubai," Khalid added, "it will be easy enough to get a hire car and I know the access codes to the Circus' arms cache in Jebel Ali,"

"Good," replied Tom.

"The subsequent Egyptian operation will be more difficult, as we'll have no access to Circus resources."

"Can't we press gang Ahmed into to assembling some supplies?"

"I'll see." Khalid left and went to find Ahmed to ask for more favors.

Chapter 24—Heartache and Pain

Far away, Karin woke early that morning, as the first sun filtered through the curtains at about 6 am. She was unable to get back to sleep. After ten minutes, she didn't bother trying to rest anymore and went straight to the bathroom to shower. She dressed casually in shorts and a tank top, as befitted the climate. She wandered out onto the terrace to take her breakfast, which the maid had just started to lay out for her. She sipped on the tangy *suco de maracujá*—or passion fruit juice—that was already poured into her glass. Then she glanced over at the paper, which had been placed there for her. As she gazed at the headlines, she didn't quite take it in at first: "Al-Qaeda Bomb Attack in Suez—Two Britons Killed." There were two headshots, one of Tom and one of another man she didn't recognize, and beside them was a photo of a bombed-out vehicle. It was as if she were dreaming. She even pinched herself to see if she was awake. After about five seconds, as the news began to sink in, Karin felt an intense stabbing sensation in her abdomen, her stomach tightening into an unbearable knot. Her mind went numb. She tried to scream out in her pain and anguish. Her mouth opened, but nothing more happened.

"Nooooo," she cried, as sound finally came out, "not my Tom!"

She broke down on the floor, weeping uncontrollably. The maid came rushing forward and tried to do her best to comfort Karin. However, it was impossible, as she was completely distraught.

"What's wrong, *senhora*? Do you need a doctor?" the maid asked.

Karin was irritated by her presence and shoved her backward.

Finally, she composed herself. "Please go—leave me alone," she said.

She was flabbergasted. *I cannot believe it! There must be some mistake.*

She frantically grabbed the paper and started to read the article. Sure enough, they had even correctly printed his name, Tom Salter, below his photograph. The article stated that the two Britons were off-duty military officers on holiday in Egypt and were killed by a roadside bomb. One of the very active al-Qaeda cells on the Sinai Peninsula are believed to be responsible for the attack. The article also implied that al-Qaeda might have been following them for some time and deliberately targeted them. The charred bodies, left by the side of the road, had been identified by their personal effects. The Egyptian police were not very confident about capturing the perpetrators, stating they would be "long gone by now." The editorial concluded that the Middle East terror threat was ever present and that non-Muslims should think very carefully before traveling to the region, even on holiday.

Karin could not accept it. Tom could not be dead. Her sixth sense was telling her that there had been some kind of terrible mistake. She tried to calm herself and think of what to do next. If there was any possibility that Tom was still alive, it was imperative that she did not blow their cover. The article had stated there was no positive identification of the bodies. She resolved not to be panicked. She told herself that until she had definite corroboration of the facts, she would assume it was a case of mistaken identity and that Tom had not been killed.

Even so, she was floundering. She just did not know what to do or think. She was aware that she too was in danger, without understanding the true nature of the threat. Whatever had happened to Tom was obviously not a case of random targeting by al-Qaeda. He was on a dangerous mission. She knew that much. If in fact he was dead, he had almost certainly been killed in action. She had no idea what he was doing, or why she and Tom were both being hunted down. Moreover, the people that were after her definitely had nothing to do with al-Qaeda. If they had gotten to Tom, soon they might well get to her. Feeling reckless, in some ways she didn't even care. There was little point to her life without Tom.

For what must have been a couple of hours, Karin sat on the floor of the veranda lost deep in thought. She decided that the best thing to do was to go for a walk to clear her head. Only then could she make up her mind about what to do next.

As she got up, her legs felt weak. She found her way, rather shakily, down the stairs to the kitchen. She went to the fridge and gulped down a whole bottle of mineral water, which revived her a little. Via the front door of the villa, she accessed the narrow alleyways of the city. She began walking, a little awkwardly at first, but soon discovered the strength returning to her legs. She found herself wandering aimlessly around the cobbled streets for almost an hour. She advanced mechanically, placing one foot in front of the other, ignoring everything in the world around her. Eventually she reached the main exit of the citadel.

She strolled past the post office, subconsciously heading for the beach. Engrossed in her thoughts about Tom, her mind drew her toward the sea. She loved to walk along the seashore and listen to the soothing sound of the ocean. She felt comforted by the sensation of her toes digging into the soft, wet sand on the shoreline. She left a line of footprints, which as she glanced behind her, she saw gradually disappearing, consumed by the tide. She felt the warm onshore Atlantic breeze on her face, which reduced the intensity of the sun's rays and blew away some of her distress. The ancient therapeutic effect of the sea calmed her, lessening her grief and unburdening her mind.

To carry on she knew she must focus. To avoid being distracted by idle thoughts, she needed a project to occupy her while she waited for Tom. She settled on redecorating the villa. She would install a new kitchen and bathrooms in the house. She sought to impress Tom with her style and taste. They would probably live there together for many years, and she desperately wanted it to be in a beautiful and happy home. Back at the house, she began by thumbing through architectural magazines to give her ideas. She drew up lists of materials, took measurements, and went into Recife to look for construction supplies.

Completely by surprise, she bumped into Javier while she was shopping. Karin was immediately irritated with herself, for a number of reasons. Firstly, she wrongly assumed that Javier would be long gone by now. Secondly, he was the only person in Recife that could connect her with her recent past. Lastly, she was thoroughly embarrassed about having to make excuses as to why she had dumped him.

"Mari, how wonderful to see you, I thought I'd lost you forever."

"Yes, what a lovely surprise!"

"What are you doing here?"

Karin hesitated, "Oh, Javier, it's really great to see you! You're looking fantastic."

"Thanks."

"Carnival must have been good for you."

"How's the house hunting going?"

She pretended she hadn't heard his question. "So, how much longer are you here for, Javier? Hasn't the photo shoot finished yet?"

"Well, yes, two days ago, actually. But I like it so much here, and I met this fabulous Brazilian model, Nicole," he said with a glint in his eye.

Karin grinned. "Oh, really!"

"I've decided to take a break from the rat race for a little while. I'm taking a few weeks' vacation."

"That's nice."

"Why don't you meet us both for dinner tonight?"

This all seemed harmless enough to Karin and in any case, she needed the company to keep her distracted from her darker thoughts about Tom.

"I'd love to. Where will we meet?"

"Let's go to the *churrascaria* where we went to before? I enjoyed it so much."

"That's fine by me."

They parted company with a kiss on both cheeks. This chance meeting curiously cheered up Karin. *Maybe things are going to turn out all right for me here in Brazil after all.* She remembered Tom's insistence that she trust no one. Despite this, she had developed a soft spot for this self-centered pretty boy and she needed a friend. He was incapable of guile, she reckoned, and by now, he would be completely occupied with the model, turning his attentions away from her.

* * *

Karin was first at the restaurant that evening and was guided to a table that Javier had reserved for them. She sat down and accepted the waiter's offer of a drink.

"*Capiroska, por favor—vodka Absolut,*" she ordered.

She started to sip on the cocktail as Javier entered the restaurant, with a gorgeous, leggy blonde that she assumed was Nicole. Karin thought that in the vacuous modeling profession—where only looks matter—one beautiful thing clearly attracted another. Javier was an extremely handsome man and had that spark that attracted women like a magnet. In this instance, even Karin had to admit that he'd outdone himself.

Moreover, Nicole was not as empty headed as Karin had immediately assumed. She was a businesswoman in her own right, having her own store in São Paulo and collection of women's fashion. She kept her hand in modeling to stay in touch with the latest trends and to promote her own brand of clothing.

They had a most enjoyable dinner together, with a wide-ranging conversation, flipping from Portuguese to English as the mood took them. Javier again behaved like the perfect gentleman, making Karin feel comfortable from the outset and staying relatively sober. Karin enjoyed the dinner and her mood was lifted so much that she decided to take a further risk.

"Javier, why don't you and Nicole come and see my new home this weekend?" she asked.

"Mari, you're full of surprises! Of course, we'd love to," he replied.

She was desperate for good company.

* * *

At noon the next day, Karin went into the ABN bank to withdraw some money from her account to help pay for the redecoration. As she was withdrawing ten thousand *reals*, the clerk said to her, "Excuse me, Ms. Van Hasselt, we have a message for you from your Swiss Bank."

"Oh, yes?"

Puzzled by this, Karin decided to play along nevertheless. She was handed a sealed envelope marked CONFIDENTAL FOR YOUR EYES ONLY and tore the seal strip down the side of the envelope. It was like an old-fashioned telegram. She read the words slowly and deliberately, understanding their significance instantly.

> ++ MY BABY + DO NOT WORRY I AM ALIVE AND WELL + I'LL BE THERE WITH YOU SOON+ I HAVE SOME UNFINISHED BUSINESS FIRST+ WILL BE IN TOUCH IN A WEEK+I LOVE YOU+TOM++

Her heart leaped for joy. *I knew it! I knew it! Yes, he's alive!* Karin's thoughts raced in a million directions as she headed for the door. In a daze, she heard the clerk call her back.

"Don't forget your money, *senhora*!"

Driving home, she was elated. She drove with confidence, weaving in and out of the traffic along the coast road. The news from Tom had given her actions new meaning and provided an added urgency for her to complete her project. Once home, she breezed into the house, almost as if in a trance. She went to her room and threw her bag down carelessly by the bed. After a quick shower, she got on the phone to the building contractor. She was going to make the most of the week or so that she had.

*　　　*　　　*

Javier and Nicole joined her for a barbeque by the pool on Saturday evening. She had selected fresh fish from the market earlier that day: sea bass, prawns, and lobster grilled simply with butter and lime juice—they were wonderfully delicious. They sat on the veranda in the gentle sea breeze, soaking up the tropical warmth and drinking Sauvignon Blanc, its slightly acidic bite accompanying the seafood to perfection. Throughout it all, she could not stop smiling.

Chapter 25—
The London Eye

The chairman was just getting home to his Kentish Manor after attending a rather stuffy dinner at the Foreign Office with some of his political masters. Consequently, he was already in a bad mood. His chauffeur was turning the corner, easing the *Jaguar XJ8* into the driveway, when he noticed that the small warning light on his communications device was illuminated. It was the protocol in cases of extreme urgency. Sir Peter's heart sank when he saw it, as this was rarely good news. It would undoubtedly ruin what was left of his evening. Sir Peter clicked on the urgent message from Dubai and pressed "Unscramble." Bad news indeed, he determined, as he read the report of Tom and Khalid's violent death.

Sir Peter was angry and suspicious at the loss of two of his best agents. He immediately fired back a message to Dubai, demanding a full investigation into the incident. This whole operation had a nasty smell surrounding it. He instinctively knew that the Yanks were holding something back. There was clearly some sort of cover up. Frankly, he had been astounded when they had declined to finish the job at Madain Saleh. Tom and Khalid were true professionals, and they had done a fantastic job cornering their high-profile target. He was even more perplexed when he received the message from Brad saying that they were under no circumstances to go in for the kill. He had tried to put a positive spin on his message to his two men in the field, but he was left wondering what was going on. He had also reluctantly agreed with Brad to let Tom and Khalid continue the chase, implying that somehow they'd be able to take UBL alive. Yet he conceded to himself that this was pure fantasy. He hated it when people took him for a fool, particularly when they tried to play such obvious games.

As soon as his Jaguar came to a halt, he launched himself abruptly out the car. His footsteps crunched on the loose gravel in the driveway, as he strode purposefully toward the front door. He draped his coat and scarf on a chair in the hallway, then headed straight for the booze cabinet in his study. Sir Peter was old school and liked a stiff drink in times of stress. He poured himself a slug of single-malt whisky, added a splash of soda, and took a large gulp.

"Bloody Yanks. They think they own us … well, we'll see about that," he murmured.

*   *   *

The next day, Sir Peter was in a pensive mood as he sat in his office at Vauxhall Cross. He gave a wry smile as he received a new message.

From: Javier Solano—WA/4 xxx Scrambled xxx 14:03 GMT
To: Wood, Peter—C +++MOST CONFIDENTIAL+++:
Made contact again with Ms. Duval. Will keep under close surveillance. Expect she is aware from the press of the Suez incident.
J.
+++

Sir Peter wondered if Karin had even the slightest inkling about Javier's identity. Javier was in fact one of his most successful agents in Latin America, a role he had managed to disguise for some time now.

Sir Peter called Javier to discuss progress.

"Karin may be an amateur," he said. "Yet, she's clearly no fool. Make sure you are as convincing as possible playing the airhead. I don't want you hamming it up so much that you blow your cover."

"Don't worry, sir. I'm certain that she suspects nothing."

"How can you be so sure?"

"I have been following her for over four weeks now, and I would have sensed some hesitation on her part."

"I'm still baffled by the Yanks' attempt to kidnap her. What on Earth was Brad thinking about, using British Special Forces?"

"Agreed, it's very odd. Did he really expect we wouldn't find out?"

"Thank God the AIVD alerted us on both sets of Dutch passports."

"We've been lucky, it's made tracking her a simple matter."

"Javier, you've done well so far. But don't get overconfident."

"No, sir—"

"Remember, you have more than one role. Besides finding Tom, you must be careful to protect Karin against another kidnap attempt."

"Yes, sir—"

"And never forget that your mission is strictly confidential, between us and only us."

"I've told no one."

"Most importantly, Operations must never get an inkling of what's going on, as they leak like a sieve."

"Okay, sir—understood."

This was the first time in his career that Sir Peter had suspected his erstwhile allies in US Intelligence of being up to something behind his back. He plainly didn't like the implications. Lack of trust across the Atlantic set a precedent that undermined the whole basis of the transatlantic alliance. The damage done could be irreparable and undermine sixty years of post-war intelligence collaboration. All the evidence clearly pointed in that direction, but he failed to see a link between the deaths and the Agency's participation in Operation Sheikh. He resolved that he would search harder to find the connection.

* * *

The next time he spoke to Javier, Sir Peter was more encouraged.

"We were invited to dine at Karin's new house," Javier reported.

"Good, it shows that you've got her confidence."

"Well, it was impossible not to notice the change in her mood—she was euphoric. Her face was radiant. She had a broad smile almost permanently stuck on her face."

"Well now, how interesting!"

"For me there is only one explanation. It must be good news about Tom. He must be alive."

"So the bodies left by the roadside in Suez were switched at the last moment."

"Almost certainly—"

"I wonder if the Yanks suspect that they've escaped too."

"I wouldn't be surprised."

"In any case, Javier, this is wonderful news. It's now more important than ever that you stick close to Karin."

"Of course, sir."

"My next concern is that two of my best agents could be at large somewhere, as loose cannons."

"Yes, I can understand the seriousness of the situation."

"We must bring them in before they do irreparable damage to themselves or the Circus' interests."

"Do you think Tom will try to meet up with Karin?"

"I'll wager a month's salary he will."

"Okay … you're on."

"No, on second thoughts, I'd be betting against myself."

"He won't be easy to catch."

"That's your job. I still believe Tom's our best chance of unraveling this mystery. My task is to discover the Agency's motives. Although, right now, I admit that I'm completely bamboozled."

Sir Peter hung up and then swiveled his chair around, turning his attention to a document his assistant had just delivered. As he digested its contents, he was pleasantly surprised. The Egyptians were not nearly as inept as their reputation suggested. Because of the sensitivity, their report on the Suez ambush had been passed to him exclusively, as the most interested party. He read the summary very carefully.

We exhumed the bodies from the Canal Zone site. It was not clear who had buried them. First, we carried out DNA testing on the two corpses believed to be of two MI6 agents. We rapidly determined that the two bodies were of close relatives, possibly belonging to the Yemeni Bin Hassan tribe. This clearly refutes the idea that the bodies belong to Salter and al-Querishi. We also positively identified a third body as belonging to Abdul Rahman al-Falah, the al-Qaeda commander who was turned by the Americans last year. Some thirty depleted uranium rounds were also discovered at the site using a Geiger counter.

Our analysis suggests that there are many puzzling aspects to this case. It appears the ambush was executed by al-Qaeda, while there are some distinct signs of American or possibly even Israeli involvement.

Sir Peter was at once delighted to validate the hypothesis that his two agents had somehow escaped and still furious at the apparent participation of the Yanks. The presence of al-Falah seemed to confirm his worse suspicions. His priority was still to bring his men in and debrief them. In the meantime, to cover his back, he wrote a note to the Cabinet Secretary explaining his darkest fears about American duplicity. Although it was inconclusive, it was better to prepare the ground and warn his superiors of an impending political storm. The Prime Minister would surely back him up to the highest levels within the US administration, but only with irrefutable proof.

Before raising the stakes, he also decided to confront his opposite number—the director of the CIA—to see if he would be more forthcoming than Brad. It was worth a try at least. He paged his assistant and asked her to get Langley on the hotline.

Chapter 26—Payback Time

The Emirates flight from Cairo to Dubai landed in the late evening. Tom and Khalid were both sitting comfortably in first class, traveling as British executives in the electronics field on a routine visit to their Middle East agent in Dubai. As is the privilege of those in the front of the aircraft, they deplaned before the remaining passengers. After a hike through the terminal, they arrived at the long line of immigration desks. It became apparent that several wide-bodied jets from the Indian sub-continent had gotten there just ahead of them. A line of Indians and Pakistanis snaked around the terminal in front of them. They waited for nearly an hour before they could get through to collect their bags and clear customs. Tom was in a lousy mood, frustrated and tired after this agonizing experience.

He soon cheered up though, as he got to their car. Khalid had hired one of the new BMW 650i convertibles, which would have looked ostentatious anywhere else in the world but was commonplace in Dubai. Tom swung out into to the fast lane as they left the terminal, heading out of town along the coastal freeway to Al Jumeirah. He stopped at a traffic light just before entering the Sheikh Zayed Road, pulling up alongside a Bugatti Veyron 16.4. The sleek lines and the roar of the engine mesmerized him. In a split second, as the lights changed, the supercar disappeared into the distance; it must have reached nearly two hundred and fifty kilometers per hour along the straight desert highway, leaving the BMW standing.

Traveling at a more sedate one hundred and forty kilometers per hour, they took about twenty minutes to reach the Palm Islands. They passed through security, giving Martin's name to the guard, and cruised quietly through the residential streets until they arrived at Martin and Paula's villa. Glancing at his watch Tom saw the time was precisely twelve midnight. The gates opened automatically and they parked their car in the driveway.

"It's late and we're all tired. Why don't we catch up later?" suggested Tom.

"All right, I'll show you to your rooms," Paula replied.

*　　*　　*

Tom and Khalid got up late and made their way downstairs.

"Wow, what a sumptuous breakfast!" Tom said, observing the feast laid out for them on the kitchen table.

"We'll soon demolish that," Khalid replied.

"Look at the time," said Tom. "It's more like brunch than breakfast, I guess."

"I wonder where Martin and Paula have gotten to?" asked Khalid.

"Look, there's a note on the fridge—Martin's gone to work and Paula will be back from her tennis lesson around midday. She suggests we make ourselves completely at home."

"No problem!" said Khalid, tucking in to the food.

After breakfast, they sat around the breakfast bar, planning their next moves.

"I propose we pay a visit to the arms cache this evening," said Tom

"Agreed," replied Khalid, "it'll be best after 9 PM, as there's less security."

"We can commence surveillance of Kurt tomorrow. We'll start with his departure from home in the morning."

"Okay, I imagine we'll need about three days to perform sufficient observations before we make the grab."

"Let's get hold of a less conspicuous vehicle for tailing him," said Tom, "a pickup—they're everywhere in Dubai. To blend in we'll need to dress like itinerant workers, see if you buy some suitable clothing."

"I'll get right on it." Khalid got up and headed for the door.

*　　*　　*

The cache was in a small bonded warehouse in Jebel Ali Port. Khalid was a frequent visitor to the bonded area and was well recognized, so he only had to flash his pass at the security gate to gain admission. They parked the car out of sight, at the side of the building, and entered without a problem. Khalid input the code on the access door keypad. The arms were stored behind a wire cage, which Khalid was similarly able to penetrate using the appropriate codes.

"Thank God that the codes only change monthly," said Khalid.

"Yes, next week we'd be screwed!" observed Tom.

They removed two of Tom's much-loved Sig Pro automatic pistols, together with ammunition, and were extremely careful in relocking the cabinets so they would appear undisturbed. Tom watched as Khalid helped himself to ten kilos of plastic, plus detonators, from the cases on the floor at the back. They were again careful to close the lids and not move anything. Tom also took half a dozen grenades and, finally, Khalid selected a M82 lightweight sniper's rifle. They were in and out in less than five minutes. They inserted the pistols into their shoulder holsters and stashed the rest of the arms in the trunk of the BMW. They were now fully prepared for the next phase of the operation.

* * *

Keeping Kurt under surveillance was painstaking job. After the second day of shadowing him, Tom concluded that he was a very cautious operator and especially good at following evasive security procedures. Every day he arrived and left by car, varying the route to and from his home, even exchanging vehicles on the second day. It was going to be a difficult task to set up the snatch. Meanwhile, they observed that one of Kurt's reports, who they had identified as Todd Major, a mission specialist, was not nearly as careful. They witnessed Todd leaving the office around 4:30 PM in a Ford 250 Crew Cab, with flame decals down the side. Spinning his wheels as he left, he drove three kilometers to his apartment building along the same route daily.

Khalid suggested a new plan to Tom. "I think we agree that Mr. By-the-Book Schneider is going to be a tough nut to crack."

Tom nodded. "Uh huh…"

"We need to try an easier target. I think if we take Todd Major, he'll not be missed as quickly and should be able to tell us at least something from the mission briefings."

"Okay, let's give it a shot. We'll pick him up tomorrow evening."

To avoid their easy identification, and to provide a cover story, they planned to disguise themselves as members of Islamic Jihad. The next day, Tom rented a vacant apartment in a nearly empty block on the Corniche. He also bought a video camera with tripod and a desktop PC from the electronics *souk*, which he installed in the apartment.

*　　　*　　　*

When Todd arrived home at about five that afternoon, two masked Arab gunmen confronted him in the underground car park of his apartment building. One held a pistol to his head, while the other handcuffed him. They stuck a black hood over his head, gave him a shot in the arm, and bundled him into the trunk of their car. It all happened in less than sixty seconds.

Todd was lightheaded but still conscious; he must have received some kind of sedative that dulled his reactions without putting him out cold. Their tires screeched as they exited his apartment block. Todd was being bumped around in the trunk, but he didn't feel any pain. Despite the fog in his brain, he was genuinely scared for his life.

Conventional wisdom was that Dubai is a relatively safe haven for Americans, and there had been no kidnapping incidents to date. Nevertheless, Todd was aware from NSA security briefings that it was all only a matter of time. Soon terrorists would start to function with a similar modus operandi as the one they employed in Saudi and start targeting westerners. Although Islamic militant organizations could not rely on the disaffected local population in Dubai to do their dirty work, they could draw on itinerant Palestinians, Lebanese, Pakistanis, and other Muslims.

Could it be his misfortune to become the first victim of this new trend? *Shit! Why was I so careless?* He knew the answer already—he had been lulled into a false sense of security by the easygoing tourist atmosphere in the small but cosmopolitan Emirate. Todd was a single and had been in Dubai for twelve months. He was enjoying the work—he had a great social life and he was taking home good money to support his new lifestyle. He could travel around the world in his vacations and was becoming quite a celebrity back home in Butte, Montana.

As they drove him around, he became disoriented. He was extremely claustrophobic and very uncomfortable with his arms cuffed behind his back. He could still just move his legs, but he was sedated and restricted by the limited space. He spent the journey trying to recall the instructions from the Agency manual on what to do in the event of abduction. It was extremely difficult in his numb state, yet he fought the drowsiness and forced his neural paths to function by counting backward from one hundred in fives, fours, and then threes. He remembered the simple things from his training—for example, he should not look them in the eye and avoid sudden movements—but he could not remember much more than that.

It was only when the car stopped and he was manhandled out of the trunk that he realized how unsteady he was on his feet. His legs were like jelly. He couldn't walk. He was being hauled across a concrete floor. Each of his kidnappers took one arm and draped it over his shoulder, leaving his feet dragging behind them. After about one hundred feet, they arrived at an elevator. He was bundled inside; they must have gone only a couple of floors and then he was dragged out again and into an adjacent doorway.

Inside, he was sat on a chair with the cuffs still on. He was tied down and then his hood was removed. He almost could have guessed the scenario: the room had bare walls, a single ceiling fan/light, and a video camera pointed straight at him. Nothing else was evident except his two kidnappers, who kept their masks on. One of the men approached and gave him another shot in the arm. This time it had the opposite effect; within about thirty seconds, all his senses were alive. His mind started racing and his thoughts were screaming at him that he was as good as dead; he would never get out of this alive.

The first kidnapper spoke to him in an American accent. "Todd, if you co-operate with us you will not be harmed. We are members of Islamic Jihad and we know that you are a member of the Great Satan's hated secret army, the infamous CIA."

Todd had a sinking feeling, as his worst fears were confirmed.

"We also know that you have been part of a task force that has been hunting down a friend of ours, Usama bin Laden."

He realized that they were well informed.

"Don't ask us how we know, but our sources are good."

His palms were sweaty and he was feeling very agitated.

"I want you to tell me slowly in your own words everything you know about this operation—and remember, our information is accurate, so if you are lying and we catch you, there will be a penalty, which I guarantee you'll find extremely painful."

At the same time as the first kidnapper was speaking, the second was attaching, what looked like a polygraph to his upper wrist and small electrodes directly to Todd's nipples with some cold, water-based jelly. He then plugged them into the device on the floor, which was connected directly to the power supply. This left Todd in no doubt that they were absolutely professional in their interrogation techniques and serious in their threats. In Todd's now heightened state of awareness, the menace was magnified a thousand times. His Agency recruiter would have observed that he had a low pain threshold, even under normal circumstances, and was one of the most pathetic candidates in the endurance entry test he had come across, barely scraping a passing grade. Todd also was keenly aware that he was not courageous and would crack immediately under duress. He decided to tell them straight away, whatever it was they wanted to know. Perhaps he might just escape with his life.

"Okay, I'll co-operate," he promised.

While trying to fight the sensation, he wondered, *Damn, what's that stuff that they gave me?*

The first kidnapper turned on the video camera and commanded, "Go ahead, talk."

"Well, the first we all knew was when we were called into the briefing room to discuss the Level Four situation—sorry, Level Four is a direct order from the Commander-in-Chief—and it was the first time we'd had such an order in Dubai."

"Stop!" interrupted the first kidnapper. "Your orders came directly from the President of the United States?"

"Yes, sir, that is correct." Todd was trying to speak matter-of-factly and be deferential, as he thought the circumstances demanded.

The polygraph, or whatever the device was, was whirring away behind him. Todd had a dry mouth and a lump in his throat. His heart was thumping, as he anticipated some sort of shock at any moment.

"Go on…"

"My boss, Kurt, told us that we were to target two British agents who were following UBL, I mean Usama bin Laden."

"All right, so what next?"

"Kurt wanted us to work out an operational plan that would make it look like they had been the victims of an ambush by the al-Qaeda faction they were chasing."

His head was spinning as he felt the effect of the drug.

"We were given three hours to come up with something, and then we were back in the briefing room again in a huddle."

"Continue," ordered the kidnapper, this time with a hint of a Middle Eastern accent, which Todd could not quite make out—either Saudi or Jordan.

"We agreed to put a man inside the al-Qaeda group and use him to direct the ambush in Sinai."

"Who did you place in the convoy?"

"We used Abdul Rahman al-Falah, a former al-Qaeda commander that we had turned."

"So, how did they get to Sinai?"

"We arranged free passage across the Gulf of Aqaba with the Jordanians. Kurt was in charge of that part of the operation."

"Was Kurt in overall command?"

"No, sir, Brad Hartman, the ADD or deputy director, himself, flew in to supervise the attack."

"Why was the mission protecting Usama bin Laden?" the interrogator asked.

"I don't know that was the puzzling part, along with targeting our allies."

"Didn't that worry you?"

"Many things about this operation made us all feel uncomfortable, but, hey, we were following orders from the highest level."

Todd prayed that he was convincing enough to avoid shock treatment. He felt his left eye twitch, as it always did when he was nervous.

"See how the CIA is full of treacherous scum that even targets their friends. Ha! How do you sleep at night, with all the blood on your hands?"

The interrogation was taking a wrong turn; the last thing Todd wanted to do was offend the sensibilities of his captors.

"You'll never win in the Middle East. We'll drive you American dogs back home, and even then you'll not be safe from our mujahedeen," his interrogator said, repeatedly pounding his fist into his other palm.

Todd froze.

The first kidnapper handed Todd a piece of paper while the second kidnapper took up position behind the video camera. "You will read this confession."

"I am a member of the CIA. My job has been to lie, kill, and maim innocent Muslim brethren in the Great Satan's crusade against Islam and its people. I repent of my ways and realize that I fully deserve the sentence for my crimes," Todd read.

They had positioned a banner with Arabic script behind him, as a backdrop to the video. He was becoming really scared by this time, and his voice began to crack as he read the final words. He had seen exactly such scenes at Terratec, in amateur videos, prior to ritual executions that were either posted on the Web or broadcast on al Jazeera.

"*Allah akhbar.* Wait, we'll be back," said the first kidnapper. They both trooped out of the room, taking the video camera with them.

Chapter 27—
The Perfect Squeeze

Tom and Khalid had adjourned to the adjacent room after the interrogation and discussed what they had heard.

"I believe him. I think he is telling us straight—all he knows," said Khalid.

"I agree. I think we have him so shitless in there he wouldn't dare lie. The polygraph tends to confirm it too," Tom responded.

"So we're not the victims of some rogue station chief in Dubai; this goes all the way to the top."

"Yes, we're in much greater danger than we thought."

"You're right, except they still don't appear to know that we escaped the ambush in Suez."

"I'm sure they'll find out sooner or later, and when they do, we'll be number one and two on their most wanted list."

Tom stroked his chin. "We need to follow through this little charade with Todd and then get the hell out of here!"

Tom sat in front of the PC and connected the video camera via a USB cable. He uploaded the confession onto the Internet, together with a statement from Islamic Jihad expressing determination to continue the armed struggle against the infidel and in particular the forces of the Great Satan. He demanded five million dollars for the safe release of the murderous CIA swine and signed off with *There is only One God and His Prophet is Mohammed—Allah akhbar.*

Tom then sent an e-mail from a dummy address to al Jazeera with the URL. He also printed it out on a piece of paper, with a message addressed to Kurt, saying that the execution could be watched via Web cast on the Islamic Jihad site, to take place at Friday noon. Kurt could secure Todd's release if he paid the ransom before that time into a numbered Swiss account. As soon as Islamic Jihad received confirmation of transfer, they would release Todd. However, there would be no deals or bartering; he must follow the instructions to the letter or be responsible for Todd's death.

Khalid paid a night watchman at a building six blocks away to deliver the note to Kurt's home mailbox in the morning. It was now a waiting game. Khalid returned to the apartment with several shish kebab, some Arabic bread, and water. Tom offered a little food to Todd, but he would not eat, he only drank the water. Todd looked like he was in a highly tense state, and although Tom sensed that Todd would have been considerably more relaxed out of his chains, he decided to keep him tied up to make the scenario as realistic as possible.

Tom suggested to Khalid that they take it in turns in guarding Todd overnight. Tom slept at Martin and Paula's house the first night, rotating with Khalid the second night. Tom had explained to Martin and Paula on the evening after they arrived that the less they knew about their activities, the better. They were smart enough not to ask in any case.

The time before the deadline passed too slowly for Tom's liking. The Agency would be frantically searching for clues. Despite the extra precautions Tom and Khalid had taken, eventually the relentless US intelligence machinery would stumble on something. He was taking a calculated risk that three days were insufficient for Kurt to track them down.

*   *   *

Kurt received the message at his breakfast table, before he went to work. He immediately logged on to the Internet to see the film of Todd. He knew straight away that it was the real thing. Just then, he heard reports on CNN that al Jazeera were broadcasting footage of an American who had been kidnapped in Dubai by Islamic Jihad. The nightmare that the Agency's Middle East Region had been concerned about had just begun. Radicalism had spread to the moderate Gulf States.

Kurt called Brad over the secure line from his house with an initial briefing and then put the Dubai station on red alert. He called a crisis meeting with all the section heads at the Terratec office for 0900 hours.

When Kurt arrived at his desk, he had a couple of puzzling reports. Firstly, there was a M82 rifle missing from the Circus arms cache at Jebel Ali, with no sign of a break in. On the one hand, this could be just an oversight by the quartermaster; on the other hand, it could be a serious breach of security. An investigation would have to wait until later. Secondly, he received an analyst's report confirming that depleted uranium rounds had definitely killed four al-Qaeda members at the ambush in Suez. He had already determined that there was no such ammunition stored at St Catherine's Monastery, so he concluded that there was a third party who took part in the skirmish.

As a rule, Kurt was on top of the detail and he did not like the inconsistencies at Suez. He called his Egyptian counterpart, the station chief in Cairo.

"Can you get a more thorough analysis of the site and the bodies?" he asked.

"I'll need to get clearance through Egyptian channels."

"I'd like for a NSA forensic team to go over the scene of the ambush more systematically. I'm convinced we've missed something of vital importance."

"I warn you this could take time."

Kurt stepped into the briefing room punctually at 0900 hours. Brad was already there, with all the senior team.

Kurt started, "Well, gentlemen, we know that Todd was probably taken about 1700 hours yesterday, as he arrived back at his apartment. We have an eyewitness account from another tenant who saw two Arabs hanging about in the car park at 1645 looking suspicious."

"Next steps?" asked Brad.

"We now need to see if we can find someone who actually saw the abduction," Kurt replied. "Frank, I want you to take direct charge of the search for leads at Todd's apartment."

"Yes, sir," he responded.

"We also need to follow up on the note," said Kurt. "Ron, can you get the comms team working to find out who set up the Web site and see what other information that you can get from the note itself—typeface ID, the usual?"

"I have a security camera video of a man dressed in a Pakistani *kurta*, who delivered the note to my house at about five this morning." Kurt said. "I'll follow that lead wherever it takes me."

Brad raised his arm and said, "And I'll get the Treasury Department to prepare for the transfer of funds on Thursday, just in case."

"Okay, let's go!" Kurt clapped his hands twice. "We have forty-eight hours to come up with something. It's barely possible we'll get Todd back alive, but let's do everything we can guys."

Looking around the room to see if anyone had something to add, Kurt then wrapped up the meeting. "Next get-together of the crisis team is at 1500 hours, for report back."

There was little positive to report in the afternoon. Nonetheless, Kurt listened carefully as Frank was debriefed first.

"I was accompanied by a member of my team. When we arrived at the apartment building, we interviewed the security guard. He was located in the first floor reception area and had nothing to tell."

"How come?" asked Kurt.

"Well the CCTV monitors show the car parking area and the exit ramp, but there is no taping done. The guard had not seen the kidnappers come and go yesterday, so there was little that he could tell us."

"Okay."

"We then went to the car park itself to look for clues. We found some signs of a scuffle near Todd's pick-up," he said. "I checked for distinctive foot prints or any dropped items, but there were none."

"Not much to go on, then," said Kurt.

"I deduced from the light covering of sand and dust on the floor that Todd had been dragged to an adjacent parking spot."

"Anything else to report?" he asked.

"Yes, as a matter of fact there were some curious tire prints there, of a low profile type that is only fitted to expensive sports cars. I took some photos to send to the lab boys."

"Not much, but worth following up," said Kurt.

"We also enquired door to door in the block, but most of the residents were out for the day and only the maids were at home. As you might imagine, none of them had seen anything strange the previous afternoon."

"Why don't you go back early this evening to interview the occupants when they return from work?" asked Kurt.

"Yes, sir, I was planning to."

Ron was next to debrief.

"Well, I made little progress with the Web site. I discovered that it was rented by a Syrian freight forwarding company, but the lead went cold in Damascus."

"Predictable," said Brad.

"Next, the printer is a standard HP model sold all over the Middle East and so difficult to trace. The paper is also HP—again from a batch that was imported into Dubai at the end of last year, which was distributed widely to local vendors."

"Nothing out of the ordinary there then either," observed Kurt.

"No, sir—there were no fingerprints or DNA traces from saliva or sweat. Whoever printed the note had probably handled it with gloves."

Kurt then admitted to drawing a blank on the security video, "It could have been anyone of nearly two million itinerant workers from the Indian sub-continent on the tape. It's virtually impossible to ascertain an identity."

They reconvened again at 2100 hours, and this time there was some better news.

Kurt announced, "The research team in Langley has identified that Frank's tire print was from a set of Michelin tires, exclusively fitted to the new BMW 650i."

"It's slender evidence, but at least something unusual," said Brad.

"Frank, crosscheck with the residents of Todd's block to make sure no one has such a Beemer," ordered Kurt.

"Sir!"

"Ray, see how many were sold in Dubai in the last few months since its launch, and to whom."

It was an unlikely clue. Kurt appreciated that it was a strange and very conspicuous car for the kidnappers to use, but it was their only substantive lead. They must follow up.

Early the next morning, Kurt called personally at the chief of police's office near the Creek. The UAE authorities were bureaucratic and slow at coming back with any data, and this was no exception. The chief of police was polite but did not promise anything. He merely said he would do it as soon as possible. Repeatedly he finished his sentences with the word *Inshallah*—meaning, literally, "when Allah wills it"—but didn't convey any real sense of urgency. Kurt then called the emir's head of protocol to try to speed things up. Despite his best efforts to pull strings, he was advised that twenty-four hours was the quickest such a request could be processed.

"Shit!"

He banged the receiver down in anger and frustration after talking to the minister. Then he stormed into the open plan office.

"Will somebody get hold of BMW and see if we can get something from their sales records," he shouted at nobody in particular.

"Okay, sir, I'll get onto West European Region to contact the head of sales," responded Ray.

In due course, Kurt discovered that the Munich firm was about as uncooperative as the Dubai authorities were. When they were told a life was at stake, they reluctantly had agreed to produce their sales statistics by the end of the business day.

Thursday morning arrived and the most Kurt had was a list of 162 BMWs sold in the last year, 30 of which had gone to hire companies, 65 to company fleets, and the remainder to private buyers.

Ray suggested to Kurt, "Why don't we eliminate the others from the initial inquiry and concentrate on the hire cars."

"Good thinking. We need to use our intuition, as we have so little time," replied Kurt. "Get going as soon as possible."

However, by Thursday evening they still had nothing definite. Time was running out. While it was Agency policy never to admit that they paid ransom money, it happened all the time. In fact, there was a large contingency budget for just such eventualities. Brad sat in Kurt's office discussing the situation.

"As ADD, I can approve the five-million-dollar payment," said Brad.

"Although Todd might not be released; I think that there's still a reasonable chance that the money will secure his freedom," responded Kurt.

"Yes, I agree, Islamic Jihad is known for outrageous demands but also for being good to their word," Brad observed. "They clearly do not want to kill the goose that laid the golden egg."

"Yes, sir and we're fast running out of options."

"I believe they'll let him go if we pay the ransom, so I'm willing to take full responsibility."

Kurt watched, as Brad prepared an encrypted e-mail to the Treasury Department to make the wire transfer immediately.

Brad heaved a big sigh, "There goes five million bucks courtesy of Uncle Sam!"

"We can only hope it does the trick." Kurt frowned back at him.

As they returned to the Operations Room, Ray called his attention.

"Sir, I think we just got lucky. We're hot on the trail of a rented blue BMW 650i convertible, now overdue with the hire company."

"Excellent."

"Also we intercepted a local police message that they have been called to an apartment block on the Corniche, reporting an abandoned BMW. What's more, one of the residents is complaining of muffled screams from next door, late at night."

"Sounds like it could be our man. Let's get down there right away."

Kurt oversaw the operation, as one hour later the doors were broken down and a shaken but otherwise safe and healthy Todd was rescued from his ordeal. They also found the blue BMW in the basement car park.

"The kidnappers must have received the payoff," said Kurt, "and then fled immediately."

"I'm sure that's the last we'll ever see of the money," replied Frank. "But at least Todd's still in one piece."

"You're right … it's a good result. Get me a full medical and psychological evaluation on Todd, as soon as possible," Kurt ordered. "I'm heading back to the office."

Chapter 28—
The King Is Dead

Tom heard the breaking news on CNN after he got out of the shower the next morning: *American hostage found safe in Dubai…*

"Okay," Tom said to Khalid, "time for us to get moving again."

"What's the rush?" asked Martin.

"We've put you in enough danger already. The longer we stay, the more perilous it is for you," replied Tom. "I can't accept that responsibility."

"If you think it's for the best," said Martin.

"Soon they'll be searching for us everywhere. We need a back-door route out of Dubai," Tom said.

"Easy enough—take my power boat," said Martin.

"Great idea!" replied Tom.

Tom and Khalid packed only the essentials, carefully hiding their weapons and explosives aboard the boat. They set off shortly after 9 AM, among the typical pleasure boaters on Friday out for a day's scuba diving or a picnic up the coast. Initially they were accompanied by a small flotilla. It was easier to hide in a crowd.

Khalid charted a course north-northeast from Dubai through the Strait of Hormuz, leaving Abu Musa Island off the port beam. Sitting comfortably in the white leather pilot's seat, Tom eased open the throttles of the Profile 280 powerboat; the BBC B-Max drive responded smoothly, as they reached fifty-five knots in the calm waters of the gulf. By hydroplaning over the surface of the sea at high speed, the powerboat could ride out any choppiness. They had indeed made a swift escape. No one could catch them now.

Meanwhile, to achieve maximum range, they had stowed as much fuel as they could on the back seat, in plastic containers covered with a tarpaulin.

"Once we get out into the Arabian Sea, we'll hug the coastline of Oman as far as Salalah," said Khalid.

"Good idea. We can refuel there," replied Tom.

"Then we must head out into open water, across the Gulf of Aden and the mouth of the Red Sea. We'll be heavily dependent upon the weather. Such a flimsy powerboat will flounder in heavy seas."

"I hope for both our sake that the forecast is good!"

"Don't worry, Tom. I'm confident that we'll get safely as far as Djibouti."

"And from Djibouti, we'll be able to make our way overland to Upper Egypt."

"That's exactly what I'd planned."

*   *   *

The sixty-kilometer wide Strait of Hormuz is one of the most congested shipping lanes in the world, with nearly twenty-five percent of the world's oil supply passing through it every day. It is transited by the world's largest ships, which can take several nautical miles to change course. These include the massive ULCC supertankers and the equally huge Malaccamax container vessels.

In contrast, the craft Tom was piloting was highly maneuverable and could easily stay out of the path of any of these oncoming monsters. Khalid's course kept them on the Omani side of the strait, close to the Musandam Peninsula. On Goat Island, at the northern tip of the Musandam, there was an American listening post. It carried out surveillance on the traffic through the strait and monitored any Iranian naval activity from Bandar e Abbas military base on the northern shore. Although they were unlikely to arouse much suspicion from the Americans, Tom was not taking any chances. He planned to avoid detection by shadowing one of the gigantic vessels exiting the gulf.

Tom could see the dark craggy coastline looming to starboard, just before he entered the strait. Four large tankers were visible from his position—two outbound and two inbound. He picked the closest outbound, which thankfully was less than a kilometer away. Then all of a sudden, Tom spotted an Iranian C-14 high-speed missile patrol boat, appearing from nowhere on a course to intercept them. It must have approached from the other side of the tanker out of his line of sight. These Chinese-built high-speed catamarans were formidable, carrying up to eight C-701 anti-ship cruise missiles, with one gun mounted forward.

They were signaling for him to stop. Tom knew it was impossible to outrun them, and he had nothing to pit against their superior firepower. Although they were well outside Iranian territorial waters and the Iranians had no jurisdiction, Tom effectively had a very large gun to his head.

"We'd better see what they want," Tom said.

"Do we have any option?" asked Khalid.

Tom cut the engine and the powerboat drifted forward about three hundred meters before stopping dead in the water. It was bobbing about like a cork as the gunboat pulled alongside. A group of sailors was lined up on deck, pointing automatic weapons at them, while a lieutenant barked through a megaphone in a strong British accent.

"Gentlemen, it is useless to resist. If you cooperate, you will not be harmed. We have someone who needs to talk to you urgently. Kindly consider yourselves guests of the Iranian Navy. Please climb aboard, up the netting, and we'll take your craft in tow."

Tom and Khalid complied without hesitation. Fifteen minutes later, they were tying up alongside in the naval base at Bandar e Abbas. The lieutenant politely invited them to accompany him and they walked down the gangway, across the quay, into what appeared to be the command center. They followed the lieutenant through a maze of corridors until they arrived at an open door.

He gestured for them to go inside. "Don't be concerned; we take good care of our guests. I leave you in good hands."

From behind a large desk, a short stocky man with a moustache, dressed in the uniform of a colonel in the IRGC leapt up to introduce himself.

"My name is Malek, and I'm with Iranian military intelligence. It's a pleasure to meet you two finally face to face. You probably don't realize it, but you've become real celebrities around here."

"I wish I could share your pleasure. I don't like meeting anyone at the point of a gun," replied Tom.

"I'm genuinely sorry for the heavy-handed tactics. I hope you'll forgive me when you've heard what I've got to say. By the way, you're not prisoners; you're free to go whenever you choose."

"You've gone to a lot of trouble to get our attention," said Tom. "So, I'm prepared to listen, but it had better be good."

"Gentlemen, I must confess that we've been watching you for some time now," Malek beamed. "Now please take a seat."

"If we must!" Tom glared back at him.

"Would you like some mint tea?" asked Malek, helping himself to one of the cups on the table.

"Not for me," said Tom, looking at Khalid.

"Nor me," said Khalid.

"I have got to say," Malek said, "as a fellow professional, I admire your tenacity—in particular the clever way that you managed to extort several millions out of the US Treasury."

Tom maintained a poker face, concealing his surprise that Malek knew about the money. Meanwhile, Malek remained silent for a moment and squinted at Tom.

"By now you must be wondering what else can go wrong with your mission. You have been double-crossed by your American friends and have become a target yourselves."

Tom froze. Malek seemed to know all about them. His information sources were excellent.

He continued, "I am sure you have already figured out that you could implicate senior members of the Agency in their efforts to protect Bin Laden. Moreover, you suspect that the corruption goes all the way up to the top, but you are not sure how the pieces all fit together."

Malek paused again and just sat there grinning inanely at the two of them for a few seconds, before he said, "As you know, in the field we normally never get the full picture."

Tom was wide-eyed. He was taken aback by Malek's revelations and wondered where all this was leading.

"In this respect, what I am about to tell you is a rarity in our profession. Yet I feel you deserve a fuller explanation of what is really happening, if only to make more informed decisions about your future."

"Okay, I suppose we've nothing to lose by listening to your story," Tom said. "We can then make up our own minds."

"Quite right!" replied Malek. "Firstly, let me start with the facts. In September 2005, we launched a raid on the Jundallah, our homegrown Sunni terrorist menace. During the attack, which occurred in eastern Iran close to the Afghan border, Usama bin Laden was shot dead by our Special Forces. He would have almost certainly died soon enough, anyway. He was terminally ill, suffering from congestive heart failure as a complication from kidney disease."

"Whoa, hold on a minute. How's that possible!" asked Khalid. "We've just been chasing Bin Laden across the deserts of Arabia."

"I can assure you I'm telling you the truth. I personally commanded the elite force that carried out the attack, and I myself supervised the recovery of Bin Laden's body to Chah-Bahar military base. We can even show you DNA evidence later, if you don't believe me."

"I don't understand. So who were we following?" asked Tom.

"I am afraid that you have fallen for a common ploy in the Middle East. You were following a doppelganger—a double, or a phony—although this time with an extraordinary twist. Intriguingly, the double was planted by the Americans."

"What!" Tom and Khalid sat staring at him, their mouths hanging open.

"You will recall the bogus press conferences and the appearances by Saddam's rather unconvincing doubles during the Gulf War. Possibly a more relevant example is your own Sandhurst-trained Sultan of Oman, who dresses up as a common soldier in his support unit, riding shotgun in an armored car, while the bulletproof Mercedes contains his double in all the official regalia."

"I don't understand. Why would the Yanks want to keep Bin Laden alive, so to speak?" asked Tom. "It all sounds highly implausible to me."

"I can understand your skepticism," Malek replied. "As soon as the reports started filtering back about new sightings of Bin Laden toward the end of last year, we assumed that it was the Agency spreading disinformation."

"Huh!" Tom grunted.

"I freely admit we were highly curious as to why they were doing it. We still maintained our silence about the genuine fate of Bin Laden. We would never have suspected that it was the Americans who had planted a double, but for pure chance."

"So how did you find out?"

"The Israelis are not the only ones with a robust intelligence network in Washington, and we are fortunate to have an agent well placed in the office of the vice chairman of the Armed Services Committee, Senator Littleton."

Tom shifted back in his seat and gazed at Malek.

"Well, there were regular private meetings between him and the US President, in a building on M Street. We assumed that it was related to the Armed Services Bill going through on Capitol Hill. Littleton had been lobbying hard for the presidential agenda."

Malek lowered his voice to a whisper, "About a month ago, Senator Littleton's chief aide, who normally accompanied him to these meetings, was suddenly taken ill. Our agent was asked to stand in as bag carrier."

"That sounds like it was a stroke of luck."

"Now, Littleton is an arrogant sonofabitch, with an unshakeable faith in American supremacy, and that makes him a careless on occasions," said Malek.

Tom was aware that Littleton had a reputation as a maverick. He was also rumored to be running for the Oval office in 2008.

"During the talk with the President, he called for some additional papers to be delivered to the room," Malek said. "I'm sure you gentlemen appreciate, this was contrary to standard security procedure. The room had already been swept, and the security detail had been stationed outside the door."

"Sloppy maybe, but only a minor indiscretion, I'd say," Tom said.

"Well, as you would expect, our man duly complied with the order. Meanwhile, as he leaned over Senator Littleton's shoulder to place the papers in front of him, he was able to secretly photograph the documents already on the table using a concealed camera."

"Very enterprising," remarked Tom.

"You can imagine his astonishment when he scanned the images to discover that it was not about the Armed Services Bill at all, but about something called Operation Twin Brothers."

"What's that?" Khalid's eyes widened.

"It turned out to be a smoking gun. We suddenly had conclusive proof in our hands of a plot by the US President and his co-conspirator, Littleton, to use a bogus Bin Laden to influence the outcome of the next elections."

"Wow, that's political dynamite!" Tom said.

"It appears that our agent had unwittingly obtained a copy of the salient parts of a JSOC—or dirty ops—briefing paper."

Malek took a sip of mint tea.

"The paper explained in some details how they had recruited an Omani with similar stature and appearance to Bin Laden. They had trained him carefully, even giving him a speech impediment and a limp to simulate the aftermath of a stroke. It seems that as soon as they became aware of Bin Laden' demise, their plan to replace him with their own man swung into action."

"It sounds like a very clever scheme to me," said Tom.

"I agree, if only they had used their double just to penetrate and neutralize the effectiveness of al-Qaeda's inner circle, they could have been heroes."

"So, where did they go wrong?" asked Tom.

"It appears that they became overambitious, deciding to use their new clout within al-Qaeda to manipulate American public opinion as well."

Malek's version of events was consistent and it corroborated Todd's story. Now Tom had an apparent motive behind the Level Four orders to eliminate them both.

"We realized immediately that we had a powerful weapon in our hands, but weren't sure how to use it to the best effect. We decided on a policy of wait and see, and we continued to monitor the situation as it evolved."

"Why would the President take such a risk?" asked Tom glaring at Malek. "Surely he must realize that if he ever got caught, it would be ten times worse than Watergate."

"People in power can easily become overconfident and do not expect to be discovered," replied Malek. "I believe multiple factors played into their decision—and besides, who in truth can justify the actions of our politicians? Remember, the GOP is under a lot of pressure, with an election coming up and with the US bogged down in their disastrous war in Iraq. Presidential popularity ratings are so low that they're almost off the chart."

Tom stroked his chin. "Yes, the Republican's desire to win the election must be strong, whatever the cost."

"What's more, I am sure that the current US Administration would hate to have to admit that we Iranians, and not Uncle Sam, were responsible for the death of Bin Laden."

"For sure ... you're right."

"On the contrary, as a consequence of their plan, they would be able to control everything that happened to Bin Laden, even whether he lived or died. They would also be secure in the knowledge that al-Qaeda was fully infiltrated. At some point, they must have concluded that they could even engineer a well-timed victory over al-Qaeda, just prior to the US vote."

"It was a bold strategy," said Tom.

"The answer to the prayers of a presidential candidate like Littleton, I guess."

Tom shook his head. "But, it was also a very risky approach. A lot could go wrong."

"I agree. The difficult part for dirty ops was introducing their double to the al-Qaeda leadership and explaining how Bin Laden had somehow managed to escape our ambush," Malek responded.

"But if Bin Laden suffered a stroke, the change in his appearance and speech would be more believable. Brilliant!" said Tom.

"Nonetheless, I can understand why JSOC must have wrestled with how to get their man into place," added Khalid.

"It'll have helped them that the al-Qaeda leaders were well dispersed and that there were no survivors from our attack to tell the tale. At this point, your American friends became very creative. They delivered the bogus Bin Laden to one of the Afghan drug barons, paying to have him smuggled across the border into Pakistan. They also coerced an Egyptian nurse, who had previously been taking care of Bin Laden and was well known to al-Zawahiri, into accompanying him."

“That was resourceful,” said Tom.

“As was their cover story: upon reaching al-Zawahiri’s hideout, the nurse gave an account of how they had both managed to escape the assault, as Bin Laden—praise be to Allah—had left the compound to pray a timely ten minutes earlier.” Malek gave a little smirk. “The Omani must have been very good, because they appeared to believe every word.”

“Okay, so what’s in all of this for the Iranians?” asked Khalid staring intently at Malek.

Malek turned to face Khalid directly. “It turned out that playing the waiting game was the right decision. We knew that the President would only deny US involvement if we made our move too soon. Without irrefutable evidence, we realized that such a story would readily be dismissed as Iranian propaganda.”

“I can appreciate your problem,” said Khalid.

“It’s worse than you think—we’d already failed to convince the Americans once before. When Usama bin Laden's son, Saad, was under house arrest in Tehran, along with other al-Qaeda figures, Ahmadinejad tried to exchange the prisoners for guarantees of US non-aggression, but Washington rejected our advances.”

“Quite a dilemma,” Khalid said.

“Yes and as we waited to see what might transpire, you two gentlemen arrived on the scene, almost by chance. Have you thought about what you will do next, where you will go?” Malek asked.

They were extremely vulnerable. Assuming Malek’s account was true, not only the Agency but also JSOC, Littleton and others close to the US President would stop at nothing to shut them up.

“You are both in serious danger. The Circus can no longer protect you, as they’re incapable of hiding anything from the Yanks. To my mind, your best bet would be to disappear on your own. You’re both capable professionals, with five million dollars at your disposal, but I’d only give you six months before they located you, no more.”

It was a realistic assessment, and Tom knew it.

Malek made his pitch. “Think about it. We can help you. I am authorized on behalf of the Islamic Republic of Iran to offer you protective custody until the threat diminishes. Then you’ll be free to find your own place of safety.”

Ah … that’s their game! Meanwhile, Tom was trying to absorb all the implications of what he’d just heard.

“Well, have you thought about Karin?” Malek asked.

Tom felt the blood drain from his face, as Malek touched his Achilles’ heel.

“What has she got to do with this?” Tom asked.

"Come now, Tom, loved ones are never safe—we all know the rules of the game," responded Malek.

Again, Tom had no doubt that his analysis was correct.

"As part of the deal, we'll also agree to recover Ms. Duval to join you—as our guest in a safe house—far away from the prying eyes of Uncle Sam."

"So what's the catch?" asked Tom.

"There's none, except we'll use your evidence to give us the credibility we otherwise lack with the Americans."

"I realize that this is a lot to take in at once. Please take your time to think about our offer. Feel free to discuss it privately between the two of you."

He indicated toward the door at the back of the room that led outside and said, "You can wander around the parade ground if you like, where you can be sure that there are no microphones."

They stepped outside into noonday heat. Tom was sure they would not want to spend too much time discussing anything in these temperatures.

"Well, what do you think? Is this guy for real?" Khalid asked.

"Do we really have a choice but to believe his story?"

"I suppose we already know with some certainty that the Yanks are after us."

"And Malek is right; it is only a matter of time before they catch up with us. We desperately need a secure refuge, and I have no idea where else we are going to find a better proposal than this."

"It's your call. You have much more at stake than I do. I'm on my own and you have Karin to think about."

"All right let's do it."

Without further discussion, they returned to Malek's office.

"Well, it looks like you've got yourself a deal," said Tom. "So, what happens next?"

"You will need to be patient, as I require a little time to get things organized. In the meantime, can you please prepare a message to Ms. Duval?" asked Malek.

"Of course," replied Tom.

Malek's professional approach eased Tom's discomfort about being under Iranian protection. Moreover, they now shared a deep distrust of the Americans, and he reasoned that their mutual self-interest would be sufficient to keep them safe, at least for the time being.

Chapter 29—Once More

KARIN HAD ENJOYED JAVIER AND Nicole's company so much that she had entertained them at home twice more in the past week. She was glad of the company, which was a welcome distraction. She missed Tom dreadfully and constantly worried about him, wondering when they would finally be together again.

Karin drove into Recife early. She was anticipating news from Tom and wanted to be at the bank when it opened. She tried to be nonchalant when the clerk passed her a new message, tucking it into her bag for reading after she left the bank. As she exited, she walked briskly to her car, trying hard not to run. Once she was in the driver's seat, she opened the envelope and read as quickly as she could.

++ MY BABY + YOU ARE IN GREAT DANGER + YOU MUST LEAVE IMMEDIATELY + DO NOT GO HOME + IMPERATIVE YOU GO STRIAGHT TO THE AIRPORT + BUY A TICKET TO MANAUS + CHECK INTO HOTEL TROPICAL + AWAIT CONTACT + CONTACT WILL IDENTIFY + DO NOT TRUST ANYONE ELSE + I LOVE YOU + TOM++

"God damn you!" she exclaimed, thumping the steering wheel in frustration so hard that she hurt her hand. It was typical Tom—enigmatic, with no attempt at explanations. *How can he expect me to drop everything, yet again, and set off on another wild goose chase?* Now she felt even more threatened by the ever-present menace of those hunting her. She was in no doubt about the determination of her pursuers. Although she hadn't any clue about their real identity or what it was that they wanted from her, she guessed they were close. She was not even sure anymore why she was running. Yet Karin had no option but to trust Tom. She literally would follow him to the end of the Earth. Obediently, she reversed out of the parking space and set off in the direction of the airport.

Once in the airport terminal, Karin checked the departure board and then went straight to the TAM ticket counter to purchase a ticket on the next flight to Manaus. Her heart sank when she found out that the flight was delayed and she would have to wait six hours.

"Is that really my only option?" Karin asked.

"I'm sorry, *senhora*," said the ground hostess.

"Excuse me," said a woman waiting in line behind her, "I couldn't help overhearing."

"Yes."

"Well there's still a possibility you could get on an earlier flight. The morning GOL flight has been delayed too. It's not due to leave for another forty minutes."

"Great!"

"You've got no bags. I'm sure if you hurry there's still a possibility for you to get on directly at the gate as a standby passenger."

"Thank you," Karin said as she eased her way past the other passengers and hurried off in the direction of security.

During the flight, Karin sat in the window seat. She had gone over and over the whole situation in her mind and was feeling despondent. It did not look good from any perspective. *Here I am, faraway from anyone I know, heading off alone to the heart of the Amazon, for Christ's sake, on an improbable search for someone who just might eventually lead me to Tom. How on Earth did I ever agree to this?*

Upon arrival, she had no baggage and so progressed rapidly after disembarking the aircraft. She jumped into a waiting taxi. She asked the driver to take her to a good place to buy a few personal items and change of clothes, and then wait to take her on to the Hotel Tropical. It was late afternoon as they headed southward along the main highway from the airport into the city. They stopped at the Amazonas Shopping Mall, where she was able to buy some stylish clothes, some toiletries, and a suitcase.

She discovered the Hotel Tropical in a tranquil setting surrounded by lush gardens on the banks of the Rio Negro. After checking in, she sat alone in her room, very uneasy and anxious for some sort of message from Tom. She was above all scared to be here on her own in this unfamiliar place, constantly haunted by the specter of whoever was chasing her. She was not comfortable in the restaurant or wandering around the public parts of the hotel. She ordered room service, even though she had little appetite. She just picked at the food when it came. She then unpacked her few purchases, arranged them in the closet, and sat down on the bed to start an indefinite wait for her mysterious contact.

* * *

The message that Sir Peter had received on his communicator put him in a foul mood.

From: Solano, Javier —WA/4 xxx Scrambled xxx 15:45 GMT
To: Wood, Peter—C MOST CONFIDENTIAL:
Ms. Duval left Recife in a hurry, probable destination Manaus. No longer in pursuit.
J.
+++

He called Javier to get more information on what had gone wrong. Javier described how he had tailed Karin to the airport and then lost her. He'd discovered from the check-in personnel that she'd taken the flight to Manaus.

Sir Peter was very curious why she went to the airport without going home. It was odd behavior. Like she had been tipped off, but by whom he had no idea. Javier had done his best. It would have been much worse if he'd been tempted to conceal his failure and not communicated right away. He called GCHQ to verify Marina van Hasselt's flight details from their routine monitoring of passenger manifests. They came back quickly, placing her on the GOL flight to Manaus at midday.

Sir Peter's temper had improved a little after talking to Javier, but he still had mixed feelings about the news. He was particularly concerned that Javier was now out of play. This presented a major problem, as he had no one else he could trust within four hours flying time of Manaus. At the same time, he took heart from the possibility that Karin was heading to a meeting with Tom. He needed to get someone to the Amazon to intercept her quickly.

He put in an urgent call to Caracas Station, Mac MacDonald. Mac was a seasoned operator with a mixed reputation in the Circus. He was slightly unconventional in his approach, eschewing a low profile. He could frequently be found sharing a bottle of whisky and smoking Romeo y Julietta cigars with a contact in one of the fashionable bars or nightclubs of Caracas. His previous posting had been in Cuba, where the head of mission had continuously complained that the Secret Service should be just that—*secret*—and that Mac was just a loud-mouthed drunk and a disgrace to his profession. Many chose to ignore that Mac's methods yielded results. Even so, Sir Peter knew that Mac was good in a tight spot and was his best option under the circumstances. The call came through on his private line.

"Hey, Mac, I've got a critical mission for you—but I need you sober," he said.

"Don't worry, boss, I've not touched a drop all day," came the good-humored reply.

"Good, get yourself on tonight's flight to Manaus from Maiquetia. I need you to track someone down for me. Coded details are being sent to you right now."

"Aye, sir!" Mac responded in a broad Scottish accent.

"I want you to report back exclusively to me. Call me when you are in position."

After he replaced the receiver, Sir Peter gazed across the river from his corner office window at Vauxhall Cross toward Westminster. The situation was becoming more critical. The Prime Minister had called him yesterday to express his concern about a possible rupture in the relationship with the US. Meanwhile, he was wondering where on Earth his two illustrious agents had disappeared to. They were still his best chance of untangling this mess before it got out of hand. It was now vital that he make contact as soon as possible. Their instinct would likely be to go underground, lay low uncertain who to trust, making his task of locating them much more difficult.

It was a long shot, but Sir Peter still hoped that Tom would attempt to make contact with Karin and they would be able to bring him in soon. Sir Peter recognized that this was counter-intuitive to all Tom's training and experience; however, the stakes were high enough to provoke such an uncharacteristic response. Then again, he was cautiously optimistic that even if Tom did not show himself in person, one way or another, assuming he made contact, Mac might at least find a clue that would lead them to Tom. The alternative was unthinkable—he would have to wait until Tom and Khalid surfaced from deep cover, months from now.

He was uncharacteristically bewildered by the whole affair. *Why, for God's sake, did Brad let UBL escape when they had a clear shot!* He knew the director of the CIA well, and in both his professional and personal judgment, he was sure that the director was not lying when he had told him that he was not in the loop on this one. *So who was … dirty ops, fronted by Brad Hartman? I don't bloody believe it!*

Chapter 30—The Reckoning

Brad was basking in glory after the safe release of Todd. He was recalled to Langley to debrief the director. Prior to his departure, Brad met with Kurt to discuss the ballistics report on the high-velocity rifle found at the scene.

"The rifle was part of a batch sold to the Israelis a couple of years back. It was recently used to fire depleted uranium rounds," Kurt reported.

"Where the hell did Tom and Khalid get hold of such a weapon?" Brad had demanded.

"It's still a mystery to me, sir," Kurt replied.

"I suspect somehow the Israelis were involved at Suez."

"In that case, it casts uncertainty about the final outcome of the encounter."

"Surely, from what we saw, the two Circus agents could not have escaped."

"It's impossible to say with any certainty based upon the current data."

"For Christ's sake, Kurt, stop sitting on the fence! We'll need to bury this report, or the Brits will be all over it. Damn that greenhorn lieutenant!"

Brad was mulling over the whole situation on his flight back to Langley, keenly aware that his own career hung in the balance. What were the chances that either Tom or Khalid was alive to testify to the actual events?

Brad thought back to his meeting in Washington last month. It was not the first time he had been summoned to an audience with the President, but it was the first time under a cloak of complete secrecy. They had met anonymously in an office block adjacent to the St. Gregory Hotel on M Street. If that wasn't odd enough, Senator Littleton, the vice chairman of the Armed Services Committee, had accompanied the President.

Brad was not unnerved that easily, but the outcome of the meeting had left him feeling distinctly uncomfortable. All the same, whatever he felt was largely irrelevant. He was nothing if not a good soldier who understood what a direct order from his Commander-in-Chief meant. His assignment was classified as Top Secret, in the highest possible interest of national security. He was ordered to protect Bin Laden from possible assassination by the Circus, who had located UBL and had two of their best field agents en route for the kill.

He'd asked the obvious question, "Why in God's name do we want to protect UBL?"

He received a rather patronizing reply from Senator Littleton. "Son, throughout history we have been a stronger nation when we have been able to focus on an enemy. The very fact that Bin Laden is out there gives us a sense of purpose, wouldn't you agree?"

"Sir," Brad responded.

"In reality, UBL has been effectively neutralized," continued Littleton. "Take my word for it—the al-Qaeda organization is infiltrated to such an extent that we know his every move. There could never be a repeat of 9/11, Madrid, London, or anything else on that scale."

"That's good news, sir."

"So for us it's convenient to keep him as a bogeyman. Saddam's gone, and if Bin Laden goes too, we would have no one left to demonize, unless we wanted to pick a fight with the Iranian regime over their nuclear ambitions, or even more questionably with Kim Jong-Il."

"If I might add, both of those alternatives sound far too risky, sir," he said, nodding gently.

"Good, we seem to understand each other. Iraq has turned into a longer-term deployment than we ever imagined, and we certainly cannot afford another war. The American people would crucify us at the polls."

"So, what are you proposing?"

"Well, I'll be running for office standing on this President's record and a platform of keeping America strong. We're the only party with the will and determination to win the fight against terror."

"But what has this got to do with the Circus' attempt to assassinate UBL, sir? Surely that's what we want too?" Brad raised his eyebrows.

"It has everything to do with it. Our plan is to continue to hunt down the elusive Mr. Bin Laden, who will conveniently be detained by our military just prior to the election."

"Hmm, I see," Brad said. "That'll reinforce the GOP's credentials in the war on terror."

The senator lifted his chin. "Exactly, the American public will be frightened to vote for the Democrats, who they see as fickle and indecisive when it comes to national security measures."

Littleton then looked him straight in the eye, "So now you've got the idea. Your job is to make sure that he's not taken out of the picture too soon."

He had handed him an envelope with his briefing papers.

"And what do our British allies think of the idea?"

"Naturally, they are unaware of our intentions. Sir Peter is in the dark. As far as he's concerned, his boys are close on the heels of the world's most wanted fugitive."

"But, you're asking me to take out two of his best guys? He ain't gonna just lie down and take it from us."

"That's why he must never know we're behind it. The operational detail is your own affair. Suffice it to say, we want no repercussions."

Brad had known better than to push back any harder. The greater good was at stake here. It wasn't a question of moralizing about what they do. Sometimes you had to bend the rules. Brad was mindful that the Republicans had offered the only consistent approach to the terror threat and that the clear objective of Littleton and the President was to protect American lives and interests. Brad took his leave and headed back to Langley.

As he examined his orders, he had been given a direct Presidential mandate and his own director did not know. This was common practice, as it provided deniability. If the shit ever hit the fan, the director of the CIA could get up in front of a Congressional hearing and say that in all honesty he was not involved.

* * *

Brad's flight from Dubai landed at Langley Air Force Base and he went straight to his office to monitor developments. In the early afternoon, he received a summons to see the director. He went to a small bedroom adjacent to his office, normally reserved for night ops, to shower, shave, and change before his meeting with the boss. Considerably refreshed, he wound his way through some of the extensive corridors at CIA headquarters, until he reached the director's anteroom. The director's assistant asked him to take a seat. As he turned around, he was surprised to see Kurt also waiting in the reception area.

"When did you get in from Dubai, Kurt?"

"About half an hour ago."

"You're the last person I was expecting to see here."

"The director will see you both now," the director's assistant said, leaving no opportunity for further questions from Brad.

As soon as they entered the room, it was evident that the director was in a rage.

"Brad, what the hell are you trying to do to me! I have had Sir Peter on the phone for nearly two hours this morning, and to say his pissed off is an understatement. He went ballistic on me, asking why we have been targeting his agents."

"What's going on? Why's Kurt here?" Brad asked.

"Brad, you don't get it, do you?" said the director. "I already read Kurt's report on Operation Moses. What in God's name were you thinking, Brad, protecting UBL?"

"Well, sir..."

"Don't give me any of that Level Four crap. I've checked with the President and he just laughed out loud at the suggestion that he had issued such a direct order."

Brad opened his mouth to defend himself but couldn't get the words out.

"It gets worse. According to Sir Peter, he now has two rogue Circus agents on the loose who are aware that they were targeted by their own side. They could easily denounce us publicly, and who would blame them, given what they have been through?"

Brad decided it was better to be discrete. "Sadly, I've nothing to add, sir."

The director's tone changed. He spoke more solemnly. "Brad, you've far exceeded your authority, possibly even set back Anglo-American intelligence relations permanently. You've become a serious liability to the Agency."

"Yes, sir," Brad murmured.

"If the Brits want to make something of this, then you were clearly acting alone. Do you understand me?

"Crystal clear." Brad hung his head.

"Meanwhile, I want you to sign this resignation letter. I am relieving you of your duties. Consider yourself lucky that there are no disciplinary proceedings."

"If you say so, sir," said Brad.

"I can only hope that this is enough to pacify Sir Peter, who is baying for blood," the director said squinting at Brad. "Kurt will assume your responsibilities as ADD. His first task will be to head an investigation into these events. Naturally, you will make yourself fully available for any further inquiries."

The director pushed the letter across his desk to Brad, who read it, smiling to himself at the irony of the wording: *to spend more time with my family*. His signature was a brief scrawl on the page.

The director collected the letter and flipped the switch on his intercom. "Send in the two MPs to escort Mr. Hartman."

Brad became quickly reconciled to his fate. There was no point in contesting the director's decision. He was the fall guy, and as Senator Littleton had so clearly put it in the meeting with the President on M Street, they wanted no repercussions.

Even so, Brad thought it remarkable that the director had chosen to make Kurt ADD and put him in charge of the investigation. He had a squeaky-clean reputation, for sure, but he could hardly be considered impartial under the circumstances. In some senses, it was a shrewd move, as Kurt would have to defend himself and his future prospects. Thus, Kurt would be obliged to sweep as much as possible under the rug or to point the finger directly at him. Since his own reputation was irreparably damaged, this mattered very little.

Brad was distraught as he left the building under escort. During his long drive home, he slumped behind the wheel of his car, lost in thought. It was an ignominious end to his twenty years of dedicated service with the Agency. He had always fantasized that he would leave the CIA with full honors after an illustrious career. Even in his wildest dreams, he never imagined being marched out in complete disgrace. There was no hope of redemption and he knew it. He had plenty of time on his hands now to repent at leisure all that had happened.

Chapter 31—Whisky Mac

Domingo Navas was an agent for the Venezuelan Dirección General de Inteligencia Militar—or DGIM. That evening, as he boarded the Varig flight to Manaus, Domingo instantly recognized one of his fellow passengers, lining up just in front of him. It was definitely Circus head of station—Mac MacDonald—an unmistakable character in Caracas intelligence circles. Realizing that Brazil was well outside Mac's normal remit, he immediately signaled his superiors with the news. As a rising star among DGIM field operators, he had been specially selected by DGIM Director General Hugo Carvajal for this assignment. His orders were to make contact with Ms. Duval in Manaus and then escort her on the flight back to Caracas. He had been told little about the background to the mission, except that the Iranian president had made a personal request to President Chavez.

The overnight flight from Caracas touched down in Bogota before proceeding to Manaus. Domingo slept fitfully because of the short sectors; nevertheless, a seasoned traveler, he shook off his tiredness on arrival. As they left the aircraft, he followed Mac MacDonald observing him from a distance. Then after they collected their luggage, he lost Mac, who melted into the crowd of disembarking passengers.

Claudia, the local DGIM agent in Manaus, met Domingo and drove him to the Hotel Tropical. During the half-hour trip, she briefed him.

"I received a message from Caracas that says that MacDonald is almost certainly on the trail of Ms. Duval too," said Claudia.

"Hmm … that's an unwanted complication," said Domingo.

"You're right," said Claudia. "I expect that all flights out of Manaus are now being watched."

"We'll have to find a new escape route. If we take a plane, it will be too easy for the Circus to locate us."

"Our least conspicuous route is to make the two-day trek by car through Roraima to Ciudad Bolivar in Venezuela."

"Can you organize a four-wheel drive, maps, and supplies on short notice?"

"No problem. Just give me a few hours."

"Okay, I want you to be ready to leave at dawn tomorrow."

"It's a dangerous journey—the border country between Brazil and Venezuela is rather a lawless area."

"That's precisely the reason nobody will expect us to opt for this route."

At the Hotel Tropical, Claudia had arranged for Domingo to get the room adjacent to Karin. From here, he could easily keep an eye on his subject until he judged it was time to make contact.

*   *   *

Mac was on his own, without local support, and still had to locate Ms. Duval somewhere in the city. He went to the hotel's desk at the airport and started calling all the major hotels, asking to be put through to a Senhora Van Hasselt. After about twenty minutes, he was successful in finding her at the Hotel Tropical.

"That was not all that hard, now," Mac whispered to himself.

He paid for a taxi at an adjacent desk and was soon on his way toward the hotel. Once he had a positive ID, he would send a message to Sir Peter. He couldn't wait to hear the boss' reaction when he found out how quickly he'd gotten a result.

Mac checked in and was given a room a few doors down from Ms. Duval. Passing by on the way to his own room, he observed that there was a Do Not Disturb sign hung on her doorknob and a breakfast tray waiting for collection on the floor. This was a good sign, as it was clear that the room was occupied.

After taking a few minutes to unpack his bag, Mac silently slipped out of his room, went back down the corridor toward the elevator and set up an infrared alarm on Ms. Duval's door. That would give him sufficient warning if she decided to make a move or anyone tried to contact her. He returned to get some well-deserved rest and to ponder the best way to smoke her out.

The simultaneous sounds of the alarm going off and someone sliding a piece of paper under his door woke up Mac. He opened his door to take a good look down the corridor and saw that room service delivering to Ms. Duval's room had activated the sensor. That was nothing to worry about. As he re-entered his own room, he casually picked up the flyer that had been posted under his door and smiled to himself as he read the contents.

Manaus Scotch Whisky Festival. 6 PM in the lobby bar—entrance R$20—all the whisky you can drink.

Well now, there's a special treat. All work and no play make Jack a dull boy. As a whisky lover and connoisseur, he could not miss such an excellent opportunity. After an uneventful afternoon resting, he made his way to the lobby bar. There was little evidence of a full-blown festival, merely a banner announcing the event over the bar and a line of whisky bottles sitting below it. Other than that, there were a couple of people sitting at tables and a young exec sitting at the bar, stirring the ice in his Scotch with his index finger. Mac immediately recognized this as an idiosyncratic Venezuelan trait and wandered over to strike up a conversation.

"Hi, I'm Mac," he said, offering a handshake.

"Domingo. Pleased to meet you," he replied in perfect English, shaking Mac's hand.

"Can I offer you a Scotch," Domingo asked.

"I'd love an Islay Malt, straight, no ice," he said, looking the barman directly in the eyes.

Mac then turned to Domingo, "Let's see if a wee dram of the true nectar has made its way this far south."

The barman was better prepared than Mac had anticipated. He reached for a bottle of Laphroaig and poured a generous measure for Mac.

"Well, I'll be damned!"

He shook his head in astonishment, chuckling quietly.

"I guess that you're not from these parts. Let me see … Caracas?" Mac said.

It was the Domingo's turn to appear surprised.

"How did you know?"

"Just the way you were stirring the ice in your drink," he remarked.

"Oh that!" responded Domingo.

"So, what are you doing in Manaus?"

"I work for a company in Caracas that sells air conditioning units. I am here in Manaus trying to do a deal with a manufacturer in the free trade zone."

It sounded tedious, so Mac didn't ask for more detail.

"What about you?"

"Oh, I work for an oil services company in Caracas, as the manager of human resources. I'm here as a tourist. I've always dreamed of visiting the Amazon one day and this is it."

They continued with the polite chitchat: Mac talked about his love of good whisky, living in Caracas, and his enthusiasm for being in Manaus. As he consumed about half the bottle of Laphroaig, strongly encouraged by Domingo, he became rather garrulous. Mac eventually went to the bathroom. About ten minutes after he returned, he began to feel strangely queasy and got up to head for his room. He excused himself to Domingo.

"Are you sure that you're okay?" enquired Domingo. "Would you like me to get the hotel to call you a doctor?"

"No, I'm sure I'll be okay. I think it's probably drinking on an empty stomach, compounded by the effect of the flight. I'll lie down for a bit and I'm certain I'll feel better in a wee while."

Mac made a crooked line for the elevator.

* * *

When Mac woke, he had a splitting headache. He had no idea what time it was, glancing at his watch and assuming he had slept all night. His first reaction was to stick his head out the door. The Do Not Disturb sign had been removed from Ms. Duval's doorknob. He made a quick call to her room, but there was no answer.

"Oh shit!" he swore under his breath, fearing the worst.

He couldn't figure out what had happened; he normally held his drink well. He cursed his own stupidity for being tempted by the Whisky Festival, wondering how he would break this news to the chairman without appearing like a complete idiot. He'd played straight into the hands of his critics, and this incident could easily spell the end of his career in the Circus. Somehow, he needed to recover the situation quickly and pick up Ms. Duval's trail again. He decided to wait for a few hours before making the call to Sir Peter; in the meantime, he would calmly search for clues as to Ms. Duval's whereabouts.

Mac first called at the front desk to confirm that Ms. Duval had checked out two days ago.

"How's that possible! What day is it?" he asked the clerk.

Mac thus discovered he'd been out cold for more than forty-eight hours. His predicament was now much worse than he first thought. Someone had probably spiked his drink. He severely rebuked himself, as only a complete amateur would normally fall for a trick like that.

On closer questioning, none of the hotel staff remembered seeing Ms. Duval leave.

"Damn!" he swore.

Mac racked his brains for where to go next in his hunt for clues. He again cursed himself, as his mind was too slow, his head still fuzzy and throbbing from being drugged. Ms. Duval was being helped and then it dawned on him that his courteous Venezuelan friend had had the most opportunity, even if he could not yet ascribe a motive. He bribed the clerk at the front desk into showing him the register, and he was able to corroborate that Domingo had checked out five minutes before Ms. Duval. Mac took note of Domingo's details and sent them to Caracas station. He had the response he was anticipating within five minutes.

From: Sanchez, Aurelio—Caracas OPS xxx Scrambled xxx 13:02 GMT
To: MacDonald, Mac—Caracas HOS
Sources confirm subject is DGIM—one of the brightest. Also he is "out of town," and due back in a couple of days.
A.
+++

Domingo most probably was still with Ms. Duval. But, where had they gone? Deciding he could not put it off any longer, he signaled the chairman.

From: MacDonald, Mac—Caracas HOS xxx Scrambled xxx 14:15 GMT
To: Wood, Peter—C MOST CONFIDENTIAL:
Ms. Duval left Manaus two days ago, probable destination Venezuela in company of DGIM. Aiming to pick up trail locally.
Mac.
+++

In reality Karin could be anywhere by now. There was little hope of catching up with her and Mac knew it.

Chapter 32—
The Long and Winding Road

It was early evening at the Hotel Tropical when Karin heard a knock. She cracked open the door on the security chain and saw a smartly dressed young man, who looked like he was Brazilian.

"What can I do for you?" she asked.

"I'm sorry to disturb you," he said in perfect English. "I'm in the adjacent room. I've been waiting for some time now to speak to you."

"Who are you?"

"Well, my name is Domingo. I'm Venezuelan and I have an important message for you."

"How do I know I can trust you?"

"Tom said to tell you: '*The next time we go to Château Bouillon, I want to do the tour of the Abbey of Orval.*'"

Karin immediately recognized Tom's perverse sense of humor. She was relieved that her anxious wait was finally over.

"Okay, you can come in," she said, undoing the chain.

Domingo started to explain, "I'm sorry, but there has been a last-minute hitch."

"Why?"

"I'm not the only one who's aware of your presence in Manaus. You were followed to the hotel."

"Oh!" Karin's heart skipped a beat.

"Please don't worry," said Domingo. "I've taken care of it."

"How?"

"Well, let's just say the man following you should be out of action for at least a couple of days."

"I won't ask for more details," she said.

"The good news is that's more than sufficient time for us to make our getaway."

"When do I get to see Tom?"

"I regret I cannot tell you anything more about your final destination. The first step of your journey is to escape from Brazil undetected."

"You have a plan?"

"Yes, we're going overland by car to Venezuela."

"Why don't we take the plane?"

"They'll be watching all the flights. Leaving by road it should be difficult for anyone to track us."

"I see."

"Get yourself ready for a long car journey. I'll be back at six tomorrow morning to collect you."

"All right," she responded.

"Please don't whatever you do, answer the door to anyone else," he said, gently closing it behind him.

* * *

Karin embarked on the road trip with a real sense of adventure. Their journey would take them through some of the most remote and spectacular geography on the planet.

Before their departure, Claudia explained some of the details of their itinerary, "The road through Roraima to Venezuela used to be dirt road north of Boa Vista. It was paved with asphalt only in the last few years. After the construction of the new bridge over the Rio Branco, it now gives a clear run from Manaus through to the Venezuelan border."

"Good, at least it will make the journey a bit smoother," Karin replied.

"That's right, but as you'll soon find out, the first hundred and fifty kilometers through the state of Roraima can be very treacherous. It has the reputation of being one of the worst roads in Brazil."

Karin raised her eyebrows.

"And, the last part of Amazonas and the first fifty kilometers or so in Roraima is a reserve for indigenous tribes," said Claudia.

"Now that sounds fascinating!"

"Well, there's a catch. Traffic is only allowed on the highway between 6 AM and 6 PM. We have to be there well before nightfall, so we must get going as soon as we can."

While Claudia and Domingo took turns at the wheel, Karin took the back seat of the pick-up and tried to stretch out. She was constantly buffeted from side-to-side by the twists and turns of the vehicle, as the drivers attempted to skirt the many potholes in the road. It was the rainy season, which meant that for about six hours that day, a continuous deluge engulfed them. Karin could hardly see where they were going most of the time. Even with the windscreen wipers at maximum speed, they were barely coping with the torrential rain. There were several centimeters of water on the road for much of the time and inevitably, their pace was slowed dramatically.

"This surface water makes it even more treacherous. There's a danger of losing control without four-wheel drive engaged," Domingo said, gritting his teeth.

"I'm just happy I don't have to drive," Karin responded.

"With all this rain, I'm worried it'll take us three days instead of the two we'd planned," Claudia remarked.

During most of the first day, they were surrounded by steamy Amazonian rain forest. After the rain, the low cloud hung over the tree tops and it appeared as if vapor was rising from ground level. They passed through the Waimiri-Atroari Reserve just before the curfew. Eventually they stopped by the side of the road near the missionary post at Catramani. Claudia fed them with dry crackers, processed cheese, and some fruit, washed down with cartons of juice that she had brought along in a cooler. Although it was uninspiring fare, Karin tucked into the food with gusto, her appetite strangely stimulated. After their snack, the drivers then settled in for some well-earned rest in the front seats, while Karin reclined at the back.

Karin was woken abruptly by the sound of car horns. She glanced at her watch and saw it was 5:30 AM. She quickly realized that the noise was coming from two vehicles with an array of spotlights, approaching fast along the highway.

"Shit!" exclaimed Domingo.

"Let's get out of here—now!" screamed Claudia. "Go! Go! Go!"

Domingo reacted on instinct; he swiftly coaxed the engine into life and hit the accelerator hard. Karin could hear the sound of loose gravel being kicked up from the tires, as their wheels spun on the shoulder of the highway.

Claudia pulled out a semi-automatic pistol from the glove box.

As they drew near, armed men appeared in the back of the trucks. The two oncoming vehicles were advancing directly toward them, blocking both sides of the road. There was no room to pass.

"What the hell do we do now?" Claudia stared at Domingo.

"Aim for the windscreens," he replied, "and leave the rest up to me."

Domingo put his foot to the floor, steering straight at their aggressors. Claudia started firing. In the same instant, Karin saw the first flash of opposing gunfire. Her heart was in her mouth. She hadn't a clue why they were under attack. What is more, she couldn't understand why they weren't fleeing. Instead, they were closing in on their adversaries at breakneck speed. Just then, she heard two sharp clunks and winced as their rear passenger door was hit. In return, Claudia dispensed rapid fire out of her window, successfully hitting one of her targets. The windscreen of one of the oncoming trucks crazed over. Karin held her breath as Domingo steered them through the narrow space between the middle of the two pick-ups. She heard a loud bang as their wing mirror caught one of the opposing vehicles and flew off backward.

Karin was trembling as they raced away from the scene. She twisted around to look out of the rear window and saw the two trucks pull to a halt.

"What the hell just happened!" asked Karin, breathless.

"Well," responded Claudia, "there are frequent muggings by armed gangs in this region."

"What! Now you tell me."

"Worse, these bandits operate with complete impunity, as they have the local police in their pocket."

"Why did they pick on us?" Karin asked biting her lip.

"Their attacks are fairly random. If it's any consolation, I think they made a big mistake," replied Domingo. "I bet one of their spotters noticed us parked at the side of the road and thought we were tourists. They won't have expected us to be armed."

"So what happens now?"

"I imagine they've learned their lesson. We'll not be followed."

"How the hell did you manage to squeeze through that tiny gap?" asked Karin.

Domingo just shrugged as they gathered speed along the highway. They soon left the bandits far behind.

Karin was completely unnerved by their narrow escape. She sat huddled on the back seat, lost in thought, fearful of what might happen next.

"Karin, don't worry—you're perfectly safe with us," said Claudia. "It's our job to protect you, and we take it very seriously."

Karin shook her head. "I was just wondering how I ever got into this mess in the first place."

After a while, she recovered enough of her composure to gaze out the window and follow their progress. Once they crossed the Rio Branco at Caracari, the sky cleared. The road ran along the course of the river toward Boa Vista. Karin watched the powerful waters surging in full flood, heightened by the rains; they rushed downstream to join the Rio Negro and in due course the mighty Amazon.

Following the incident, Domingo and Claudia kept a lively conversation going, undoubtedly to make her feel better. Karin began to enjoy their company and found them both amusing. Although she was still nervous, their companionship eased some of Karin's trepidation, and she gradually became more comfortable. By the time they arrived in Boa Vista, she was able to regain most of her good humor. While they drove through the city, the broad avenues and green spaces impressed Karin. The normality of city life helped reassure her too.

"We're relatively safe here," said Claudia. "Let's take a breather. I know a small hotel in the center where we can get a meal and there's a chance to clean up."

"Sounds good to me," responded Karin.

* * *

As they left Boa Vista behind them, the terrain started to unfold into wide-open grasslands.

"We're trying to reach the Venezuelan border town Santa Elena de Uairén, by nightfall," said Domingo.

"Can we stay there?" asked Karin.

"Yes, there are a couple of hotels. Santa Elena is the jumping off point for tourists visiting the *Gran Sabana*."

"Isn't that the scene for Arthur Conan Doyle's novel *The Lost World*?"

"Yes, it's a vast savanna surrounded by mysterious tabletop mountains called *tepuis*."

They crossed the border with minimum of hassle and once in Santa Elena they checked in to a tourist hotel for the night. The next morning after a substantial breakfast, they made an early start.

"Today we should reach our final objective; Ciudad Bolivar on the Orinoco," Claudia informed her. "I'm sure you'll enjoy the fabulous scenery along the way."

Sure enough, in the dawn's early light they had a spectacular view of

Mount Roraima, the biggest tepui, with sheer cliffs rising vertically to three thousand meters.

"That's truly awesome!" Karin said. "I just wish I was here under different circumstances."

"I understand perfectly," replied Claudia.

"I'd love to take some time to explore this stunning landscape."

"I know, it's a pity we're in such a hurry," she responded. "Otherwise we'd be proud to show you more of our beautiful country."

At that moment, all Karin could really think about was how desperate she was to be reunited with Tom. While impressed by the incredible setting, she could not give it the attention it deserved. She decided to plan a trip with Tom when they had the time to enjoy it.

"I was listening in to the tourist guides' conversation at the adjacent breakfast table," Domingo announced.

He looked over his shoulder at Karin. "It seems the tourist's bus to Ciudad Bolivar was hijacked last night. They forced the passengers to strip at gunpoint, robbing them of their valuables and raping two of the women."

"My God—I thought we'd left all that behind in Brazil, but Venezuela is worse!" Karin flinched.

"Unfortunately, such assaults are a regular occurrence here too."

"I'm shocked! This place is otherwise deceptively peaceful."

They arrived at a Venezuelan National Guard roadblock, which made her feel even more uneasy.

"What are they looking for?' asked Karin.

"Contraband," said Domingo.

"They look pretty shifty to me. Are you sure that they are not exacting some form of toll?"

Karin could see that there was little attempt at real policing. She assumed from Domingo's silence that she had guessed correctly. Even so, she was extremely thankful for her escorts. As when Domingo and Claudia flashed their IDs, they were immediately waved on—and saluted too.

Later that afternoon, as they approached the banks of the Caroni, Karin saw two abandoned shantytowns.

"Illegal diamond and gold mining is the principal activity in this region," said Domingo. "When there's a discovery, makeshift dwellings like this spring up overnight and the gang lords move in to control the local economy."

"Huh," Karin gave a small shrug, "It's just like the Wild West out here."

She remained very frightened by the risks of traveling in this country, especially after listening to Domingo's stories. Despite the immense natural beauty, she started to re-evaluate her decision to return. She felt hugely relieved when finally they turned into the Base Aérea Libertador, just outside Ciudad Bolivar, at the end of her road journey.

They passed a line of ancient DC3 aircraft.

"Look at those planes, they're amazing!" said Karin.

"Yes, many of them are still fully functional and take tourists to fly by Angel Falls," Domingo replied.

"It's like a scene from an old movie."

Farther down the apron, beyond the old planes, they pulled up in front of an Aviación Militar Venezolana hangar. They got out and wandered toward the air force headquarters.

As they arrived, the commandant welcomed Karin with a warm smile. "*Ola, Sra. Duval. Bienvenida. Tú estás lista para un viaje supersónico? Entonces, chévere.*"

Karin looked blank.

"We have a wonderful surprise for you," he said. "You'll need to put on this flying suit. Please use my office to change. It's the first door on the right."

Karin was not really in the mood for surprises, but she did what she was told and pulled on the ill-fitting flying suit over her jeans and T-shirt. She kept on her trainers, which seemed to go with the rest of the outfit. As she finished dressing, the commandant came in to his office and offered her a flying helmet to complete the outfit. He then led her out into the hangar, where she stood open-mouthed at the sight that greeted her.

"It's one of the Sukhoi Su-30, air superiority fighters that we just acquired from the Russians," the commandant said.

"Wow!" replied Karin, staring at the incredible aircraft.

Domingo and Claudia were waiting to say their farewells.

"You're now moving so fast that nobody can catch you," said Domingo laughing.

"Thanks for taking such good care of me," Karin smiled back at him.

"The Cubans have arranged a connecting air force flight from Havana to Moscow Sheremetyevo Airport, leaving soon after you land. *Buena suerte*," said Domingo.

"*Vaya con Dios*," said Claudia.

They both gave Karin a big hug. Then the pilot guided her up the steps into the copilot's seat. As he helped her get comfortable in her harness, connecting her oxygen and headphones, he cautioned her, "This is one of the most sophisticated fighting machines on Earth. Please do not touch anything unless I tell you to."

He needn't have bothered with his little speech, as Karin did not intend to touch anything. Her heart was in her mouth and she had butterflies in her stomach, as the powerful swing-wing jet taxied out onto the start of the runway. Then there was an unbelievable sensation as the fighter gathered speed down the runway and took off, rotating skyward with full reheat. Karin felt the g-force push her hard back into the seat, and as she looked down only a few seconds later, she saw the airstrip fading as a tiny speck in the distance.

"Our destination is Havana, Cuba, and our flying time is about twenty-five minutes at mach 2.2," the pilot said. "We'll be flying at an altitude of forty-two thousand feet, so I'm afraid you'll not see much because of the cloud base."

"Okay," replied Karin.

"Please keep your oxygen mask on the whole way," he reminded her.

* * *

Sitting on her flight to Moscow, Karin was astonished by Tom's ability to mobilize resources from military and intelligence organizations halfway around the world. At the same time, she kept wondering where on Earth she was heading and when she would get to Tom. While she appreciated the need for secrecy, she wondered why she was being kept in the dark. Then, finally, after her plane touched down in Moscow, the Cuban intelligence officer on her flight informed her that her final destination was Tehran. She wouldn't have cared if he had said Baghdad; she just wanted to be with Tom, so much it ached. He gave her a boarding pass for her connecting Aeroflot flight and told her that she would be escorted to her departure gate.

Upon disembarking, two clean-cut, athletic-looking types with broad shoulders dressed in smart suits and wearing security badges met her at the end of the ramp.

"Ms. Duval?" the first man asked in a thick Russian accent.

"Yes."

"Please come with us," he commanded.

They walked quickly to the elevators in the middle of the concourse. She noticed out of curiosity that her escorts were doing their best to shield her from the view of other passengers. The two Russians appeared menacing, and Karin felt very uncomfortable. They entered into what looked like a small service elevator and selected the third floor. She was trying not to shake. It seemed like she would have to go through yet another terrifying experience before she would finally get to see Tom. *Where are they taking me, for God's sake?*

Karin clutched her bag, as the doors of the elevator slid open to reveal a large room filled with computer monitors and bustling with what looked like one hundred or more armed police.

"What is this place?"

"My name is Alexei," said the first of her escorts. "We are FSB."

Karin gulped.

He waved toward the group of agents. "We monitor all arriving and departing passengers from Sheremetyevo here."

"I was told that I would have an escort, but I feel like I'm under arrest!" she said.

"Not at all … don't worry. This is just a precaution for your own safety," said Alexei. "Let me show you."

He motioned for her to join him at one of the monitors.

"Look there."

He clicked the mouse and zoomed in on one of the passengers waiting by immigration control. Karin could see that he was continuously searching around, as if he was looking for someone.

"He's a CIA agent. Four of them have been watching the airport for about three weeks now. From our sources, we believe they're after you."

"What the hell does the CIA want with me?" Karin asked, open mouthed.

"It's not you that they're after, but Tom Salter. They believe that you can lead them to him," said Alexei. "You would both be in great danger if they spotted you."

"Ah ha," she said.

She nodded gently as pieces began to fall into place for her. *Of course, I'm just a way for them to get to Tom. I should have realized.*

"But why are you helping me?" she asked.

"Well, let's just say we like to help our Cuban friends from time to time," he replied. "Also we get a certain pleasure out of frustrating the plans of our old rivals in the Agency."

Alexei laughed quietly.

"Wait in this room, you'll be quite safe," he instructed, leading her into a private office in the corner of the floor. "In half an hour I'll take you to your plane."

He closed the door and left her alone inside. She sat behind the main desk, rocking back and forth in a swivel chair, pondering her fate. She hated the fact that she was not in control of her own destiny. Despite Alexei's courteous approach, both he and the FSB scared her. She was completely in their hands, and it made her very uneasy. Nonetheless, she was well aware, even under such trying circumstances, she must keep her faith in Tom. She was sure he would not let her down.

At the appointed time, Alexei came for her.

"Okay, time to go," he said.

She gave a quick start, as she had not seen him entering the room. She swiveled around to meet his gaze.

"I'm ready when you are," she said, collecting her bag from the desk as she got up.

They traveled down to the ground floor together in the goods elevator. She felt a blast of cold air as she exited the building. She was ushered into the back of a black Mercedes sedan that was waiting nearby. Alexei jumped into the front passenger seat. She was grateful that the FSB appeared to be taking no chances by escorting her the whole way to the aircraft. It was snowing, as she climbed the steps to board her scheduled flight to Tehran. Alexei guided her as far as the first class cabin. The crew literally closed the door behind him as he left the aircraft. Within seconds, the pilot had started the engines and was taxiing away from the stand. Only then did it strike her that in little more than three hours, she would see Tom. The plane lumbered down the runway and Karin breathed a huge sigh of relief as the wheels departed Russian soil. There was no turning back now.

Chapter 33—Back Together Again

Malek had settled Tom and Khalid into their accommodation, a newly constructed housing compound nestled below the snow-capped Alborz Mountains. It was situated among the high-rise condominiums in the affluent suburbs of northern Tehran. Malek beamed with pride as he showed them around the complex. Tom was amazed by the facilities—it had three villas, a swimming pool, a tennis court, and a recreation building, all sitting behind a high wall topped by an electric fence and security cameras.

"You have your own bar, computer room, games room, library, mini-theatre with flat screen TV, and more than two hundred satellite channels," Malek said, stopping to catch his breath.

"Every creature comfort imaginable, and more," Tom said, grinning.

"If you desire anything else in the way of provisions, just fill out this form and it will be delivered by the following day."

Malek handed them some instructions and a wad of forms.

"It's not a prison. You can leave the compound whenever you like." Malek pointed to the first page of the instructions. "But please call me on this number first."

Tom thought it unlikely they would go out. Foreigners would receive an uncertain welcome on the streets of the Iranian capital, and regardless, it was just not smart for them to be seen in public, lest they be recognized.

"It's a gilded cage," said Tom after Malek had gone.

"You're right—it's a moot point as to whether the security is to keep others out or to keep us in!"

"No matter what, Malek is trying very hard to please. I trust him and believe he's doing his best to take care of us."

* * *

Even though Malek informed Tom daily about the progress of the rescue attempt, during his first week in the compound, he was very edgy knowing that Karin was still in danger.

Iranian intelligence reported that Karin had immediately caught the flight to Manaus on receipt of Tom's message. However, he was not greatly comforted, sensing how she would be feeling, alone, frightened, and on her guard the whole time against an unidentified enemy. He desperately wanted to speak to her and reassure her, but couldn't without placing her in greater jeopardy. He kept imagining the worst—that Karin had been intercepted by the Agency or the Circus and was being tortured to reveal his location.

Worse, Malek then had no news at all for the next few days. He explained that Karin was making her getaway overland and although she was in safe hands, there was no easy way to communicate with her. Initially this heightened Tom's anxiety but he quickly recognized he had no option other than to place his faith in the system. After all, they were professionals who were arranging her escape. Worrying didn't solve anything. Only on the fourth day did he start to relax when Malek told him that Karin had safely reached Cuba and was boarding a flight to Moscow en route to Tehran. The worst was over.

"Is she okay?" he asked.

"She's been through a very testing time and had a couple of close calls," replied Malek. "But as far as I know she's in good shape."

Malek patted Tom on the back, smiling.

"Stop worrying. The Cubans are taking good care of her. They've even arranged a special flight to get her to Moscow."

"Ha," he scoffed. "Life is full of surprises—even in my wildest dreams, I never thought I'd be grateful to the Castro regime!"

* * *

It was a rainy spring day, and Tom was due to meet Karin. Malek drove him to Imam Khomeini International Airport, thirty kilometers to the south of the city, and arranged for Tom to stay out of sight in one of the VIP waiting rooms. They had arrived about an hour before the flight was due, so Tom sat and flicked through some magazines and sipped on a coffee that the ground hostess served him. His mouth was dry and his palms were sweaty; he felt like a nervous schoolboy on a first date. Meanwhile, Malek made him feel worse, as he kept popping in and out of the room to check up on him.

"Pull yourself together, man," Malek said. "I can't believe that a seasoned professional like you gets this flustered by a woman!"

"Go away, Malek," he replied.

Tom hated the wait. He could hear the clock ticking slowly. *Why is it taking so long?*

Karin was finally ushered into the room, dressed casually in jeans, a sweater, and trainers, and carrying a heavy coat. At first glance, she seemed to have survived her ordeal remarkably well. He leapt out of his seat and rushed forward to give her a big hug. Simultaneously, she threw out her arms and shrieked with joy.

"Oh, my God!" she said,

"I can't believe it!" said Tom. "At last—"

He felt Karin trembling as he touched her.

"I just can't understand why I'm so nervous," she muttered.

He folded her in his arms and she nuzzled in against his chest.

Karin sighed softly. "You can't imagine how much I've dreamed about this moment for the last few weeks!"

"I'm so sorry for the nightmare you must have been through," Tom said. "If there had been another way, believe me—"

"I know, my darling," she said, "all that matters now is we're together again."

Karin leaned back and smiled. She had that mischievous look in her eyes, which Tom recognized only too well. Then slowly she pressed her warm lips firmly against his. They kissed for what seemed like an eternity, clinging desperately to each other. His mind drifted back to the intense joy of their first kiss in the Grand Place. He'd loved her from the first moment, and he loved her now more than ever. Any remaining fears evaporated. Karin made him complete. She was his touchstone. Together with her, he could face any hardship.

"I love you more than life," she whispered in his ear, with tears streaming down her face.

"I love you too and missed you so much," replied Tom. "I promise I'll make it up to you."

He gently wiped away her tears, "Sssh, it's all right now."

At that moment, Tom noticed that Malek had been watching them discretely from the corner of the room. He smiled gingerly at Tom.

"I guess it's time to go," said Tom.

Malek drove Tom and Karin back across the city to the compound. He kept a running dialogue going in the car, which Tom assumed was largely for Karin's benefit. Malek made observations on a multitude of topics, about the surrounding sights of the city, Persian history, and the facilities in the compound, the climate, and the mentality of the Iranian people. Even though Tom could see she was tired, Malek's banter appeared not to bother Karin. Tom wondered how much she was really taking in, as she snuggled up to him in silence. He still could not believe that she was there by his side. Even the bizarre circumstances of their reunion, in such a strange hostile place, did not bother him. All that was important was she was here, safe with him again.

As they arrived at the compound, Tom was overwhelmed by his desire for Karin. He desperately wanted her. A fire was burning inside him that needed to be put out. Tom showed Karin to their villa and they went straight upstairs to the bedroom. Without saying a word, she immediately locked the door, pushed him back on the bed and began undressing him.

He was determined to absorb all the excitement, to consume her totally. They made love, gently, erotically, delicately. It was exquisite, and he maintained his state of arousal for almost an hour. Her touch was like electricity, sending shockwaves of pleasure over the surface skin and softly caressing his body beneath. He experienced a new sexual awakening. Carefully he entered her, sensing her warmth and softness closing all around him, the ecstasy growing until final release. Afterward he lay beside her, basking in the warm glow of their love. After the separation, the coming together again was always blissful. This time it was sweeter than ever.

Chapter 34—Dead or Alive

Even though the director had not overtly instructed Kurt to cover up any damaging evidence, by choosing him to head the investigation, he was clearly trying to protect the Agency. Kurt had to ensure that the integrity of his findings could not be challenged. To achieve this, he would need to dig deep and not be afraid to reveal any painful facts.

All the same, the idea that Brad was somehow acting independently and on his own authority, did not hold water for a second. All indications pointed to Brad's complicity in some sort of plot to shield UBL. Hence, Kurt decided to talk with him and get his version of events first hand. He arranged for a car to take him to Brad's home in rural Virginia, about half an hour's drive from Langley. He was optimistic that he would find some significant clue to this mystery. However, he hardly recognized the Brad that opened the door to him. He was scruffily dressed with tousled hair. He looked as if he had not slept in days. His shoulders were hunched and his head bowed. Manifestly, the Agency had been his *raison d'être,* and once removed there was only the empty shell of a man left.

The first thing that Kurt asked Brad was, "For Christ's sakes why were we defending UBL?"

"I had Level Four orders and cannot divulge any more."

"But, Brad the President denies issuing any such order."

"Then draw your own conclusions," said Brad.

Although the implications were extremely disturbing, Kurt was almost certain that Brad's orders for Operation Moses had been Level Four, or at least he appeared sincere in this claim. Obviously, Brad wasn't insane, which was the only other possible explanation he could think of.

"Give me something to go on," he said. "Maybe I can salvage something of your career."

"It's too late for that and you know it," he replied.

Kurt was convinced that someone high up had been playing Brad. There was no other rationale for his behavior.

"I can't pretend to understand your reasons."

"Then don't even try—go—leave me in peace!" Brad responded.

"Okay, you've got my number. Call me if you want to talk," he said. "I'll let myself out."

In amassing evidence for his investigation, Kurt was provided with the NSA's account of the Suez incident. He also read the confidential report on the bungled attempt to detain Karin Duval. If this document was ever to be disclosed it would point the finger directly at the Agency. He ordered all copies destroyed. Kurt also had tried to get some intelligence out of the Israelis. However, Mossad had met his inter-agency request for information on the Suez incident with a polite but firm response that they had to protect their sources.

He was sure that searching for Tom and Khalid would be an unproductive waste of his time—watching, and listening, until one of them was spotted. Besides, he preferred to leave the job of finding them to his Circus colleagues. He rightly assumed that both agents would be unwilling to talk with the CIA.

He had few options left. His best chance was to search for answers within the convoy. Although Operation Sheikh had been aborted, secretly Kurt had continued tracking the five Land Cruisers. He was kept regularly informed by the NGA. Based on the latest update, the convoy could be found in a small town near Luxor in Upper Egypt. Apparently, UBL and his entourage had been there for the last couple of weeks.

Kurt pressed the button on his intercom, "Can you please arrange for the Beechjet to take me to Cairo."

"Right away, sir," his assistant responded.

Then he called Frank in Dubai on the scrambled phone.

"Frank, assemble a covert squad of eight men with logistics support to travel to Luxor tomorrow," he instructed.

"Affirmative."

"And we'll need sufficient materiel for an amphibious night raid."

"Roger that."

After Kurt hung up, he sat back in his chair and pondered the possible holes in his plan. Although he was taking some big chances with this operation, he was confident that he had a good handle on most of the details. He was usually meticulous in his preparations. Based upon his experience, he'd found this was the most effective way to manage the risks.

* * *

Kurt's aircraft made a refueling stop at Cairo airport and then took off straight for Luxor. As his flight arrived at the general aviation area, he instructed the pilot to park on the apron alongside the aircraft from Dubai. After disembarking, he spoke with one of Frank's men, keeping a watchful eye from the terminal.

"Hey, Lee, keep a careful lookout," said Kurt.

"Yes, sir—and congratulations on the promotion, sir!"

Lee had arranged a car to the Winter Palace Hotel.

"Welcome to Upper Egypt and the fabulous antiquities of Luxor," his driver said.

"Thanks," replied Kurt.

"American?" the driver asked.

"Yes."

"May I compliment you on your choice of hotel, sir? It's one of the most beautiful in the whole of Egypt. If there is anything I can do to make your stay more pleasant, my name is Mustafa," he said, handing over his card. "You can ask for me by name at the concierge desk. I'm an official tourist guide and would be happy to show you the sights."

Shortly after their arrival, Kurt convened a meeting in one of the hotel conference rooms. They appeared to be yet one more American tour group visiting the fabulous ancient sights of Luxor. However, their true purpose was unquestionably more menacing.

"Well, gentlemen," he began, "we have an intriguing problem to solve. I want to find out why were we ordered to protect UBL and who was really behind this scam?"

"That won't be easy, sir," replied Frank.

"You're right, and besides, our mission is incredibly sensitive. I needn't remind anyone that Brad was using the Commander-in-Chief and Level Four orders as his cover."

"Could the President really be involved?" asked Ray.

"I don't know. He might be."

"And if he is?" asked Frank.

"I'm prepared to accept the consequences in the interest of finding out the truth," replied Kurt.

"Listen up," he said. "My plan is to kidnap UBL and hold him hostage. We can find out what he knows and use him as a means to smoke out whoever's been shielding him."

The whole room was left speechless for several seconds.

Frank interrupted the silence. "It's a daring plan, but is it realistic?"

Kurt was undeterred. "I want you to look at these surveillance images from the town of Qinā, about thirty five kilometers north of here."

Kurt switched on the projector.

"This is a two-week-old time sequence, focusing on the outskirts of the town."

He flipped through the shots.

"Watch, as the five Land Cruisers arrive," he said. "Afterward you can see that the vehicles are concealed from view in a nearby warehouse."

Kurt highlighted the actions on the screen using his laser pointer.

"Now watch, as the main party is escorted into a large villa overlooking the Nile."

He circled a building about six hundred yards away from the house.

"This is the bodyguards' quarters."

Even though he had watched the sequence several times, Kurt continued to be impressed by the NGA technology and the clarity of the images from space.

"We've been keeping a twenty-four-hour vigil for the last two weeks, and we've seen no significant movements since al-Qaeda's arrival."

"Al-Qaeda appears to be complacent then," said Frank, "as if no one can touch them."

"You're right, Frank," Kurt said. "A couple of our best agents from Cairo Station have been on the ground in Qinā for ten days now and observed a very relaxed attitude."

"What have they got?" Frank asked.

"Well, they have ascertained that UBL is a guest of Mohammed Mahdi Akef, the leader of the Muslim Brotherhood."

Kurt then put up a floor plan of the villa on the screen.

"UBL, Abu Musab, and two others are housed in the rear of the villa—here," Kurt indicated on the plan. "They only have three guards at the villa during the night, two stationed at the front entrance and one at the rear, so it should be a piece of cake for us to approach from the river unseen."

"So what's the timeline?" asked Frank.

"We need to go as soon as we can, tonight, before they prepare to move on," Kurt replied.

*   *   *

To say that Kurt was lucky and that Brad was not would be an over-simplification. Arguably, the fact that Frank's men executed his plan with flawless precision was an important factor. Moreover, on this occasion, there was no interference from the Israelis. Al-Qaeda appeared to be taken completely by surprise. Frank met Kurt back at the rendezvous, behind Luxor General Aviation Terminal, by 3 AM with his valuable cargo in tow. They had sedated UBL, so he was in a semi-conscious state, able to be manhandled but not lucid enough to hold a conversation. They bundled their hostage on to the Beechjet and took off with haste, heading for Diego Garcia in the Indian Ocean.

Kurt had thought the US base on the island was an ideal choice for his purposes, because of its remoteness and his ability to keep a lid on the presence of such an infamous prisoner. Furthermore, Diego Garcia had a special holding pen and a secure interrogation center that had been set up at the start of the Afghan war specifically for questioning terrorists. The center had been decommissioned following the Abu Ghraib scandal, so it was unmanned and free from prying eyes.

Kurt ordered that UBL be kept fully sedated for the flight. As an added precaution, he told them to handcuff him and chain him to his seat, with Frank and one of his men taking turns to watch him. Hardly a word was spoken in the cabin for the whole journey.

When they deplaned, UBL was stretchered across to the military hospital and held in a secure room under a close guard. The base physician examined him.

"He'll be able to talk tomorrow," the doctor told Kurt.

"I'd like to speak with him as soon as possible. But I suppose a twelve-hour wait isn't a problem," Kurt replied.

Time was on his side. Whoever was covering for UBL had to make the next move and he knew it. What Kurt had not anticipated was the surprise that greeted him the next morning. As he entered the hospital room, UBL was sitting up in bed smiling.

He began to speak in perfect English, "I'm not who you think I am. My name is Said bin Thabour. I'm an Omani working for Joint Special Operations Command."

"What!" Kurt flinched.

"I belong to Task Force 121—you might have heard of us? If you need, you can verify with my commanding officer, General Doug Broom," the Omani said.

Kurt was stunned. Of course he had heard of Task Force 121, which had been set up as a covert op in 2003 to hunt down UBL and Saddam. The repercussions were enormous. It was now obvious why they were protecting UBL—he was one of our own.

He felt a surge of admiration for JSOC that they had managed to plant a double in UBL's place. He had to admit that the likeness was uncanny.

"Whatever happened to the real UBL?" asked Kurt.

"Sir, I am afraid you are going to need clearance before I can answer your questions," replied Said.

Kurt immediately understood. He wondered how much Brad knew about this little escapade. He was sure he must have been aware of what was going on, as otherwise nothing made any sense. However, why did he say nothing when he had questioned him? It could probably have gotten him off the hook. Perhaps Brad knew only part of the story, not enough to explain what was really going on—or perhaps he had fallen on his sword to protect the secret. Kurt would probably never know.

Certainly it was one of the most daring and successful operations in the history of espionage. The operational details would have been kept within a very tight circle. This was why his own director was apparently unawares. Yet, how could he forgive himself—in the search for the truth, he had inadvertently put an end to JSOC's brilliant scheme.

He must talk with Doug Broom as soon as possible to limit the possible damage. Without hesitating, he marched straight out of the hospital heading for the communications building. The heat was still bearable at that time of day. Yet, when he arrived at the Comms Room, he had patches of sweat on his shirt and was uncharacteristically red in the face. Brusquely, he asked the technician to patch him through to JSOC headquarters in Florida. He entered the soundproof booth and hastily closed the door behind him. Kurt did not usually let his irritation show, but at that moment, he would have confessed to being completely flustered.

It took about ten minutes to go through the usual screening procedure and then to locate General Doug Broom. Kurt was listening in to the intermittent conversation with Doug's staff, as they pulled him out of a mess dinner and got him to a secure communications booth, like Kurt's.

"There had better be a damn good reason for this!" Doug Broom snapped on the other end of the line.

"Doug, please accept my apologies for having to get hold of you like this, but I must inform you that we have Said bin Thabour in custody," Kurt said.

"No shit! We'll hell, that won't go down well with the boss," Doug replied. "What are you damn spooks doing poking around in other people's business anyway? Ain't you got something better to do, like taking pot shots at Kim Jong-Il!"

Kurt paused for a few seconds without responding, hoping Doug would calm down.

"You'd better hang on to him and breathe a word to no one. I'll send someone to collect him," Doug said.

"Can I debrief him?" Kurt asked.

"No, definitely not!" was the stern reply. "You're way out of your depth. If I were you, I'd be a good soldier and let us take care of it, unless of course you want to go the way of Brad Hartman!"

The call ended abruptly. Kurt then instructed the comms officer to patch him through to the director. Kurt suspected the fallout would reach his boss quickly, and he wanted to get his side of the story across first. Kurt also knew that he should then do exactly what Doug had suggested and keep his head down, if he wanted to survive.

* * *

A priority message went from JSOC to the Commander-in-Chief and Senator Littleton thirty minutes later.

MOST URGENT From: Broom, Doug—JSOC xxx Scrambled xxx 23:15 GMT
To: Rambler—MOST CONFIDENTIAL
cc: Littleton, J.
Operation Twin Brothers aborted. All evidence destroyed.
D.
+++

Chapter 35—Trump Card

Back in Tehran, Mahmoud Ahmadinejad sat in his office contemplating his next move. The Americans were becoming more and more vociferous in their demands that he dismantle Iranian uranium enrichment efforts. Yet he was adamant that he would not give in to mounting diplomatic pressure, which he perceived as unwarranted interference in Iran's right to self-determination. It was a geopolitical game with high stakes, and he needed more influence.

A few moments later, he received a call from Malek informing him that the British agents and their dependants were now secure, so the next phase of the operation could begin. This was the news he had been waiting for. He remembered being astonished by the intelligence on Operation Twin Brothers, which he had received a couple of months back. He was equally disappointed knowing that he could not use it on its own. Now things were different. He was extremely pleased with Malek's work. The two agents were living proof of a conspiracy and provided him with just the bargaining chip that he'd been looking for. Now he had to figure out how and when to use it to his best advantage.

Ahmadinejad summoned Malek to a meeting of the Supreme National Security Council the following week. He decided to use Malek's remarkable testimony as a way to disarm his critics—some of the ministers in the council were highly volatile.

The meeting started promptly.

"Firstly, I'd like to welcome Colonel Malek Kalbasi of the IRGC on behalf of the council and to congratulate him on the successful detention and turning of two British spies," said Ahmadinejad.

He watched as Malek fidgeted nervously.

"Hear, hear, he's one of our best officers," the minister of defense added. "I too would like to highly commend him for his role in the Bin Laden affair and now for creating convincing leverage over the US President."

"Please give us your report," said Ahmadinejad.

Malek cleared his throat as he started his discourse. The council listened while Malek described the events leading up to the agents capture and how he'd taken them into protective custody.

"Well done! I'm convinced the Americans can no longer deny the accuracy of our information or the validity of our sources," said Ahmadinejad.

There were nods of assent around the table.

"Colonel Kalbasi, please stay and listen to the rest of the proceedings, as our honored guest," Ahmadinejad said.

Most of the discussion that followed was about a public statement he was planning to make, to the effect that *Iranian scientists had successfully enriched uranium to the 3.5 percent level, which was pure enough to run a nuclear reactor.*

"We are closer to forty percent enrichment level," said the minister of defense. "But, it's still a long way from the ninety percent required for a nuclear bomb."

"I agree, but the Americans are sure to ignore the facts of the case, no matter what we say," responded the minister of justice.

"I'm certain we can anticipate a continuing war of words from Washington and possibly even sanctions," said Ahmadinejad.

* * *

Ahmadinejad knew that the reaction of the international community to his announcement was political theater managed by the Americans. As he had predicted, it was completely disproportionate to the content of his statement. The following week he learned that a fresh proposal for a trade embargo was circulating around key missions in the UN. Diplomatic pressure was rising daily. He also realized that unless he played his trump card soon, he would be rapidly isolated and any vote at the UN Security Council would inevitably go against him. He decided to act.

He called the Iranian ambassador in Washington. "I want you to schedule a confidential conference call between you, me, and the US President, as soon as possible."

"Mr. President, coincidentally, I have a monthly meeting with the secretary of state tomorrow," he responded.

"Excellent. You can raise it then."

"But it's an unusual request, sir. She may reject it."

"If she does, tell her to inform the President that it concerns his *twin brother*," he declared. "He'll take the call, I'm sure."

Ahmadinejad paused for a few seconds.

"I need you to help me confront the US President with the hard evidence of his own treachery and force him to stop his diplomatic campaign against us."

Ahmadinejad had correctly assumed that the US President would agree to the call. It was all set up for the following day.

"I'm fully aware of your Operation Twin Brothers and the plot to influence the elections," the ambassador translated Ahmadinejad's opening statement.

There was a curious silence at the other end of the line.

"I'm sure you appreciate that should this information leak out, it would cause you and the Republicans untold political damage," he continued.

"I'll just deny it," responded the US President. "It's too farfetched."

"Mr. President, this time we can back it up with witnesses," responded the ambassador.

"Oh, I don't know."

Ahmadinejad couldn't understand why the US President didn't seem more concerned. He went for the sting.

"Look, in exchange for our silence on this matter, the US must withdraw the UN resolution on sanctions and halt their attempts to block Iran's peaceful uranium enrichment program."

The Iranians heard a hollow laugh on the other end of the line.

"Gentlemen you are far too clever for your own good. However, you have nothing on me. It's no deal," the US President replied.

As the line went dead, Ahmadinejad was perplexed. *What the hell just happened?*

* * *

On the other side of the world, the US President replaced the receiver and a wry smile came across his face. He'd successfully called their bluff. He was relieved that all traces of Operation Twin Brothers had been eradicated. So easily, it could have been different. Gently rocking back on his chair, he reflected: *Serendipity, it's all about timing and luck!*

www.ingramcontent.com/pod-product-compliance
Lightning Source LLC
Chambersburg PA
CBHW020613310726
48979CB00008B/1460/J

* 9 7 8 1 4 4 0 1 2 7 5 0 2 *